REDEMPTION

A Story of the Oregon Trail
& the Fraser River Gold Rush

REDEMPTION

A Story of the Oregon Trail & the Fraser River Gold Rush

Love is better than anger, hope is better than fear;
optimism is better than despair,
so let us be loving, hopeful and optimistic.
—Jack Layton, 2011

Redemption is a tragic story of loss and redemption and of love and revenge, inspired and based on true historical events that took place on the Oregon Trail, the Donner Pass and Canada's Fraser River between 1846 and 1858.

DRAGON
HILL

YVONNE HARRIS

The Publisher: Dragon Hill Publishing Ltd.

Library and Archives Canada Cataloguing in Publication
Harris, Yvonne, 1935–, author
    Redemption : a story of the Oregon Trail and the Fraser River Gold
    Rush / Yvonne Harris.

Includes bibliographical references.
Issued in print and electronic formats.
ISBN 978-1-896124-65-0 (softcover).—ISBN 978-1-896124-66-7 (EPUB)

        I. Title.

PS8565.A6524R43 2017   C813'.54   C2017-903432-4
                                            C2017-903433-2

Project Director: Marina Michaelides
Project Editor: Kaija Sproule
Maps: Tamara Hartson
Cover Images: Compass background, Irina Tischenko/Thinkstock;
covered wagon, mppriv/Thinkstock

Produced with the assistance of the Government of Alberta, Alberta Media Fund.

Alberta
Government

PC: 32

To my husband Paul and son Shane

And to Sweeney Scurvy

Of Kwanlin First Nations

A Poet and a Survivor

Prologue
Crossing the Atlantic 1661

In 1661, David Ackerman, his wife Elizabeth and their six children sailed from their home in North Brabant, The Netherlands, to be able to worship freely in the New Dutch Reform Church. It was a rough crossing in the sailing ship *De Vos*, taking 74 days, which was longer than the *Mayflower* trip of 1620. The Ackerman family landed November 4th in New Amsterdam (now Manhattan Island).

David Ackerman died either on the ship or shortly after they disembarked, leaving his wife Elizabeth with the care of the family. She fed and sheltered the children until the boys were old enough to work. It was here where the first Ackermans lived before spreading out across the United States.

The author is a descendent of David Ackerman, and research shows that an Ackerman crossed the Oregon Trail in 1846.

Two hundred years after the Ackerman family landed in the New World, a different adventure was underway: the settling of the northwest. In the mid-nineteenth century, four hundred thousand emigrants crossed the continent in search of a better life, and in 1858, miners from California, Washington and Oregon stormed up the northwest coast to the Fraser River Gold Rush.

In the path of the emigrants and miners were the North American tribes, who had lived here since time immemorial and whose lives were irreversibly altered by these historical events.

Redemption is an historical novel of three fictional Ackermans: David, Robert and Alice, who traveled over two thousand miles on the Oregon Trail, over the treacherous Sierra Nevada Pass, and north to Canada and the Fraser River War.

It is also a story of Chief Spintlum, a little known Kumsheen leader at Lytton, who stopped the Fraser River War.

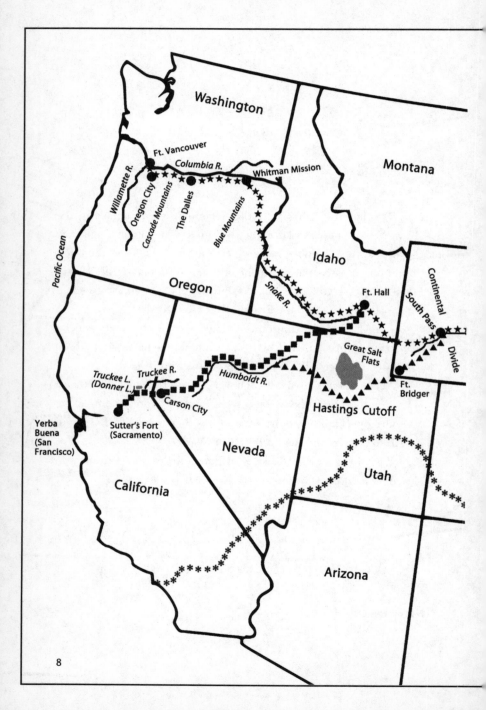

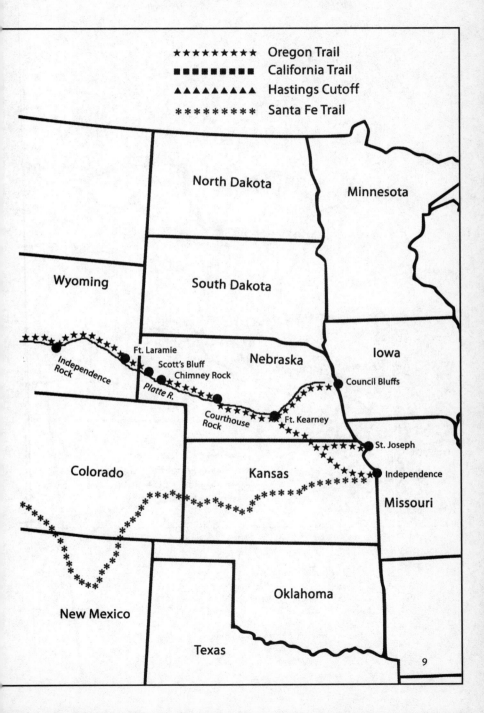

★★★★★★★★★ Oregon Trail
■■■■■■■■■ California Trail
▲▲▲▲▲▲▲▲▲ Hastings Cutoff
✱✱✱✱✱✱✱✱✱ Santa Fe Trail

North Dakota

Minnesota

Wyoming

South Dakota

Iowa

Ft. Laramie

Scott's Bluff

Independence Rock

Chimney Rock

Platte R.

Nebraska

Council Bluffs

Courthouse Rock

Ft. Kearney

St. Joseph

Colorado

Kansas

Independence

Missouri

Oklahoma

New Mexico

Texas

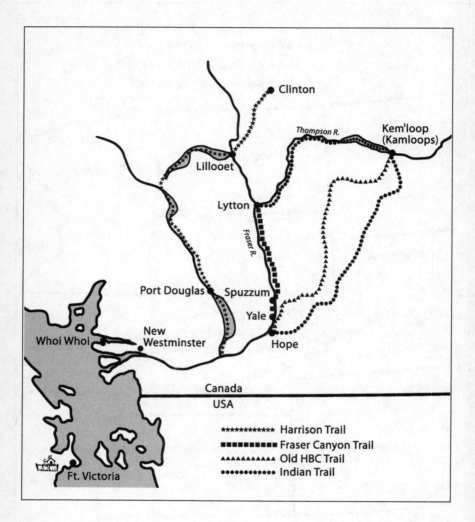

Dramatis Personae

Fictional Characters

Addie: Single, on Oregon Trail and Sierra Pass.

Alice: Widowed and then married to Saxby; on Oregon Trail and Sierra Pass.

Amelia: Alice's daughter, age seven. On the Oregon Trail.

Americus Chablis: Married to Charlotte; crossed on Oregon Trail.

Andersson: Robert's teacher in Bedford.

Anna and Jan: Married couple on Oregon Trail and in Fort Victoria.

Annabelle Lee and Elizabeth: Twin daughters of Olive and Dudley. History tells us that twin girls were separated on the Oregon Trail during the trek across North America.

Billy and his three younger brothers: Sons of McNair and Dorothy.

Blackberry: Yana girl who survived the massacre. Blackberry is fictional. However, the Yana massacre is part of history, and only one person from the Indian village survived.

Campfire Woman: Horatio's Pawnee wife.

Carreena: Educated London woman, deceived by Stuart; took the Oregon Trail; later married Swede.

Charlotte: Rich girl married to Pat, divorced and married Americus; crossed on the Oregon Trail.

Christian: Single, on Oregon Trail and Sierra Pass. Christian's character is based on a real life hero, who carried several children over the Sierra Pass, rescuing them from starvation.

Constance: Alice's sister-in-law; married to Elijah.

David: Guide for Swede's wagon train on Oregon Trail and a special constable posted on the Fraser River; father of a little boy and husband to a Yana woman who died of smallpox.

Dorothy: Married to McNair; mother to Billy and three smaller boys. On the Oregon Trail and Sierra Pass.

Ella: Daughter of wealthy parents. Ella worked for Anna in Fort Victoria.

Elijah: Alice's brother-in-law in Springfield.

Eliza: Mormon woman; head of a large extended family; on the Sierra Pass.

Elswa: Musqueam boatman who guided Alice, Walter and McNair up the Fraser River.

Ferris: Minor character; one of the low-lifes who arrived in Truckee in search of valuables.

Horace: Minor character; one of the low-lifes who arrived in Truckee in search of valuables.

Horatio: Ferry operator on Missouri River who hired Robert.

Issachar: Bullwhacker on Sierra Pass.

Jake: Killed by Saxby before reaching the Sierra Pass.

Kiowa: Blackberry's mother; killed by Fremont's men in the Yana massacre.

Kraut: On Hastings Cutoff; died before reaching the Pass.

Leanne: Married to Siederleggen; mother of Gertrude and one son. All died on the Sierra Pass.

Louise: Charlotte's daughter; crossed on Oregon Trail and then north to Fort Victoria.

Maggie: Musqueam woman; married to Walter.

Mary: Hired help on the Sierra Pass.

Mathew (Badaway), Ruth and Adam: Sioux children adopted by Addie's father; crossed on the Oregon Trail several years before Addie.

Marguerite and Herman: On the Sierra Pass route; remained behind at Truckee.

McNair: Married to Dorothy; father of Billy and three younger boys; on Oregon Trail and the Sierra Pass. Captain of the party from The Parting of the Ways to Sierra Pass.

Nelly: Married to O'Malley; mother of Adam and baby. Nelly emigrated from Ireland during the potato famine, then died of starvation at Truckee.

O'Reilly: Robert's father; husband of Winifred.

O'Malley: Married to Nelly; father of Adam and baby; on Sierra Pass.

Penelope: Walter's common-law partner; crossed on Oregon Trail; separated from Walter before reaching Oregon City.

Robert: One of the three main characters in the book. Thirteen years old when he joined Swede's wagon train; fell desperately in love with Annabelle Lee; crossed on the Oregon Trail and Sierra Pass and settled in Fort Victoria.

Rose: Young, beautiful, part-Aboriginal woman; crossed the Rocky Mountains to Fort Victoria and then up the Fraser River; married Christian.

Saxby: Dr. Saxby Chablis; married to Alice; crossed on Oregon Trail and Sierra Pass; led the ill-fated trip over Hastings Cutoff.

Siederleggen: Married to Leanne; father of Gertrude and one son; crossed on the Sierra Pass.

Sofia: London seductress; Carreena's rival for Stuart's affection.

Stuart: Abandoned Carreena for Sofia.

Swede (Sven Osterberg): Captain of the wagon trail on the Oregon Trail; married Carreena and settled in Fort Victoria.

Walter: Penelope's partner until their breakup; married Maggie and settled in the British Colonies.

Winifred: Robert's mother, an Ackerman; related to David and distantly related to Alice.

Yoletan: Salish man from Fort Victoria; worked for Anna

Historical Figures

Chief Spintlum (Cxpentim) of the Kumsheen at Lytton, a village at the confluence of the Thompson and Fraser Rivers: History documents record the meeting of Captain Snyder and Chief Spintlum, albeit in Snyder's words. As well, oral history from the Lytton First Nation tells us more about the meeting and the promises made and broken.

The so-called treaties are controversial. A written version has not been found; it is likely they were verbal.

I take the position that the American Captains Snyder and Graham, along with their militia, were prepared to exterminate the Fraser River people. Captain Snyder believed it was not in the interest of the miners that all out war be waged. Certainly the terms were not kept, and the miners did not stick to one side of the river as agreed to. "You the White man shall not pass over here, and we will not pass over there."

There is a monument in Lytton in honor of Chief Spintlum . In recognition of the chief's role in stopping the Fraser River War, Queen Victoria sent the chief presents and told him he should be chief forever.

Hanna, Darwin and Mamie Henry, eds. *Our Tellings; Interior Salish Stories of the Nlha7kamax People.* Vancouver,1995: UBC Press.

Letter from Captain Snyder to Governor Douglas, dated August 28, 1858. British Columbia Archives.

Christian (John Stark): Christian is a fictional depiction of the 1846 hero John Stark, who was a rescuer at Starved Camp during the Donner tragedy. Rather than leave anyone behind to die, he herded and carried all nine people to safety, at times carrying four children along with supplies, an axe and a blanket.

Rarick, Ethan. *Desperate Passage: The Donner Party's Perilous Journey West.* New York, 2008: Oxford University Press.

Bridger: Jim Bridger is a known mountain man who was on the fur trading expedition on the Platte River and was later the owner of the fort bypassed by the re-routed Oregon Trail. He was one of the two men who took Hugh Glass's kit and arms and left him to die (*The Revenant*). History also recounts the story of the letter left at Fort Bridger warning the emigrants of the dangers of the Hastings Cutoff. Some historical accounts of Bridger are sympathetic; this novel is not.

(Rarick, Ethan, Ibid)

Douglas, James: Governor of Fort Victoria during the 1858 Fraser River Gold Rush. Initially, he took steps to protect the Salish Tribes. Later, he abandoned this stance under pressure from colonialists and miners.

Freemont: An explorer and military man in the mid-19th Century, called the Pathfinder. He led the massacre of the Yana people, killing all but one.

Graham: American militia captain, intent on ridding the Fraser River of the tribes. He was killed on the Fraser River, and his assailant was never caught.

Hastings: Led immigrants over the cutoff to Sierra Pass. History portrays him as a mere promoter, careless of the lives of the emigrants who followed his route across the salt flats to California. The pass through the Sierras, known as the Donner Pass, is now a major highway.

Kit Carson: Well-known Indian fighter who in his later years regretted the treatment of the North American Tribes. History does not confirm or deny that he was at the Yana massacre.

McLaughlin: Governor of Fort Vancouver and later the founder of Oregon City. He assisted many of the emigrants who arrived hungry and destitute on the Columbia River shores.

Snyder: Captain Snyder was an American militia captain and journalist. He was with thousands of miners who came to the Fraser River in 1858. He led a militia up river to meet with the tribes, telling them if they did not stand down and let the miners up river past Hell's Gate, he would return with reinforcements to remove the river people forever. There are differing opinions of Snyder, with some depicting him in a positive light. This novel looks at his words both in the letter and as recounted by the Nlha7kapmx people with the clear message that if they did not give up the land they would be killed or driven out.

(Hanna, Darwin & Mamie Henry, Ibid)

Snyder, Capt. N., *Letter to Governor Douglas.* August 28, 1858; British Columbia Archives, Victoria, BC.

Sutter: Emigrated from Switzerland to California. In the mid 19th Century he had a large land holding on the Sacramento River with an associated, substantial fort. Sutter met and sheltered the survivors of the Donner Pass tragedy. Fort Sutter is now a tourist site in the city of Sacramento.

Woodworth: Captain Selem Woodworth was one of the would-be rescuers of the Donner Party. While starving people waited for food and supplies, he lingered at Bear Camp so long that the hundreds of pounds of necessities for which he was responsible never reached their destination. He nevertheless took credit for the rescue.

(Rarick Ethan, Ibid)

PART I
THE OREGON TRAIL

Chapter One

Alice

Alice's heart pained as their covered wagon pulled out of Springfield heading west. She sat quietly beside Saxby, her husband of three months, and held her seven-year-old daughter's hand. She was relieved the road out of town did not take them past her home, now sold by Saxby and occupied by strangers, with unfamiliar smells and strange voices filling the rooms she'd so loved.

Alice choked back a sob, recalling that her parents and James, her beloved husband, had died in that house; her babies had been born there, and her little son had died there at the tender age of two. Her chest tightened at the memory of her beautiful son, his sweet face clearer to her than the features of her deceased husband. Ingrained in her heart was the vision of her son, his beautiful cheeks cold, his tiny heart stopped. She'd held his lifeless body for hours until James gently took him, whereupon she'd fallen to the floor sobbing. Never again would she smell the soft sweetness of his face or brush her lips across his downy hair. Beside her, five-year-old Amelia, patting her mother's back, had been crying along with her. Within months, James succumbed to the same disease that had taken their son. Two loved ones snatched from her within a year.

There were days when Alice had difficulty picturing James's face. She remembered he was tall and handsome, but most of her memories of him were of words and touches, not his physical appearance. The house she left behind, however, she would never forget. She cherished the memories of the clean hardwood floors, the window seat where she'd nursed her babies, the kitchen with its ornamental wood stove, the surface polished and gleaming black, the cupboards she and James had built together and the cool light of the astral lamp on the sand-polished surface of the pine table.

She had walked by the house last week for one final look, although she knew it would bring a renewed flood of tears. Even from the street she could detect odors wafting from the house, strong spices and garlic, smells that offended her. The loss of the home she had grown up in hardened her some.

Don't cry, it will anger him. Try to make this new marriage work.

Leaving her cherished home behind forever created a leaden lump in her chest, but she held back the tears of regret and masked the pain of sorrow that filled her heart. *I am turning my back on my home and my dear friends, and facing the unknown west with a two-thousand-mile trek through Indian country and wilderness.*

As the heavy wagon lumbered out of Springfield, Alice felt a sting of regret over her hasty decision to accept Saxby's marriage proposal. She felt no physical attraction to him, certainly not the wild love she and James had shared. Alice had remained deep in mourning for more than a year after James died. It was her brother-in-law, Elijah, who'd invited her to the dinner where she'd met Saxby. She had told Elijah that she had no wish to marry, but he and his wife Constance did not heed her.

"Dr. Chablis is well positioned in society, and a bachelor with means," Elijah told her. "He will make you a fine husband, someone to protect you."

Alice wondered why she would need protection. She had a comfortable home and a fortune that would keep her and her daughter fed and clothed, and would also provide for Amelia's education.

"You must come to dinner without the veil and the widow's weeds," her sister-in-law cautioned. "It has been almost two years since James passed, and it is time you were settled in life. You are not getting any younger."

"I am only twenty-two. Surely there is no need for me to rush into marriage."

"Well, you rushed into your first marriage, if I recall, marrying my brother before you were little more than a girl, and now here you are alone with a daughter to care for." Constance spoke in a dismissive tone, treating Alice like a child. "Springfield is much like the Old Country. Widows are looked upon with suspicion. Already I hear the women talk about you. They worry that with your fine looks, their husbands will be attracted. Widows have always been viewed this way. A husband will put an end to the wagging tongues."

At the dinner, Alice ate sparingly of the gigot of lamb and listened politely to Saxby boast of his exploits in Africa and the wild beasts he had felled. Later in the evening, as Saxby and Elijah sipped brandy, Alice busied herself with her needlework, bored and wishing she were home reading her new calfskin-bound volume of Byron's poems. Since James's death, Alice had avoided social gatherings. Instead, she preferred to remain home with Amelia and the housekeeper.

She had not been repulsed by Saxby's appearance. He was of medium stature, well attired in a double-breasted wool suit, a striped silk vest, a white shirt with a stiff white collar, his black hair and beard groomed and oily, and his hands meticulously manicured. He was more than twenty years her senior and, although thick about the waist, he was still in his prime, an observation Alice made out of a sense of fairness rather than admiration.

But Alice disliked the jut of his jaw and could barely stand listening to Saxby's self-centered sludge of words. As she took note of Saxby's self-congratulating comments, she realized that she could not marry the man, as the thought of bedding with him repulsed her. The following day Alice shared this opinion with Elijah and Constance.

"I don't dislike Dr. Chablis but I prefer to remain independent, care for my daughter, and manage my own fortune. James left me well provisioned and I have no interest in a husband, at least not yet."

"I've always contended that you Ackerman women are too independent," Elijah replied, "believing you have the brains and skills to manage money, even run a business. What nonsense your privileged parents stuffed into your young heads."

"I am able to care for myself and my daughter." Alice felt the blood rush to her head and her voice grew tight with anxiety. "Leave me be, Elijah."

"I will manage your funds until you are married," Elijah said, crossing his arms around his ample chest. "I know James was a fine husband to you, but before he died I convinced him not to burden you with the family finances. I promised I would see you well married. I have his signed agreement according me power-of-attorney. A woman is not equipped to manage a house and funds, even a modest fortune such as yours."

"You can't be serious! James and I were soulmates." Alice tried to quell her anger. She had never cared for Elijah. He had married James' middle-aged sister after a hasty courtship, and Alice had watched her sister-in-law wilt within months of the marriage. That Elijah also intended to control her was more than Alice could accept. She tried to hold in the rage she felt, wanting to scream at him and convince him that she was capable and could care for herself and Amelia. Instead, she held her temper and continued in a calm voice.

"James appreciated my intelligence and my ability to manage the household accounts. Leave me run my own affairs, Elijah. There is no need for me to marry and absolutely no need for you to control my estate." Her voice was tense and high pitched.

"I will look after you until you are wed; I will sign every note and authorize every purchase. That is how it will be." He turned his back on her and walked away. This escalated Alice's anger. She could not hold back and yelled at him. "How could you have been so devious as to go behind my back and pressure my sick husband to relinquish my rights to our property and fortune?"

Elijah turned back, startled by her loud outburst. "You are being hysterical." His voice harsh and unfeeling. "I always believed James was too lenient with you. I will look after your affairs hence forward. It is the proper thing to do. Women should not be troubled with bank accounts and investments. That is the task for a man. I will be your protector until you marry, and both Constance and I believe that Saxby will be the perfect match."

Alice could not bear the thought of having Elijah manage her life; marrying Saxby was the lesser of two undesirable choices. In an angry rejection of Elijah's authority, she accepted Saxby's proposal, convincing herself that sharing her life and wealth with Saxby was preferable to suffering Elijah's dominance.

But why had she agreed to Saxby's decision to make this desperate journey? She remembered well the day he'd returned from that first meeting, all fired up over a journey across the continent.

"You should hear what they are saying about Oregon Country! The beauty of the land, free land," he emphasized. "I have joined the American Society for the Encouragement of Settlement of Oregon Territory, and I am taking us across America. We'll settle in the West and increase our fortune," Saxby announced proudly.

Her fortune, not his. That is what rankled. The ancient English rule of male progenitor had survived the Atlantic crossing and its sick seeds taken root in America.

Why couldn't we be like my Dutch ancestors who passed the family inheritance to the surviving spouse, not to a brother-in-law or distant cousin? If only I had insisted on a contract. My mother's marriage was covered by a contract, but when I broached the subject with Elijah and Saxby, I was scorned.

Now with her funds under Saxby's control and her life dominated by her husband, she was not asked if she wished to go west. She was told.

When Alice protested that the journey was too hazardous and that the Indians might harm them, Saxby grew angry.

"Alice, I will make the decisions and you must not concern yourself. The journey is safe. Kit Carson crossed on this trail all the way to Oregon, taking the South Pass. Kelly, the fine gentleman who writes about the West told me that there had not been a single Indian attack in five years. We'll be in a wagon train with night watches and expert riflemen to deal with the Indians should they trifle with us. We will be safe; we will prosper in this new land. To dispel your doubts, read Mr. Greeley."

He pulled out a wrinkled copy of Horace Greeley's 1838 article from the New Yorker and slapped it on the table.

"He urges young men to go west to seek a better place in the world. Since you swallow every word he writes in opposition to slavery and in defense of women's rights, why can't you accept his word on the prospects of emigrating west? Look around you, Alice," Saxby continued, pacing back and forth across the living room floor as if delivering a lecture. "Our economy is failing; people are out of work and no one can afford to pay a doctor with anything but a scrawny chicken. I can get a good price for our house, and when we go west we will get free land and a chance for me to make a fortune. Stop being obstinate and help me with our plans as an obedient wife would do."

Alice's face grew hot with tension. James would never have dreamed of telling her to be obedient, and now this rebuke. For a minute she was at loss for words before she mustered the courage to speak up.

"You are giving me a great deal of advice that is free of charge, but is also, I would grant, free of common sense. When I agreed to your marriage proposal, I thought I would stay here in my family home, in the town I grew up in, that I would be near my friends. I see no need to disrupt our lives for the unknown. We are well off. At the death of my parents, I inherited the Ackerman family home and considerable funds. The house we live in is free of debt, and the small fortune James left me will to tide us over through these bad times."

"There is much less money than you think. I had debts to pay and still have creditors writing me. We must go, and you must stop opposing me."

"You can't have unpaid debts. The Ackermans have never had debts. Surely my fortune is not gone." Alice balled her fists at her side in frustration and disbelief.

"No, of course not, but what is left will finance our trip and outfit us. If we are to be comfortable, we must have a proper outfit and sufficient supplies to last us during the four-month journey." Once more, Saxby took up pacing across the floor. "I have researched this well. We will have the best wagon that ever traveled west. It is wonderful. Like a stagecoach because the entrance is at the side. Comfortable leather seats with storage areas underneath. And another feature only the newest and best coaches can boast of, a second floor for more storage. I ordered the wagon custom-made from a skilled wainwright in St. Louis.

"As well," Saxby continued with enthusiasm, "I made an investment in our future. I bought the most beautiful Canadian purebred horses. A team of four will pull each wagon and when we reach Oregon, I will sell the horses at three times their cost."

"Horses! Don't the emigrants use oxen? Last year I saw the wagon train leave Springfield. No one was pulling a heavy covered wagon with horses, always oxen. But I guess I know little about the overland trail."

"Yes, Alice, you don't know anything about the Oregon Trail, so trust me. It you need further assurance you will be won over by the words of Aster, the great entrepreneur of the western fur trade. He claims Oregon is the Garden of Eden. You will love it there, and I shall make sure you and Amelia are happy. Now, assist me to prepare for our journey."

"Please could we take more time to think this over? It seems so very rash." Alice felt her stomach tighten. She was unaccustomed to the unbridled authority Saxby wielded. She was right to fear him, for his response was explosive.

"Be silent, woman. You are like a stone in my shoe." Saxby loomed over her, his face contorted in anger, his fist raised as if to strike her. "I will not be questioned further, and that is the end of it." The force of his words and the fierce, wild look in his eyes frightened Alice.

She felt sick from tension. She could not oppose him as she had no experience with confrontation and no legal say over the disposal of their resources.

"If need be, I suppose I must go." Her voice was cold, her sense of herself diminishing. "Show me what else you have for me to read so at least I can start off with my eyes open and with our family prepared."

Alice spent days studying the list of items needed for the journey and working in the kitchen to prepare food. With young Amelia's help, she salted enough beef and pork to feed them for the five months on the trail, then measured and packed flour, rice, beans, sugar and coffee. Alice added shirts and pants belonging to James, clothes she had not before been able to part with but now did not mind using as trade goods. She conversed with the trappers returning from the headwaters of the Missouri River, asking them about relationships with the tribes. They told her to bring goods to trade, most importantly tobacco. She stored the supplies in wooden boxes and wicker baskets, labeling them in her neat hand before marking the items off her list. By early April, Alice had the outfit ready.

Amelia was caught up in the excitement of the trip. Annabelle Lee and Elizabeth, the eleven-year-old twins from her school, would be joining the wagon train. The three girls looked forward to being freed from school; they spoke of the endless blue Pacific Ocean and a rich green land of fruit trees and gardens.

Throughout the preparations, Saxby continued to tout the advantages of settling in Oregon. At times, Alice wanted to plug her ears rather than listen to his unbridled enthusiasm.

"We have friends who will leave in two weeks, and Sven Osterberg has agreed we can join his wagon train if we are ready in time. At least six other Springfield families are planning to leave as soon as the roads are dry enough and there is grass for the stock. I've written my brother in Manhattan, asking him to join us on the Oregon Trail. You will have a sister-in-law, and then may not miss your friends as much. They have three children, two boys and a girl a little older than Amelia. Now cheer up, and tell me this is what you desire as well."

Alice offered no further resistance regarding the trip west, but had difficulty believing the Oregon hype perpetually circulating among the townspeople and fueled by exaggerated accounts in the newspapers. The promoters spoke of Oregon as a land of milk and honey, not only with fat pigs but pigs already roasted.

Greeley's descriptions of Oregon were more credible, yet still did not convince Alice that their lives would improve if they migrated west, and she feared Saxby's rashness and his reluctance to seek her counsel on plans for the family.

Chapter Two

Robert
Bedford, Iowa

"Robert, I want you to keep this with you. Two hundred years ago, my family brought this bible to America." Robert's mother placed the worn old bible in the boy's hand. "The family bible has always been passed down to the oldest Ackerman son." She paused, and thirteen-year-old-Robert saw the emotion in his mother's eyes. It seemed she was near tears, but his mother was never one to cry. She cleared her throat and continued. "I was the eldest daughter in a family of six girls, so my father gave me the bible. It represents hope in this new land and my hopes for you and for our family. The mistakes I made in my life are costing my children their future. My wish is that you will help us break free from our poverty." Winifred steadied her voice, knowing that she had to school herself not to weep, not to let Robert know how difficult this was.

Robert thought back on the events of the past week, starting with a confrontation in his school room that had reshaped his life.

Robert had been sitting at his desk in the one-room school in Bedford, concentrating on his history book, when his father had burst into the room and begun yelling at the teacher.

"I need my son in the fields, not wasting his time burying his head in books!"

While his father had railed at the teacher, Robert slunk lower in his seat, his textbook a shield in front of his face. All he wanted was to remain in this comfortable environment of books and not be forced to take up the hopeless job of the farm laborer—out in freezing rain and baking sun, pulling tree roots, picking rocks, plowing, stacking hay at harvest and trying to keep the large family in food. Robert had no aversion to hard work as long as there was hope for the future; however, he knew that the hard-scrabble parcel of land his family farmed would never do more than feed the family, if that. Robert was the oldest of ten children, with the youngest still a nursing baby.

We need more than food and a roof over our heads. We must be schooled, not just me, but my sisters and my little brother. We are not meant to be buried in poverty and ignorance.

"The boy's out of school this minute!" Robert's father was a sinewy man, his head balding slightly, his homespun clothes hanging loosely on his frame. He had a wild temper and although he cherished the baby and the toddlers of the family, he had grown to be envious of his older son, even showing hatred at times.

"If only my father would leave me be," Robert thought, humiliated in front of his classmates. His fellow students had always admired Robert as his marks exceeded everyone else's, even when he challenged the tests taken by the students in the higher grade. Three of his younger sisters were in the room, silent and frightened by their father's anger. Robert had to endure his father's rant played out for all to hear.

"There's fields to plant," he stated emphatically. "I need the boy at home to work the farm. He don't need no education to build fence posts."

"But Mr. O'Reilly, your son is a scholar, the best student I have ever taught, both in the Old Country and in Iowa. He could be a teacher, a doctor. All he needs is a chance at an education. Leave him be until he completes the exams in two weeks. Take a farm worker in. There are men looking to work, asking only for their bread."

"I ain't likely to hire anyone when I have a healthy son, and I ain't goin' to put another plate on the table when I already have twelve mouths to feed. He'll be a farmer like me, like my father and his father before him back in Ireland. I don't want my son to be putting on airs like them Englishmen do, and moving out of his station in life."

The teacher stood his ground, his expression calm but stern. The students were quiet except for the nervous shuffling of feet as they witnessed the uncomfortable confrontation.

"Your wife is from an old respected New York family, educated and prosperous, a family which sends the children to school, girls as well as boys. Robert comes by his studious nature through his mother, not only because he is her flesh and blood but because she has prepared him well for an academic career. I know Mrs. O'Reilly studied science herself so she could teach Robert. She is an intelligent woman able to use the Jacotot method of teaching."

"What the Hell is Jacotot teaching?"

"*Tell me and I forget; teach me and I may remember; involve me and I learn.* Winifred learned the method from her educated mother, as did all the Ackerman women in her family."

"If you mention one more word about the Ackerman family and their wealth and power, I'll flatten your ugly Dutch face."

As his father's voice grew in volume and angst, Robert quietly shouldered his books, hung his head and walked to the back of the room. His teacher, Mr. Andersson, continued his defense of education, but Robert knew there was no hope of reversing his father's position. Mr. O'Reilly was a man who did not tolerate opposition.

Mr. Andersson was new to the country, having emigrated from Holland last summer. He was proficient in science and Latin and had mastered the English language with only a slight accent. He was a pleasant man in his twenties, with a broad face and a beard closely clipped to the shape of his chin. Although he dressed neatly in grey wool pants and a black vest and jacket, he was sturdy and muscular, more like a farm hand than either Robert or Mr. O'Reilly. Robert felt a kinship with his teacher, because Robert's family on his mother's side had also emigrated from Holland. Robert had learned to speak Dutch from his proud mother and occasionally answered his teacher in the language of their common forebears.

"Now, Mr. O'Reilly, you must not address your son's teacher in that manner. I have to ask you to leave now. I do not have to put up with such audacious rudeness." Mr. Andersson moved to his desk and was about to pick up a textbook when he turned back to address Mr. O'Reilly once again.

"But wait. Before you go, let me show you something. I will give Robert this list of the kings and queens of England and allow him two minutes to study them. He has not covered this in his studies, so you will be able to see what a quick mind he has."

The teacher did not wait for an answer. Instead, he lifted a paper from the neatly stacked pile on his desk. "Robert, come forward and take a look at this. You will have two minutes to study the list, after which I will ask you questions."

Robert crept warily from the back of the room, avoiding his father's angry glare. He took the paper. His face became a picture of concentration while the teacher kept his eyes on his pocket watch.

"Time's up. Give me the paper and tell me the names of all the kings and queens of England from Henry the IV to the present monarch."

Robert recited the names without hesitation.

"Thank you, Robert. Now, Mr. O'Reilly, do you see what a brilliant mind we have here? Someone who would be top of his class should he be allowed to finish school and have a chance at university."

"I give not a damn for these parlor tricks that a parrot could be taught. He is my son, and it's long past time I put an end to the foolishness that robs food from the mouths of my family. I am removing Robert from school, and I will hear no more from you."

Mr. O'Reilly grabbed Robert's arm and pulled him from the school, out into the brilliant sunshine of the spring day and onto the road leading out of the village.

Robert was tall for his age, with long legs and a slim but muscular body. He had never considered fighting his father or voicing his objections before, but now he had to speak up. He had been walking a few steps behind his father and quickened his stride to catch up.

"Pater, I really want to stay in school. Please let me. I will be up at first light to help on the farm and back home working till dark if you would just let me study. Mother wants me to be educated. She told me."

"Your mother should mind her household duties and leave the decisions about my son up to me. She can't forget she comes from her hoity-toity New York family and can't accept a husband's authority. I will make sure she keeps her nose out of this."

Robert's shoulders slumped as he followed his father home. With every step, Robert felt the hopelessness of his life. Every dream he had of being educated and being successful in life was dashed. He saw himself in his father's boots, grim and unhappy, working year after year to make a farm produce enough to feed a big family.

Supper that night was a strained affair. His father sat at the head of the table silently scooping his food, his mother at the other end, her hair neatly rolled in a bun, sitting upright and proud despite the washed-out and frayed pinafore she wore. Around the hand-hewn wooden table were Robert's nine siblings. The youngest was ten months, content in his mother's lap, the twin girls, aged two, were looked after by the oldest daughter, then the five other girls ranging in ages from four to eight.

Too many girls and too many mouths to feed. Robert picked at his food, unable to choke down his helping of boiled onions and a tough piece of mutton.

"Eat up there, boy. There's work to be done, and I need you up at sunrise and out in the back quarter. Mrs. O'Reilly, this boy is out of school and will plant the fields with me this year."

A dark look crossed Winifred's once beautiful face but she said nothing. What was the point? If she argued with O'Reilly, it would make it even tougher for her firstborn, and she had her own plans for Robert, plans that did not include working like a hired hand and taking over a farm that refused to produce enough food for a family of twelve. She pushed the food about her plate as she thought of the many financial struggles they had faced, recalling that O'Reilly frequently moved the family as one farm or enterprise after another failed.

Early in their marriage, they had lived in the tenements of New York, freezing in the winter and sick from the heat in the summer, never enough work for O'Reilly and always too much work for Winifred. To feed the family, she had foraged for berries and dandelion greens, baked and sold bread and pastries. After the fourth child was born, she took in washing. Winifred worked from early morning, feeding her family and caring for the children, and toiled till the tallow candle fluttered out, sewing and knitting to keep her growing family clothed. Hard work was the driving ethos of the Ackerman family, and although a small inheritance from her wealthy family had released them from the misery of the tenements, it was only to throw them once again into poverty when O'Reilly sunk her fortune into a feed store on the Potomac and then sunk the feed store.

I must stop dwelling on the past. I will place my hopes on my first-born. Despite the long hours she had worked that day, mulling over the family's financial failures took away her appetite. She placed the drowsy baby in his crib and cleared her plate into the slop bucket before lifting the water kettle from the hearth. She filled the metal wash basin on the wooden sideboard and washed the dishes as the older girls cleared the table and dried and stored the plates on the makeshift shelving that lined one area of the log cabin wall. As she washed the dishes and tidied the kitchen, Winifred thought about Robert. *He must finish school; I cannot let him rust away in this poverty.*

A week passed before Winifred approached Robert. "My son, what I have to say, you are to keep between you and me." Winifred smoothed her apron with her red and worn hands before continuing. "I know you are unhappy, and I grieve for you. You are a good worker and would be appreciated by anyone needing a strong and willing hand."

"My nephew David is a guide on the Oregon Trail. I am certain he will take you on to help him with the wagon train to the west. I want you to meet him at Kanesville just before they cross the Missouri, and I want you to leave tonight. Look for a situation at the crossing to fill your time until David arrives."

"But Pater will strike you if he knows you arranged this."

"Who will tell him? Not I. And you will be long gone before he knows you have left. You are a fast runner. Put distance between you and this piece of dirt, and use my maiden name, Ackerman, so you can't be traced."

Robert took this in with little to say. There were suddenly too many unknowns in his future for the young boy to process. He worried that a job would not fall easily into his hands. Who would hire a lad of thirteen when so many experienced workers were searching for a situation? After a long silence, Robert stood up and threw his arms around his mother, trying to hold back his tears.

"Don't be sad, Robert. Your journey is a promise that all of us will have a better life someday. Now, I want you to go to your room and pretend to sleep. I put a pack under your bed with food and as much money as I could spare. You must go, my dearest son. You are meant for a better life than bending over a plow. Follow your fortune. Work hard, and find a way to finish your schooling and prosper in Oregon Country. When you make your start in life, we will find a way to bring the family west so we can be together again." Winifred put a hand on his shoulder. "I have something for you."

That was when his mother gave him the old bible with the names of his Ackerman ancestors dating back two hundred years.

～

"Beg your pardon, Sir," Robert said to the man at the ferry. "Would you have a situation for me working on the ferry?"

The man had a fierce black mustache, a bushy beard and a dome as hairless as an egg. The ferry operator paused in his work to look the boy over, and decided he had never seen a more distressing picture of poverty. The boy wore a tattered coat several sizes too large, shoes with soles that flapped as he walked, and pants soggy from the rain and too large for his thin frame. In spite of all that, his wheat-colored hair was brushed, and he carried himself proudly, not like a beggar boy.

"Boy, you look like something the cat dragged in. How is a puny kid like you goin' ta lead a team of oxen off the barge, or handle the oars?"

"I drove oxen on our farm, and I used to row my father's boat on the Potomac River. I know boats and currents. I'll show you, Sir."

With surprising nimbleness, Robert ran up the bank to where a man struggled to lead his team down to the landing. It was a covered wagon similar to hundreds of others gathered at Kanesville waiting for the ferry. Robert introduced himself to the man and asked if he could help. "Back in Bedford, we had a team like this," he said, smiling warmly at the owner of the wagon. "What are their names?"

"Billy and Jane there in the front, and Jack and Jill behind."

Gently and with authority, Robert coaxed and prodded the four lumbering beasts down over the soft, loamy soils of the Missouri River bank.

"Easy now, Billy. Step lightly there, Jane," Robert said softly as he brought the team onto the barge. It was difficult for anyone to dislike Robert, given his manners, his self-confidence and his engaging smile.

"You did good, Robert." The bargeman had stood watching, his big hands tucked into his back pockets. "You're an energetic boy on your feet; I don't truck with lazy workers. A dollar a day and you work dawn to dusk all save the Sabbath, and maybe even on the Lord's Day if them emigrants will pay enough. Now help load one more team before we push off. By the by, the name's Horatio." He offered Robert a meaty hand and gave the boy a hearty handshake and a grin. "Looks like I've hooked a good lad."

Over the next month, Robert proved himself as a worker. Good food gave him the strength to handle the oars, and his eagerness to jump in and help with whatever was needed won him Horatio's respect.

Horatio wanted more than a day's labor from his worker. His Pawnee wife spoke only a little English, and Horatio knew only enough of her language to ask for a cup of tea. He wanted a patient listener, someone interested in politics, inventions, and the news of the world.

Campfire Woman's reason for rising early in the morning was to bake the tastiest biscuits, cookies, and bannock. What Horatio and Robert did not eat, she sold to the emigrants. She had no wish to learn about world politics, even if she could read English. Her life was safe and comfortable compared to the death and starvation that had followed Captain Leavenworth's military campaign against the

Pawnee and the expulsion of her people from the south of the Platte River.

Although Horatio had grown up in poverty in a London sweathouse, he was a scholar of sorts. He had learned to read from a kind but educated aristocrat sent to the sweathouse for failure to pay back a loan. When the teenaged Horatio was released from the sweathouse, he took every opportunity to read, scavenging for newspapers that the rich tossed carelessly aside, and saving his pennies to buy a cherished book. Now that money landed in his hands from the ferry traffic, Horatio had arranged for the *New York Tribune*, carried by trappers and mountain men to the Missouri crossing, and he spent the evenings discussing the news with Robert.

"You know boy, that Horace Greeley, he's some important writer. He encouraged young men like you to go west, but tried to tell the world the West was no place for women. And look'a here. We got women, children and old grandmothers all crossing two thousand miles of the continent, seeking free land. If it weren't for them explorers, Lewis and Clark, paddling and walking to the Pacific, we might have been content to stick with the thirteen colonies. Thomas Jefferson sent them two explorers on their way. He was a slave owner. Did you know that, boy?"

Horatio was not looking for an answer. He only wanted an attentive audience to talk to in the evenings, and Robert was a quiet, willing listener who took information into his head like a sponge soaks up water. Campfire Woman sat quietly by the sperm oil lamp, beading moccasins, occasionally getting up to refill Horatio's tea cup or offer the skinny white boy another biscuit.

"We owe the Oregon Trail to them explorers, including that man Freemont. Lewis and Clark, they were different." Horatio hoisted himself out of his armchair, moving to the shelf of books. "Got a copy of the book, *History of the Expeditions of Captains Lewis and Clark*. Bet'cha haven't seen that, boy, have you? That man Biddle ended up publishing part of the journals 'cause Meriwether Lewis, well he kept promising Jefferson to write up the journals, but never got around to the job, then up and died."

He passed the worn book to Robert, who reached out, taking the volume as reverently as if it were the Holy Bible.

"Lewis and Clark," Horatio continued, warming more to his subject, "they never had anyone die from an Indian arrow. Freemont, he's decisive, a strong leader but he's a hot head. He'll make trouble with them tribes, and you can bet my bottom dollar on that, son." Horatio knocked his pipe against the stone wall of the hearth and slowly filled it with fresh tobacco.

"And now we got President Polk," he continued as he settled back in his chair. "They call him an expansionist, annexing Texas, then next he will be snatching Oregon out from the grip of the Brits and kicking the Hudson's Bay Company north to Fifty-four Forty. You know where that is, Robert?"

"Way north in New Caledonia at the south end of Russian Territory," Robert answered in a modest tone. Horatio nodded, pleased to have a companion with book learning.

"So you think the British will give up so much territory?" Robert asked.

"The British rule Canada from across the ocean and won't stick up for the Canadians. The Brits argue that the Columbia River should be the US-Canadian border, but Poke won't hear of it and the Brits will back off. Poke calls it the country's Manifest Destiny— add more and more territory, extract the golden pearl of California from the Mexicans and push north until we are the largest and strongest nation in the world. Still, Polk's detractors say they wouldn't accept Vancouver Island as a gift and called the British Territory a mere pine swamp." Horatio gulped his tea before continuing.

"Those Hudson's Bay Voyageurs and them Scots, they be one tough bunch of frontiersmen, sorta like our Jedediah Smith crossing the Sierras, Bible in his hand and vinegar in his veins. Men with mustard. You got mustard, boy, and you got brains, too. Same as them Scots up north in British Territory. I heared they crossed the entire continent, paddling through canyons, walkin' along the side of the cliffs."

Robert looked up from the dying embers in the hearth. "That was Simon Fraser who crossed the Rockies in 1808 with his Canadian Voyageurs, canoeing all but the most dangerous canyons. Fraser would have reached the Pacific Ocean if the Indians hadn't pushed him back. The other explorer was Alexander Mackenzie who crossed all the way to Bella Coola on the Pacific Ocean. I studied their journals and look forward to meeting Hudson's Bay men when I arrive in Oregon City."

"They'll be there, but I'll bet my gumboots, it'll be the United States of America that makes the rules. You know boy, the fur trade is near over and the settlers will push aside the trappers, traders, Indians and mountain men. Someday America will lay down train tracks all across the continent from east to west. Then Americans will pour into Oregon, so pick your land, boy, while there is still good land to be had."

"Yes, Sir. I will stake land as soon as I am of age."

With hope in his heart, Robert worked his days at the ferry landing. In the evenings, he continued his education under the tutelage of the scholarly trapper turned ferry master and teacher. At night, in the hay shed next to Horatio's and Campfire Woman's cabin, Robert dreamt of a future in the West and the fortune he would earn for himself and his family.

Chapter Three

Annabelle Lee and Elizabeth
Springfield, Illinois

The twins were identical, with curly black hair that fell to their shoulders, long black lashes and eyes a mysterious blue. The girls carried themselves with considerable poise. From the time they turned nine there had been nothing awkward about the twins, and by age eleven, young men were noticing their poise and beauty.

The twins were mirror images of each other except for their attire. Elizabeth wore tailored gowns of deep blues and greens, cut to fit snugly about her waist. The dresses were decorated with intricate braiding and shiny copper buttons. Annabelle Lee chose a romantic style in pale rose colours, blues and mint green. Her gowns reached to the mid-calf, revealing delicate silk slippers for indoor wear or beautifully crafted leather boots with buttons for outdoors. Their dress and their natural beauty were not lost on the young men in Springfield, and as they approached their twelfth birthday, both girls had blossomed into sought-after beauties, tall and graceful as young debutants.

While they were copies of each other physically, they were dissimilar in character. Annabelle Lee was the romantic. She read poetry and memorized Shakespearian poems. She lit candles by her bed at night and read penny dreadfuls—mass produced novels about romance and tragedy. If the novel was of a young woman dying of pneumonia, she would weep tears over the pages. She enjoyed reading *Pride and Prejudice* so much that she read the book slowly to prolong the enjoyment and then turned the book upside down to read it. When she wasn't reading, Annabelle Lee liked to create frames for pressed flowers, cutting delicate pieces of bright material and collecting shells or pebbles to paste onto a frame. She would present these works of art to her mother and Elizabeth.

Elizabeth was the homemaker in the family. She studied her lessons but eschewed novels and poetry. When Annabelle Lee curled up on the window seat with a volume of sonnets, Elizabeth was in the kitchen helping her mother cook. Elizabeth was more conscious of her beauty than her twin, and planned to use her fair looks to advantage. She hoped to find a prosperous husband, some-one who would ensure her life would be one of privilege and comfort.

As their birthday approached, their mother asked Annabelle Lee how she would like to celebrate. Alternate years, each twin would have her chance to decide. For their eleventh birthday, Eliza-beth had chosen an elaborate picnic in the backyard with fine linen on the tables and an array of delicacies—lemon cakes, strawberries and cream and rich pastries. This year, their twelfth, was Annabelle Lee's turn.

"Mother, I would like to have a picnic at the cemetery with only you and Elizabeth. I want to sit on the grass close to grandmother's grave and sing her a hymn and then enjoy a picnic lunch."

Her daughter's request did not surprise Olive. Annabelle Lee had never accepted that her grandmother would die, spending hours by the bedside, cooling her grandmother's forehead with cloths dipped in ice water and reading aloud to her. Her grandmother asked Annabelle Lee to read certain passages of the bible, but the words were too often about death and salvation. Annabelle Lee preferred to discuss the fun times they had enjoyed and the fashions her grandmother would adopt as soon as she was well.

Before the death of their grandmother, Annabelle Lee had always been able to heal the sick. She'd nursed a new-born calf struggling for life, so tiny and sick the farmhand advised putting it out of its misery. Annabelle Lee would not hear of it, and had fed the frail calf from a bottle and kept it warm in her bed until it gained weight and survived. As a spindly eight-year-old she'd saved the neighbor's dog from a grisly death by stitching a dreadful gash after the poodle was struck by a speeding carriage. Annabelle Lee believed she had the gift of life and was devastated when her grandmother took her last breath. The visits to the cemetery comforted Annabelle Lee in the losses of both someone she loved and the treasured illusion of her life-giving gift.

Despite their differences, Elizabeth and Annabelle Lee were inseparable. They walked to school together and shared their lunches in summer under the shade of the Springfield trees, or in winter in adjoining desks in the one room schoolhouse. When their father announced that the family was to sell their business, the farm and the house to go West, Annabelle Lee and Elizabeth were happy and excited. Having known very little in life but safety, admiration and pleasure, they had no fears or insecurities to project onto the upcoming journey. Annabelle Lee took to reading Washington Irving's *Adventure of Captain Bonneville*, while Elizabeth diligently studied the maps showing the trail they would take. However, the day came that caused tears.

Aunt Dorothy and their uncle, McNair, travelled to Springfield from their farm and arrived at the house to make plans for the trek west. McNair was barely through the door before he began to extol the advantages of settling in Oregon.

"Out west I can git myself a square mile of land and a quarter-section for this wife of mine. Dad burn me, I am done with this country. Winter's frost freezing my behind. Come spring, the muddy river flooding half my fields. So I tells Ma here, let's go out yon where the Injuns be."

McNair spoke in a voice so loud that the twins wanted to plug their ears. Both Annabelle Lee and Elizabeth loved their uncle but often commented to each other about his rough language and equally unattractive attire. He wore overalls that were tattered at the hems and a misshapen hat over his bushy brown hair.

"Dudley and I are also planning to claim free land, but we have other reasons to relocate," the twins' mother explained. "Our business had been doing well up to now, but this recession is cutting into our profits. Dudley wants to relocate to Oregon Country where opportunities will be greater and where farming will be much easier—no winter to speak of." Olive paused to place her embroidery on a side table before continuing.

"Now that our decision is final, I must tell you how pleased I am to have my younger sister with me," she said smiling at Dorothy. "I know we are as different as Annabelle Lee and Elizabeth, but having each other on this long journey will be a comfort." Olive got up from her chair, smoothing her printed muslin skirt. "How would you like a nice a cup of tea and a chat while McNair goes about his business in town?"

"That would suit me fine as I have something to ask you." Dorothy held her newborn and sighed tiredly as she sat down in an overstuffed chair. Her simple homespun smock crumpled loosely about her thin frame.

"Elizabeth, please stoke up the fire and put the kettle on." Elizabeth was up in a second, walking gracefully into the kitchen where she tied a white apron over her brilliantly colored muslin dress.

After McNair left to purchase provisions for the journey, Dorothy shared her misgivings about the journey.

"I hardly sleep at night thinking about taking our four young'uns through a country with Indians crawling through the trees ready to snatch them. And who knows what they'll do with us women?" Dorothy said, nervously twisting her handkerchief. "Are you not worried, Olive?"

The twins' mother placed a finger on her lips to silence Dorothy and spoke to Annabelle Lee. "Dearest, please take the three boys outside to the swings. I will bring a snack out in a few minutes."

Annabelle Lee placed her book on the cushioned window seat and looked up to see the three boys running through the parlor, with Billy, the oldest, leading the chase. Annabelle Lee smiled at their antics. She gathered up the boys, taking the two youngest by the hand and leading all three out the door.

Olive resumed speaking once the door closed behind the children.

"We don't talk to the girls about the dangers, and I don't dwell on what might happen. Dudley told me it has been safe. No Indian attacks for the past year. Besides, I am looking forward to the adventure, and so are the twins. It will be exciting to pass through country seldom seen before by Christian folk, and then reaching the blue Pacific Ocean."

"With my four children to care for and all the chores of cooking and washing, I fear the trip. Olive, I beg you to let me take Elizabeth with us. I need her to help with the cooking and to mind the young ones." Dorothy had a look of awful tiredness, and spoke in a whiney voice.

"Ask McNair to bring a young woman to cook for the bull-whackers. We will have at least four hired hands, including a cook."

"You know my husband, Olive. He won't spend a gold piece on anything but the farm. Always buying more land and expanding his herd of cattle and flock of sheep and goats. Likes a good table of food, but I never had more than pennies to spend on anything but the very basics."

"Dudley runs his hardware business and farm efficiently, and makes a good living for us while still seeing that his home and his girls are well provisioned. He takes pride in seeing me and the girls in fine dresses and is pleased that I can set a fine table."

At that point in the conversation, Elizabeth came from the kitchen holding a tray of fine Limoges teacups along with a plate of lemon cakes.

Dorothy looked with more than a small serving of envy at the expensive china. "When we settle in Oregon, it is my hope that I shall have a big house and the funds to buy a china set like yours, and maybe even a bolt of calico so I am not dressed in an outfit that looks like a flour sack." Dorothy noticed the elegant design of Elizabeth's dress and felt embarrassed that a young girl of twelve years should be so beautifully attired while she was fitted out in the dress of the commoners.

Elizabeth served the tea and placed the tray with the teapot and treats on the table.

"Thank you, Elizabeth," Dorothy said. "You are a blessing to your mother."

"Annabelle Lee is equally helpful, Aunt Dorothy. She does fine stitching, braiding and embroidery on our dresses and has a gift for designing clothes." Elizabeth did not appreciate their aunt ignoring Annabelle Lee's talents.

Dorothy thought back on her teenage years when she was a pretty, carefree young girl filled with hope. All too quickly, she had married McNair at sixteen and by the age of twenty-one, had four children, all boys and no one to help the young mother with the kitchen duties. Run ragged on her own, Dorothy seldom withheld her opinions of Olive's indulgent parenting, insisting that

Annabelle Lee was being spoiled and should do her part in keeping house and cooking.

Now, of course Dorothy wanted Elizabeth as a helper on the Oregon Trail, not a dreamy child who had her head in a book. But at this request, Olive thought about the months without Elizabeth by her side, trying to manage with no proper kitchen or washhouse.

"You could take Annabelle Lee with you. She loves children and will care for them well. She cooks naught except to boil water for tea and even then will boil the kettle dry. She will fetch water and gather wood for you. She is a good girl."

"I don't want to tell you this Olive, but you've spoiled Annabelle Lee, and she would be little use to me with her head in a Jane Austen book and her mind off in the clouds." Dorothy's approach to child rearing was *spare the rod and spoil the child*.

"You take Annabelle Lee or no one," Olive said firmly, getting up from her chair and picking up the tray of china. "Elizabeth will stay with me. And Dorothy, I won't have you or McNair raise a hand to our daughter. We have never once struck the twins, and I will not put my child in your care if there be a strap in that wagon."

"Really, Olive! How can you raise a child without discipline? I tell you that is exactly why Annabelle Lee is less than useless, and if I wasn't so desperate I would do without help for the children. However, it is clear to me that I cannot nurse the baby and see the boys don't fall under the wagon wheels, so I suppose I am stuck with your dreamy child."

"I am trying to do you a favor, Dorothy," Olive said, already regretting her offer. She preferred to keep the girls close to her side. "One more thing, Dorothy. The girls do not like to be separated, so you must make certain our wagons stay together. Dudley intends to be near the head of the wagon train so that we get the jump on the others for the best campsite and have a better road. We plan to leave as soon as the trail is dry and grass available. Mid-April at latest. Hopefully your team will leave with us and keep up."

"How will you have a better road at the front?"

"Dudley was told that the last wagon in the train must deal with bigger ruts and deeper mud holes, and that often there is little grass for the oxen when you travel at the back end. Just make sure we camp together. Before the girls came into this world they were together, and they want to remain together."

With that, Olive and Dorothy agreed. Annabelle Lee and Elizabeth accepted the arrangement, but not without shedding tears over the approaching separation.

"Elizabeth," Annabelle Lee told her sister that night as they lay in their beds, "you must come to Aunt Dorothy's wagon every night. Promise me."

"You come back to Mom and Dad's wagon." Elizabeth didn't like their sharp-tongued aunt any better than Annabelle Lee did.

"I can't, Elizabeth. I will be looking after the children. Promise."

"I promise." With that, Elizabeth turned on her side, covered her head and yawned. Annabelle Lee opened her book, the candlelight shedding a faint glow across the two beautiful girls.

Chapter Four

Addie

Addie removed her black leather buttoned boots, hitched up her riding outfit and gracefully swung her leg over the saddle of her Arabian horse before she clicked her tongue to urge Pierrot into the wide Missouri River. She rode astride, not side-saddle as was the custom for women of her social standing.

The water was muddy and dark. Upriver, the ferry crossed the turbid waters, carrying two wagons and several cattle. Addie reached the western bank before the ferry landed. Pierrot shook his mane and snorted as he reached the shallows. The soil on the riverbank was a loose, deep mixture of loam, and the horse sank up to his fetlocks as he carried Addie from the muddy shoreline and up the bank. Addie dismounted and found a grassy area where she could sit and dry out in the warm sun. Pierrot stayed close to Addie, munching the sweet spring grass. Addie talked softly to her horse and gave him a piece of her bread, his mouth soft when he accepted the food.

Downriver she spotted a steamboat stuck fast in a sandbar, and across the muddy Missouri she could see the line of wagons like a long white snake, winding from the riverside up the bank, and into the distance. She saw hundreds, maybe even a thousand Prairie Schooners, looking like ships at sea, white sails open to the wind. Instead of sailing across the ocean, they would cross the continent.

From her perch on the top of the bank, she had a clear view of the landing and watched as the rope and pulley system, along with two rowers, drew the ferry onto the landing area on the Nebraska Territory side of the Missouri River. A slightly built boy, appearing to be in his teens, leapt onto the shore and hitched the rope around a pole, securing the barge. She watched him direct the first wagon off the barge. At times, he had to help the team by gently leading the frightened oxen off the precarious barge and onto the spongy shoreline where the big clumsy beasts struggled to pull the wagon up the embankment and on to the west side of the Missouri River. This was the beginning of the Oregon Trail.

With her feet and legs dry from the sun and air, she smoothed out her riding skirt and petticoat, and pulled on her knee socks and boots. Addie wore a close fitting doublet buttoned to the waist and a long skirt split at the back to permit her to ride astride. Below her dark blue woollen skirt, a fringe of white petticoats peaked out. She noticed the boy glancing up at her and gave him a warm smile. He smiled and waved at her then turned to assist the second wagon disembark. She couldn't help but notice his fine features.

That boy will have all the young girls enticed.

Addie stood up and stroked Pierrot's neck. He was a graceful horse, gleaming black in color and both strong and beautiful, a descendent of the horses brought over by the Spaniards in the 17th century.

"Pierrot, this was the widest river you will have to swim. You were wonderful; we're a better couple than most of the men and women on the wagon train." She stroked his coat and kissed Pierrot's muscled neck.

Addie was distracted by a commotion on the Kanesville side of the ferry crossing. She watched as a wiry-looking, middle-aged man hitched up a team of oxen to a heavily loaded wagon in preparation for the crossing, seemingly ignoring the nearby woman's angry harangue. The woman's pumpkin-shaped figure was difficult to miss, as was her high-pitched, complaining voice. Addie wondered if this ill-matched couple was part of her wagon train.

Addie had met David, the guide, and Swede, the wagon master, on the Iowa side but had not yet met her traveling companions. The emigrants joining the wagon train had all traveled to Kanesville from towns and cities east of the Missouri. After the river crossing, they would form into a wagon train before heading out on the Oregon Trail that would take them to the Pacific Ocean.

Addie rested on the bank, waiting until her guide and the wagon train captain crossed the river. Watching the young lad working on the ferry reminded Addie of her Sioux foster-brother. The last time she'd seen Matthew, he'd been about the same age as the boy on the ferry.

While she waited in the warm sun for Swede's wagon train to get underway, she recalled her childhood at her father's mission and the three Sioux orphans that were brought to her house and had now been adopted by her father. When the Reverend first told her that a twelve-year-old Indian boy would live with them, she imagined a handsome, dark-eyed young warrior who would capture her heart. Romantic love had often been on young Addie's mind from the day she turned eleven. Yet now at seventeen, she was unmarried and crossing the continent alone.

Five years ago, the three Sioux orphans had arrived in a horse-drawn carriage with her father driving the team. The two youngest, five and seven, were helped from the wagon by her father while the oldest boy jumped down, landing with light feet. His movements were graceful and strong, but he was far from handsome with his crooked nose and stringy hair. Addie watched from the doorway as the children gathered their meager belongings and followed her father towards the parsonage.

"Addie, I want you to meet our guests. This is Matthew," her father pointed to the eldest. "Well, that is not the name his mother gave him, but we have given them biblical names that are easier to pronounce. What is your real name, Matthew?"

"Badaway, Sir." Matthew smiled, not at all offended at having a new name.

"Thank you, Badaway. I must try and use your real name. Our youngest is Ruth," he continued, patting the dark shy girl on the shoulder, "and here is our strong boy, Adam."

Addie's enthusiasm was dampened. The children were filthy and ragged. They wore torn and dirty cotton clothing. Ruth had snot smeared under her nose, and all three reeked of smoke.

Addie had romanticized the Sioux, admiring the portraits of brave warriors with handsome, aquiline noses, bright ribbons in neat braids, and beautifully adorned skin leggings and vests. These orphans looked nothing like them. They seemed like children from the poorest and most desperate streets of New York.

"Addie, please welcome our guests and don't stare. Let them see your beautiful smile."

Matthew gave Addie a wide, warm smile, while her own smile was strained. Little Ruth looked like she was about to break into tears, and Adam stood by his older brother with his head down. When Addie realized these children needed friendship, she took Ruth's hand and smiled genuinely. Ruth returned her smile, clutching Addie's hand with her little fist.

"That's better. I put your old clothes away in the attic when you outgrew them. Find something to fit our littlest guest. Then I want you to fill the tub and bathe Ruth in the kitchen. I will see that the boys are cleaned up down by the creek."

Addie willed herself to get through this distasteful task.

"Sit here and wait for me." Ruth looked at her with a puzzled expression. "Father, please tell her in her own language to sit until I prepare her bath water."

Addie dipped water from the reservoir in the wood stove, undressed the shy child and motioned for her to get into the tub. Ruth stood stoically beside the tub but did not move. Addie felt overwhelmed by the mothering tasks suddenly thrust on her.

"Come." Addie put her arms out and lifted the brown skinned child into the warm water, then placed a roughly carved miniature canoe beside Ruth and smiled. This time, Ruth returned the smile and grasped the canoe, pushing it through the water.

"Now I will scrub a-dub-dub you. Here we go. Scrub-a-dub-dub three men in a tub. The butcher, the tailor, the candlestick maker. Scrub-a-dub-dub."

Ruth smiled at Addie and repeated, "dub-dub." Addie picked up the canoe. Then in her Sioux language Ruth said, "wa'ta." Addie repeated, and Ruth gave an appreciative smile that brought tears to Addie's eyes. Forgotten was the odor, the ragged look of the child and Addie's disappointment that the only authentic Indian attire were the worn moccasins that the three had arrived in. She hadn't had a mother to bathe her when she was Ruth's age and began to enjoy bathing her new little sister.

Addie's mother had died of cholera when Addie was four years old, and since that time she had lived with her kind but over-tasked father. The memories of her mother were fading, but not Addie's longing for more family. Addie had always wanted a sister or a brother, and now overnight she had three siblings.

The Sioux children settled into the household like hungry kittens taken in out of the rain. There was ample food at the Reverend's table, toy soldiers for Adam, dolls for Ruth and a garden and kitchen for Matthew. At the Indian reserve, which was more like a prison camp, the growing boy had been deprived of food. Now he had all the food he could want.

Reverend Appleton taught school at the Mt. Pleasant Mission. His class included the three Sioux orphans, five children from nearby farms and Addie. Classes were in the Anglican Church hall located next to the parsonage. Addie's father interpreted for the Sioux children, but even as they picked up English, Addie learned to speak Sioux.

Meals were a mix of the two languages and cultures, and although boys rarely cooked or cleaned in either culture, under the Reverend's roof all tasks were shared, whether in the garden or the household, and regardless of whether you were a girl or a boy. Within a month, Matthew assumed all food preparations and happily sat with his new family, explaining the dishes he presented. Over the next two years, he watched over his younger brother and sister, scolding them if they did not eat everything on their plates or if they neglected tasks.

Matthew never fulfilled the romantic image Addie had dreamed of, but he was a good friend who never complained about household chores. He was different from the other boys Addie knew, and she wondered how this homemaker could have ever hoped to be a warrior. He was soft spoken and more cautious and fussy than Addie's elderly aunt. It was as if an old maid had joined the family, but a very useful one. He not only cooked, but learned to read recipes and come up with remarkable dishes.

When guests visited they assumed Addie had prepared the food and were surprised when Reverend Appleton brought Matthew into the dining room to be praised for the meal. When one of the matrons at the table questioned Matthew about his preparations, he gave elaborate explanations.

"I made for you Scrapple. It has boiled hogshead and liver, seasoned with cayenne, marjoram, coriander, salt and pepper, and thickened with corn meal and buckwheat. Your dessert will be Federal Pan Cake served with stewed apples and thick maple syrup. I've made the dish to celebrate our freedom from the King who thought he could rule us from across the sea." The occasion of the dinner was July 4. The guests, who were the deacons of the church and their wives, smiled at this elaborate explanation then stood up and clapped in appreciation of the amazing meal.

"Matthew has become a more dedicated American than my own daughter," Reverend Appleton explained to his guests, "but he keeps his Sioux mother's custom of using all parts of the animal, and he serves up food fit for the president."

This pleasant life ended abruptly the following spring, when officials from the Department of Indian Affairs arrived at the home.

"The children are to be transported to the reservation as ordered." The two men, armed with rifles and government papers, traveled in a carriage pulled by a team of horses.

"The children are happy with us," Reverend Appleton argued. "Leave them be. The older boy is doing well and will soon earn his own living as a cook, or even a chef. The younger two are in school. Forcing them to the reservation will cost the government money. Besides we know what conditions are like for the Indians moved to reservations: illness, not enough food, no game left for the men to hunt. Please. I beg of you in the name of God. Don't send them there."

Addie and her three foster siblings listened to the conversation from the upstairs balcony. Matthew looked stunned, and Adam and Ruth crowded against Addie.

"Hide," Addie whispered. She led the children into her bedroom, her finger to her lips to silence them. They understood. Addie closed the door slowly and silently.

"You know where the root cellar is, back of the house? Hide till we come for you. Don't make a sound." She tied sheets together and with Matthew's help, lowered the two younger children out the window and down into the back garden.

From the bedroom window, Addie watched them walk away towards the cellar and disappear. She removed the sheets, straightened up the room and sat on her bed reading.

The officials searched for the children until dusk. When Addie was questioned, she remained cool and composed.

"No, sir, I have no idea where they are. I guess they were frightened of you and have likely left forever. Their parents were killed by men like you, men with guns."

"Yes, of course we will let you know if they return. But I don't expect them to come back."

When the officials left, Addie confided in her father. "I've hidden them and I am begging you, don't let those men take them to the reservation. It will be a life of misery for them, and I couldn't bear it."

"I won't, of course. But what can we do?" He stroked his short grey beard and puzzled over the predicament. "You fetch the children and let me think on it."

Next day, the Reverend spent the early morning at the church and returned for breakfast to announce his decision.

"I will take them West with the wagon train. In Oregon, no one will question us when I say they are my adopted children. However, part of this plan involves you, Addie."

"Whatever I can do to help." She wanted with all her heart to save the children from being taken to a reservation, where so many perished from disease and starvation.

"I must leave with the children within the week. There will be no time to settle my affairs. I built this house and the church with my family's fortune. The church I will donate, but I want you to sell the house and all our belongings, that is, everything that's left after I pack the wagon for the overland trip. The proceeds from the house will give us a start when we reach Oregon. Once you settle our affairs, stay with your aunt and take the wagon train next spring to join us."

On hearing of the Reverend's plans to go west and leave Addie, little Ruth clung to her big sister's pinafore.

"Addie, come with us. We mustn't leave you because the bad men in the wagon may take you to the reservation. Come."

"They can't take me Ruth, so don't worry. You will love seeing the beautiful mountains and the blue ocean. Soon I will come."

Matthew was sorry to be leaving the comforts and routine of the household, but Adam took the decision well, thinking about the adventure of the trip. For Addie, it was a relief that the children would not be taken away to the reservation; they would remain in her family, even if Addie would be parted from them for a year.

"Thank you, my dear father. Thank you." Addie hugged her father and the two younger children. "Matthew, I want you to look after not just your brother and sister, but also my father. In one year, I will join you."

But Addie did not join the wagon train the following spring.

It was three years since her father and the Sioux children left. One year which Addie spent in hospital close to death from small-pox, and two years of recovery in her aunt's home. During her convalescence, she corresponded with her father through letters carried around Cape Horn. One of the letters she sent contained bank notes from the sale of their property, money that her father needed to carry on his missionary work and care for his adopted children. Through these long years, Addie carried with her the memory of her father, and of Matthew, Ruth and Adam. Finally, she was well enough to endure the hardships of the journey across the continent.

Addie had already arranged to leave with the Swede wagon train to Oregon when a letter arrived from her father. It was posted at Yerba Buena, telling Addie that she should come to California where he had opened a church and mission. It was too late to find a wagon train taking the overland route to California, so she decided to remain with the Swede wagon train. She had been impressed by Swede's measured and thoughtful manner. Everything was discussed with the guide and nothing done in haste. It was also Swede's reassuring bulk that gave her a sense that all would be right. Yes, she would stay with Swede's wagon train and find some way to get to Yerba Buena later, either by taking a boat south down the coast or by crossing the Sierra Nevada mountains.

Chapter Five

Crossing the Missouri River

Kanesville, Iowa

Emigrants waited impatiently for the ferry operators to load their wagons onto the scow. Each time the ferry reached the far shore, Horatio urged Robert to unload quickly and return for the next customer. When Robert assisted the next wagon onto the shores of Nebraska Territory, he asked about David Ackerman, the guide for the wagon train.

"And why would a boy still wet behind the ears want to talk to our guide?" one of the teamsters asked, eyeing the lad.

"He's my mother's nephew, an Ackerman like me." Robert's spoke in a soft respectful tone, not shy but not brash either.

"Guess you might be." The teamster recalled that he was not much older than Robert when he'd left home to work as a farm hand. He had watched Robert work and judged that the boy more than earned his wage. "Our guide is Ackerman, alright. I'm told that David always crosses near to the last," he told Robert, "then watches from the Nebraska Territory side of the river until everyone on his wagon train is safely over. He's on a big white stallion and wears an Indian vest. Can't miss him, sonny."

But Robert was seldom given a rest and wondered how he would be able to leave Horatio and the barge for even a minute in order to talk to David. Robert would not consider offending the man who had been kind enough to hire him.

Horatio and Robert worked from dawn to dusk moving the barge along the tow line that stretched tautly from shore to shore. In minutes, they would have the empty scow on the east shore and ready to load the next two teams. They were waiting for one of the last teams of the Swede wagon train when Robert spotted David swimming his white stallion across the Missouri and galloping it through the water's edge in a curtain of spray. Robert watched as David crested the bank on the Nebraska Territory side of the river, rider and horse both shedding water. David dismounted and turned to watch the scow carrying two of the wagons that would join him. He was a tall, lean, lanky man in his mid-twenties. He wore his blond hair shoulder length and was clean shaven except for a narrow mustache.

"Our wagon will be the next to cross, McNair." Dorothy was out of breath, having dashed back to the wagon, carrying their infant in her arms. "Come, dear. Hurry or we will miss our turn." She was the mere shadow of what she had been when McNair had swept her into an early marriage. Bringing four babies into the world in five years gave her no time for herself, and sleepless nights with a colicky baby left dark shadows under her eyes.

They had been waiting two days at Kanesville, Council Bluffs as some called it, and Dorothy had used the time to wash the children's clothes, reorganize her supplies and purchase fresh vegetables. "Four young ones to feed, and now Annabelle Lee, an extra mouth drawing on our provisions."

"She takes good care of our rambunctious young'uns, don't she?" McNair offered.

"I'll give her that," Dorothy said, grudgingly.

Annabelle Lee was at the wagon minding the McNair boys, not an easy task given the tendency of Billy, the oldest, to run off in every direction with the two younger brothers in tow.

It is like chasing birds, Annabelle Lee thought as she ran after the three boys, one of them still a toddler.

What Annabelle Lee wanted to do was search for her family and her beloved twin sister, Elizabeth. Since she couldn't leave her little wards, she called out to anyone passing nearby.

"I don't want to trouble your conversation, Ma'am, but please tell me if you have seen my sister, Elizabeth. She and I are the spitting image of each other; even our father can't always tell us apart. I was to meet my family here at Kanesville, but I am responsible for these little ones and can't search for her. Please would you keep your eye out for her and tell her where I am? I miss her so."

The pleading in Annabelle Lee's voice struck a chord with many of the women but was ignored by the men who were weighing their choices for crossing the Missouri River. Now that a steamer had arrived at the jumping off place, another option was available— a safer way across the wide river, but a much more expensive choice.

Annabelle Lee overheard one of the new arrivals discussing the crossing. "If they weren't soaking us so much for the steamer, I would load my wagon this minute and get on the road. But paying fourteen dollars will near clean me out."

"I hear that the crossing upriver is less crowded. I'm taking my wagon up there and try and beat the crowd. Too many people here with their stock, and soon there will be no grass."

A third man argued for the lower crossing at Trader's Post. Annabelle Lee listened with little interest. Her eyes scanned the wagons, looking for her parents' wagon with the name, "Bound for Origen", scrawled in red paint on the white canvas cover. Annabelle Lee smiled at the misspelling, thinking back to the day their mother suggested the twins make up a name for their wagon and write it on the cover. Annabelle Lee had come up with flowery slogans, like "Searching for Paradise" and "Journey to the Unknown." Elizabeth argued for a simple slogan and scrawled the letters while Annabelle Lee held the paint can.

"You're spelling it wrong, Elizabeth."

"No, I'm not. You always think you know better." They argued, and then Elizabeth's hurtful words that still pained Annabelle Lee. "I am happy you are to travel with Aunt Dorothy. It will be a relief not to listen to you tell me how much more you know 'bout everything."

When their father decided to leave a day ahead of the McNair wagon, Annabelle Lee and Elizabeth had begged him to wait and keep the two families together. "Not to worry, girls," their father told them. "We will all meet up at Kanesville, and from there I promise we will travel together." Despite Dorothy's promise to meet her sister, McNair delayed their departure, arriving a full week after Olive, Dudley and Elizabeth had crossed.

"So where are you, Elizabeth? Why aren't you looking for me?" Annabelle Lee was often close to tears, missing her parents and pining for her twin sister. Annabelle Lee was anxious to cross the river, as there were hundreds of wagons on the Nebraska Territory side, and she thought it was likely that Elizabeth would be waiting for her when they reached the far bank.

"It is like Noah's ark," Annabelle Lee joked, as Dorothy returned with her husband and baby and climbed onto the wagon seat. Dorothy urged McNair to move the team to the ferry landing while Annabelle Lee led the three boys onto the ferry and herded and pushed their three best milk cows and their four goats on board. The teamsters drove the rest of the stock into the river, trying their best not to lose any prize oxen or cattle to the flooding Missouri.

Annabelle Lee had the care of the boys as well as the cows and goats and was not sure whether it was the children or the animals causing the most problems.

"Robert," a rough voice boomed out, "keep an eye on them young'uns." It was Horatio, who was pulling hard on the oar. On the opposite side of the scow from where Robert worked an oar, five-year-old Billy leaned out over the side watching the water swirl against the flatboat.

"Go back to your mother, boy," Robert ordered in a firm but pleasant tone. "There are bad beasts in this river that you don't want to meet up with. Big beasts."

Billy, with eyes wide, looked at Robert and stepped back from the edge just as Annabelle Lee ran across the deck to grab her young charge.

It was if a vision had appeared, as if lightening had struck. He was speechless for a moment before finding his tongue. "Keep a close eye on that one, Miss. He has no fear of water. Luckily, he has a healthy fear of unknown beasts," Robert said, a sweet smile on his face.

She was struck by his fine looks, his blue eyes and blond hair. Their eyes locked and a flush rose to Annabelle Lee's cheeks. Her heart gave a jump. She looked at him for a moment then took Billy's hand and led him away. During the rest of the crossing, Annabelle Lee kept glancing at Robert. Each time, he was also looking at her with an engaging smile on his lips.

Robert watched intently as Annabelle Lee minded the several goats and cows, and the three boys. It was love at first sight. When he glanced across the crowded deck of the scow, their eyes met. She did not look away, but smiled, raising a slender beautiful arm in a graceful wave. Was this the love of Romeo and Juliet, who in one short glimpse had fallen hopelessly and dangerously in love? Robert was so smitten by Annabelle Lee that he could barely handle the oar.

"Robert, heads up there, boy. We're losing to the power of the Old Muddy. Put muscle into your rowing."

Robert felt embarrassed and turned to his work with renewed vigor. When the scow reached the landing, Robert hitched the barge to the dock and after leading the McNair wagon off the barge, he turned to look for the girl who had captured his heart. She had taken the children on shore and was busy holding onto the two toddlers and minding Billy. Robert desperately wished he could go on shore and speak to her. *What is her name?* He needed to know. The meeting with Annabelle Lee unhinged him. She had taken him over, heart and soul.

But Horatio was anxious to move the barge into the river. When Robert bent to untie the ropes, he looked to the shore. Again their eyes met. There she was, even more beautiful with the late afternoon sun falling on her bonnet and casting a shade over the fine lines of her face.

"Annabelle Lee. My name is Annabelle Lee. And you?"

He only had a moment to call out his name before Horatio pushed the barge into the swollen murky river.

From that moment, Robert whispered her name over and over. *Annabelle Lee. Annabelle Lee.* He replayed each moment on the barge and at their parting. He wanted to remember every detail of this heavenly creature—blue eyes with dark lashes, black hair that curled over her slender shoulders and her graceful steps as she moved up the bank with the brood of children. He wanted to store that picture of Annabelle Lee in his heart, from her small feet in buttoned black boots to the crisp white apron she wore over her pale pink dress of fine wool, and the blue bonnet that covered her black curls.

I was a child and she was a child,
In this kingdom by the sea;
But we loved with a love that was more than love-
I and my Annabel Lee;
With a love that the winged seraphs of heaven
Coveted her and me.

He hoped she would still be on the bank when the scow returned, but when they brought the next load of emigrants, Annabelle Lee and the McNair wagon were no longer in sight. Soon he was busy loading the wagon owned by the quarreling couple.

"Walter, can't you see that the stubborn beasts need the quirt to get them moving. Be more of a man, not a weakling. It's embarrassing me to hold up the ferry." Her high pitched and reverberating voice drew the reluctant attention of many. The sound traveled up the bank and was amplified by the wide, slow moving Missouri.

"Please not so loud Penelope," his voice muted. "If you yell a little louder, they'll hear you back in Springfield, Illinois."

Addie listened to the quarreling couple. She also heard the reasoned, calm advice from the young boy, who offered to lead their oxen onto the barge. He was so fair his hair looked white under the late afternoon rays of the dazzling sun.

What took Robert's sudden attention for the next hour was far less welcome than his infatuation with Annabelle Lee. Walter and Penelope were to join the Swede wagon train but, like the McNair family, they had arrived late. This prosperous couple traveled with their two wagons, four teamsters and a herd of forty cattle. They could never agree on anything, a fact that slowed them down. If Walter wished to leave early, Penelope insisted on a late start. If the road became rutted, Walter, a cautious man, would wait up, hoping for a better trail while Penelope would demand they continue.

"Not sure if we can load all of your stock on one scow, Mister," Robert told Walter.

"And what are we supposed to do with them if we can't get them across?" Penelope interjected.

"Ma'am, you might swim them. That is regular. Cattle can upset us, and a fine lady like you won't want to be swimming in the Ol' Muddy, now would you?"

Penelope gave him a wan smile. She was annoyed at the prospect of a further delay, but pleased to be called a fine lady for this is how she felt about herself despite her pudgy figure and squat stature.

"Maybe so young man, but I want the prize stock on the scow and will pay extra to bring them. I just saw a cow being swept downstream and around the next bend. I don't want to lose even one of our valuable milk cows."

"Have your teamsters swim them over, Ma'am," he entreated her again.

"Our fellows are not used to crossing rivers with the herd and will surely lose one or more. Farm boys, not river men. They will swim many of our animals, but not our precious milk cows. They will cross in the scow, and that is the end of the discussion."

After a rush of activity, with Robert warily at the oars, the scow entered the water, tipping slightly to one side with the weight of the wagon on one side and the cattle on the other. The cattle instinctively moved to the lower side of the scow shifting the equilibrium of the craft.

"Herd your cattle on the upper side, Mister!" Horatio yelled urgently, as he pulled hard on the oar. "We're overloaded on the downriver side."

Walter hooted and then whipped the animals, but they crowded around the familiar wagon, fear preventing them from taking a step up the slanted deck of the scow.

"Walter," Penelope yelled in panic. "Do something, or we'll tip. You boatmen! What in God's name are you doing? Are you trying to kill us?"

Just then the scow tipped precariously to the downriver side, and the wagon with Penelope perched on top, slid to the edge of the scow, teetered for a second before plunging into the swollen waters, followed by Penelope's furious screams.

Once the heavy wagon was off, the scow righted itself. Walter did not hesitate. There was Penelope clinging to the wagon as it was propelled down the Missouri's spring runoff, her round body looking like a giant pink ball attached to the wagon. Walter plunged into the water but couldn't reach the wagon, which bobbed a couple of times before being swept into a back eddy and caught by an overhanging tree. Penelope continued shrieking as she grabbed the branches and pulled herself onto the Nebraska shore, dripping wet and furious.

While she was safe, Walter was not. He was not a strong swimmer, and the grip of the river caught him. "I won't make it!" he screamed. "Help me!"

Robert saw Walter's sinewy arm reach up then disappear into the dark swirling water. He emerged again, some distance away, flailing desperately. McNair was on the shore and flung out a rope, but it fell short of the struggling swimmer. Robert stripped off his shirt and removed his boots. He was about to go after Walter when Horatio stopped him.

"No, boy. You won't reach him in time, and if you leave the scow, we will lose the rest of the load. Stay where you are. One drowned man is 'nuf for one day. Too bad it's the man and not the niggling wife."

Walter's stricken face emerged once again out of the murky water, no longer struggling, seemingly prepared for his fate. Watchers on both sides were sure he was lost to the river, when a horse and rider plunged down the bank, and in a wild spray of water, headed downriver in pursuit of the drowning man.

"Grab the horse's tail and hang on for dear life!" David yelled, when he reached the exhausted man. Walter had only enough strength left to grasp the end of the stallion's tail, first with one hand and then the other. He clung in desperation to the coarse, thick hair as David swam the horse to shore. A few feet from the riverbank, Walter almost lost his grip.

"Hang on there, man. Not much further and your feet will hit river bottom. For God's sake, don't let go."

The horse struggled to find purchase on the muddy shoreline. Snorting and shaking its mane, the big stallion dragged Walter to shore. Walter was initially too weak to get a foothold, and knelt on his hands and knees in the shallows, panting and exhausted. Men rushed to the shore, reaching out to grab Walter's hand. He staggered to his feet, swaying uncertainly. McNair grabbed Walter and steadied him until the exhausted man was able to walk on his own.

Downriver, a group of men worked to pull the wagon out of the willows and onto shore, while the women brought towels and dry clothes for Penelope. She said nothing about Walter's narrow escape from drowning. In their relationship, everything was about Penelope.

Penelope and Walter were not the only couple to reach Kanesville late. Saxby's team was even slower, bringing up the rear of the Swede wagon train. David watched from the Nebraska side of the Missouri River, concerned that three of the wagons had arrived late. On an earlier trip, David had guided emigrants who believed that the loss of a week or two in a trip of five months would not matter, but these miscalculations early in the journey could prove disastrous as the months passed and winter approached. David had planned to begin a week earlier. Now it was late, and they risked hitting snow when they crossed the Cascades.

Robert watched the western sky, anxious for the sun to set so he could search for Annabelle Lee and see her once more before her wagon train headed off. As well, he had to find his cousin. One more wagon to take across and he would be free till the next morning. As the scow moved across the river and the night shadows fell on the Missouri, Robert noticed an inexperienced horseman begin the crossing.

Saxby edged his beautiful Canadian horse into the silt-laden water. The horse sniffled and stalled. Saxby dug his spurs into its flank and then into the horse's barrel. Gingerly, pawing and tossing its head, the stallion walked into the water, wild-eyed and frightened. Saxby wanted to cross the river boldly, but the purebred Canadian horse was used to a paddock, not a muddy river with unsure footing.

David was on the west shore watching Saxby swim his reluctant horse into the Missouri's muddy waters. The horse spooked and tried to back out of the swirling waters. "Goddamn you!" Saxby yelled, his cussing reverberating over the water. Saxby dug his spurs hard into the horse's flank. The horse, snorted, shook its head and slowly swam its heavy rider to the Nebraska shore.

Amelia sat on the wagon while her mother stood alongside the team of horses. Alice's face flushed with embarrassment at hearing her husband's angry voice.

Robert and Horatio drew the ferry to the Kanesville landing, where Alice waited to cross.

"Where be your man or your teamster?" Horatio asked her, taking in the pleasant curves of the pretty young woman.

"My husband is riding his horse across," she answered, pointing to Saxby, "and our teamsters are taking our other two wagons. I'm driving this team," Alice said smiling at the rough-looking boatman and urging the team onto the barge with a light flick of her quirt.

"Robert here will give you a hand, Ma'am, if that be to your liking."

Alice was happy to have the amiable boy lead the team onto the barge. Amelia, several years younger than Robert, looked on, thinking that this boy had the sweetest looking face she had ever seen. At her age, boys were considered bothersome and ugly. This boy was different.

Robert carried out his job quickly and efficiently, and bent to the oars as if his life depended on crossing the Missouri in record time. This trip across the river was the smoothest and fastest of the day. He was so distracted by his obsession for Annabelle Lee that he momentarily forgot about contacting his cousin. After he walked Alice's team onto shore, he turned to Horatio expecting his employer to call it a day.

"Just two more trips lad. Still enough light to make a safe journey. Are you ready Robert?"

His heart fell and he hesitated for a moment. "Oh, yes. Of course," he agreed, concealing his disappointment from Horatio.

"Good lad. You are a boy with mettle." Horatio gave Robert a friendly cuff on the shoulder before they set off once again.

By the time they completed the last crossing, David was no longer in sight, and the fifty wagons in the train had already headed west into the wilderness. Robert felt torn, not wanting to desert Horatio but committed to joining the western migration. He would eventually have to leave his employer, and it would be a more difficult parting than leaving his father's farm. The man who'd given him his first paying situation and conversed with him as if they were equals was someone Robert would remember fondly throughout his life.

"Sir," Robert said nervously to Horatio, "I truly regret having to tell you this, but my cousin is the guide of the wagon train that crossed earlier. I must try to find him. If he will take me west with him, I must leave your employment."

Horatio was not taken by surprise at this. Robert had shared his plans with him, but now that the time had come, Horatio was concerned about losing not only a hard worker, but also a good listener.

"You're making good money, boy. Why not stay and catch up to the guide later? Besides, as soon as more steamers arrive here, we will be out of work, or at the least we will pick up one or two of the less prosperous. I expect most of the emigrants will be through in two weeks. Staying on won't delay you overmuch."

Robert gave this serious thought. He wanted to find David and ask about joining the wagon train. More important, he had to see the girl who had stolen his heart. He struggled with his conscience, torn by his loyalty to Horatio, his infatuation with Annabelle Lee, and his promise to his mother. He desperately wanted to see Annabelle Lee again, and he knew he must follow his dream and go west with David's wagon train.

"I will even give you a fast horse," Horatio offered, "if you stay for two weeks."

This persuaded Robert to alter his plans.

"Thank you. I will stay, but please, I must run ahead, catch up to the wagon train and ask my mother's cousin if I might join him later."

"They will be miles down the trail, boy," Horatio protested. "How will you get there and back and still catch some sleep before sunrise?"

"I'm a runner Horatio, Just watch. You will see."

With a happy heart, Robert ran west, following the tracks of the covered wagons. He was satisfied with his employer's terms, confident he would find David and the wagon train, and be back in time for a short sleep before Horatio's early call to work. Robert's slim build, hard work and healthy meals lent him a natural and effortless running style. Fit from his job as an oarsman, and with his lean, long legs, he covered the six-mile stretch in well under an hour. Throughout the run, Robert thought about the beautiful girl with the dark eyes.

~

"You look as starved as a bird abandoned by its mother. Sit. I will give you a corn biscuit." It was Anna, one of the women whose wagon had crossed earlier that day. Robert remembered this pleasant woman and her congenial husband. While many travelers thought only of pushing to the front of the line, never giving a thought to the boatmen, Anna and Jan had thanked him for his good work.

"I appreciate that, Ma'am," Robert said, catching his breath, "but please, just point to where I can find David."

Jan overheard this conversation and walked up to the boy. "Over there by the river, son. He's arranging for our wagons to be taken across the river. It seems the Indians here want to extract a toll from us when we cross tomorrow."

"Thank you, Sir. Much obliged. And, Sir, where would I find a girl about my age? Her name is Annabelle Lee."

"They're early to bed types, so you won't find anyone in that wagon up and about at this time of night."

"Then I'll be off to find David." Robert thanked the couple and jogged off. Disappointment filled his heart as he realized it would be weeks before he would see Annabelle Lee once again.

"Now, isn't those polite words coming out of a young lad," Anna said, watching him go.

"He told me he ran from the Missouri River to our camp and intends to run back this very night. That is a lad with determination."

"Now you go take that boy our leftover corn muffins and that chicken breast," Anna told her husband. "The poor skinny soul will need some nourishment if he is to make it back to the Missouri crossing. He's the lad on the scow, a competent lad who has been brought up proper."

"Your wish is my command, Madam," he grinned. "But why not come with me to see the boy and find out what he is up to?"

There was nothing dainty about Anna. At five foot ten, she was taller than her amiable, rotund husband, but there was no extra flesh on Anna. She was a big-boned, muscular woman, with a beautiful bearing and a classically sculptured face. Jan often joked that, if need be, she could throw a horse over a fence.

Anna and Jan, the most compatible couple in the wagon train, walked hand in hand to the river, where they found David conversing with the Sioux warriors in a mix of Sioux, Chinook, sign language and English. Addie stood beside David as interpreter; Robert remained off to the side, waiting patiently.

The Sioux were adorned with feathers, beaded furs about their necks and brass rings around their wrists and arms, and even in their ears. Anna viewed them as exotic and thought if she had any artistic talent, she would love to paint them. They spoke quietly to David, and although they all held rifles and spears, the guide was not at all intimidated. As Anna and Jan watched the group of warriors and the tall guide converse, they were impressed by the quiet and respectful demeanor of everyone, Sioux and white alike.

"Look Jan, they call them savages, but they are not aggressive. They are businessmen negotiating a sale." In fact, it was a sale. David passed over a purse of money, and the leader of the group counted out the coins.

Anna could make out the chief's response. "Six bits each, fifty wagons." Then the leader, with his painted face and decorated vest, offered his hand to David. They shook, and the chief turned his horse and motioned to his warriors to follow. One of the young warriors hesitated and spoke to Addie in Sioux. Addie replied in his language and smiled at him before he galloped off to join the others.

"Looks like the trading went well, and that we can cross the river tomorrow," Jan offered. "David was gifted with a big chunk of self-confidence to stand up to a band of warriors like he does, to look them in the eye and not show a sliver of fear."

"What of young Addie? She stood by his side as if she's spent a life with the likes of them," Anna remarked smiling, "and besides, it looked like she stole the warrior's heart." By this time, Addie had turned to watch the young warrior gallop his pinto away from the camp. When he reached the top of the hill, he reined in his horse, looked back at Addie and waved to her. She waved back at the graceful young warrior, horse and rider silhouetted against the night sky.

David turned to notice the boy, standing aside with Jan and Anna. "And what do we have here?' he asked, sizing up the boy and cupping his chin in his hand.

"He's related to you, David," Anna told him. "Says he's your cousin, and he has your name."

"And what name would that be, son?" David took the cigarette end from between his lips, dropped it and ground it out before looking again at the boy.

"Robert Ackerman, Sir. My mother sent me to you and asks that you take me on as your helper, only I can't come now but will catch you up if you will have me. I promise I will work hard from dawn to dusk and more. I wish I could come now, but my boss, he asked that I stay for two weeks to help him until the last of the emigrants cross. He will give me a horse, and I will ride hard and find you." These were more words than Robert had ever uttered at one time.

"So you're loyal to your boss. What do you think of this boy, Jan?" There was a twinkle in his eyes, as it was clear that the boy had made an impression on the adults. "Should we take him on if he is able to catch up with us? Can we trust his word?"

Before Jan could reply, Anna spoke up. "I am a good judge of character. He is from good stock and will be the best young man you will ever find."

"I agree," Jan added, thinking that it would have been more appropriate if Anna had waited for him to answer. *But,* he thought, *she is always the one to give an opinion, and her views are invariably the same as mine. She feels as I do on all subjects, and I am proud to feel as she does.*

David nodded. "It seems my advisors approve of you, so I agree. Swede's the wagon master and has the final say, but he asked me to find a rider to hurry along the slow teams, and you fit well enough. Our terms will be worked out later, when or if you catch up to us." David stepped a little closer, the better to see the boy in the dim light. "So, you are Winifred's oldest. Your mother is a fine woman. I don't want to say anything negative about your father, but I know it has been a hard life for your mother. She has plans for you; that I can be sure of."

Robert nodded, keeping his thoughts of his father to himself.

"Do you know why I have always liked her?" David pushed his hat back on his head. "My mother and sisters stuck by me when I married my dear wife, but many of the so-called upper-class aunts, uncles and cousins in the Ackerman clan disowned me. Called me a squaw man. Winifred stood by me. She is Dutch to the core and doesn't view someone with a dark skin as a savage, or a man who married an Indian woman as a fallen man."

"Your father was my mother's brother, right? I am to tell you she will miss him dearly, and sends her condolences."

"Thank you, son. My father was a fine person, very like your mother, and I miss him each day." Robert was surprised to hear the emotion in David's voice as he spoke about his loss. Robert thought of his own father and how little affection there was between them.

"Mother said I must go west. That I must go back to school and better myself." He paused for a second and smiled at them, his unassuming nature impressing the three adults. There was something so very engaging about this boy who was being thrust into the role of a man when barely past his childhood.

"Thank you for agreeing to take me on," Robert continued. "I will find you no matter how hard and long I have to ride. I must go now as I must be at work before sunrise. I think I ran six miles to get here and must run back the six miles to the crossing."

"Robert, take this." Anna passed the package to Robert. "Have a bite before you go."

"Thank you, Madam. I'll eat when I get there. If I eat now, I won't be able to run." Robert pocketed the small greasy, cloth bag with its generous gift of food, smiled, and with a graceful and measured pace, retraced his steps back to the Missouri River.

Chapter Six

Charlotte and Americus

Manhattan, NY

Charlotte grew up knowing she was attractive, and from a young age had used her beauty and her skill at deception to get what she wanted. Soon after learning how to talk, she told fibs to her parents, and she only honed her skill during her years at school. Her parents were gullible, telling teachers that their daughter was high strung but brilliant. In fact, Charlotte was not studious; Charlotte simply knew how to manipulate her teachers, especially the male instructors, smiling suggestively until they gave her a higher score. By fourteen, Charlotte realized the tremendous power she could wield over men. Heads turned when she walked with her parents through the streets of Manhattan.

Charlotte's thoughts were preoccupied with ball gowns and gold braid, and her life was occupied with parties and dinners. She loved attention, and by age sixteen, had numerous suitors at the door. One young man was so smitten that he walked back and forth in front of her house all night. Pat was a fine looking young man with eyes as dark as hers were blue. He was tall and dashing, his hair thick with pomade. He was done out in the slim-fitting pants and checkered waistcoat that were considered smart among the young men. To Charlotte's parents, he was obviously a flimflam man, unsuitable for their daughter.

His downfall was his love of gambling, but this fault piqued Charlotte's interest. She loved risk and was exhilarated by someone who took life less seriously than the young men deemed acceptable in her society. Her parents discouraged Pat, but Charlotte, who never accepted authority, ignored their concerns. When Pat proposed, Charlotte waited till her parents were away, packed her wardrobe of gowns, shoes and hats, hired a carriage, and left with as many gold coins she could find. Charlotte convinced the minister that she was eighteen, and they were wed in Saint Peter's Roman Catholic Church on Barclay Street.

That their daughter had married an Irishman was enough injury to her parents; for her to abandon the Anglican Church and convert to Catholicism was unforgivable.

At sixteen she was a bride, and at twenty-two she had three children and lived in a rundown tenement in Manhattan. They had little money, and whatever Pat earned was often wasted at the racetrack or in gambling halls. Pat was never mean to Charlotte, and was always apologetic when he lost money and generous when he won. The children loved him because he spent time with them, and when he had cash in his pocket, he took them to Brighton Beach and treated them. Louise was the oldest and his favorite.

"You're my babe. Just as pretty as your mom and the best little girl a daddy could have." Louise was the hard worker in the family. She did not take after her mother or her father and was less gullible and forgiving than her grandparents.

The boys wanted to be just like their father, carefree and funny, while Louise was a serious five-year-old. The boys at ages four and three were gregarious and uncontrollable. Louise could manage them, but Charlotte was too despondent and frustrated to deal with two rambunctious boys.

Charlotte's figure remained perfect, and the expensive silk and muslin gowns she'd removed from her parents' house continued to look stylish. Secretly, Charlotte hoped she might find another man who could be dependable and give her the life she felt she deserved. Their poverty ate away at her. She did not visit her old school friends from Fifth Avenue, as she could never invite them to the stench and poverty ridden tenements. She felt trapped.

The tenement was sickly hot in the summer and freezing in the winter. Pat missed a rental payment one month, and the landlord threatened to evict them. If they lost the apartment, the next step down was the Piggery District with its hog yards and shanties, a disturbing possibility that haunted Charlotte day and night. Each time they faced eviction, Pat sought out the men who ran Tammany Hall to make a deal for a few dollars. Digging into debt with the likes of those men hung over Pat's head, while living on the brink of eviction weighed Charlotte down.

Charlotte also had nightmares about the ugliness of their fifth floor apartment. At times, her frightening dreams seemed so real. She would sometimes find herself walking through a mess of garbage in her kitchen trying to clean it up, yet no matter how hard she worked in this dream, there was always a mess, the children were always filthy, and at times she saw herself as no longer beautiful, but fat and in rags. She awoke from these dreams in a sweat. Soon, she realized that the reality of her life was beginning to mirror the horror of her dreams. Charlotte, the beautiful girl who was a princess to her father, was soon to be an ugly matron, living out her life in abject poverty.

Her parents also realized the destitution Charlotte faced, but they refused to help her, arguing that she had made her bed, and now she must sleep in it. Charlotte's wealthy parents also knew they could not abandon their grandchildren to such a destitute existence; they had to be properly educated.

Charlotte was eager to accept their help, and when Louise turned seven and the youngest five, the grandparents enrolled them in private schools in Manhattan. Louise's seminary was on the other side of a high fence from the boys' school—they shared the same principal, but had separate schools and instructors. Their grandmother outfitted them in school uniforms, and each morning, Louise brushed her brothers' hair, made sure they washed up and checked that their knickerbockers were the accepted length. She would also inspect their fingernails and straighten their cravats.

Louise was always dressed early and ready to leave. The boys took their time and exasperated Louise, and it was only when they reached the school grounds that she was finally free of her motherly duties. Now she could study. Louise was not a brilliant student, but she applied herself. Her favorite subjects were science and art. She was fascinated by plants and animals and loved to draw pictures of birds and exotic beasts from around the world. She could identify every bird she saw when her father took them on outings.

Louise felt happy now that she was in school and relieved of the constant care of her brothers. The boys made friends easily and were the clowns of the playground, popular with the other boys but always getting into trouble with the playground supervisor and the teachers. Eventually, the principal pulled Louise out of class to give her a note regarding the boys' behavior. But, like her grandparents, Charlotte made excuses for their behavior. "Boys will be boys. Don't concern yourself, Louise, you are far too serious for a young girl."

The next note from the principal required that the parents attend a meeting to discuss their sons' behavior. Charlotte had ignored the first note, but when Louise brought home the second letter, Charlotte realized that the boys would be expelled if she did not attend.

Charlotte did not want Pat to go with her to the school. She feared it would be too obvious to the principal that the family was not from the proper side of town. In preparation, Charlotte curled her hair and dressed in her most attractive outfit. It was a black silk dress that was too revealing for a school meeting. Around her tiny waist was a red silk sash that emphasized Charlotte's figure. She hired a carriage and sashayed into the principal's office, pleased at the effect she had on the men she passed in the hallway, while ignoring the scornful looks from the modestly attired female staff.

When Charlotte was ushered into the principal's office, she flashed a charming smile at the principal.

"Mrs. Kelly, thank you for coming. My name is Professor Chablis but please call me Americus." With one look at Charlotte's voluptuous body, Americus was infatuated. He could not take his eyes off Charlotte. She was beautiful beyond anything he had ever seen. Her way of gazing directly into his eyes made him believe that Charlotte was also enticed by him.

What Charlotte saw was a man who had power and money but was far from handsome. He was fat and short, in fact, almost her height. He had cold, grey, watery eyes that looked fish-like. He was dressed expensively in a fine wool double-breasted suit with wide black satin lapels and a neatly tied black cravat.

He offered a well-manicured hand to Charlotte. At the touch of her smooth, warm hand, desire overwhelmed him.

"What a lovely woman you are, Mrs. Kelly. Please have a seat. Should I ask my girl to fetch you iced tea or a glass of cool lemonade?"

"Nothing at all. Thank you. And Professor Chablis, you may call me Charlotte." She crossed her slim legs and allowed the silk skirt to pull up enough to show her attractive ankles. Americus' face flushed with ardor at the sight of the few inches of silk stocking on Charlotte's beautifully shaped ankle. But he had to take control of his emotions in order to remember the purpose of the meeting.

"Now, the boys. They are full of energy, and we must find a way to have them settle down. Is Mr. Kelly willing to discipline them?"

"My husband is away most of the week, and when he is home, he only encourages the boys to be unruly. I doubt that he will be able to change them."

"Then allow me to make a proposal. I will take the boys under my wing and ensure they are no longer troublesome either in the playground or in class. Would you give me your permission to treat them as my wards?"

"You are too kind, Professor Chablis."

"Americus. Please remember to call me Americus. I will be here for you whenever you have time to visit, and I encourage you to drop in often to see how your boys are developing." Charlotte directed her gaze at his pale-lidded eyes and smiled fetchingly.

During the year that followed that first meeting, Charlotte visited the school each week, spending most of her time in the principal's office, and a few minutes in the classroom. Indeed, the boys had changed. They were no longer full of laughs and high jinks. They sat quietly at their desks, heads down and pencils busy.

A few days before summer break, Americus asked Charlotte to take tea with him at Delmonico's. The restaurant was everything that Charlotte had missed since her elopement with Pat. The tables decorated with roses and set with crystal glasses. Fine china elegantly placed on white linen. Women wore fashionable crinolines, and one of them stood out in the new bustle that was replacing the hoop skirt; men doffed their expensive beaver hats at the door, and sported thigh-length frock coats suitable for a casual outing at a restaurant.

"My dear Charlotte, you belong in places like this all the time. I want to help you and your children. You must have guessed my feelings for you."

Charlotte could not answer at first as the misery of her life was so raw and her desire to return to luxury so overwhelming. He could save her. Take her away from the wretchedness of the tenements.

"What are you thinking, Charlotte? Would you leave that useless man and become my wife?"

"But how can I divorce him? There are no grounds for divorce," she said, looking vulnerable.

"Let me worry about that. I will contact Mr. Kelly, and he will see reason. He cannot keep such a delicate, beautiful creature trapped in a life she doesn't belong in. I will put you in a mansion overlooking the ocean and see that you have everything you desire. So tell me, my beauty, will you accept me?"

"But what about the children? They love their father and won't want to leave him."

"Don't you think Louise and the two boys will be better off with the future I can provide them, able to attend fine schools and be part of society?"

"Yes, of course. I worry about them. I fear that Louise will end up in poverty and that her life will be the misery that mine is. And the boys, as well. Since you began to watch over them, their marks have improved. They are not as carefree as before, but life cannot be filled only with laughs and good times. Children must learn to do as they are told. You have done a wonderful job giving them direction and discipline."

"I could see that the children needed a strong hand. Having a father like they've had, one who doesn't take up his role in disciplining, is tantamount to having no father at all."

"Is it really true that you will buy me a house on the ocean?" Tears pooled in her eyes at the thought of an escape from a life of destitution to one of wealth and comfort. "Americus, I would be so happy."

"Yes, my angel. A mansion in Manhattan overlooking the water."

"You are offering to save me from a life that has become unbearable. Yes, Americus, I will be your wife, but you and I know what New York is like when it comes to divorce. Don't we have to petition Congress, and won't that take years?"

"Ah, my dear. I have a plan that will see you freed from that wretched husband in the time it takes to travel to Indiana. That state is advanced, and judges there will give you a divorce in a day. Stuck up New Englanders call Indiana the "Midwestern Sodom," but to my mind, they are modern and going with the times. Please read this." He passed Charlotte a newspaper clipping.

> Unhappy husbands and wives can obtain a divorce without crimination or publicity: incompatibility of temper only required. All cases guaranteed. Advice gratia. Apply to G.H. Bacon, No. 6 Pine Street, Room 21.

Charlotte finished reading the ad, smiled at Americus and gave him her hand.

Before school commenced in the fall, Americus and Charlotte were married. Charlotte never felt any sexual desire for Americus. He gave her what she wanted, security and a fine house; she offered her body whenever he desired her. His sexual appetite was unrestrained. He could not get enough of her, asking her to undress and pose for him, or wishing to role play when he would order her to tie him up and beat him with a strap. Charlotte carried out her duties without complaint. The mansion on the ocean made up for the humiliating sexual exercises. Whatever he wanted, Charlotte complied with a thin obliging smile.

Louise and the two boys were cared for by the maid, and seldom saw either Charlotte or their stepfather. That was quite alright with them, for they despised him. Americus used the whip on the boys to make them behave and, despite Louise's perfect behavior, he found an excuse once a week to put her over his knee and spank her.

"Mother, please, you must help me and the boys," Louise had begged, certain their mother would protect them. "Professor Chablis whips the boys every day, and yesterday he punished me just because I dropped a book on the floor."

"I knew when I married the Professor that you would cause problems. Don't you appreciate what he has done for us? This beautiful house, your schooling and fine clothes? Do you want to go back to the stench and misery of the tenements?"

"As a matter of fact, Mother, I was happier with father and so were the boys. We didn't know we were poor. Now there is money, and yet we are not even fed properly. I know you and your new man eat lobster, steaks and crab, but he is miserly when it comes to us. Maid feeds us leftovers, bits of meat and rice and more rice. I haven't eaten a fresh vegetable since we moved here, and the boys don't even get milk."

"Complaints and more complaints. Be satisfied with your life, Louise, because I can't ask the Professor for more than he is giving us. This house costs a fortune. Although he is well off, payments are taking most of his salary. Try and accept your circumstances. Now, I must go. Professor Chablis insists that I am at the dining room table on time, looking my best."

Louise watched her mother sashay along the marble floor of the hallway leading to the heavy double doors of the dining room.

She doesn't love him, and I hate him. She traded our Daddy for this ugly man and for a fine house.

Louise found refuge at school. Her artistic skills and her knowledge of birds and animals impressed her classmates, and she developed a special friendship with Suellen, who hoped Louise would teach her how to draw.

It was the noon break, and the bright spring sun shone through the trees in the schoolyard. Louise and Suellen had just finished eating their lunch when Suellen leaned forward, placed a finger on her lips, and whispered to Louise.

"The Professor whipped me last week although I did nothing. I told my mother that he likes to whip the girls and not because we misbehave. My mother and father had a meeting with him. The Professor became angry, yelled at my father and threatened to expel me. Of course, my father did not cave in to the Professor's bluster. Now my parents have gone to the school board with a complaint. I am telling you this because he is your stepfather, and I wondered if he also beats you."

"He's a monster," Louise said softly. "When he whips me, I have to bend over his knee and I feel his thing poking me. I can't bear it, but my mother turns her head and I have no one to protect me." Louise broke down at last, crying in front of the friend who had finally given her acknowledgement of the Professor's despicable behavior. She'd borne her despair for so long it was a relief to finally let it out.

Suellen placed a comforting hand on her friend's shoulder. "I am sorry for you, Louise. Maybe my father can do something."

"Professor Chablis doesn't only whip the young girls," Louise said in a shaky voice. "Last week I saw him touching Olive's bottom. I swear it is true, but I was afraid to tell anyone, and my mother won't believe a word I say."

"Come to my house and tell my father about this. Tell him that Professor Chablis touched Olive and about you being whipped."

"The Professor will beat me till I bleed if I say a word against him."

"You must find help, Louise; you must stay away from him. My mother told me there are men who try and hurt young girls like us."

"I can't risk saying anything. Stepfathers are allowed to beat their children, and he will deny touching Olive. That is the way it is. He has power. My mother will ignore me. I am just child, and no one will believe me over a school professor."

But it wasn't a student who finally brought the matter to the school board. One of the male teachers walked into the principal's office and caught him kissing an eleven-year-old student.

That was the end of his position at the school. He was dismissed by the school board, but not charged with an offense. The twelve-member board did not want the school's reputation to be damaged, so it was all done quietly. One day, Americus was in power in an exclusive school with over one hundred students, the next day he was at home, sulking and trying to find a way out of his dilemma. He couldn't tell Charlotte he had been dismissed, and he knew he had to come up with something.

"I want to move away, Charlotte. I have great plans for us, and I hope that you will support me. The position of principal is too stressful, and the pay minimal compared to what I can make out west."

"Leave Manhattan and my house?" Charlotte's dismay was palpable. "But Americus we mustn't."

"I know you love your house by the sea. But we will join a wagon train for Oregon, and I will take you where it never snows, and build you a house on the beautiful blue Pacific."

"What are you talking about, Americus? Surely you don't want me to travel across the country with the wagon trains. It will be such a harsh life. Think of the lack of civilization in the West, and the murdering savages! It will be too much for me. Days in the blazing sun. And how will we manage without the cook and our maid? Really Americus, I couldn't."

"Of course you can. My brother wrote me from Springfield. He is taking his new wife and stepdaughter. He sold their house at a good price, and they are getting ready to leave this spring. We will make a fortune in the West. I've already sold the house, and I want you to prepare for the journey. We are to meet my brother at the Platte River crossing. It is all planned. The children will see wild savages and buffalo, and your nature-loving daughter will see birds she has never laid eyes on before.

Chapter Seven

Carreena
London, England

S tuart settled back on the ornate couch that was the first piece of furniture they had bought together. He took Carreena's hand in his.

"I need to talk to you, my dearest friend."

She could tell this was a serious conversation, and she hoped he would ask for her hand in marriage. After all, they had lived as man and wife for six years, and she loved him dearly, although she knew he was no longer satisfied with the physical aspect of their relationship.

Carreena vividly remembered the day they'd met. It was in the British Museum in London. She'd recently returned from a trip to Egypt and was excited about the new archeological discoveries. There was so much new information she was anxious to impart to her students at the Academy.

They'd met by chance and struck up a conversation about the Egyptian exhibit. After leaving the museum, they shared a table at the Athenaeum. Carreena had almost lost hope of finding a soulmate, with her life taken up by her duties at the Academy and her passion for travel. Yet there he was, a handsome solicitor who loved to travel and, like Carreena, was an excellent equestrian. What was most amazing was that he loved her.

That was years in the past; this was Christmas Eve, in the Reign of Queen Victoria, a day when women received engagement rings. It was also Carreena's thirtieth birthday. If she and Stuart wanted to have a family, there was little time left for Carreena. But she quickly found out it wasn't a proposal he had in mind. Instead, Stuart delivered the cruelest words she had ever endured.

"I am so sorry, my friend of many years, but I have found someone else, and I cannot pretend any longer. I need this other woman, and although I view you as my very finest friend, I can no longer live with you."

Carreena could only gasp and try to maintain her composure. She'd always kept her thoughts to herself. She was not an emotional woman, although she loved Stuart deeply and had been sure they would spend the remainder of their lives together. Their sexual life had changed; much of the passion she'd felt in their first two years had been supplanted, at least for Carreena, by her need for companionship and loving hugs. Carreena suffered from sleep deprivation, and would regularly move onto the couch in order not to disturb Stuart. She'd never imagined those nights apart would affect their long-term relationship. Now his words cut deep into her heart.

"I cannot believe you would hurt me like this." Her voice so soft that Stuart strained to hear her. *How dare you!* she wanted to scream, but she schooled herself. Her face was pale, and her entire body ached. Tears rolled down her cheeks. She wanted to lean into him, have him hold her once more and soothe away the intense pain. *He'll never hold me again. I'll never make his meals again or rub his back. I can't bear it.* She sobbed uncontrollably, letting herself fall into the couch, covering her face so Stuart could not see the suffering he had inflicted.

"But who is she?" Carreena muttered through her sobs. "I saw you walking in the park with Sofia. Surely you are not leaving me for someone like her?"

"It is Sofia. I need more than what we have, Carreena, and I am truly sorry I have hurt you. I didn't think you cared that much for me. There is so little passion in our relationship, and it has been that way for a long time. Only our shared interests have kept us together. Please don't be so sad."

"I am not sad. I am devastated. I am not jealous of Sofia. If she is the type of person you want, then go. You can't be the man I thought you were. For God's sake, Stuart, everyone knows that Sofia is a hopeless gossip, with morals as loose as her tongue. Surely not her!" Hot tears flooded down her cheeks. She held her head in her hands and sobbed.

"Carreena, please don't despair. I was sure you also realized our physical love was not strong. I am truly sorry that I am causing you such misery. You will get over this."

"You have hurt me beyond anything I could imagine. I never want to see you again. Please spare me the pain of seeing you by clearing out your belongings today while I am at the Academy." She cried quietly, holding back until she heard the door close behind him, then she collapsed on the couch sobbing uncontrollably.

After Stuart moved from their flat, Carreena closeted herself lest she meet up with Stuart and Sofia. She had always been distant and aloof, but now she isolated herself from her friends. She could not bear the thought of seeing Sofia and Stuart holding hands, kissing, salting her wounds. Life in London became unbearable. To avoid seeing Stuart and Sofia at the stables, she gave up riding her horse, Velvet. She no longer attended the theater or visited the art galleries, although she knew Sofia's interest was in the new nightclubs, not Renaissance paintings. If she met up with the two lovers, her heart would truly break.

I can't believe he could choose that woman—anyone else and I might understand. Carreena mulled over their separation as night after night her thoughts centered on losing Stuart to a woman everyone said was a vixen and a gossip. *Yes, she is sensual with her blond hair and gowns that expose her bosom. But so indiscreet! So crude! Can he truly care for a woman like that?*

Time was not healing Carreena's wounds. Instead, she became increasingly hysterical over the loss, feeding her sorrow with thoughts of the lovers in each other's arms. She imagined them talking about her, because Sofia could not resist commenting on the misfortunes of others and was incapable of holding her tongue.

Carreena became despondent and listless. Nights were the worst. She tried to fall asleep, but visions of Stuart and Sofia dominated her thoughts and fueled her anger at Stuart for the pain he'd inflicted. Because she couldn't sleep, her teaching suffered to the point that her supervisor recommended a leave of absence.

"Take a break, Carreena," he suggested kindly. "You look so distressed, one would think your best friend had died. I saw you crying before classes commenced this morning, and I am very concerned for you."

Yes, Carreena thought, *my friend might as well be dead, for he is lost to me.*

"Why not go to the continent?" he continued, placing a comforting hand on her shoulder. "Go to America, not the British Colonies. New York is a bustling center of art and culture. They need educated teachers like you. A change would help you heal."

McPherson was a kind supervisor. Old, but wise. Carreena pondered his advice over the next few weeks but did not make a decision until the fateful day when she decided to return to the riding stable. They were there, Stuart and Sophia, holding hands as they walked from the stables. It was more than Carreena could bear. The next day, she paid her thirty guineas and booked passage to New York.

On the voyage across the ocean, she listened to fellow passengers talk about the migration west and decided she needed to put more than the Atlantic Ocean between herself and Stuart. She needed an entirely new adventure, not another city full of happy couples and museums. When she arrived in America, Carreena thought that the expenditure for her passage was the wisest purchase she had ever made.

In New York, there were booklets and articles regaling the wonders of Oregon Country, as if gold were in every creek and a roasted pig on every table. Carreena read every available article on the Oregon Trail. She wondered how she would manage the trip on her own, when she suddenly came upon an advertisement in the *New York Herald*.

Wanted: Educated governess, fluent in French and Latin, accomplished in music and needlework, to care for three children of Professor Chablis and his wife during their journey to Oregon. No Irish need apply. Testimonials to be presented at 60 Rockaway Blvd., Long Island.

The next day, Carreena knocked on the door of a grand house by the ocean. For the interview, Carreena wore a light brown, three-piece walking suit made of fine wool. The vest had a high collar, and the skirt fell past her ankles just above the foot of her polished buttoned leather boots. She'd swept her hair up into a chignon, which was partly covered by a small-brimmed brown hat she'd purchased before her departure from London.

Her knock was answered by a woman who reminded her all too much of Sofia. Charlotte, with her low cut gown and tightly ribboned waist, brought back painful and vivid memories of the blond voluptuous woman who had usurped Stuart's affections.

"What is it you want?" Charlotte asked, not offering a smile.

"My name is Miss Percival, and I am following up on your advertisement for a governess for your children."

"Come this way, Miss, I want my husband to meet you, and we will see if you are suitable."

Carreena's initial thought was that she would refuse the position as she had no desire to spend months in the wilderness in the company of a woman who could have been Sofia's twin, but Charlotte motioned for Carreena to follow her into the parlor. A white Pomeranian lapdog pattered after them, yapping at Carreena.

Americus rose from a roomy chair, stubbed out his cigar and extended a sweaty hand. "Pleased to meet you, Miss. I am Professor Chablis." Carreena concluded that this squat, unattractive man had likely won the hand of the voluptuous woman not through love, but because of wealth or power.

He launched into an enthusiastic monologue of the value of going west. As his gaze wandered frequently to his wife during the lengthy lecture, Carreena wondered if it was delivered for her benefit or his wife's.

Carreena was repulsed by this short, round little man with the watery, sick eyes. She decided not to take the position after all, no matter how providential it had seemed in the newspaper. She went through with the interview, unsure of how to extricate herself politely before hearing all the particulars. However, she reversed her decision when she met the children. It was not the boys that changed her mind, it was Louise.

Charlotte led Carreena to the nursery where the children lived behind a locked door. Inside, Louise sat at a table, drawing pictures for her two brothers. The room was bare of toys and looked much like an orphanage Carreena had once visited in London. The light in Louise's eyes and her pleasant manner contrasted sharply with the gloomy room.

"Louise is excited about the trip and has been drawing maps for the boys," Charlotte informed Carreena. "They are young and innocent and don't know what we face. However, I must warn you, Miss, there will be threats by savages and a hazardous road. I am not looking forward to our departure from Long Island, nor to leaving behind my house and the city of my birth. But we follow our husbands and do their bidding."

Carreena wished she could have followed Stuart all the days of her life, and if she could be with him now she would face any number of fierce savages and unknown trails.

"Surely we will be safe," Carreena demurred. "Your husband mentioned that your wagon train will include your sister-in-law and her family, and that there will be fifty wagons or more and over one hundred people in our wagon train. There must be safety and comfort in such a large number of travelers."

The two women walked together to the parlor where Americus presented a letter of employment to Carreena. She would go west, and her life would start anew.

As Carreena walked back to her hotel in Manhattan, she felt a sense of comfort at making this decision. A tiny slice of the hurt and anguish inflicted by Stuart took flight from her injured heart.

Chapter Eight

Saxby and the Guide

David rode alongside the wagon train, guiding the emigrants over the rolling hills and into valleys—valleys carved through the loess soil by small streams leading to the Missouri River. He had been hired by Swede to find the fastest, safest route to Oregon. An Overlander, they called him, as he had been west several times before. This was Swede's first trip. He relied on the guide to choose between the many new trails and cutoffs that had opened up during the past two years. Swede's job was to see that the wagon train got underway each morning, and to settle any disputes.

Alice often saw David riding alongside the wagon train, horse and man looking as if they were made for each other. It was easy to pick him out in his distinctive beaded Indian vest that seemed to be part of him. He wore leather chaps, a black Stetson, a red scarf tied at his neck, and at his waist were a Bowie knife, his leather possibles sack and a holster with his prized Colt revolver. His fair hair contrasted sharply with his wind and sun-darkened face. A long-barreled Sharpe's rifle, always within reach, was in a leather boot strapped to the right side of his saddle.

He kept a sharp eye on the wagon train and on each of the participants. Frequently, Saxby's team was slow, and David had to ride to the tail end of the train to hurry them along. It wouldn't do to let the wagons be spread out over too far a distance, lest the ones at the back get into trouble or the ones at the front miss the trail. A loose wagon train caused nothing but trouble.

Saxby was driving the team of four horses over the soft soil when the wheels got stuck. Saxby whipped the team, cursing at the purebreds. He was a man quick to anger when the slightest barrier got in his way.

Alice, who had been walking alongside the wagon, lifted her cooking box out, hoping to lighten the load. Still the horses could not pull the wagon. Their other two wagons, driven by hired teamsters, had managed to pull through the difficult slope after they hooked up a third team of horses. Alice wondered why Saxby didn't ride ahead to where the teamsters drove the other wagons and retrieve two extra horses to pull the rig out of the rut. She surmised that Saxby did not have the skill to drive a team of six. She bit her lip and decided to hold her tongue.

"Goddamn them to hell!" he yelled, his face hot and sweaty. It was late in the day, close to the time when the wagon train would stop for the night. Alice watched as the other wagons disappeared over the hill. It nettled her that once more they would arrive late at the campsite. Saxby cursed and whipped the slender-shanked black steeds, but the beautiful horses could not budge the wagon. After an hour, Alice noticed a rider cresting the hill at full gallop. She recognized David from a distance by the relaxed way he rode and from the Stetson that fit his head like it was cut just for him. As he rode closer, Alice thought that he looked finer than many of the men she had met at the theater, men who wore velvet jackets and expensive black beaver top hats.

"These beauties don't have the muscle for the Oregon Trail," David said, stepping down from his horse and dropping the reins on the ground. David walked about the rig to check the back wheels of the wagon. "Dug in deep it seems," David paused and bent down on his haunches, carefully inspecting the mired wheels.

"Saxby, hand me an axe. I need to cut branches to place under the wheels." Saxby kicked at the soft soil with his boot, hesitating. He did not take well to being ordered about.

David eyed the older man, taking account of Saxby before reaffirming his orders. "We are late," David said in a manner that showed he would brook no opposition. "I need your cooperation, man, not more delays. Get me an axe."

Alice pressed her palm on her forehead, annoyed at Saxby's lack of cooperation. Saxby eyed David with contempt. He clamped his arms over his chest and glared at David, refusing to be ordered about by a man he thought of as a mere laborer, a man with no education and no abilities other than to ride a horse and find a trail.

"Here's the axe." It was Alice who had climbed nimbly into the wagon, jumped down and handed the axe to David.

"Thank you, Ma'am." David looked at her for a moment, noticing the frustration in her eyes before turning to walk down the slope to the copse of willows.

Alice followed him. "I'll help carry the branches if you wish."

"That will be fine, Ma'am."

Saxby stood by the wagon, filled with anger at this reversal of roles. On the wagon train, Saxby was just another member of the group; no longer was he the doctor in command of others. This rankled him.

Alice returned with an armload of branches. "Will you not help us, Saxby?"

Saxby had been sitting on the side hill, smoking. He butted out his cigar and helped Alice arrange the branches, not speaking, a dark look on his face.

David returned with another load of branches that he placed in front of the other set of wheels. He took the reins of the lead horses and called them by name, gently urging the graceful purebreds forward out of the soft soil of the Missouri floodplain and onto firm ground.

David did not wait for Saxby to thank him and likely no thanks would have been forthcoming. He tipped his hat to Alice, mounted and galloped away, dust flying from the horse's hooves.

Saxby drove the team forward, arriving late at the camp. Alice could find only a rugged, uneven space to put up Amelia's tent. She sighed tiredly as she noticed families sitting comfortably by their fires enjoying the evening while she still had to build a campfire and prepare dinner. Thankfully, Alice did not have to cook for the two teamsters, as Saxby gave passage and food to Mary, a young woman who was tasked with preparing the teamsters' meals.

"Why did we use horses when everyone else has oxen?" Alice asked as she passed a plate of savory beans to Saxby. Alice rarely spoke to Saxby, let alone queried him, but this had been a long, tiring day.

"Don't question my judgment." The harshness in his voice frightened Alice.

Alice's chest tightened and she checked herself, not wanting to escalate the conflict. She was relieved when, after his curt words, Saxby gulped his dinner and retired to the wagon. He did not even take the time to help with the chores. Alice pitched a tent for Amelia and, weary of Saxby's gloomy nature, Alice found refuge in reading *The Pilgrim's Progress* to Amelia. At last, when there was no longer enough light to read, she kissed Amelia and closed the tent flaps. "Sleep well, my darling."

Each day, Saxby's wagon trailed behind. In rough sections, rocky, marshy or steeply descending or ascending, most of the emigrants walked. Because Saxby's team could not keep up, Alice and Amelia seldom sat in the wagon even when the trail was smooth and flat. The team of four purebred Canadian horses was part of the herd Saxby had intended to sell in Oregon for a high price, but horses could not pull the same weight as oxen no matter how much they were whipped up the hills and through the swampy terrain.

A week passed, and once again they arrived late at the camp. It was time to crawl into bed beside Saxby. Alice felt stressed from the day's events, and she hoped he would be asleep and not make any sexual demands. Although she slid quietly under the covers, he was waiting for her. Every night he wanted her, but he seldom had an erection without her ministrations. Laudanum was an anti-aphrodisiac, and most nights Saxby would take her hand and place it on his flaccid penis, expecting her to arouse him. After he finished, Saxby rolled over and fell asleep.

Despite her physical exhaustion, Alice couldn't sleep. She thought back on the day's events, angry over Saxby's obstinate behavior, how he had taken them close to a violent confrontation with the Pawnee at the Papeo Creek crossing. The Pawnee had constructed a bridge over the creek and demanded a toll. It was only fifty cents, yet Saxby refused to pay. When the Indians blocked Saxby's wagon, he grabbed his gun and threatened them. Alice was on foot, and Amelia on the wagon seat beside Saxby.

"Please Saxby, pay them. It is a pittance compared to a fight."

"Shut up, woman. When will you learn?"

She stood on the makeshift bridge beside the horses, feeling helpless in the face of Saxby's anger and full of fear for her daughter, who faced the band of armed Pawnee. The minute Saxby raised his rifle, the leader of the Pawnee, his expression as implacable as stone, motioned to his four warriors. The Pawnee aimed five muskets at Saxby, Amelia and Saxby both directly in the line of fire. Alice, her heart pounding, placed herself between Amelia and the Pawnee warriors, but the confrontation ended quickly. David rode up to the bridge, dismounted from his horse and leapt onto Saxby's wagon, firmly pushing aside the rifle.

David and Saxby grappled for the rifle. But now it was pointed away from the Pawnee. In a quick, decisive move, David smashed Saxby's arm with his other hand and grabbed the rifle.

That evening David approached Saxby. "There will be no fights with the tribes while you travel in Swede's wagon train. If you start a battle with the Pawnee, the dead will cover the prairies—dead emigrants and dead Pawnee. If you don't give offence to the Pawnee, they won't touch a hair on your head."

"You don't know what the hell you are talking about," Saxby's eyes were hard. "We need to exterminate those vermin down to the last woman and child before they rape our women, gut our children and mutilate their victims." Saxby's face flushed in anger. Being scolded by David rankled him. "I may not have traveled the West before, but since joining the wagon train I've heard from others of the atrocities and brutality of the Indians. Eyes torn out, noses cut-off, entrails placed on rocks, arms hacked off, feet decapitated. You are defending these savages!"

"In battle, the Cheyenne will mutilate bodies and the Sioux torture captives. They are experts at butchery, and you would not want to look at a battlefield after they have finished. For the most part, they simply want to trade and be compensated for strangers crossing their land. A treaty with the Pawnee ended the conflicts with the tribe. There are peaceful tribes and warlike tribes. A man can be tried and hanged for killing an Indian just because he is an Indian, so best that you learn the difference."

"That isn't the case. Indians are killed in California, and no one cares. Why should they?"

"Maybe that is the case while California remains part of Mexico, but when the Americans take over California, the state will come under the authority of President Polk of the United States of America. I expect there will be laws against the senseless murder."

"You're a squaw man," Saxby said, scornfully. "Who can believe you?"

David struggled to contain his patience. *Trying to talk sense to this man is like lecturing a stone.* David wanted to send his fist into Saxby's jutting jaw. Instead, he gave Saxby a cool glance and walked away.

As Alice replayed the picture of Saxby's angry encounter with David, the fury and malevolence on her husband's face sent a sick feeling through her stomach. His actions had placed Amelia in danger; to Alice, this was unforgivable.

In the tent, as Alice opened the book to read, Amelia asked her about the confrontation.

"Mom," a worried look on her sweet face, "were the Indians going to shoot me?"

"No, darling. Their bullets would have found Saxby. Still, it was scary, wasn't it? I shall make certain nothing like that happens again." She hugged Amelia and kissed the child's worried brow. At the same time, she wondered if indeed she would be able to protect her beloved daughter from Saxby's rashness.

I must stop dwelling on Saxby's faults. It will get better. He will learn to get along with others. He may even conclude that oxen would pull our heavy wagon better than a team of parade horses.

Saxby did not learn. The next river crossing was even more difficult. Saxby and Alice had to unhook the horses and transfer a team of McNair's oxen to pull the wagon across the sandy bottom of the river. As usual, Saxby's wagon was at the end of the train. This left Dorothy alone with the children on the opposite side of the river. During the hours it took to bring the wagon across, a band of Pawnee arrived to watch. Dorothy was terrified and quickly hurried the children into the wagon, then sat at the entrance to the wagon, a rifle across her lap.

Annabelle Lee peeked out from the canvas opening of the covered wagon and watched the Indians with curiosity.

"They are Pawnee, peaceful Indians. David said so. I think they may want to trade with us or ask us for food."

Annabelle Lee watched two young women who carried their infants in decorated canopied baskets suspended from their backs by a band around their forehead. "Look, there are several Indian mothers and their babes." Annabelle Lee stared at the Pawnee, fascinated by their exotic dress and elaborate decorative beading on their skin clothing. She also admired the men with their feathered headdresses and beaded buckskin jackets and leggings.

"Annabelle Lee, you are every bit the fool I've always thought you were. I told my sister that she was raising you and Elizabeth with no sense of the real world. Indians will kidnap our children, torture our men and do the unthinkable to our women."

"But, Aunt Dorothy," Annabelle Lee said in a soft respectful voice, "surely some are kind and good."

"Listen to me, Annabelle Lee," Dorothy said firmly. "They have no mercy, and even young girls like you are in danger. Don't ever let your guard down around savages."

"David says that in the village where his son lives, the mothers say the same thing about us. When a wagon train passed her village, one of the mothers hid her two children in a hole in the ground and covered them with branches. She told the children that if they were captured, the white people would eat them. David told us that he knows when they intend harm and when they just want to trade, steal a horse or ask for food."

"David is a good guide, but he is a squaw man and might lead us to our deaths with his goodwill to all Indians."

"I heard that his wife died of smallpox and that he was cared for by his grandmother."

"Yes. I know," Dorothy said. "It's sad, but it makes him even more sympathetic towards Indians."

That night, Dorothy expressed the same view to McNair as they settled into their bed.

"Dorothy," McNair said, "I heared a story about David that will set you back on your heels. Swede and him, they were crossing Sioux country when the savages surrounded the wagon train, wounded two of the men and captured a young woman. Our guide, he up and chased them Sioux. Picked off six with that Sharpe rifle of his, caught the young brave that kidnapped the girl and sliced off what them savages take from us, the young warrior's scalp. The girl was rescued, and the band of Sioux never bothered Swede's wagon train agin."

"Well, I'll be gob smacked," Dorothy said with a wry smile.

~

Saxby's parade horses continued to slow down the Swede wagon train. Since crossing the Elkhorn River, Alice and Saxby had struggled through miles of flood plain, where the horses sank up to their fetlocks. Each time the wagon got stuck, Saxby had to call on other men with oxen to pull their wagon out of the mud. Saxby never thanked them; instead he became defensive and then aggressive when David suggested a team of oxen would work better on the trail than horses.

That night Alice had a small measure of relief as Saxby left the camp, walking off into the grove of trees bordering the swamp. He carried his gun, but Alice knew he would not bring back even a rabbit to add to their diet of salted meat, beans and rice.

Although travelling with Saxby was frustrating, Alice loved the camp life and the beauty of the land. She was an energetic camper, always waking with the first rays of the sun, often humming or singing as she prepared breakfast and loaded their wagon for the day's journey. One morning, as Alice sang the "Yellow Rose of Texas," she noticed David watching her and listening. He smiled and held her eyes for a moment. She waved and continued her work, moving easily around the campfire, elegantly as a ballet dancer, her skirt sweeping as she lifted the boxes into the wagon.

The wagon train moved west, first through cool spring weather and wild rainstorms, then into the dusty bright sunshine of the Nebraska Territory's great plains. As long as Alice did not have to be near her husband, she enjoyed the long hours walking with Amelia, admiring the spring flowers and varied terrain of this new land. Alice was a woman who smiled easily, never given to complaint. With so many pleasant distractions, she thought less and less often of her childhood home.

She also felt less trapped by her marriage to Saxby. He did not socialize with the other emigrants, instead taking his gun and wandering about the edge of the encampment, or spending the evenings in their covered wagon, often too drugged to appreciate the beauty of the land.

Alice threw herself into the work of cooking and caring for Amelia. In contrast, Saxby grew increasingly withdrawn and morose. Saxby did not seek out her company, so once Alice completed her household tasks on rest days, she took Amelia and Annabelle Lee in search of berries and plants.

Amelia was a gregarious, lively child, who delighted in everything she saw along the trail. She adored the beautiful Annabelle Lee, and the older girl was in turn entertained by Amelia's vivacious personality despite their difference in age.

They picked strawberries and Alice took scissors from her possibles sack and clipped the leaves to dry for tea, never moving completely out of sight of the camp. Although some of the Pawnee they had met along the way had been petty thieves and beggars, they were not violent. Still, it would be foolhardy for a woman with two young girls to wander alone too far from the protection of the wagontrain.

It had been a month since they crossed the Missouri when the team of horses struggled to pull the wagon up a rise at the crest of a valley. Alice and Amelia walked together behind the wagon, while Saxby sat on the wagon seat, driving the team. Amelia was strong for her age and able to cover several miles each day. When the girl tired, Alice lifted her onto the top of the feed box for a rest.

"There's the fabled Platte River," Alice told Amelia as she glimpsed the slow-moving, silt-laden water flowing through a tree-less valley. Amelia jumped off the wagon to see this new sight.

As the Oregon Trail left the basin of the Missouri River to fol-low along the Platte River, a new concern replaced the fear of attack. Cholera struck the emigrant trains, and graves became distress-ingly common along the trail. One grave in particular upset Alice. It was a small gravesite surrounded by a rude fence of pickets. There was an inscription scratched on a board:

On reading these words, Alice's eyes filled with tears, remem-bering her own dear little son who had died at that age. Amelia stood by her side and took her mother's hand.

"I miss him too, mother. Remember how he hated to eat his veg-etables, but when I fed him, he would smile and eat the peas or carrots?"

"Yes, Amelia, he was God's sweetest creature, as are you, my dearest one." Alice hugged her daughter as they stood beside the gravesite.

Before leaving, Alice and Amelia added a pen of logs about the gravesite to discourage the prowling wolves from digging up the little child.

"What a lonely, desolate place to bury a sweet, little boy. At least our little William is safe in a cemetery. He is not out here, miles from civilization with only strangers to place flowers on his grave."

As the wagon train wound along the valley, more graves appeared.

"Saxby, please stop," Alice called to him. "The wolves dug up the grave. We must bury the bones. It is a little child. It will only take a minute."

"We are already too far behind. Stop looking at the graves. It's making you crazy."

"But if it was our child, you would want someone to stop," she entreated.

"You are wrong, woman. I would tell them to press on, and that the dead are dead."

Alice tried to accept Saxby's cold response but wished with all her heart that he could feel as she did. Saxby seemed unable to share her sadness at the hardships and death that surrounded them or experience any joy in the beauty of the land. There was a gloomy melancholy that enveloped him every hour of his waking day.

If she spent all her days with him, the distant earth of this endless river valley would soon drink her blood. To preserve her normal positive attitude and love of life, Alice stayed with Amelia and distanced herself from Saxby. Walking the trail with Amelia allowed Alice to open her mind to the beauty of the Platte River Valley. She thrilled to the early sun lighting up the hills and the prickly pear blooming on the treeless river edges—sharp to the touch, but beautiful to the eye.

As she walked day after day, she contemplated her marriage to Saxby. She had never experienced even a tremor of sexual desire for him. Now, a new worry occupied her. She carried his child. *I have no wish to bear a babe and have the child grow up under Saxby's harsh discipline and gloomy nature. If only I had taken more care douching myself.* It wasn't really the child she wished to be rid of, though. Her thoughts turned again to her growing anxiety over her marriage. *If only I could free myself from Saxby, I would welcome another child.*

Chapter Nine
Robert and Annabelle Lee

Annabelle Lee could not believe her eyes when she saw Robert ride into the camp on the Platte River, a dollop of foam flying from his chestnut gelding's mouth. But here he was, boy and animal alike, dusty and out of breath. Every waking hour since leaving the Missouri River, Annabelle Lee had been thinking of the boy with the engaging smile. She watched Robert from the shadows of her aunt and uncle's wagon, too young and shy to approach him.

Anna was the first to greet him. "You're the boy who worked on the ferry and ran forward to see David. You're even skinnier, son, although I am pleased to see you've outfitted yourself with new clothes. Why not wash yourself up and sit down for a good meal? Put some fat on that frame."

"Thank you, ma'am. But please, where can I find your guide? After I speak to him, may I accept your offer?"

"Yes, son, of course. David is over there," Anna said pointing to where David sat, a coffee cup in his hand and a roll of maps spread out on a makeshift table.

"Let me take your horse. Jan and I will see to it while you talk to our guide."

"That is most generous of you," Robert said, tipping his hat before walking over to David. He passed between several wagons, always watching out for the enchanting Annabelle Lee.

"I hope I am not disturbing your work, Sir. I want to let you know I'm here and hope you're still able to take me on as a helper? I have a good horse and will work hard. If I may have my victuals, I need no pay."

David stood up, maps clutched under his arm, his right hand extended to Robert. They shook hands, and David smiled at Robert, thinking that the boy's light hair and blue eyes closely matched his own when he was a skinny thirteen-year-old.

"Welcome to the Swede train, Robert. I watched you at the ferry. You're a good bullwhacker, and that is just what we need. We've lost time crossing the rivers; a lad like you will be just the ticket to work with the slower teams. Then there's this worry over cholera. So far we've not been hit, but the women say we need to move faster and leave behind the Platte River and its murky waters. There are also concerns about our timing. I must get the wagon train over the mountains before snow falls in the Cascades."

"I've seen the graves, but did not know it was disease striking the wagon trains."

"Women worried about the Indians, and little did they know that for every one emigrant killed by an attack there would be twenty times as many dead from cholera or carelessness." David returned to his maps.

"I didn't know there were maps of the Oregon Trail."

"Not sure if they have it right, but most guides pick up a copy of this. It's the Topographical Map of the Road from Missouri to Oregon drawn by Preuss, the cartographer with Freemont. I have a friend with us who is an expert with maps. Name's Christian. When I can't figure where the next good water and campsite might be, I call him over for a confab. You'll meet him soon because one of your jobs is to ride ahead and locate our campsite. Now you find yourself some victuals, and have a rest. You take the watch at midnight."

Robert tipped his hat to David and walked back to Anna and Jan's campsite, again watching for Annabelle Lee.

The late evening sun sent slanted rays over the hilltops bordering the Platte River, casting shadows across the campsite. The evening was quiet except for the soft murmur of the slow-moving Platte and the low chatter of voices.

"Come sit yourself down, Robert," Anna offered, turning to the campfire to fill a plate with fried steak and a mound of rice with onions. "Eat this up and then there's dessert. We camped early today so there's food a'plenty. Jan put together a pie that beats anything. Flaky crust filled with strawberry preserves."

"I suppose you are surprised that I am the chef in the family," Jan said, getting up to shake Robert's hand.

Robert doffed his hat and shook Jan's hand before accepting the plate of steaming hot food from Anna.

"Many thanks," Robert smiled engagingly. "The food smells mighty fine, Sir. I'm on my own now, so when I reach Oregon, I will have to cook for myself."

Robert had only eaten a few pieces of jerky and hardtack over the past several days and was famished from his long ride. His mouth watered at the sight of the food, and despite his mother's high standard of table manners, Robert heaped his fork with a piece of steak and a mound of rice, savoring the taste of the dinner which he consumed in record time.

"Never tasted the like of it since leaving my mother's table in Bedford, Iowa," Robert told them, handing the plate back to Anna. While Robert felt obliged to chat with Anna and Jan, his mind was elsewhere. All he could think of was Annabelle Lee.

"I guess you are a little young to find a wife," Jan said with a chuckle, "but I see our little beauty across the way can't take her eyes off you."

Robert's heart missed a beat. He scanned the campsite anxious for a glance of the girl he loved. And there she was, sitting in the shadow of the covered wagon, more startlingly beautiful than he remembered. Robert's entire being yearned for this young love of his, this first love.

Robert smiled and waved to Annabelle Lee. She gracefully lifted her arm and waved back. She smiled at him, gathered up the three boys she looked after and led them away. Robert felt as if his life was beginning anew. His heart filled with hope for the future and love for this girl. It mattered naught to Robert that he was still a decade from marrying age. He had found his true love and knew he would be bound to Annabelle Lee till the end of his days.

Robert's first day on the job was long and occupied with duties that included riding ahead to locate a suitable camp. Each night, they needed grass for the stock. He was competent at finding campsites flat enough for tent sites and well stocked with buffalo chips for the fires.

Water was a problem because the Platte River ran slow and murky through its low-lying valley. The silt in the water ruled out the possibility of a clean bath, but when left overnight in a bucket to settle it was clear enough for cooking. Robert tried to find campsites with a clear stream running into the Platte, so the cooks would not have to waste time settling water, and mothers would be able to bathe their children and wash the day's dust from their own faces and hands. Once the wagons were circled, he helped the emigrants drive their herds of cattle and sheep into an enclosure, and staked out the oxen and horses near the wagons.

Robert performed all his duties so conscientiously that over the first few days, the sun had set before he was free to look for

Annabelle Lee. By that time, she was in the tent reading to the boys or already asleep.

He wanted with all his heart to be with Annabelle Lee, so the following day he rode up to her as she walked beside the McNair wagon with two of the boys in her care.

"Do you remember me?" He remained on his horse and smiled, noticing every detail of this beautiful girl who had captured his heart.

"Robert. Of course. Why would you ever think otherwise?" Annabelle Lee returned his smile. Robert's heart beat faster. *Never have I seen anyone so beautiful.* Despite the oppressive heat, she looked cool in her light, blue cotton frock and gleaming white pinafore.

"I want to talk to you tonight after I finish work. Are you free once the children are in bed?'

"Unfortunately, my aunt demands I go to bed and stay in the tent with these two young ones." She motioned to the boys aged six and five. "They love to have me tell stories, and then we all fall asleep. Maybe tomorrow we can talk; Aunt Dorothy told me it will be a rest day."

"Tomorrow then." Robert made a clicking sound with his tongue, and horse and rider galloped away, heading to the back of the wagon train. Word had passed down the line of wagons that once again Saxby's wagon was bogged down, this time mired in the sand dunes.

Robert rode back along the trail, passing dozens of wagons before meeting up with two riders, a man he did not recognize and the woman from the Missouri Crossing, seventeen-year-old Addie on her graceful Arabian horse. She was decidedly unhappy with the man's company, spurring her horse into a gallop in an attempt to leave him behind. Each time she galloped away, the man whipped his mount and caught up to her.

"Miss, is everything alright?" Robert asked, as he reined his horse in beside them.

"No, it is not, Robert. I have asked Finis to let me ride alone, but he insists I need protection. Finis, I will tell you once more," she said, turning to the awkward-looking rider, "I don't want you to ride with me; I want to ride at my own speed and with only my own company." She spoke sternly, a look of annoyance in her clear blue eyes.

"This young woman must have a man to ride shotgun, and Addie here and me, we don't need no gypsy wet behind the ears telling me a young woman don't need a man by her side. The Oregon Trail ain't no place for a woman on her own. Now skedaddle, you little hobo."

Finis rode uncomfortably, with the posture of a lamppost as if riding was foreign to him. His hair was short cropped, and his close-fitting denim shirt and pants added to his awkward appearance.

Robert noted how uncomfortably Finis perched on his a big, powerful palomino. *If that beautiful horse belongs to Finis, I'll eat my shoe.*

"Robert. Please insist that he leave me be. I can't bear being followed and watched every moment."

"Sir, did you hear the lady's wishes?"

"I ain't takin' no orders from a tramp. You ain't even a man, so don't be telling me what I kin do. I suppose you think yourself old enough to be chasing a woman of her age, a skirt that has already been spoken for. Git yourself off, boy, before I whip your little ass."

Robert did not reply. Instead, he pulled the whip from his saddle and slapped the back of Finis's horse. The palomino lunged forward suddenly with Finis clinging awkwardly to horse and saddle. Robert continued to chase the horse and rider, slapping the palomino's hindquarters with his whip until Finis was a mile away. Robert turned his horse and rode back to Addie, tipping his hat at her with a sweet smile on his lips, before continuing back along the trail in search of Saxby and his team.

Robert found Saxby cussing at the team, and Alice and little Amelia pushing the heavy wagon from behind. Extracting Saxby's wagon was an almost daily event, and Robert had learned how to handle the team of four horses, discovering that whispers and gentle treatment worked far better than whipping and cursing.

That evening, Addie walked over to where Robert was carefully applying liniment to the leg of one of the horses that had gone lame. Addie noticed that horses were calm around the boy.

"Thank you, Robert, for assisting me today. Finis should not have spoken to you that way," Addie told him. "I appreciate you, and I know you and Annabelle Lee are friends. I would say more than friends, while you and I are friends, like brother and sister."

"I miss my little sisters, Addie, and am pleased if I can be your young brother. Let me know if Finis bothers you again."

That night Finis shared a campfire with two bullwhackers, young men hired in Illinois to drive the oxen. Finis pulled out a bottle of whiskey, took a hefty gulp and passed it to the others.

"Did'ya know what that little snot Robert is doing? He is hanging around Addie like a fly around a sugar bowl and putting on airs. I heared he talks to Christian about reading the law, but he'll be lucky if he can work in the trades. A professional? No way." Finis sucked from the whiskey bottle, the liquor loosening his normally taciturn nature. "The little fuck is just a runaway. Bet my bottom dollar. He should learn to live with what he's handed."

"David gave that kid the plum job," the youngest of the bullwhackers complained, fanning the fires of Finis's hatred for Robert. "Riding ahead to find the campsite ain't no work."

"He's gittin' above his station," Finis scowled. "If anyone is going to lift up Addie's skirt, it won't be that little tramp, and don't think he ain't trying to get into her cunt just 'cause he only has fuzz on his cheeks. I had my first when I was his age." Finis gave a sly

chuckle before continuing. "You know what happened? After breakfast one day, my aunt took me into the pantry, closed the door and
showed me how to use my peter," Finis said, with his characteristic,
irritating braying laugh. He staggered to his feet, barely able to stand.

Finis realized his tongue had loosened too much, and checked
himself. No good divulging his past life. More drink and he would be
telling them about burning his uncle's farm to the ground and avoiding the sponging house by hitting out for the West with the beautiful
palomino and the gold coins from his dead aunt's kitchen jar.

The men drank late into the night because the following morning was a rest day, and they could sleep in to recover from their
over-indulgence.

Robert waited impatiently for the rest day, taking to his tent
early and getting up as soon as the first rays of the sun lit the Platte
Valley. His duties were light: turn the stock out to graze and remove
the hobbles from the horses and oxen staked out beyond the circle
of wagons.

At last Robert was free to seek out Annabelle Lee.

"Annabelle Lee," Robert said softy as he walked up to where she
sat sewing buttons back on Billy's cotton shirt. "May I visit you?"

"You are most welcome. My aunt is caring for the children, and
I have the day free."

"Come with me," he offered his hand. Annabelle Lee no longer
felt shy. She placed her sewing on the makeshift bench and took his
hand, which was toughened from work, but not sweaty. Annabelle
Lee's hand felt cool in his. He held her hand lightly and smiled at
her, his heart filling with love. It felt natural to them. It was as if
they had walked together like this, hand in hand, all their lives.
They strolled to the Platte River and sat beside the lazy river.

"I don't know what to tell you," Robert said, with a loving look,
"but meeting you was like being struck by a sunbeam. Have you any
idea how much you have affected me?"

"If it is anything like the feeling I have for you, then I understand. I always believed that I was destined to love at first sight. And dear Robert, I do love you, and I am not afraid to tell you."

The two young lovers spent the day together, sharing their feelings. They talked about the families they were parted from and then planned their future, both unconcerned that years would pass before they would be old enough to marry. Robert and Annabelle Lee had found true love.

Nights remained cool, but the June sun parched the prairies. Alice longed for the shade of trees at her Springfield home. On the Platte River trail, they found little relief from the hot sun.

Annabelle Lee, blessedly relieved of childcare for the afternoon, walked with Alice and Amelia. As they made their way along the flat bank of the river, they passed a sobbing mother burying her child.

"I heard the mother say the child died of diarrhea, Mrs. Chablis, but I think it is cholera. How do people get the disease?" It was Annabelle Lee who had realized that the people on their wagon train might become infected by the disease.

"It is like the black plague," Alice shared with her, "but not carried by rats as happened in London. I think it might be in the water. I look at that dirty Platte River and wish to leave it far behind to reach the Sweetwater River."

"They have collar?" Amelia asked.

"Cholera. Not collar," Annabelle Lee corrected. "It is a bug that makes people sick."

"I like bugs."

"I won't let this bug near you, my sweet girl," Alice told her, kissing Amelia's rosy round cheek. "It is a bad bug."

"Your father is a doctor," Annabelle Lee noted. "Does he tell you how to stay free of cholera?"

"He's not my father," Amelia pouted. "My father died."

"Dr. Chablis has offered no advice," Alice told them. "I am careful to boil the water and not use food that may have been touched by someone that has the disease. I hope to keep my family safe from that dreadful scourge, and I dearly hope that no one in our wagon train becomes infected. I only wish we would move faster and get away from this deadly river."

"You say that you want to go faster, Mrs. Chablis," Annabelle Lee said. "I don't want to offend, but my aunt says it is your team that holds us up. She says you and Saxby must change to oxen as the horses cannot pull through the sand and mud."

"You have not offended me, Annabelle Lee. I know we're slow."

Annabelle Lee and Amelia spent the next hour chatting enthusiastically about Oregon. Their parents had often told them about the fruit trees, the winters without snow and the blue ocean.

"I want to see the tree that has apples, oranges and plums, all on one tree, and I will climb the tree and eat the fruit all day and just come down at night." As Amelia spoke, she waved her arms, mimicking a climbing motion. She was an animated child whose arms, fingers and legs were never still until sleep enveloped her.

"It is not like that, Amelia." Annabelle Lee liked Amelia, but she was much younger and sometimes talked like a baby. "There are apple trees and orange trees. Trees only have one kind of fruit." Amelia adored Annabelle Lee, and if Robert and the McNair children did not take up Annabelle Lee's day, Amelia would have been glued to her older friend from dawn to dusk.

"When we get to Oregon, we will have a farm with fruit trees and a big garden, and Elizabeth and I will be together again," Annabelle Lee said longingly.

"Why didn't they wait for you at Kanesville?" Amelia asked.

"David told me that the first of the wagons in our train made it across the Missouri two weeks ahead of us. My uncle was late getting to Kanesville. Aunt Dorothy had word that my parents joined an earlier wagon train and kept moving to give their stock enough grass. They will meet us at Grand Island, and if that is not possible, at Fort Laramie."

"My mother said there is a store there," Amelia said with a smile. "I want to buy a new pair of moccasins with lots and lots of beads." She waved her hands expressively as she spoke. "I hope it will be cooler there. It is blistering hot, hotter than ever it was in Springfield." She fanned her face in a clown-like gesture, and grinned at Annabelle Lee.

~

The heat *was* punishing and the road dusty. Penelope, with rolls of fat about her girth, suffered more than anyone, although Penelope rode in the wagon and did not exert herself physically. For her, the heat was unbearable. Every few minutes, she mopped her face with her kerchief sighing in misery and informing Walter of her discomfort throughout the long, hot day as if the heat wave were his fault.

Even the nights were hot, robbing many of a restful sleep. Penelope could not sleep because of the unrelenting heat. Instead of bedding down in the wagon, she placed a rubber sheet under the wagon bed, lay down and covered herself with her best quilt.

As the sun dipped below the hilltops and the valley darkened, Little Wolf swam across the shallow, muddy river, slithered up the bank and hid in the willows waiting till the white people took to their beds. Little Wolf, a slim twelve-year-old, was intent on proving his courage and skill. He waited patiently until all was quiet in the emigrants' camp. Slowly, Little Wolf crept towards the circle of wagons.

Little Wolf saw the horses hobbled outside the enclosure of wagons. He also saw the young boy pacing among the herd, always on watch. A full moon lit the camp, falling on the horses and the vigilant night watchman, and glinting off of the rifle Robert carried. Little Wolf figured that if he tried to steal a horse, he might end up with a bullet in his belly. He looked around for an easier prize and spotted Penelope's round form under the wagon bed. In the dim moonlight, he picked out the brightly colored quilt. It would be perfect for his old grandfather.

Little Wolf crawled across the treeless area between the river and the wagon and slowly, ever so slowly, slid the quilt off the large woman. He touched her ample arm. Penelope gave a throaty snort but did not wake. Little Wolf had his prize. In minutes he was fording a shallow part of the river, holding the quilt high off the water, happy and proud.

Morning broke to Penelope's loud screams. "Where on earth is my quilt?" Penelope yelled as the first rays of light awakened the camp. "Did you come and take that quilt off me, Walter?" Penelope was standing beside her bedroll, her arms wrapped across her ample chest. She wore a billowing nightgown, her lank hair covered by a nightcap.

Walter emerged from the wagon, wearing only his long johns. "What is it now, Penelope?" Walter shook his head, knowing that another issue was about to be added to Penelope's growing list of grievances.

"My quilt! The one my mother gave me. It's gone!"

"I don't have it. Last I saw, you were asleep with your quilt tucked up to your chin."

By this time, neighbors had arrived to see what the commotion was all about. David walked over, searching around Penelope and Walter's wagon and then squatting on his haunches to get a closer look at the ground.

"Ah! I see the footprints of a young brave," David said as he came to his feet. "Penelope, looks like you had your quilt stolen by a young Pawnee, who snuck up on you in the night and then melted away into the woods with his prize." David had a wry smile on his tanned face. Penelope was not smiling.

"He will be back at his camp counting coups along with the other warriors. Sneaking up and touching an enemy—that is you, Penelope—without harming you is considered by the Plains Indians one of the greatest feats for a young warrior. Think of it as the young boy's entry into adulthood. Little harm was done, but he earned a place of honor in his tribe." David chuckled, thinking about how proud the young boy would be.

"Don't laugh. It's not funny," Penelope said sharply, her lips tight with anger.

But many of their fellow travelers could not help grinning over the young brave's skill at stealing items out from under the emigrants' noses, as long as it didn't happen to them, of course.

"The Indians are making a regular business of stealing from us, but really I don't think we should begrudge them a little pot, a piece of calico or that quilt," Addie remarked. "Can you imagine sneaking into their camp and stealing their horses? Is there even one of you brave enough? I think not."

"I'll show you how to treat the Injuns," Finis bragged. "Git me a gun and a few men, and we go and clear out those thieves. That's what I mean to do." He pasted a smear of a smile on his face.

"No Indian hunting," David commanded in an unmistakably firm tone. "We need to pack up and move on and get ourselves over the mountain ranges. As long as we keep our guns in our holsters, I expect little trouble from the tribes. We are crossing their lands, and up to now, the Pawnees have honored the treaty and have kept the peace. And that is what we will do. We will keep the peace."

"What you don't realize, David," Addie interjected, "is that the settlers will take the Indian land, treaty or no treaty. That is what happened in the States, and my guess is that is what will happen across the territories and in Oregon Country."

"I agree," David responded, "but if their land is given to the settlers, there will be war."

"Why should the Indians have land?" Saxby ranted, coming in at the tail end of the discussion. "They don't farm it; they don't use it!"

"They hunt, fish and pick berries," David said in his reasoned voice. "On the coast, they have houses built of cedar trees, big houses with potato patches in the village. That is their land as much as your farm is your property. They…"

"Their property," Saxby butted in. "Indians don't own land."

"You talk bullshit, David," Finis blurted.

By this time, David was too angry to continue. Talking to Finis and Saxby was like throwing words into the wind. They refused to listen; they had made up their minds about the tribes, and nothing would change them.

It was not only the differences of opinion that caused friction; the hot weather and dusty winds caused tempers to flair. Dorothy did not cope well. The baby developed a rash on his bottom from the heat, which was made worse by the lack of clean water to bathe the infant. He was uncomfortable and cranky, waking Dorothy several times during the night and leaving the mother's nerves frayed.

Alice withstood the hot sun and driving rain with little discomfort. She had always been resilient in the face of adversity. Like her mother, Amelia endured the blazing heat without complaint. However, Alice wondered if Amelia, being a congenial and well-mannered child, would refuse to complain no matter how difficult the circumstances. Alice brushed her lips across Amelia's soft curls and thought, *She is such a joyful, uncomplaining little girl, such a joy to be near. I would give my life for her.*

To find some relief from the intense heat, Swede decided they should take to sleeping in the day and setting out as the sun dipped below the hills. That evening, the travelers wearily walked through the night. Even in the cool of the night, they could smell the stench of death. Graves dotted the route; at times bodies were strewn across the surface, rotted after being uprooted by wolves. Little Amelia averted her eyes. It was a sight she could not bear without her stomach lurching.

Annabelle Lee found the corpses a curiosity. She thought of her own life and her childhood fascination with cemeteries. Now she faced the brutal reality of death.

"They must take the time to bury their loved ones deep and grace the graves with a fence and flowers," Annabelle Lee said. "It is not respectful to expose the dead to wild beasts."

"Look, Mother," Amelia whispered, as ahead in the shadows they passed a family, heads bent in prayer over a newly buried loved one.

"Don't worry, my love. I will keep you safe from harm. Let us pray that we will all escape the disease and arrive safely in Oregon Country. Now, my darling girl, time for you to sleep." Alice lifted Amelia into the wagon as it rolled slowly along the trail. A lone wolf howled, its eerie wail frightening Alice, although she was not a woman to be easily scared. She continued walking, shaking off the sense of foreboding. Saxby was on his horse, leaving Alice to drive the team of horses.

As the first faint morning light rose on the eastern horizon, David loped by on his white stallion. He pulled up the reins and stepped down from his horse, tipping his hat to Alice and letting the column pass by. He was checking on the wagon train, making sure no one had fallen behind and that all was well during the long night march.

When the eastern sun lit up the valley, Swede called a halt. They drew the wagons into a circle, made breakfast and slept till mid-day, waking under a cloudy sky. Swede ordered the wagon train to form up. The clouds grew darker as the wagon train moved west, buffeted by a swirling, dusty wind. They covered a difficult ten miles before making camp in a poplar grove. The canvas covers over the wagons flapped in the wind. Alice decided to keep Amelia in the wagon, as the wind was too fierce to pitch the tent.

That night a windstorm swept across the valley, scattering belongings and drenching the camp in a pounding downpour. For half the night, driving gales of wind and rain howled down the Platte Valley, shaking the covered wagons and whipping the canvas covers. Finally, the winds died down, allowing the exhausted travelers to fall into a peaceful sleep.

As the first faint rays of morning light seeped into camp, Annabelle Lee woke to Billy's cries. She tried to sooth him back to sleep, but the six-year-old curled up in agonizing pain, his body feverish.

"My tummy; it hurts. I dirtied myself, Annabelle Lee." He cried first in remorse as he was the big boy of the family, and it was shameful to lose control of his bowels. Then he cried in sheer pain as the disease made his legs cramp and his head ache. Annabelle Lee cleaned up the mess, washed Billy and sang to him to try and sooth him back to sleep. He tossed and groaned until the June sun streaked crimson across the eastern horizon. Billy was worse, and she realized she must call his mother. Annabelle Lee crawled from the tent she shared with Billy and his brother.

"Billy is sick with the cholera," Annabelle Lee yelled into the covered wagon where Dorothy slept with McNair, Billy's younger brother Charles, and the baby.

In a moment, her aunt had emerged from the covered wagon carrying a satchel of medicine and home remedies.

"Oh my God, please not my Billy! Annabelle Lee, pour a little water in a cup and add pepper. I'm told that might help." Annabelle Lee was quick to comply.

"I will stay with him every minute, Aunty. I won't let him die; I promise."

Although Dorothy thought Annabelle Lee foolish and dreamy, now it seemed the girl had spunk. Anna came over and offered to help with the baby and Billy's other two brothers.

"They say corn meal and whiskey is a cure," Anna remarked.

"I tried that," Dorothy said. "Billy couldn't keep it down and simply got worse. Annabelle Lee gave Billy the pepper water. It did no good. I am beside myself."

"Don't worry so, Aunty," Annabelle Lee said. "I've saved others; not my Granma, though. She was old, and my mother said I cannot save old people."

"We need a miracle to save my darling boy," Dorothy said, her voice choking.

Annabelle Lee and Dorothy stayed by Billy's side until he fell into a fitful sleep. "Let him rest, Annabelle Lee," Dorothy told her niece.

"It seems like the laudanum is helping Billy sleep, but I used it up and we need more," Annabelle Lee said, a worried look on her sweet face. "If he is able to rest, maybe he will fight off the disease."

Convinced that her niece was right, Dorothy rapidly made her way to Saxby's wagon.

"Saxby, please, we need your help," Dorothy's voice high pitched and frantic.

Saxby emerged from the wagon, a scowl on his face. "What is it?"

"Billy has cholera, and we believe you can help. I've tried pepper, camphor, ammonia and peppermint. Nothing works. Billy's condition is getting worse. The laudanum helps him, but I have no more. Please give me a little for my boy?"

The emigrants in the wagon train knew that Saxby used laudanum every day, and it did not surprise Dorothy when he took several minutes before handing over a tiny vial of the opium elixir.

Dorothy took the small offering and acknowledged the gift with a cool thank you.

"Is there anything I can do, Dorothy?" Alice asked. "I could look after Billy. I know you have the other children to care for."

"No, Alice. You won't," Saxby barked.

"Thank you, Alice, but Annabelle Lee is staying with Billy. I know Swede will have the wagon train moving soon. I will make Billy as comfortable as possible, and Annabelle Lee promised to stay by his side in the wagon."

Anna and Jan listened to this exchange as they sat by their morning campfire feeding Billy's younger brothers and caring for the baby.

"Saxby is as reluctant to part with laudanum as a miser is to part with his gold." Anna sat on a packing box, bouncing the baby on her ample knee. "Did you hear how he controls Alice's every move? Not a leaf falls from the tree without Saxby determining where it will land."

The storm had dumped a deluge of rain on the trail. The earth of the Platte Valley did not absorb moisture; it collected in puddles, turning the road into gooey mud, slowing down the wagon train as the teams had to pull through the wet, muddy ruts.

Annabelle Lee was true to her word and cared for Billy, wiping his fevered forehead with a wet cloth, cleaning up when he vomited and soothing him to sleep after giving him a dose of the precious laudanum. Gloom hung over the Swede wagon train. No one wished to stop for lunch; they wanted to quit the Platte Valley as soon as possible and leave behind the frightening disease. But now the disease traveled with them.

"The McNairs must drop out," Penelope announced to Walter. "If they stay with the wagon train, we're as good as dead."

"The parties behind us and in front of us have the disease," Walter told her. "There's no escaping it until we quit this deadly river. Annabelle Lee may be a slip of girl, but she said the water carries the bugs that infect us, and that young one is wise beyond her years."

"I hear there is a man taken sick at the end of our train. His family should leave as well." Penelope spoke in a bitter tone, her once pretty smile long since replaced by an angry scowl across her pudgy cheeks. Walter looked over at her, noticing her eyebrows plucked to the thinnest of lines, giving her the appearance of being constantly annoyed.

There is so little we agree on, Walter thought. He felt trapped, thinking about the months ahead on the trail, days without end in close quarters with Penelope.

"We can't make them leave. They have paid, just as we have paid. If they don't keep moving west, they will not make it over the mountains and the entire family could perish. We must be more Christian-like and help one another."

"Maybe they could turn back like those people." Penelope pointed to four wagons traveling in the opposite direction.

Walter turned to look at the destitute family, treading wearily east, back to Kanesville and to the eastern towns. "The turnarounds are a sad group. All the men dead, and the women and children half starved."

"But they are heading home, and I would give my wisdom teeth to be back in Springfield instead of on this trek of death and misery."

"Penelope, it was your idea to go west," Walter said in his quiet voice.

Penelope chose to forget she had pressed Walter to make the trip and launched into a lengthy monologue of complaints ranging from the weather to their companions in the wagon train, and even to comments on Walter's lack of attention to her needs. Walter listened quietly, not revealing his own thoughts about Penelope's constant criticism. His thoughts were with Billy and Annabelle Lee, hoping that the lovely young girl would be careful and not contract the disease herself.

Annabelle Lee remained by Billy's side throughout the long day's trek that started at six in the morning and ended late that evening.

Dorothy walked behind the wagon carrying her baby and holding the hand of five-year-old Charles. McNair drove the team of oxen while their four-year-old son sat on the wagon seat under his father's watchful eye.

"Billy is sleeping quietly," Annabelle Lee reported, poking her head out of the back of the wagon. However, long before they reached camp, Annabelle Lee had used up the laudanum and Billy was screaming in pain. His stomach churned and his legs ached.

When Swede brought the wagons to a halt for lunch, Dorothy approached others in the wagon train, begging for laudanum. Strangers handed over what they could spare. With the soothing drug, Billy dropped to sleep for a blessed healing hour, only to wake once again, crying out at the pain.

June brought long days that enabled Swede to push the wagon train hard. As the sun sent its final rays into the Platte Valley, David rode back along the wagon train, encouraging the travelers and telling them the camp was only a mile ahead. It was the third day of Billy's illness. Annabelle Lee, the most patient of caregivers, remained with Billy.

"Did you hear that, Billy? Soon we will stop, and you won't be jolted and bumped about."

But Billy was so ill he did not hear Annabelle Lee. He moaned faintly as McNair drove the team into the circle of wagons.

"We need more laudanum, Aunty. Ask Anna. Maybe she has some to spare." A worried look crossed Annabelle Lee's face.

And, of course, Anna and Jan were more than generous, handing over their entire supply of the poppy's soothing drink.

"My Jan does not use the drug, and I only had it for emergencies. Little Billy is an emergency."

That evening, Robert finished his camp chores and rushed to the McNair wagon. Throughout the long trek, he'd worried about Annabelle Lee. He remembered Annabelle Lee telling him that she was a healer. She'd told him how she'd mended the dog's leg and saved a calf's life.

Robert joined Annabelle Lee at the campfire. The moonstruck youngsters sat close together on a packing box, their hips touching, Robert's bare arm brushing Annabelle Lee's delicate elbow.

"Annabelle Lee, please take care when you're near Billy."

"Dear Robert," she whispered to him, touching his arm lightly with her fingertips. "Please don't worry. I am doing what I must. Billy will live, and that's what is important."

"No, Annabelle Lee. That you live is important. I could not bear it if you became ill. I would give my life for you, but I don't want you to risk your life for Billy."

"I am not foolish, Robert. I often wash my hands, and I take care not to catch the disease. But I must stay with him. It is my destiny to help the sick."

"Your destiny? No, Annabelle Lee. Your destiny is to be with me. Give me your hand, Annabelle Lee." Robert held the small hand in his and kissed her soft fingers.

"I want you to hold this with me." Robert held out the old Bible and placed his hand on the worn cover. "Put your hand over mine. When we marry, we will write our names in my family Bible, and when we have children, we will write their names and dates of birth. This will be our first kiss, and it will be our promise to pledge our love till the day we die and beyond." Robert continued in his earnest tone. "My dearest Annabelle Lee, my only love, I commit my life to you."

"My darling Robert, I am yours forever." The two young lovers held the Bible together as their lips touched. It was a long, sweet kiss, a gentle and beautiful kiss.

The following day was equally grueling. The summer heat scorched the valley, and gusts of wind sent dust scurrying about the wagons. The heat in the covered wagon was almost unbearable. Billy's temperature rose, and his little body poured with perspiration. Annabelle Lee kept him as cool as she could, wiping him with a cloth dipped in tepid water and mopping him with a soft towel.

The wagon train made camp later than usual that day. Dorothy went to check on Billy immediately; he was asleep.

"You have been a good nurse to my boy. Please rest and enjoy the evening while I sit with Billy."

Robert waited at the McNair wagon for Annabelle Lee to step down. He took her hand and led her to a bench beside the campfire. They sat close together, Annabelle Lee's head resting on Robert's shoulder.

"Those two look like they are joined at the hip," Anna remarked to Jan while they enjoyed a rest after their evening meal. "When you were that age, Jan, did you have a girlfriend, someone who stole your heart?"

"You are the only woman for me," Jan said, a twinkle in his eyes. "Until we met, I did not even look at a girl."

"I think you are pulling my leg. Girl or boy, no one avoids Cupid's arrow for twenty years." She paused for a moment, thinking back to her youth. "When I was eleven, there was a choir boy that I could not take my eyes off. He had beautiful blond hair and a voice like an angel. Even his name, Kent Twelves, had an angelic sound."

"I knew it. You are still in love with young Mr. Twelves," he teased her. "Admit it."

"I love only you, dear Jan. You are the best thing that ever happened to me." She gave him a warm hug and moved closer so he could put his arm around her waist.

"That Annabelle Lee might be a slip of a girl, but she has turned out to be a tower of strength. I don't blame Robert for having a serious case of puppy love."

"They are acting like they are well beyond the puppy love stage. Watch them."

Jan looked across at the McNair campfire and saw Robert lean over and kiss Annabelle Lee. It was a long, gentle kiss. When they pulled away, Robert ran his hand along her cheek, and Annabelle Lee rested her head on his chest.

"They are in love," Anna said smiling, "just like you and me when we first fell in love, and couldn't resist touching each other."

"I still can't resist touching you," Jan said as he moved his hand down her buttocks, "but maybe we should take to our bed before we become the center of attention for all the busybodies in the caravan."

Morning broke over the Platte Valley. The eastern sun caught the treeless hills bordering the river and moved across the flat valley, lighting up the white covers of the wagons and tents. A curly-haired boy peeked out of the tent and watched the sunrise.

"Annabelle Lee! Tell Mommy to make me breakfast. Tell her I'm so hungry I could eat a horse."

"Oh, Billy," Annabelle Lee cried, hugging him. "Aunt Dorothy! Come quick! Billy's done with cholera. He's well."

"Oh, my darling boy. My sweet boy." Dorothy held him so tight and so long that Billy wiggled out of her embrace.

"Please, Mommy, will you make pancakes for our breakfast?"

Chapter Ten

The Loup River Crossing

Word of Billy's recovery spread throughout the wagon train, and with it, joy and relief at every campfire. Dorothy, who had never been outwardly affectionate with her children, now hugged young Billy and kissed his cheeks until Billy wanted to escape from his mother. Her view of Annabelle Lee had changed. She raved to everyone she spoke to about the courage and strength her niece had shown during Billy's illness.

The sun still blazed down on the line of covered wagons, but the emigrants walked with light steps and a sense of joy in their hearts. It was a pleasant journey to the Loup River, until the men riding in the vanguard spotted a band of Pawnee.

"Injuns up ahead!" they yelled back. Men took out rifles, and women gathered up children and lifted them into the wagons.

The Pawnee band waited at the Loup River crossing asking each wagon owner for money or a gift before waving them on. Annabelle Lee and Billy watched, fascinated by the strong warriors who had decorative beads adorning their necks and waists.

"Look, Annabelle Lee! Even the dog helps carry." Billy watched a massive dog with a pack the size of Billy.

Annabelle Lee watched the women riding bareback and pulling teepee poles, piled with supplies. "They are moving their village just like we are."

"Billy, Annabelle Lee. Get into the wagon and stay away from the savages. They love to snatch little children."

"They're harmless, Aunt Dorothy. They only want two bits. I heard him. But I think McNair should watch the young warriors because they will lead off a horse or cow right under our noses. David says that the young warriors are not allowed to find a wife until they've stolen at least one horse."

Dorothy was about to tell Annabelle Lee that David was an Indian-lover and that Annabelle Lee was as silly as a goose, but then she thought about Billy's remarkable recovery. She checked her tongue and resolved never again to scold her niece. Dorothy knew only too well that her little boy had been snatched from the brink of death. Gratitude replaced the bitterness and resentment she'd harbored towards her sister's child.

Addie rode up to one of the Pawnee women. "Where are your people going?" she asked, in a combination of Chinook, Sioux and sign language.

"We move from the valley to the buffalo hunting ground," the young woman replied in Pawnee. "Not far. In winter, we move back with our dried meat. We laugh about the wagon train people, going all across the desert and mountains to make a new camp."

The two women smiled at each other, and Addie rode alongside the band of Pawnee, smiling at their children on the travois and thinking about her Sioux stepbrothers and little sister Ruth.

Saxby brought his team to the crossing. "Not another toll," Saxby fumed. "I don't want to pay out more of my money. It will all vanish before we reach Oregon. And, Alice," his voice bellowing, "stop giving those savages food every time they put out their hands."

Alice looked back at her husband's hard face, her stomach tightening. He had seen her approach one of the women to ask in sign language if she could trade a piece of calico and cookies for a pair of moccasins.

Alice had a store of trade goods as well as baking in the wagon and often traded for dried meat, a fresh fish or berries. Addie, who seldom cooked, assisted Alice as an interpreter and, in exchange, Alice supplied Addie with bread and cookies.

"I give little in exchange for the fish or fresh meat that I know you relish. Today, I traded for a new pair of moccasins and for you, a piece of fresh venison." She wanted to scream at him in frustration, but it was no use confronting him. She continued in as calm a voice as she could manage, while her entire body tightened. "I fail to understand why that is a problem, just as I can't understand why you don't pay the toll. Saxby, please pay them, and let us move forward?"

"Be quiet, woman," Saxby growled. This silenced Alice. She had no skill at facing his controlling nature.

He refused to pay the fifty-cent toll to cross the Loup River. Instead, he drove the team north to a shallow crossing, but this crossing was fraught with difficulties. The riverbed was quicksand that swallowed the horses to their shanks. It was clear to Alice that the horses could not pull the wagon out of the riverbed.

"Saxby! We are about to lose the horses and our wagon!" Alice yelled, easing herself off the wagon seat and into the water-soaked sand. Alice tucked her long skirt into her bloomers and waded precariously to the front of the team, sinking up to her knees.

"I'm unhooking the horses and leading them to safety," Alice told Saxby. "I don't want to watch these beautiful beasts get sucked down. The elephant continues to follow us on this trail." Amelia, slight but muscular, jumped from the wagon and waded into the water to assist her mother.

"Mommy, why are you talking about the elephant following us?" Amelia asked, carrying a basket from wagon to shore.

Alice smiled. "It is a strange story. Years ago, a ship's captain sailed from Africa to our land and brought an elephant to Manhattan.

Everyone was amazed by the elephant's size, its mystery, as well as the potential for harm. From that time on, we talk about an elephant following us when we see strange and wonderful things or when bad things happen."

"Nothing bad will happen to us, will it?"

"Of course not, my sweet." But as Alice reassured her daughter, she looked at Saxby perched awkwardly and helpless on the wagon seat. *When I met him, he seemed so cocksure of himself; now I find he is useless on the trail. How can I protect myself and my daughter from his rash decisions?*

"Damn those Indians. I'd like to put a bullet through their filthy skulls." Saxby fumed while remaining rooted to the wagon, afraid he would be sucked into the quicksand should he attempt to make it to shore. He was a heavy man who lacked athleticism.

Why is he blaming the Pawnee? Alice asked herself. *It is his fault we are stuck in the river, not the fault of the Indians. But I fear to tell Saxby what I think.*

"Saxby, let me fetch a board from the wagon to make a platform for you to step on so you can make it to shore." Alice tried to sound reasonable, while concealing her frustration at her obstinate husband.

Alice waded to the wagon, found the crow bar and pried a board off the back of the feed box. She watched as Saxby awkwardly eased himself down from the wagon and onto the board, walking precariously to dry land. He lowered himself onto the sloped ground of the riverbank, drops of sweat beading on his forehead.

"You will have to help me, Saxby." He remained rooted to the ground. "We will need your help, Saxby," she said with an edge to her voice. "Amelia and I will move the supplies from the wagon and pass them to you. We are light and only sink a little in the quick sand. If we remove the load, the horses might be able to pull the wagon free." Alice waded to the wagon and carried a heavy box to the shore. Alice's smock, wet on the bottom, was still tucked into her bloomers, revealing her slim muscular legs.

At last Saxby stood up and took the load from Alice. There was a gloomy look to his face. He disliked being ordered about, especially by a woman, but as the hours passed, with Alice shouldering most of the work, Saxby's attitude changed. He appeared to appreciate her efforts, and when she passed him the last box, he gave her a wan smile.

Once the wagon was relieved of the heavier items, Alice rehooked the team, but even without the weight of the supplies, the horses only managed to make the wagon shudder slightly.

"Saxby, we must ask for help, or we'll be here all night."

"I agree. I applaud your efforts, Alice. I have never seen a woman work this hard. And you, Amelia, you are strong like your mother." This was a rare compliment from a husband who, since the beginning of the trip, had never acknowledged his wife's strength and skill on the trail nor his stepdaughter's good humor and behavior.

"I'll come back as soon as I can." Saxby mounted Excalibur and disappeared up the trail. It was dusk, and Alice wondered if they would be able to reach camp that night.

Hours passed before Saxby returned with the wagon train guide and two yoke of oxen. It wasn't the first time David had had to double back to assist Saxby extricate his team of horses from an impossible crossing.

David saw Alice and Amelia on the riverbank wrapped together in a quilt. "You both must be freezing, and night is coming on."

"Amelia is cold and tired. I'm fine and will help hitch up the oxen. I am able to walk in the quicksand without sinking. You will see." David watched as Alice worked untiringly, hooking the traces from oxen to the wagon. Alice, motivated by modesty, did not tuck her smock into her bloomers but instead waded into stream, the bottom edges of her clothing heavy with water and sand.

It was another hour before the oxen could pull the wagon onto the shore. Alice lifted Amelia into the wagon, tucking the quilt around the little girl and kissing her forehead. "Sleep, my sweet girl. We will be in camp soon, and I will have a tasty meal for you."

"Would you like a hand to load up?" David asked Saxby.

"We'll manage on our own," Saxby replied ungraciously.

David tipped his hat to Alice, nodded coolly to Saxby and galloped off.

As Amelia slept, Alice worked tirelessly, moving the boxes from the ground to the wagon with minimal help from Saxby. A slight stirring of the wind dried Alice's smock, which riffled in the breeze as she worked.

By the time Saxby and Alice arrived in camp, the other emigrants had taken to their beds, but it was not the end of the day for Alice. Her family had not eaten supper, and after the hours of labor at the Loup River, Saxby and Alice wanted hot food, not a cold snack.

Despite her weariness, Alice added buffalo chips to Jan and Anna's fire, and within half an hour had a hot meal ready. Amelia woke to the aroma of food. Refreshed from her sleep, she jumped from the wagon and hugged her mother.

"Hello, my hardworking daughter," Alice said, kissing the top of Amelia's mussed, curly hair. "I have a dish of food for you." Alice passed a bowl of beans and bacon to Amelia and then dished out another plate for Saxby.

"It is just leftover beans, Saxby, but you need a hot meal as much as Amelia and I."

"Well done, Alice. And please, I must tell you that you deserve my admiration. I promise to be a kinder husband. I know I have not been myself on this trip."

"We will manage, Saxby," she said, but her inner voice told her quite the opposite.

Although Saxby's uncharacteristic kindness should have moved Alice to share his bed, she was so exhausted she remained resting by the campfire when Saxby retired for the night. Amelia was asleep in her tent and Alice sat by the dying embers of Anna and Jan's fire, her back and neck aching. She sipped chamomile tea, hoping it would sooth her muscles so that she would fall asleep the minute she took to her bed.

"I've come to see if you are alright, Alice." It was David. "Only among my wife's family have I seen a woman work as hard and as long as you."

"I shall recover, Mr. Ackerman. Just a few aches that will be gone by morning."

"I have something that might help. I grew up in a family of girls and was raised by a Dutch mother. Dutch men have no inhibitions about assisting a woman who suffers pain. I helped my wife give birth, so if you have no objections, Alice, I will rub this salve on your back?"

Alice hardly knew what to say. If Saxby woke and saw David touching her, he would likely kill them both. However, her muscles ached so painfully that she did not want to refuse his offer of the relieving salve.

It isn't just the soothing salve, Alice admitted to herself. *I desire his touch.* Alice could not help but have feelings for this thoughtful, self-assured man.

"I have no objection," was Alice's reply, uncertain and nervous. *What am I doing?*

David pulled down the back of her smock and gently massaged her neck and shoulders with camphor.

"I must lift this out of the way," he said softly, pushing aside her lacy bodice and running his fingers lightly over the nape of her neck, ever so slowly, first to one shoulder and then the other. "A woman with muscles in her back," he said with a warm chuckle.

Alice felt shivers up her neck. His touch was achingly pleasurable. She felt an intense physical reaction and gave a groan of pain and pleasure, almost swooning from his touch.

"Thank you. That is enough. I feel better." She wanted to turn to him and fall into his arms, but reason restrained her. Alice stood. She knew she could not bear his touch another second.

"Sleep well, Alice." David's eyes caught hers for a moment, his gaze unwavering and intense. That they desired each other was clear, although neither said a word. She turned away, her emotions in turmoil. David watched as she walked to the fancy wagon, climbed inside and closed the curtains.

Alice moved quietly about the wagon and slipped into bed without disturbing Saxby. She thought only of David. She yearned for his touch, for his voice, and she pictured in her mind the fine features of his face. Most of all, she enjoyed his sense of humor that contrasted so sharply with Saxby's melancholy.

Chapter Eleven

The Platte River

Summer beat down on the great plains of the mid-west with no way to avoid the punishing heat. The sluggish Platte water was too murky to provide a refreshing swim or bath, and the narrow border of cottonwood trees along the river too thin to offer shade. Alice and Amelia walked alongside the wagon, Alice striding, her daughter running with bursts of energy, then tiring and slowing down. Saxby sat on the seat of the covered wagon, driving the team of four. As the pace of the wagon train was the same as the pace of the walkers, Alice and Amelia were able to keep up with the wagon. They walked close behind, but not too close, as neither of them wanted to share Saxby's company.

As they trudged mile after mile through the dusty, hot valley, Alice thought back to the evening of the Loup crossing. The encounter with David played over and over in her mind. Each time she thought of David's touch on her neck, her body clenched with desire. The feeling of loving and being loved, for she was certain that was the case, kept her moving day after day. The future with Saxby might be dismal, but at least she had Amelia, and now, the wonder of David's love, to sustain her.

Alice and Saxby were usually the last to reach camp. In order to have food prepared before dark, Alice mixed the bread dough during the noon break. An hour down the trail, she grabbed the bowl of raised dough from the back of the slow-moving wagon, then stopped along the trail while she and Amelia punched down the dough.

"You will be a good baker, Amelia. You are very skilled at punching the bread dough with your strong arms."

Amelia smiled proudly at her mother and flexed her little arms to show off her muscles. Alice laughed and hugged her. And, indeed both Alice and Amelia grew stronger and more tanned each day from the long hours walking under the prairie sun.

When they were near camp, Alice and Amelia took the bowl of bread dough, snatched up the bread pans, then stopped to prepare the buns for the fire. It was quite easy to catch up afterwards, as the wagon moved at turtle speed. Mother and daughter finished the job and ran, laughing and happy, to catch up and place pans on the back of the wagon. By the time Saxby drove into the circle of wagons, the buns had risen and were ready to bake.

"Anna, might I put my Dutch oven on your fire?" Alice asked when they finally arrived in camp, hours after the others. "I have bread ready for baking,"

"I can't believe you are able to prepare buns while covering almost thirty miles of trail," Anna said with a smile. "About the fire, ask himself. He has our supper near finished."

"Of course you may share our fire, Alice. And I'm impressed you have bread ready to bake. I suppose you also roasted a pig while on the road," he joked.

"I will make a pan of salted beef with rice," Alice smiled, "and we would like you to share our fresh bread and the strawberries that Amelia and I picked yesterday."

"I hope Saxby appreciates you," Anna said, as she helped herself to a bowl of beans and pork.

Alice was about to tell Anna that Saxby had thanked her for her help at the Loup River when Saxby approached, scowling and kicking up dirt with his fancy black boots.

What is wrong now? Alice wondered.

"Where is our fire? Amelia, gather buffalo chips and help your mother with the fire. We don't need to accept the charity of some-one else's camp. We must make our own way."

Amelia looked at her mother, a puzzled expression on her face.

"Off you go Amelia, and do as he says. I will need the fire to heat dish water."

Alice wished she could remain with Anna and Jan, enjoy a laugh and relax. Instead she dished out the meal and served the fresh baked bread at the fire that Amelia prepared. Saxby did not acknowl-edge that Alice was the only woman able to bake fresh bread for an evening meal despite their late arrival at camp. Alice recalled how James had complimented every dish she placed on the table, even the over-baked cookies she'd made early in their marriage.

Alice found it increasing frustrating to deal with Saxby. The following day, the river crossing was especially difficult. They paid for a ferry to take their wagon across while Saxby and Alice swam the horses. The trouble started after they hooked up the wagon. The bank was unstable, and once again the team of horses was unable to pull the wagon up the incline. This time, the other teams left them behind with a warning.

"Saxby, your outfit is holding up the entire wagon train," David informed him. "Swede says we must move on to get away from the disease, so I am telling you to change over to oxen or you will have to wait for another wagon train and see if they will let you join them."

"Like hell, will I do that!" Saxby shook with fury. "I've paid my share of your wage, and I won't be paying again for another guide. Do you think me a fool with money?"

David almost answered that yes, he thought Saxby a fool. Instead, he said nothing and left to ride on to the evening campsite. Saxby had no intention of dropping back and begging another wagon train captain to let them join. Neither was he willing to spend money on oxen or admit his choice of a team of horses was foolish. After unloading the wagon and carrying all their heavy belongings up the riverbank, they were finally able to get the horses to pull the near-empty wagon up the slope. It was dark when they arrived at the camping site.

Although Alice feared Saxby's temper, she decided she had to speak to him about the horses, and pondered on how to approach the subject without initiating an outright conflict. She waited until dinner was ready and passed him a plate of beans and cornbread.

"We are so very slow on the trail and get into camp so late. Would you please trade four of our horses for a yoke of oxen? Oxen are so much stronger. With oxen we will keep up, and you will have a longer rest in the evening." Alice's stomach clenched with anxiety.

Saxby's anger erupted like a sudden storm. One minute he was about to bring a spoonful of beans to his mouth, the next he had tossed the meal on the ground and lunged at Alice, his arm raised.

"No, Saxby! Don't!"

Saxby was beyond reason. He struck Alice across the face. She staggered dangerously close to the fire. Amelia jumped from her seat, grabbed her mother and pulled her back from the flames.

Mother and daughter were stunned by the attack. Alice had a red bruise on her cheek, and for a minute she relied on her young daughter to steady her. Amelia wept and clutched her mother's waist. Alice remained silent, too shocked to speak. But Saxby spoke up immediately.

"I did not mean to hit you. Forgive me, Alice. It won't happen again. But I must tell you not to question my authority. Stop trying to manage me. Yield to my will, or we will never reach Oregon." With those words, Saxby turned and stepped into the wagon.

That night, Alice slept in the tent with Amelia, the two of them comforting each other.

"Dear girl," Alice confided to Amelia, "thank God you are with me, or I would turn and walk home, carrying my belongings on my back. With you here, maybe we will be able survive. Tomorrow, we will reach Grand Island. David said we will meet up with the emigrants traveling from Independence, and they may be bringing mail. Dr. Chablis said that his brother's family will be meeting us there."

Whether Amelia was tired or hot, her temperament remained sunny and positive.

"They have three children, do they not? The girl is about my age. It will be fun for me to have another friend, and to have boys who can play with the McNair children. Annabelle Lee spends so much time caring for the McNair children and so much time with Robert, I hardly see her."

"You must try and go to sleep, my love. It is late. Do you want me to sing to you, my darling girl?"

"Yes," Amelia replied, snuggling into her mother's arms. "Please sing 'In the Sweet Bye and Bye.'"

Alice sang, her voice low and melodious. Soon, Amelia slept, but Alice continued to relive the insult and injury Saxby had inflicted on her.

Across the circle of wagons, the men had gathered about McNair's campfire, sharing their views of the Pawnee band that followed alongside the wagon train.

Members of the wagon train had differing opinions about the Pawnee. Finis bragged that he would kill the first Indian he saw, and each time any of them approached the wagon train, Finis pointed his gun at the visitors, never waiting to see if they were intent on harm or simply wanting to trade. Saxby shared Finis' hostile attitude.

"The only good Injun is a dead Injun," Finis told the men. "The sooner we wipe the land clean of them varmints," he added, "the sooner we can git to puttin' the land to proper use."

Saxby used a more advanced argument. "The government wants all the buffalo killed because using the land to graze wild animals is a waste. As soon as we wipe out the buffalo, the Indians will die out and civilization will move in. I have heard this from a reliable source."

The men drank and talked, their voices increasingly loud, until Dorothy rose from her bed with a crying baby in her arms and told McNair that they were waking the camp. McNair bid the men goodnight, and quiet descended on the camp.

~

"Look, Mother, there are wagons on the island and more across the river, thousands of them!"

Alice smiled at Amelia's endless joy and enthusiasm for new sights and experiences, as she stood near the riverbank, looking across to the island and to the south side of the river. Gleaming in the afternoon sun were twenty covered wagons. A few families had camped on the island to take advantage of the trees that offered shade and a supply of wood.

Indeed, this was the junction of the wagon roads, where the travelers from Illinois joined with the emigrants coming from Independence. While the Pawnees paddled emigrants across the Platte in their birch bark canoes, one family crossed on a scow to join the Swede wagon train.

Chapter Twelve

At Grand Island
Nebraska

Americus and Charlotte had waited on Grand Island several days before the Swede train arrived. They'd spent most of their days sleeping in the wagon, leaving Louise and the boys with Carreena.

"Cook rice for the children," Americus ordered Carreena. "The rest of the food is to be left untouched."

"First, Sir, I remind you I am their governess, not your all-purpose maid. I instruct and care for the children. Second, the children need meat and dried fruit in their diet. Rice and more rice. That is not healthy for a child."

"I care not what you think, Miss Percival. And since I can't force you to cook," Americus said angrily, "Louise will prepare food. I am most irritated that you refuse to do as I command. You are an employee, not my equal." Carreena accepted this rebuff silently, as impassive as an owl.

Louise cooked rice for herself and her brothers, Joseph now aged seven, and Paul six. Although Carreena made the point that she was a governess and not a servant, she helped Louise with the cooking and washing up. After they completed the chores, Carreena held study sessions with the children in the shade of the covered wagon.

Louise looked forward to meeting up with the wagon train, hoping that once they were in the larger group of emigrants, she would find friends and be able to avoid being near her stepfather.

Emigrants arriving from Independence brought letters posted from Springfield and addressed to members of the Swede party. As well, emigrants who had passed by earlier left letters to be passed on to the later emigrants. A letter awaited McNair and Dorothy.

Dorothy recognized her sister Olive's handwriting and tore open the envelope, anxious to find out why Annabelle Lee's family had not waited for them as promised.

Annabelle Lee stood at Dorothy's elbow, patiently waiting to find out the whereabouts of her sister and her parents. She had missed Elizabeth every day; she had so much she wanted to share with her twin. Who else could she talk to about Robert? She wanted to confide in her sister about the love of her life.

Dorothy also hoped the letter would be a promise of an early reunion. She wanted so much to thank Olive, to tell her how Annabelle Lee had saved Billy's life. But this was not to be.

"Annabelle Lee, I have news from your parents. They could not wait for us. Your mother writes that we will all meet up at the end of the trail in Oregon."

Tears gathered in the girl's eyes. Dorothy wanted to put her arms around Annabelle Lee to ease her pain and disappointment, but she was unaccustomed to being physically affectionate. Instead, she patted Annabelle Lee on the back in a weak attempt to comfort the girl.

Annabelle Lee held back her tears. She wanted to weep and be comforted in her mother's arms, not her stern aunt's embrace.

"I'm sorry, Annabelle Lee," Dorothy said. "I know you miss your family. Maybe this will cheer you. I believe it is a letter from your sister."

Annabelle Lee took the letter and walked off to read in private. Even McNair felt remorse at how matters had turned out. He had his four sons with him and his oldest boy saved from the grave, yet the girl who had saved him was separated from her family.

"If it weren't for those slow teams," McNair grumbled, "we would have got ourselves to Grand Island in time to meet them."

"It's water under the bridge," Dorothy added firmly. "Not much we can do but carry on." Dorothy avoided reminding McNair that he had delayed their departure and caused the families to travel separately, forcing the twins to be separated for the first time in their lives.

～

Saxby and his brother Americus shook hands and introduced their wives and children. Amelia immediately took a liking to Louise, for although Amelia was a year younger, they shared a similar problem. Both disliked their stepfathers.

"Well, brother," Saxby said, taking Americus aside, "I see you got yourself a beauty for a wife. Same with me, but along with my Alice came a good-sized fortune. I surmised from your letter that Charlotte brought only her fine looks and three needy children."

"The children have a governess, so they don't bother us much."

"Now that is society, Americus. A governess. Well, I am impressed! But come and see my wagon. It is something else. Bigger and more luxurious than any on the Oregon Trail."

Saxby guided his brother through the wagon, with its double story and unique side door.

"What a remarkable palace you have, Saxby. You do everything in superior style."

Saxby beamed at the compliments, seemingly puffing out his chest with pride and thinking to himself that he had outdone his younger brother in terms of wealth and choice of wives.

Also joining them at the Grand Island crossing was a man of unusual appearance and questionable character. He was short and stooped, his pant legs rolled up and his shirt too big for his crooked, small frame. It was difficult to determine his age, but he looked as if he might be in his thirties. He had always been treated like a social outcast because of his stunted appearance and was surprised when Annabelle Lee approached him to say hello.

"Why is your back so crooked?" Annabelle Lee was always curious about physical conditions that were different or painful. Although she knew that her aunt would tell her to avoid this sinister-looking man, she could not help but ask about his disability.

"When I were a young'un, younger than you, I was a breaker boy."

"A breaker boy?"

"I am from a mining family and went into the mine when I was six years old. My father died, and my mother had to give me to the mine or else lose our house. That is the way it was back then, and maybe still is. I spent years crawling into holes and digging out the coal, ten hours a day, every day. By the time I was your age, I could not straighten my back."

Just then Dorothy called Annabelle Lee, to help her with the children. "Stay away from Styles, Annabelle Lee. I don't care for his looks."

"He is a little scary, Auntie, but I still felt sorry for him with his back as crooked as a question mark."

"I did not mean to scold you, Annabelle Lee. I only want to keep you safe, and it is not safe to speak to some of the strange-looking men in the wagon train. Come, I've made a dinner with fried potatoes, one of your favorites."

～

The trail along the Platte River was solid on this stretch, so Alice and her daughter were able to sit in the wagon alongside

Saxby. Her husband was not the type to chat, so Alice was left in peace with her thoughts about the journey ahead. The wagon train made thirty miles that day. A good day was forty, but twenty to thirty was usual. She was relieved that their team didn't struggle behind the others as much as before.

Alice calculated the number of days they would be on the trail. *Thirty miles a day, and we have not yet reached the halfway point. Unless we pick up the pace, we will cross the Blue Mountains and the Cascades as winter bears down on us.* This uncomfortable thought gave her a jolt, and she realized she had not remembered to pee before boarding the wagon.

"Please pull the wagon aside. I need to do my necessities."

"I don't want to lose our position in the train. Can't you wait till we stop at noon?" The wind stirred the dust on the trail, warning of the winds that would grow stronger in late afternoon.

"I'll try," she agreed, thinking that James would have willingly granted such a simple request. He would smile at her and ask jokingly if she needed help to unbutton her bloomers. This reaction from her new husband gave her further cause to despair about her marriage to Saxby.

The wagon reached a rocky section of the trail. Each jolt caused more discomfort. "Please, my husband, I really need to get off the wagon. I will be quick. I promise."

"Why didn't you let me know earlier, or why the hell did you not go before we left? You just have to wait. We'll be nooning soon." A gust of wind blew from the west, slightly rocking the heavy wagon.

The wagon jolted once more as it bounced out of a rut and Alice felt her bloomers dampen. She stood up from the wagon seat, poised like a swimmer and prepared to step off from the wagon. Just before she took flight, the wagon rolled over a stony outcropping, upsetting her balance. Rather than landing lightly on both feet, one foot twisted on a boulder, injuring her ankle. Despite the pain, she recovered and ran limping away from the wagon.

"Damn you, woman! What the hell do you think you're doing?" his voice cold and cruel.

Alice ducked behind a nearby bush, upset and shocked by Saxby's reaction. She emerged and hobbled towards the wagon, now brought to a halt. Her skirts flew around her, buffeted by the strong wind. Saxby stepped down from his seat, scowling at Alice as she hobbled towards him. He seized Alice by the elbow and marched her forcibly to the wagon. She winced with every step. Her face burned with indignation, but she did not utter a word.

David rode back to see what was holding up the Saxby team. He dismounted and watched Saxby propel his wife onto the wagon. David threw his cigarette on the ground and stubbed it hard with his boot.

Saxby took his seat in the wagon, whipped the team and glared at Alice sullenly, hard eyes, hard mouth.

Alice was silent, thinking that this journey was a wilderness of disappointment and sorrow, on a trail that seemed endless. She missed her cousin and her friends in Springfield and longed for their love and support. This journey could not end too soon.

"Saxby is as cross-grained as a sycamore plank," Jan offered in his congenial voice, as he and Anna unpacked their cooking pots at the campsite.

"And in his cups half the time after taking copious draughts of laudanum," Anna added. "That poor woman will regret the day she tied the knot with him. He doesn't appear to have a thimble of common sense. Dangerous, too, because his choices are made without thought except to satisfy his ego."

As evening fell, the wind abated and the travelers were able to light fires and enjoy a respite. Anna moved close to Jan on the makeshift bench they had put together beside the fire. Anna rested her hand on Jan's thigh. They were a couple who touched and cared for one another, and to see Alice treated like a slave and underling disturbed them.

"Well, at least I know better than to question that man. His feedbox was not closed, and I thought it proper to let him know. He did not thank me. Just scowled. I imagine he would slug me a good one with a shovel or the butt of his gun if I said a word to him about his treatment of Alice. Now that his brother's family has joined us, I thought his temperament would improve."

"They are a pair, those two. Both unmarried till late in life, both putting on airs as if they were lords of England. Like that would carry any weight with us. And that new wife Charlotte, abandoning her three children as if they were unwanted kittens. What a kettle of strange fish we are traveling with."

The wagons were in a wide circle, with the setting sun creating lengthening shadows behind the wagons and the campfires sending a warm glow over their faces. Anna glanced over to see Saxby grab Alice's arm in a controlling manner.

"How could someone as mean and greedy as Saxby win the hand of the most beautiful and richest young widow in Springfield?"

"I have no idea, my dear Anna, but rather than get upset over that unfortunate couple, you and I have more pleasant business to look after in our bed against the wall."

Alice limped about the campfire washing the dinner plates and pots while Amelia swooped back and forth from campfire to wagon, putting away the cooking pots and dishes. David watched the scene and thought that the young girl had inherited the energy and sweet nature of her mother.

Saxby was off somewhere with his Henry repeater in his saddle boot. Once the chores were done, Amelia asked to be excused and ran off with the speed of a deer to her new friend's wagon. Louise had brought the doll given to her by her real father, and she held it in the crook of her arm for comfort. Amelia had a box of toys in the wagon from which she selected a singing bird and a working water mill to play with.

Like children throughout the world, they delighted in the precious hours of play after chores and before night closed in. Tonight, no one called them to come to bed, so the two girls walked to the stream that trickled over a rocky bed through the campground. They built a dam with rocks and sticks, set the waterwheel to work and placed the singing bird in a willow beside the stream.

From her seat by the campfire, Alice watched the two girls, Amelia waving her arms as she talked in her animated way, Louise attentive and reserved, listening to her younger friend. Seeing Amelia's happiness gave Alice a warm feeling. *At least I have my dear girl to give purpose to my life and hope for the future.*

Alice sat beside the fire, enjoying the solitude and beauty of the evening and resting her injured ankle on a stool as she mended her bonnet. She watched the flickering lights of the campfires.

The forest was cloaked in silence. No birds taking flight, no squirrels chattered through the trees, and there was only a faint rustling of wind in the willows. Evening fell on the camp, and pods of light from the campfires lit up the circle of wagons, reflecting off each white canvas. Alice thought she should walk over to fetch Amelia for bed, but the pain in her ankle kept her by the fire. *Amelia will come home. Thank God I have her by my side, or I would go crazy on this trip.* She felt sadness and longing, remembering the ghost of her earlier home and yearning for the life she'd left behind in Springfield.

She often recalled the warmth and love she'd shared with James, whose spirit followed her across these desolate lands and who she felt shared her sadness and sense of loss. Alice kept vacillating between hope and despair. She was an optimist by nature and, despite her negative experiences with Saxby, she retained the hope that life would improve once they reached Oregon.

As the evening darkened, Alice looked over at Amelia and Louise playing happily. She had just decided to give the girls a few more minutes when she heard footfalls. *I guess Saxby's back and will expect me to arouse him because he drank too much to get an erection.*

There was little affection in these encounters. She felt like a prostitute must feel, obliged to give pleasure to someone she did not care a fig for. She felt nauseous and gritted her teeth at the thought of the nightly duties she hated to perform. She hoped Saxby would take to his bed this night and leave her in peace. Her swollen ankle was a present and bitter reminder of Saxby's treatment of her. She could not submit to him, not tonight. But it was David, not Saxby, who walked up to her campfire.

"Let me put this on your ankle," he offered. David had a cloth in his hand that he had dipped in the creek. "It will bring down the swelling." He did not wait for her answer, but knelt on his haunches and gently pulled her ankle onto his knee.

"I must move this out of the way," he said before removing her shoe and pulling off her stocking. His touch was powerfully sensual, and she was certain that he found pleasure in touching her.

She sat in silence. Although it would have been good manners to speak, no words came to her lips.

Doesn't he know that I can't help being aroused by him? He is intelligent; he must know. But then if he feels nothing, is he purposely arousing me and caring naught for my feelings? It may only be a game that titillates him and will eventually cause me heartache. But then, he is helping me cope and possibly has no motive other than easing my pain.

"Is that better?" He carefully pulled on her shoe, sliding the soft leather boot carefully over her injured ankle and taking time to attach each button.

"Yes, thank you. It was thoughtful of you." Alice stood up, gingerly putting weight onto her ankle.

"You should not walk until the swelling goes down. Will you let me fetch Amelia for you and send the other young one to her tent?"

Alice looked at him, feeling an immense attraction to this handsome, caring man. "Yes. Please," she replied, her voice husky and low.

She had no wish to share Saxby's bed, and once more crawled into the tent and sang until Amelia yawned and closed her eyes. But Alice did not fall asleep as easily. Her thoughts centered on David and his touch. Finally, she drifted off to sweet dreams, only to wake to stomach cramps. She sat up with a start and felt warm blood between her legs.

She was relieved. *At least I won't have to birth Saxby's child.*

Alice left the tent to find rags for her flow of blood. Tomorrow was a rest day, time for Alice to recover and time to assess her feelings for David.

In the weeks following this second encounter, Alice could not keep her eyes off David. She watched as he led the oxen or rode his horse at the side of the caravan. She could recognize him from a distance by his graceful posture on his white stallion. He rode as if he and his horse were one.

Alice's heart was taken over by this man who was not free to love her. *No matter how much he desires me, he will not be unfaithful. And no matter how much I yearn for his touch, should I give into my longings, Saxby would kill me.*

Her body flooded with warmth each time she looked at him. She hoped that David was not a womanizer and thought if she was free, he would make a loving husband. While she could not help but want David's company, she had to conceal her feelings, especially from Saxby. In this close group, some with sharp eyes might pass on gossip that would reach Saxby's ears.

As she sat in the wagon along the endless Platte, she watched David from a distance. When she glimpsed him riding alongside the wagon train, she recalled David's touch on her bare skin. He must have known that he had aroused her; a woman can tell when a man desires her. Each time Alice replayed last night's encounter, the pit of her stomach clenched in unbelievable pleasure.

~

"Mother, may I go and play with Annabelle Lee and Louise?" It was Amelia, her face like sunshine, smiling and waving her arms in excitement, as if all life would ever offer was happy adventure. She had helped wash and put away the pots and dishes, and now her mother was resting by the campfire sewing.

Amelia adored the two older girls: Annabelle Lee for her beauty and dresses as fashionable as Carreena's and Louise for her uncanny ability to identify birds and sketch them so well they appeared to fly across the page.

The two older girls loved Amelia because she could make them laugh, recounting books her mother had read to her. Along with giving an accurate rendition of the story, Amelia emphasized the important parts by adopting the voices and actions of characters in the story. When Annabelle Lee and Louise had heard enough of the *History of Little Henry and His Bearer*, they told Amelia to button her lips and turned to each other to revisit their favorite subject, Robert.

"He is in love with you, Annabelle Lee. I think if he was five years older he would propose," Louise said. "Girls receive proposals when they are thirteen, and you are twelve. But usually proposals come from old men with a team of oxen and money."

The three girls sat together on a bench beside the McNair wagon. The last rays of the setting sun lit their faces. Amelia listened but had little interest in the talk of love and marriage.

"I don't want to marry until I am twenty-one," Annabelle Lee said. "Look at my Aunt Dorothy. By the time she turned nineteen she had a babe in her arms and three boys at her knees. She acts and looks like a tired old woman. And then there is Penelope, twice the size of her skinny husband, whining at him all day long."

"But you love Robert, don't you?" Louise secretly adored Robert, but felt no jealousy towards Annabelle Lee.

"Yes, of course, but Robert has plans to read the law and become a solicitor. He wants to bring his entire family west—well, maybe not his father who was mean to him. I am so proud of him. He is what every young man should be: hard working, intelligent and loyal to the ones he loves. It doesn't bother me that we cannot marry for many years. When I find my family and my dear sister, I want to finish school and write stories. Robert will make lots of money because he is ambitious, and I will be home with the children. When they sleep in the afternoon, I will take pen to paper."

The mention of writing stories got the young child's attention. "I would like you to write stories for me," Amelia piped up.

The two older girls ignored Amelia and continued with their discussion of love and marriage. "So he proposed to you, and you didn't tell me?"

"Thirteen-year-old boys don't propose," Annabelle Lee said with an amused smile, "but he professed his love for me, and I will always love him till death and after death. Do you know that Juliet was only thirteen when she shared one amazing beautiful night with Romeo, and then both chose death over a life without the one person they loved beyond all?"

"But that is just a story in Shakespeare's play," Louise countered. "Normal children do not get married, although they can make a promise to each other and be faithful till they are old enough to marry."

"My mother was fourteen when she married my father," Amelia told them. "Mother said she loved him until the day he died, and she still loves him. Now my mother is married again, and she is unhappy. I'm never marrying. Especially I'm not marrying an old man." Amelia thought of her beautiful mother tied to a man twice her age, a man who never smiled, a man so much the opposite of her real father.

"There was a girl in Springfield who married the day she turned thirteen, and my mother told me about Mormon girls who marry younger than we are," Annabelle Lee added.

"Well, that's not a happy story! Mormon girls are married to men as old as their grandfathers, and the Mormons take several wives. How disgusting! Marrying someone your own age and when you are old enough to marry would be better." This was Louise, the voice of reason among the girls.

"Jan told me that when his father was fifty he married a twelve-year-old," Louise continued. "It's a strange story because they met by chance. His father was given an invitation to a dance that a friend couldn't attend. Sitting in the corner, looking sad and abandoned was Lucy, an only child who lived on a remote farm and had little contact with others. No one would dance with her because she was crippled. Fell off a horse as a child; broke both arms. Her arms healed but were deformed. Jan's father, who was past hoping to find a wife, saw this lonely, sad girl sitting by herself. He asked her to dance the waltz. Despite her disabilities, she was a natural dancer. Lucy learned to love him, and she was a wonderful mother and a loving wife until her husband's death."

"So you visit Anna and Jan and tell each other stories, do you?" Annabelle Lee asked with a smile.

"I want to have the kind of marriage Anna and Jan have," Louise answered. "Except, unlike them, I want to have lots of children. It is hard for Anna not to have a family; she loves children. No matter that she is without babies, they still care for each other. Never bickering. Besides, Anna is an independent woman. She doesn't take orders from her husband. She is Dutch, and Dutch women have their own money, and their own land and make their own decisions. That is how I want my marriage to be."

"Robert and I will be equals in marriage. Robert intends to claim land as soon as he is old enough to qualify. He wants good bottomland that is rich and will produce wonderful vegetables and fruit trees. He says he doesn't want a pile of rocks like his father's Bedford farm. He intends to aim much higher than his father, who failed at everything he undertook. Robert is such a good person, the best person in the world. We promised to wait for each other, but that will be many years from now." Annabelle Lee broke off her enthusiastic description of her future at hearing Dorothy's summons. "Oh! Oh! There's Auntie looking for me. Time to tuck the boys into their bedrolls." She ran off, light-footed as a grasshopper.

In the morning, Annabelle Lee cheerfully resumed her child-caring duties as the wagon train moved slowly west under the bright sunshine of the Great Plains. Annabelle Lee remembered the maps Elizabeth had shown her. In a few weeks they would reach Fort Laramie and soon pass the well-known landmarks of the Oregon Trail: Courthouse, Chimney Rock and the famous Independence Rock. At this prominent landmark, Annabelle Lee and Robert intended to carve their names encircled by the outline of a heart marking for the centuries their undying love for each other.

Indeed, the love between Robert and Annabelle Lee was over-whelming for both of them. She was unaware of the power she held over him. His love for the beautiful nymph was much deeper than the love of the characters in the novels Annabelle Lee read. They could not take their eyes off each other. Robert loved to look at Annabelle Lee's graceful arms, and Annabelle Lee loved to touch Robert's hair, so fair it was nearly white.

At the end of the day, when Robert's duties ended and Anna-belle Lee had the boys sound asleep, they sat together on a packing box, Annabelle Lee's downy arm brushing against Robert's. When she showed him the new pages of the scrapbook she had added that day, he would touch her fingers lightly.

In their thoughts, they wished they could hold each other like husband and wife, but each felt unprepared for intimacy. They were too young. They remained chaste, holding hands and each day allowing a kiss. It was the most tender and endearing of loves.

The following night, they camped at Lone Tree where emi-grants from the South Platte crossed the river and joined the main trail. Annabelle Lee was busy fetching supplies for Dorothy when Americus climbed into the wagon. She had never cared much for Americus. His fish-like eyes made her think of Shelley's *Frankenstein* and the monster that was inhuman but with evil, human desires. Annabelle Lee wondered how Louise could bear traveling in the same wagon as her disgusting stepfather.

"Your mother said I could borrow a pot." Americus's leering smile repulsed Annabelle Lee, and she stepped away from him, moving farther into the wagon. "Charlotte is busy learning the business of cooking over the fire, burnt one pot and needs to start our dinner over again. Not much of an outdoors type, this wife of mine." Americus chuckled as if it was a joke to burn supper. "I've threatened to fire that snooty governess who thinks herself too fine to cook and scrub. Women! If only they remained young and obedient like you." His gaze took in the girl's graceful form.

Annabelle Lee watched him guardedly, her dark eyes narrow beneath dark curls. Americus pushed farther into the wagon, moving between the supply boxes and the girl. Annabelle Lee backed away from him, but Americus followed her. When he reached Annabelle Lee, his hand brushed against her knee. Annabelle Lee, suddenly frightened, slid away from him and out the door, running on strong, thin legs to find her aunt.

"Aunty. Go see Americus. He says he is to have a pot."

"Can't you help him?" Dorothy asked. Annabelle Lee face darkened.

"What is it?"

"Nothing, Aunty, but please, I don't want to get the pot for him."

"You're a funny kitten. Elizabeth would have given him a pot, and there would be the end of it." The mention of her twin brought tears to Annabelle Lee's eyes and Dorothy's heart softened. She took her niece's face in her hands in the first physical expression of tenderness she had shown in the girl's life.

"The two of you are different parts of a whole, but you are a wonderful girl, and I love you like a daughter. We will find Elizabeth. Now, you have a break. I will get the pot for Americus."

Instead of joining Robert, Annabelle Lee lay down on her bedroll beside the wagon, and when Dorothy called the family for dinner, Annabelle Lee didn't move. Dorothy knew immediately what was wrong, and so did Annabelle Lee. They had nursed Billy through the illness and knew the signs. Annabelle Lee's legs ached, and her stomach lurched.

Annabelle Lee's illness rocked everyone in the wagon train, even the self-centered Penelope. The angel who had saved Billy was dangerously ill, and despite being worried about the progress of the wagon train, Swede did not move them out the next morning in the hopes that a day of rest would help Annabelle Lee fight off the disease.

Robert stayed with Annabelle Lee throughout the day, wiping the perspiration from her forehead and holding her as she sipped a spoonful of laudanum. He gently pushed the moist, curly black hair away from her face.

"You have the most beautiful face in the world," he told her, voice shaky and heart aching. "My dear love, you must get better. I will die without you."

"You won't die, Robert. Live and remember my love for you, and when I leave, I will still love you," she murmured weakly. Then Annabelle Lee lay quietly, resting before the next wrenching pains of the disease.

He kissed each cheek, his tears flowing onto her angelic face. That night her breath came in a muffled flutter. Robert held her small hand in his and listened in panic when it seemed she would not take another breath, then she took a small gasp of air and lay still for a few minutes, soothed by the opium. Another breath and then silence. Her fingers loosened on his grasp, and she let go her fragile hold on life.

The angels, not half so happy in heaven,
Went envying her and me—
Yes! that was the reason (as all men know,
In this kingdom by the sea)
That the wind came out of the cloud by night,
Chilling and killing my Annabel Lee.

Robert stayed by his darling throughout the night and until the eastern sun sent its first rays over the Platte River hills. He cried till he had no tears left. Dorothy found the boy kneeling beside Annabelle Lee, where she had left him hours earlier.

"I love her, too," Dorothy said, weeping as if it was her own child who had died. "She is an angel, Robert. She will join the angels in heaven." She knelt beside the distraught boy, sobbing along with him.

"She is my life," he sobbed. "I cannot bear it." He released Annabelle Lee's small, cold hand and stood up, raising his arms in utter despair.

Dorothy held Robert, both sobbing over the loss of the girl who owned Robert's heart, the girl who had saved her son.

"There, there, young man." Dorothy patted his back and stepped back, her hands resting on his shoulders. They stood together that cruel morning, clutching each other in heartbreak as the sun streaked deep red slashes across the eastern horizon—aunt and love-struck boy, tears streaming down their cheeks.

"I will never, ever love another. Never, as long as I live."

"I know, dear boy. I know." Dorothy stemmed her tears, hoping to find words to lessen Robert's anguish. All she could think of was to give him a chore so he would be able to wrest himself away from Annabelle Lee's side. "You should leave her now. I must prepare Annabelle Lee for her eternal rest. The men are digging her grave. Walk up the hill and help them. Annabelle Lee told me that if she died on the trail, she wanted to be buried deep so the wolves and Indians would not disturb her rest."

Robert kissed his beloved one last time and climbed the hill to join the gravediggers. He had been a tough boy, never crying throughout his hard childhood of whippings and misery, but now the tears would not stop. He did not care if the other men saw him.

The loss of his true love was more than his young heart could endure.

The emigrants felt no joy as the Swede wagon train passed Courthouse and Chimney Rocks. Robert remembered how Annabelle Lee had yearned to see these rocks, as well as the other famous monument ahead on the trail—Independence Rock where they were to carve their names.

Soon the wagon train would cross into Wyoming Territory, and ahead lay Fort Laramie. Robert had looked forward to reaching the Fort, where he'd planned to purchase a gift for his dearest love. He didn't know what he could have found in this remote post, and thought she might have liked delicately beaded moccasins or a bag decorated by a Pawnee woman. Now his only reason for living, his one source of joy and delight, lay buried on a lonely hill in Nebraska Territory.

David offered lighter duties to Robert during his period of mourning, but Robert refused.

"Give me more tasks, David. I suffer so that I feel I am going out of my mind. And please don't tell me that I will get over the loss. I won't."

"Then you need to help others, Robert, just like Annabelle Lee did. If there is a sick family, offer to pitch their tents or graze their animals."

"Yes, I agree. I will never feel happiness again, but I will be able to feel useful. My life has changed so much, all my hopes are gone. And David, there is something you must accept from me." Robert took the old Dutch Bible from its leather case.

"It's the family Bible brought over in 1661 by the first Ackerman family to settle in the New World. Like me, you are a descendent of David Ackerman, and you also have his name. You must take it now. You have a wife and a little son. Their names and yours should be inscribed in the family Bible and then the names of their children and grandchildren. The Bible is a promise of hope. I have no hope; I want you to keep hope alive."

David opened the old Bible and read the names of David Ackerman, his ancestor and Robert's. David accepted the gift, laid his hand on Robert's shoulder and walked slowly back to his wagon, reflecting on his family's history, pleased that his own namesake was the first Ackerman to set foot on American soil. *Yes, my dear departed wife will have her name in this fine book, as will my beautiful little son.*

Chapter Thirteen

Difficult Decisions

Fort Laramie, Wyoming

Alice was beautiful, but not the most attractive married woman on the wagon train. Charlotte was unrivaled in looks and figure, and as different from Alice as a cracked and useless piece of fine china was to a beautifully crafted clay bowl. Although Charlotte was married to Americus, she was really a kept woman, a paramour whose duty was not at the campfire, nor at the washtub, but in the bedroom. She hated cooking over a campfire, and unlike Jan, Americus eschewed those duties as well. It frustrated Americus to supply food and passage to Carreena, who had refused to take on any duties other than supervising and educating the children.

"Carreena has got to go," he told Charlotte. "Useless as teats on a bull, that woman. Why on earth did we hire her?"

"We engaged a governess, if you recall, Americus, to ensure the children's education would not suffer and to give you and me more time with each other. Carreena is wonderful with Louise and has the boys behaving properly. Is she worth her continued food and passage? I don't believe so. We can manage without her. Louise can take over care of the boys instead of sketching birds all day. She will cook for us. She's old enough to pull her weight."

Carreena was not surprised at being removed from her position. She cared little for her employers—Charlotte, the indulged wife, and Americus, the philanderer who ogled the girls and young mothers.

"That is quite alright with me, Professor Chablis," Carreena said, upon being dismissed. "I shall miss the children, but I have my own funds. I am financially independent and will ask Swede to let me pay for my passage and a spot to keep my belongings. I am a walker, and I don't need your wagon to take me to Oregon. Good day." Carreena spoke in her clipped British accent that left no doubt in Americus's mind that the governess felt nothing but contempt for him. "And Americus, Louise is a fine girl. Take care you do not abuse her."

Carreena did not wait for a reply. She removed her traveling trunk, and with the aid of a teamster, walked over to the wagon train captain, carrying herself with poise. Although many of the women on the wagon train wore homespun tunics with a white apron and bonnet, Carreena retained London fashions and stood out among the emigrants. Her clothes were practical, yet stylish. During the day on the trail, she wore a grey walking outfit of fine, light cotton and sturdy, high button leather boots. On her black hair, she wore a wide brimmed straw hat festooned with flowers and feathers.

Carreena, an experienced traveler, now had time to enjoy the journey. As she walked west alongside Swede's wagon, the pain of her breakup with Stuart disappeared, replaced by a renewed love for life. She looked forward to passing the well-known landmarks that marked their progress across Nebraska Territory and into Wyoming. When Carreena first spotted Chimney Rock, she searched out Louise.

"See, in the distance! There is Chimney Rock, far away on the horizon," Carreena said, pointing to the spirals of the unique rock formation rising above the prairie. The wagon train had passed Courthouse Rock while everyone still mourned for Annabelle Lee, but with Chimney Rock in sight, they knew they would eventually leave the misery of the Platte River. The sorrow over the girl's death still haunted them, but the wound was beginning to heal. Only Robert clung to melancholy, the loss of his dear one weighing him down day and night.

"Scott's Bluff will be after Chimney Rock and next Fort Laramie," Carreena explained to Louise.

"That's a town right?" Louise asked. "Is there a store there? My family is nearly out of anything good to eat, and I tire so of rice and then more rice."

"A store there is, Louise, and only three days from Scott's Bluff."

~

The wagon train was a few days from Fort Laramie when Swede asked David to join him for dinner. After a meal of grits and sausage, Carreena took the dishes away and set out coffee for the two men.

"Many thanks for preparing dinner, Miss. Never took you for a camp cook, and look at you now!" David smiled warmly and tipped his hat as Carreena turned to leave them.

"Sit down here with us, Carreena," Swede said, raising up on his muscular arm and patting a seat. "I'll do up the dishes later."

"You two men have business to talk about, and once I've the dishes put away, I have my book to read." Swede kept his eyes on Carreena as she walked to the wagon, back straight, head high.

Swede lit his pipe, dropped the match and ground it out with his boot. He was a big man, but handsome with a clipped beard and mustache. He never did anything in haste.

"I've come to a decision, David." Swede took a puff on his pipe before continuing, the smoke swirling up around his face. "We are later each day getting out of camp, and each day I have to send Robert back along the trail to hurry Saxby along. It has become critical because we are now a week behind schedule. We should have reached the Sweetwater by this time." He puffed on his pipe and paused.

"I have never dropped anyone from my wagon train before. It's a hard decision, especially since Saxby has a fine wife and daughter. Hard indeed." He knocked the pipe against the packing box and lifted his coffee cup from the makeshift table. "I must consider the wellbeing of the others. Unless Saxby is able to keep up, we must ask him to leave the wagon train. He could wait at Fort Laramie and join the group behind us."

The following morning, David found Saxby leading his team of four horses over to the wagon. David thought the beautiful Canadian purebreds too special to be handled by a man with little horse experience.

"I need a word with you, Saxby." It was clear that this was not to be a pleasant conversation. "If your rig falls behind again, this will be your last day with us. Swede will return half your fee," David said coldly, his thumbs hooked into his belt. "You can wait at Fort Laramie for the next wagon train."

"That suits me just fine. I despise Swede's leadership, and I don't trust you as a guide. I plan to take the cutoff to California and hope never to see any of you again."

"What are you talking about?" David could barely contain his anger. Immediately, he thought of how Saxby's plan would affect Alice and Amelia. "The cutoff to Fort Bridger is not passable to California unless everyone is on horseback or mules! You must stay with the main trail and go south to California from Fort Hall."

"I have a letter from this man Hastings," Saxby countered, his voice clipped. "He has opened up a trail and will meet us at Fort Bridger. He'll lead us through the mountain pass. I will save seven weeks on the trail and get us to Sutter's Fort by early September. You call yourself an Overlander," he scoffed. "Hastings not only knows the Oregon Trail, he also guides emigrants through to California."

"I have heard of this man Hastings. He is promoting land in California and cares naught for the safety of women and children. Don't be foolish, man. You have a wife and a child with you."

"I see you looking at my wife. That's the reason you don't want me to take her away."

"You speak with a forked tongue, Saxby. You've just been told to leave our wagon train, so how could I be plotting to be near your wife? I have a wife. My concern is for the safety of Alice and Amelia and any others you might encourage to join you in this folly. You have a good woman there and a fine daughter. I don't want to see them struggle across the salt waste. Wagon trains need water, wood and grass. All you will find is a barren waste traveling the salt flats." David crossed his arms over his chest in frustration, before continuing in a cold voice. "I tell you, but it seems you are not willing to hear me. If you would continue to Fort Hall, that route to California is not easy but is much less risky than the cutoff."

"You don't know what you are talking about. I will look after my own without your advice," Saxby said gruffly. "I am heading to Fort Bridger, where Hastings will meet me and take us across the mountains. It saves miles and miles of travel. You don't know the route, so don't tell me where I should take my family." With that, Saxby stormed off.

As they approached Fort Laramie, they met Pawnees on both sides of the road, wanting to trade moccasins for calico, guns and pots. As well, several Pawnee with canoes met the emigrants at the riverbank and offered to take the travelers across the river. Most emigrants forded the river sitting in their covered wagons, but several families paid the Pawnee for passage across the river to the fort.

The fort was constructed of large cottonwood trees, and measured over a hundred feet long. Bordering the river was a row of buildings including a warehouse and bakery. The travelers, who had walked hundreds of miles sleeping only in the open or in crowded wagons, were relieved to see buildings with four walls and a ceiling.

"Saxby, I need money to replenish our larder," Alice said, once again feeling tension at the prospect of a confrontation with her husband. "If we don't reach Oregon by October, we will need at least another hundred pounds of flour, as well as more coffee and dried fruit. Both Amelia and I need to buy moccasins. We've walked our last pair of shoes into tatters."

"We can't afford the prices asked at Fort Laramie. I have a plan to get us to California in September, so don't waste our money. Soon we will have buffalo meat to sustain us, and before you know it, I will have you and Amelia over the Sierras and into God's Country."

"What are you saying? Surely you haven't changed your mind about Oregon?" Her chest tightened, and she could feel the blood rush to her face.

"I have word from an experienced Overlander about a cutoff that will save us seven weeks on the trail."

"We should stay with Swede's wagon train. It's safer. We need a large group in case of Indian attacks. I don't want to go off on our own."

"We won't be alone. I've talked to other men willing to leave with me to head south, instead of taking a route that veers so far north. I don't want to argue with you, Alice. How did it ever get into your head that a woman is allowed to speak when men are making a decision? Why can't you just accept my judgment? It is your duty as a wife to support me, not question me every step of the way." Saxby replied, a sharp edge to his voice.

Alice wanted to tell him that she had little faith in his plans for a shorter route and doubted Saxby's ability to hunt buffalo to provide food for their campfire. *I would break off with this overbearing man if only I could find a way to provide for Amelia. He would never give me a divorce, and knowing his vindictive nature, Saxby would follow through with his threat to claim Amelia as his daughter.*

After leaving Fort Laramie, the wagon train resumed its slow progress along the Platte. Illness stalked them, grass was scarce. The summer heat punishing. The emigrants couldn't wait to leave the banks of the dirty river, knowing that ahead they would reach the Sweetwater River.

"When in God's name will I ever rid myself of this miserable river?" Anna complained to Alice as they trudged along in the heat, dusty from windstorms and aching for a drink of cool water and a bath.

"I can endure the dust and heat, Anna, as long as I have your company. When we reach the road that splits to Fort Bridger, Saxby intends to break off from the Swede train and take a short cut to California."

"Stay with us, Alice. Don't go through the Sierras with that man of yours."

"Saxby knows that I am unhappy with his plans and has threatened to take Amelia from me should I leave him."

"My dear Lord! Surely he wouldn't be so cruel."

"Under the law, she is now his daughter. Stupid though the law is."

Amelia walked beside her mother, listening to their conversation. "I am not his daughter," Amelia pouted. "Never. I won't let him take me away from you, Mommy. Never. Never." She clung to her mother, wrapping her arms around Alice's waist.

"Darling pumpkin. I will never leave you." She enclosed Amelia in her arms. "Now, let's talk of something happy. David says we'll reach Devil's Gap in a week," Alice said. "What a joy that will be."

"Louise says the water pours out of the rocky gap," Amelia said, waving her arms like a waterfall. "She said we will camp nearby. We can walk from the trail over to the gorge where the water shoots down the mountain." Alice was surprised to hear Amelia's enthusiasm over the journey. Her daughter had been in tears for days after Annabelle Lee's death, and very quiet and unresponsive for the past two weeks.

Alice took Amelia's face in her hands and kissed both of the child's rosy cheeks. "You are sweetness itself, my little muffin."

When they reached the Sweetwater, Swede called for a day of rest to celebrate Independence Day. The wonderful Sweetwater River and the promise of the celebration gave everyone renewed energy. Except for Robert, most of the company had left behind the deep sadness of Annabelle Lee's death. The emigrants had all been touched by death at some point in their lives and had learned that moving on after a period of mourning was the only way to survive.

Alice couldn't wait to wash off the dirt of the Platte Valley. She joined the other women splashing in the river, wearing only a bodice and pantaloons.

"The men have been told to leave us be, and if anyone dares to peek, Swede will exact a one-dollar fine," Anna informed them. "If they don't have a dollar, Swede will order them an extra night watch."

Alice washed the dust from her long dark hair and soaped her fingers till the nails gleamed. Amelia and Louise found a hidden spot to wash and splash. For the first time in weeks, Alice heard her daughter laugh.

"If only Saxby would give up his rash idea of taking a new trail to California," Alice shared with Anna, as they waded from the water and walked to where their clothes and towels hung on a tree. They found a sheltered spot behind the trees, removed their clothes and toweled off, skin tingling from the cold water.

"I only wish to stay in the safety of Swede's wagon train and the happy company of my friends, and that's what my Amelia wishes as well."

"Once again, I urge you to let Saxby take his dangerous trail, and you stay with us, Alice." They toweled off and sat in the sun, wearing clean undergarments and letting the hot sun dry their arms and legs.

"Don't you think I have considered leaving him? My choices are limited. I am a creature of our times, doing what is expected of me and staying with an abusive man because women have little freedom. I have no means, and my small fortune, or what is left of it, is in Saxby's hands."

"Appeal to your family for support," Anna suggested.

"If I leave Saxby, my uncle wouldn't give me bread if he found me begging on the street. I can't appeal to my cousin; they have a large family and naught to spare. I'm caught, Anna. But my main reason for following Saxby is Amelia. As I told you, Anna, should I leave him, he will claim her as his daughter, and the courts will rule in his favor. I cannot lose her. Never! I am trapped."

They finished dressing, donning clean cotton smocks and brushing their hair dry in the warm breeze. They paused near the trees, absorbed in conversation.

"Oh, dear Alice. I understand," Anna said, feeling immense empathy for her friend's dilemma. "Except for my disappointment in not having children, I have been blessed. But you, Alice, your first marriage to James was everything you wished for. Now your second marriage has become a nightmare. I can't think how to advise you."

"I made a hasty decision to take Saxby's offer. I knew it was wrong; I didn't listen to my heart, and now I may be risking my daughter's wellbeing. Why was I not wiser?"

Chapter Fourteen

The Fourth of July

The next morning, sunlight slanted into the campsite, waking Alice. She felt rested, and put aside her worries over Saxby to rise cheerfully and start the morning fire. She was not the first to wake; the other women were pulling out supplies to prepare special dishes for the Fourth of July celebration and the men rode off with their rifles in search of game.

"Injuns!" one of the men shouted. David, alerted by the commotion, sized up the band. "They're Arapaho." The emigrants watched as the band of men, women and children rode towards the camp.

"Why now," Anna moaned, "just when we are about to enjoy a well-deserved holiday?" Men stood with rifles at the ready, sizing up the warriors and braves. David walked forward to meet the leader, who approached the camp with his hand raised in greeting, indicating that they meant no harm.

Anna and Alice breathed a sigh of relief. "Let's add to our dishes; it looks like we have been graced with a dozen uninvited guests." The two women laughed and turned back to their work. The band of Arapaho made camp a little distance away but not far enough to miss the aroma of food from the emigrants' cooking fires.

The hunters returned with two deer, fresh meat that would be a welcome break from the salt pork and bacon. Three Arapaho hunters came back with a buffalo, creating a hive of activity at their camp, with the women busy removing the hide and butchering. The Arapaho leader selected a choice piece of the buffalo, the prime ribs, which he presented to Swede.

By that time, Louise, with Carreena's help, had stitched "Old Glory" with red and blue fabric found among the women's necessaries, and the men worked on hoisting the flag, laughing and kibitzing as they tried to reach the highest branches. A young teamster, sinewy and muscled, removed his shoes, grabbed the flag, and, quick and agile as a squirrel, shinnied up the trunk of the cottonwood tree. He tied the flag high above the gathering, where it fluttered softly in the light wind. He slid down to the ground to resounding applause.

Alice and Anna shared their cooking fire and chatted happily as they prepared their dishes.

"Alice, if you pour any more brandy into that tutti frutti, the children will be staggering about."

"My dessert will be perfect with exactly this dose of brandy, and besides, if I don't use it to spike the fruit and bring out the flavor of the spices, Saxby will pour it down his gullet." Alice's big laugh was contagious, and Anna burst out in laughter, carried along in the happiness of the moment.

Alice dipped a tasting spoon into the dessert and took a delicate sip. "Yum. What I love about preparing food is the finesse of a fine dish that brings together the taste, contrast, aroma and simple beauty of the dish. My mother told me that to be a fine cook, you need a quick eye, a curious nose, and most important, perfect taste."

"A fine cook must also have endless energy, like you. Busy as a bee from morning to night. I work a might slower in my preparations. I placed strawberries under a net in the sun to dry." Anna winked at her friend. "And I'll serve this delicious dessert with a splash of sweet port and vanilla pudding. In place of cream, which our cows are no longer offering up, I am substituting a beaten egg white mixed with a dollop of butter. We don't have laying chickens giving us eggs, but lucky for us, eggs keep for ages, providing we pack them properly for this bumpy trail. I'll have this scrumptious dessert ready lickety-split, whilst himself will be grilling the steaks."

"I thought you hated cooking," Alice remarked.

"I hate the day-to-day grind of preparing mush for breakfast, beans and bacon and more beans and bacon. I told Jan that I would rather clean the thunder pot than cook every day. Desserts, they are different. They allow my imagination to take flight. Speaking of people taking flight, I see that husband of yours has made a head start on the whisky." Anna and Alice watched as Saxby walked unsteadily to the wagon, bottle clutched in hand.

"Whisky and his addiction to laudanum will make a beggar of him, Alice. Best you rein him in."

"Me, tell Saxby what to do! Anna, I may as well speak to that magpie eyeing us from the branch of the cottonwood tree."

By the time they finished the food preparations, Saxby was asleep in the covered wagon, snoring loudly. Alice climbed into the second story where she kept her traveling trunk. She quietly sorted through her gowns, bonnets and petticoats, the outfits bringing back memories of James and her home in Springfield when she had been a fashionable young matron who lavishly entertained their friends and James's business partners. Alice ached for those past days of love and happiness.

She lifted a satin gown she'd worn to celebrate her wedding anniversary with James. It was creamy satin with a billowy crinoline skirt, low cut at the neck in the fashion of the day. She slipped the gown on and circled her small waist with a pink ribbon. She wound her long, dark brown hair up in a bun fastened with sparkling ruby-colored hairpins. She checked herself in the mirror and crept quietly from the wagon, thinking it was no use selecting clothes for Amelia. Before the age of five, her daughter had had her own unconventional, yet attractive, fashion sense, matching blazing plaids with purple pantaloons—whatever combination was the loudest and most unlikely.

"Well, now, look at you! Alice, you are a beauty in that dress." Anna wore a muslin dress with a delicate motif reflecting the popular influence of India. The puffed sleeves, the low neckline and snug waist flattered Anna's robust build.

Alice glanced at the other women, some in their finest gowns, others wearing homespun, with ribbons in their hair and around their waists. Charlotte stood out, resplendent in a red velvet gown that accentuated her figure.

"And would you look at that," Charlotte remarked to Americus. "There's the British snob, helping herself to beans and fried potatoes as if she had spent a lifetime on the trail. I would have thought she would only eat oysters and lemon jelly cake." Charlotte's smile was as crooked as a hairpin. Americus, acknowledged her comment with a cold nod.

Carreena wore a more fashionable gown than Charlotte, and being out-dressed at an event, even in the midst of the wilderness, nettled Charlotte. The London schoolmistress had donned a Parisian fashion of black and white stripes and a wide-brimmed hat festooned with white feathers.

Carreena, head held high and back straight, lined up with fellow Oregon Trail travelers and the Arapaho men, women and children, all helping themselves to a smorgasbord of food, including potatoes and berries donated by the surprise guests. The contrast between the Arapaho women in their beaded buckskin dresses and Carreena's London fashion would have enticed any artist.

Carreena was tall and slender, and not considered a beauty, but the fading afternoon light softened her features. After filling her plate, Carreena accepted a seat between Jan and Alice.

"Are you telling me, Jan, that when we arrive in Oregon, we will be in a state that allows slavery?"

"For the time being. But when Oregon joins the union, the abolitionists will push for a free soil state. The southern states, they'll break away from the Union rather than give up that abominable practice, and the north will not let the country split asunder." Jan paused, a worried look crossing his round face. "Some say there'll be civil war over the slavery issue."

"My! How could this happen in a country with a constitution that declares all men are created equal? Britain abolished slavery in 1833. I knew there were slaves on the plantations of America, and I've read about the poor souls being flogged and treated worse than the slavers' dogs, but I thought it was only a matter of time before good-minded citizens would end that inhumane practice."

"You are well studied in our politics, Carreena. It has been instructional to speak with you. However, I am being called to duty and must take my leave." Jan tipped his hat to Carreena and joined the men who were placing boards on the grass for a dance platform.

Paul Wiggle from Pittsburgh had loaded his wagon with Monongahela whisky that he intended to sell in Oregon. In honor of the celebration, he had opened a crate, and several bullwhackers who had been into the rye whiskey were slurring their words and stumbling as they helped prepare for the celebrations.

"You look too sober, Jan," said one of the bullwhackers, staggering and offering a bottle to Jan.

"Many thanks, but I'll pass. Whiskey goes sour in my belly."

Following the feast, the emigrants sang the "Star Spangled Banner," holding their right hands to their chests, many with tears gathering in their eyes. So far away from home, yet the pull of the country they loved was stronger than ever.

As they sang, Alice looked over at David. He wore a white buck-skin jacket that Alice thought must have taken days to decorate with needle, thread and beads. *His wife's skillful work, a wife who cared deeply.* Her heart missed a beat as she studied him, admiring the fine features of his face and the sunburnt look of a man who traveled the trails of the west.

The musicians tuned up their fiddles, brought out guitars and accordions, and played a lively rendition of the Irish Washerwomen. The men lined up, step dancing one at a time on the makeshift wooden floor. The first dancers were the young men hired on as bullwhackers and teamsters. They step danced one after another, some staggering from too much drink, their companions hooting and hollering. Walter, slim and light-footed, followed the hired men. Then, to Alice's surprise, Swede took the floor, tapping out the rhythm with quick, light feet despite his bulk. Each dancer received a round of applause, but the cheers and clapping for Swede were the longest and loudest.

Swede was the last of the step dancers before the fiddler called the Virginia reel and couples lined up on the flat, grassy field. Alice sat to the side watching contentedly, the light from the campfire sending a warm glow across her chest.

One of the young bullwhackers approached Alice and offered her a trail-hardened hand. He had a short beard, a sunburned face and smelled of sweat and smoke.

Alice smiled and accepted the invitation. *Why not?* she thought. *Saxby will never join the dance.* He had returned to the wagon imme-diately after finishing off a heaping plate of steak and potatoes.

Alice and her black-bearded partner swung around, both laughing at the fun of the dance, Alice feeling happy for the freedom she had grasped. She noticed that David was partnering the grace-ful Carreena. As they swirled over the ground, Alice wondered if David was attracted to the elegant London woman.

Alice swung down the line of men, each one spinning her about once, her satin crinoline billowing out over the grass. She reached David, whose gaze caught her eyes as he took her arm to swing her around, folding her tight against him, and holding her a little longer before releasing her to the next dancer. She felt the blood rush to her face.

The fiddler struck up a polka. Alice watched Swede approach Carreena and offer his ham-sized hand to the London aristocrat. He was a keg of a man, tall and muscular. He had exchanged his trail-worn trousers and broad-brimmed hat for a well-cut three-piece suit of dark navy blue wool. Carreena moved into Swede's arms, comforted by his reassuring bulk. Alice watched Swede and Carreena swing gracefully across the grass until David approached, offering his hand.

"Would you do me the honor?"

Alice flushed, feeling nervous and uncertain. "Yes, Mr. Ackerman. I love to dance and would be most obliged." Her heart beat against her rib cage as he took her hand and led her into the circle of dancers.

At the end of the polka, David did not release her immediately, but held her in his arms, then brushed his hand along the nape of her neck. An involuntary shiver pulsed through her chest and down into the pit of her stomach. His gaze was unwavering and intense. It was a look that left no doubt in her mind regarding David's desire for her.

Alice swallowed nervously and blushed. She stepped back and lowered her eyes. The band played the "Yellow Rose of Texas." David extended his hand to lead her into the waltz. Alice knew it would be dangerous.

"Thank you, Mr. Ackerman, but I ... I am tired."

Best to set the boundaries. She bowed her head slightly and walked away into the shadows, David's loving glance ingrained in her heart. A full moon sailed in a cloudless sky.

~

A pink streak of sunlight on the eastern hills turned the moon into a pale orange orb then blotted it out as the brilliant July sun lit up the heavens. The visiting Arapaho tribe left the wagon train, also heading west to the buffalo range, their negative view of white people mollified by the generous and warm welcome they had received at the celebration. Despite their habit of stealthily pilfering unguarded items, this time they left without stealing so much as a blanket, let alone a horse.

The emigrants walked under the dazzling sun, reliving the enjoyment of the previous evening. The trail swung back and forth over the Sweetwater, forcing the teamsters and bullwhackers to drive their teams across the stream and up rocky riverbanks over and over. No one complained as the good humor of the previous day carried them forward and kept up everyone's good spirits.

Swede and Carreena walked together beside his wagon, enjoying each other's company. Alice wondered how that relationship could work. Swede was toughened by his years as a sea captain and hard days on the trail as wagon master, a man without Latin or Greek, and Carreena was a refined student of languages, history, and music.

The youngsters in the wagon train gazed at the rock wall along the river, captivated by the strange formations. This stretch of the trail was particularly fascinating for Amelia and Louise, who looked for strange faces and monsters in the towering cliffs. It was not long before they spotted the most well-known landmark on the Oregon Trail.

"Look, Mother, there's Independence Rock." Amelia pointed to a high mound of rock rising out of the prairie. "Please could we stop? I want to write my name on the rock, and I need to have a little axle grease to write with." Alice was heartened to have Amelia return to her normal cheerfulness and enthusiasm.

"Please pull aside, and wait for us, Saxby. It would be good for Amelia to mark our passing."

"Not again, Alice. We are behind once more, and I don't want to be searching for the last campsite up ahead. Remember Alice, we have been given notice to keep up with the wagon train."

"Look! The others are pulling aside so we must stop, too."

Saxby acquiesced, and Alice and her daughter walked to Independence Rock to leave their names and a date along with the thousands of others inscribed with tar or carefully carved into the rock.

Addie was among the travelers to visit the rock and inspect the names.

"Louise and Amelia," Addie asked, "please let me know if you see my father's name, Reverend Appleton, or Matthew, my stepbrother. They may have written on the rock when they passed by years ago."

Children love a mystery, and the children in Swede's wagon train also loved Addie

Louise and her brothers had learned to be excellent readers under Carreena's tutelage, and quickly searched the rock, reading out the names and dates. The McNair boys, who pretended they could read, checked name after name, not knowing what they were reading.

"I found Matthew's name!" It was sharp-eyed Amelia, who was an early reader.

"Is that the Indian boy your father adopted?" Louise asked. "Was he your boyfriend?"

"You are a girl who loves stories of true love," Addie said with a smile. "No. Matthew is my friend but he is also my brother, and I hope to find him and the rest of my family when I reach California."

"Addie, aren't you mixed up? We're all going to Oregon, not California."

"Well, Louise, a week before I left to join the Swede's wagon train, I received a letter from my father telling me he had opened a mission in Yerba Buena. It was too late for me to find a party traveling to California, so I will leave you at Fort Hall and take the California trail."

"You can't travel alone, Addie," Amelia protested.

"Why not stay with us and take the steamer from Oregon City to Yerba Buena?" Louise did not miss much when it came to information about the West.

"Where I go, my horse comes. The trail is best for me, and Pierrot and I won't be alone. Swede knows a trapper who will guide me."

While the beautiful, independent woman was years older, she related to the children on the trail better than to the adults, some of whom were critical of a woman traveling on her own.

As Alice and Amelia walked back to their wagon, the sky cleared of morning fog. "The mountains, mother. I can see them!"

Alice looked west, and in the distance saw the blue outline of the Rockies. "Soon we will cross the backbone of the continent, and if Saxby is correct, we will be in California before winter."

"California? You're wrong. We're bound for Oregon, Mother." Amelia rarely complained, but at this news, her sweet face turned gloomy. "Everyone else is going to Oregon. Well, everyone but Addie. I want to stay with our wagon train. I don't want to leave Louise and Robert."

"We must do as my husband commands. That is the way it is."

"When I marry, I will be like Anna," Amelia stated emphatically, her firm arms planted on her hips. "She is Dutch. She has her own money and is equal with Jan." Before the conversation could continue, a black cloud of dust rose up from the prairie and sped towards them like a moving hillside. They watched, thinking it was an approaching storm, despite the brilliant blue sky and blazing sun. Then they heard the deafening noise and felt the earth beneath them vibrate.

"Buffler! Git your guns, men!"

"Amelia. Come quick! It's a buffalo stampede!"

Alice helped Saxby drive their wagon into the circle, then joined the women and children to watch the approaching herd from behind the wagons. Saxby grabbed his smooth bore gun, mounted Excalibur and rode off with the other men toward the stampeding herd. The buffalo herd passed within a few yards of the circled wagons. Dust rose up in clouds, and wild snorts and the sound of pounding hooves filled the air, making any conversation almost impossible.

The beasts thundered past, thousands and thousands of them. It was an amazing sight. The women and children watched, thrilled by the spectacle. The younger children were frightened by the noise, the older children were excited and the women were happily anticipating a meal of fresh meat. Alice, Amelia and Louise watched in amazement.

"Look at David," Louise shouted. "He rides like an Indian." Alice watched David, holding the horse's reins in his teeth, cocking his rifle and firing at the buffalo while galloping in the midst of the herd. David aimed perfectly, and the animal dropped with his first shot. Over the years in his work as a trail guide, David had trained Lightening as a buffalo horse and had perfected his own skill as a buffalo hunter. Most of the men from the wagon train were farmers, teachers or businessmen with no experience as hunters.

They did not gallop with the herd but instead remained at the edge of the stampede, firing from relative safety as the buffalo raced by.

Despite his lack of experience, Robert galloped his chestnut gelding right into the middle of the herd, the horse's hooves kicking up clumps of dirt. He rode so close to the buffalo that his gun almost touched the beast's haunches. He chased down a fat cow, surrounded by dust and stampeding buffalo.

"Oh, Mom!" Amelia cried out. "Robert's horse fell!"

Louise and Alice watched, her heart beating in fear for her friend out there surrounded by the immense beasts. The gelding staggered to its feet and shook its mane. Robert leapt back into the saddle, and horse and rider were off once again in the midst of the herd, the boy ignoring the risk, taunting death, his bravado driven by the loss of his loved one. In minutes he'd killed his first buffalo with a well-aimed shot to the head of the fat cow. He turned his horse out of the stampede and reined the gelding to a halt as the remaining buffalo hurtled past.

After the noise and dust had finally subsided, two dozen buffalo lay dead on the prairie, enough to supply fresh meat for cooking and for preparing jerky.

"Amelia, my sweet, we will have fresh meat for our dinner."

Alice picked up her skinning and butcher knives from the wagon and was about to walk out to help Saxby with the butchering when she saw him approach, a disconsolate look on his face.

Alice knew something was amiss when Saxby dismounted, said not a word to Alice and climbed into the wagon.

"He didn't kill a buffalo, right?" Amelia had a worried look on her sweet face. She knew that Saxby's lack of success on the hunt spelled trouble for her mother.

"The others will bring us some of their meat, but Saxby will not partake. I only hope he allows us to accept meat from the other marksmen. I am weary of salted pork."

Alice had biscuits baked and a pie in the Dutch oven by the time the hunters returned with buffalo meat packed on the horses.

"Ma'am." David approached her campfire. "Bad luck that Saxby's rifle misfired. He was after a fat female that would have made tender steaks. I have a front quarter for you from an old male but even so, I am sure the fresh meat will be a welcome change."

"I thank you. And I see that the others have more than enough meat for the frying pan and the drying racks."

"There will be more herds once we cross the pass. Too bad that Saxby will take you south onto the cutoff. There won't be any buffalo when you reach the Great Salt Flats. I will try and get you a hind quarter tomorrow so you can salt and dry enough meat to tide you over."

"We don't take your charity. Get out of our camp!" Saxby yelled out from his bed.

Alice did not return the meat. She and Amelia fried the steaks, and her husband said no more. She knew he was drinking laudanum to mask his embarrassment.

I care not for his mood, Alice thought. *I will enjoy my meal of fresh meat because who knows when, if ever, we will get another steak.*

The following evening, Alice sat by the dying embers of the campfire reading a book of Shakespeare's sonnets. When she could no longer read in the fading light, she watched the blaze of sunset streak across the western sky. Alice recognized David from a distance, his tall frame silhouetted against the orange and crimson glow of the setting sun. He walked towards her, his footfalls quiet.

"Ah, I see you are a student of Shakespeare. *Shall I compare thee to a summer's day?*" he grinned, his glance engaging.

"You! A trail guide, quoting poetry?" Alice smiled back and laid her book down on top of a storage box.

"You might recall, dear lady, that like Robert, I was raised an Ackerman. Seven sisters all schooled in Latin, Greek and, of course, the great bard of the 17th century. I was the middle child, the only boy in a flock of petticoats, and their sole audience during family performances of *Romeo and Juliet*."

"You are an enigma, Mr. Ackerman. A scholar and a buffalo hunter." She smiled. "Ah, I see you have brought me another good-sized piece of meat."

"I have the hind quarter for you. Dry as much as you can. Once you reach the Great Basin there will be nothing, no game animals, not even a rabbit or squirrel until you quit the desert. You will be in the land of the Washoe. They are called Diggers because they're able to find food where you will only find salt wastes. They might help you if you are prepared to learn their ways and not judge them. But be cautious; they are also a thieving bunch of Indians who will sneak your cattle out from under your nose."

"Why are you so concerned, David? The route should be safe. This man Hastings will lead us through to the Humboldt River and then over the mountains."

"The Humboldt is a hardscrabble region. I wouldn't call it a river; it has no outlet and no inlet. It is a sink of mud and despair. Hurry through that area. Don't stop for the Sabbath, and get to the mountains before the first snow. The Sierras catch the moist Pacific winds, and in a couple of days, you'll have snow up to your petticoats. Absolutely impossible to cross with wagons. Once the snow is deep, you won't even be able to cross it on foot. Yes, I am worried for you."

"I have no choice but to follow my husband."

"I wish Saxby would listen to reason and stay on the main trail. I rarely speak ill of any man, but your husband is a fool who will cause great harm to those who follow him. I can do nothing but warn you because I want you and Amelia to be safe. Please take care; Hastings is not to be trusted. He is an inexperienced traveler with a talent for self-promotion. Whatever he says or does is for his benefit alone.

Alice tried to put aside David's warning as she prepared jerky for the next stage of their trip. She cut the meat from the buffalo quarter into thin strips, salted the meat liberally and hung the pieces from the outside cover of the wagon. The dry hot air of the plains would turn the meat into jerky in only a few days. She kept the bones and buried them under the fire to cook the marrow and make a delicious meal for the following day.

She wished with all her heart that Saxby would change his mind, but instead of heeding well-meant warnings, Saxby was buoyed up by the prospect of a quick route to California, and actively promoted the cutoff to other emigrants in the wagon train. Dorothy also opted for the Hastings route to California, a change that surprised Alice as well as McNair.

"But, Dorothy," McNair asked, "I figured you to stay on the Oregon Trail and join your sister to tell her of Annabelle Lee's passing, not go off to California."

"I can't face my sister. She will hate me for the loss of her beautiful daughter, and Elizabeth will never forgive me for allowing her twin to die. I have my boy Billy alive and well, while my sister has had her child taken from her because of me. I promised to keep the two girls together, and I failed. I will send a letter to Olive with Swede's train, but I cannot join her." Tears flowed over Dorothy's cheeks, and although she was still in her twenties, she looked much older, her face lined with sorrow and regret.

"That be it, then," McNair grinned. "This is our big chance for rich land, and since it sits well with you, Dorothy, we're bound for California."

Alice wished she could continue on with Swede's party. She felt secure under David's guidance and Swede's supervision of the wagon train. She knew if she carefully rationed their food supplies, her little family would reach Oregon exhausted, but with a little food to spare and hopefully a purse of money.

They camped on the banks of the Little Sandy River where Saxby gathered the party that would turn south to Fort Bridger. Alice couldn't hide her disappointment.

"Oh, Anna, when will we ever meet again, and how will I survive without you and Jan to comfort and counsel me?"

"Break off from Saxby," Anna told her again, "Taking the cutoff is a lunatic notion."

"That is also my advice," Jan added, "and I am not the kind of man to hand out buckets of advice. I leave that up to Anna. But today I tell you to stay with us on a road that others have safely crossed. Think of your sweet daughter."

"Of course I think of her. She is all I have, and I would gladly break off with Saxby and remain with the Swede wagon train if that was possible, but Saxby will force me to go. He might not miss me, but he will not allow me to leave him, and what is worse, as I have told you before, he will claim Amelia as his and take her from me."

"I'm so sorry. It must be hard for you, Alice. But listen, if life in California doesn't work out, take a boat to Oregon City and find us. A couple like us won't be hard to find. Himself makes quite a splash in a small community—a big fish in a little pool." Anna laughed, but tears pooled in her eyes as she realized that they might never see one another again.

After a final set of good wishes from both parties, Alice walked back to their wagon, her eyes on the ground and her shoulders stooped. A cool wind blew dust across the prairie, ruffling her skirts and sending sand into her teary eyes. Alice felt trapped. She did not trust this man Hastings, and she had little faith in Saxby's judgment.

"Alice, watch where you walk. You almost knocked me over." It was David, a wry smile on his face. "I've come to say my farewell.

Swede will have our wagon train moving early tomorrow, and your man is never too quick with his departures. I hope you remember everything I've told you and that you keep yourself and Amelia safe."

"Thank you for all your help while we were on the trail together. I'll miss your company, Mr. Ackerman."

"I have something for you." David reached into his vest and pulled out a pistol. "It is a pocket pistol that I want you to keep."

"What on earth for? Saxby has a rifle and a brace of pistols."

"Does he let you use them? Has he taught you how to load and clean a gun? Does he even know how to keep his guns in good repair?" She didn't reply, but he could read the answers in her face. "I want you to have this gun. It's a Colt revolver."

"It's expensive," Alice protested. "I can tell. Saxby has control of all my money, and I can't pay you."

"It is a gift, Alice. Please accept it."

"What would I be needing to shoot? Will we be attacked by Indians?"

"Maybe the Indians, or perhaps the Mormons. There's trouble brewing between the government and both groups out here, the Indians because their land is being taken and the Mormons because they want to have their own laws and country. The Washoe along the Humboldt are a pack of thieves and not very friendly. I don't know what you will encounter, but a gun can be a peacemaker when trouble erupts. I warn you, the route you take will not be easy. It might even be just a duck or goose that you need to shoot to feed yourself and Amelia."

"I don't even know how to use a gun."

"I will show you. Come close to me, and listen carefully." David held the pistol in one hand and a small flask in the other. "This is the powder," he said, passing her the flask. "Add powder to each chamber. Try to be consistent and put the same amount of powder in each chamber. Next, add a slightly greased wad and then the lead ball. After you have a ball in all four chambers, cap each one with this." David held up the caps. "For safety, leave one chamber empty, and set the chamber on the empty one. I'll give you a case of twenty balls."

He handed a package to Alice, his fingers brushing her palm.

"The Colt will fire four shots, and each will release a cloud of smoke and kick back with a strong recoil. Be prepared for that, and steady yourself before you take the next shot."

"If I had to shoot something or someone, I would never finish loading in time."

"You're smart, Alice, and quick with your hands. I've watched you working around the campfire. You have dinner simmering before other women find the frying pan. If you can make perfect bread, soup and pie all at the same time, you can learn to load the Colt quickly and expertly. Practice loading it, and then try firing it. The noise, the kickback and the smoke will surprise you the first time, but the gun is accurate if you know how to use it and if you keep the chambers clean. I will feel better parting with you if you have the revolver."

"I couldn't shoot a human being."

"You could if Amelia was in danger or if your own life was threatened. Give me your hand, Alice."

She hesitated for a second.

David took her hand in his and placed the pistol in Alice's palm. Their eyes met, and Alice couldn't break away from his unnerving gaze. The way he looked at her was unmistakable. Alice felt a surge of warmth from his touch.

"David." Alice couldn't continue. She didn't know what to say.

"I will miss you, Alice, and I will think of you."

"I'll miss you, too." She swallowed the lump in her throat, her voice soft and emotional.

He opened his arms and gently embraced her. Alice felt pleasure and comfort from his touch. He placed his fingers on her chin and raised her face to his. She hungered for a kiss, but there would be no kiss.

Alice knew that the embrace was not between two friends parting but a man and woman who desired one another. Alice silently begged with all her being to stay with this man, to have him hold her forever. *That cannot be, but if only I could have just one kiss to remember him, to help me through the bitter months ahead.* Alice felt an overwhelming longing.

They broke apart but didn't acknowledge what had happened between them. She couldn't speak because the only words that would come to her lips would be words of love, and those were forbidden.

"Stay alive for me." Tears filled her eyes as she turned and walked away from David, back to her wagon. An eerie light shone through the trees, enveloping the camp, and a wind stirred in the old cottonwood trees, making a weird creaking sound as tree branch groaned against tree trunk.

"What are you weeping about?" Saxby grumbled.

"I will miss my friends." She looked away, not wanting Saxby to see her eyes and question her further.

Alice did not want to share Saxby's bed that night.

"Saxby, I must find Amelia. It is late. Go to sleep. I will be back in a few minutes."

But he was not asleep when she returned, and as usual he moved next to her, took her hand and placed it on his limp cock.

"Please, not tonight," Amelia protested. "I feel unwell."

"Sick? I don't believe it. You're strong and healthy. Have you not heard of the rights of the husband? Refuse me again, and I will make you regret it."

Saxby's rough sex was almost impossible for Alice to bear. When he didn't reach a climax on top of her, he tossed Alice on to her stomach, much like a butcher tosses a hindquarter of beef, and pushed into her from behind. Alice gritted her teeth, waiting for the assault to end.

Alice's body and mind were now linked to David. She ruefully remembered her aunt's advice on the day before Alice's wedding to Saxby: *Open your heart fully to no other. I cannot counsel you too strongly to take no other confidant but your husband.*

Saxby lacked the character of a man capable of being a woman's confidant, and Alice had opened her heart to David, whose beautiful face she might never see again.

PART II
THE PARTING
OF THE WAYS

Chapter Fifteen

The Hastings Cutoff

The Swede party, with David guiding, turned right at The Parting of the Ways, heading along the established trail to Oregon. Saxby's newly formed wagon train would veer left along the Little Sandy River and take the less traveled road to Fort Bridger.

Saxby held up their departure to wait for the next wagon train so he could recruit more emigrants. The man who came across as arrogant and stubborn within Swede's wagon train spoke confidently and persuasively to strangers, claiming to have a route that would take them across the mountains to California and get them to the Promised Land in just weeks. It was a compelling argument, especially for those short of supplies and money.

Before the break-off party began the southward route from The Parting of the Ways, several families had been persuaded to join them. The new recruits taking the Hastings Cutoff included an Irish family of four, an extended Mormon family led by widow Eliza along with children and grandchildren, some as young as a year old, an Austrian with his wife and children, and a German-speaking family. Single men were hired as bullwhackers or teamsters, and young women came along to cook and care for children. In total, fifty-five emigrants chose the cutoff trail to California.

The break-off party traveled for a day while sizing up their leader and fellow travelers. They knew they would have to select a wagon master for the trip to California, with one member of each family casting a vote. At the end of the day, McNair was declared captain.

It rankled Saxby. *Havn't I been the one to convince them to take the Hastings Cutoff? Why would they choose McNair? He's a man with no education, a paunchy unkempt farmer who cared little if his waistcoat was ripped and his shirt cuffs frayed.*

Saxby's air of superiority rubbed people the wrong way. They had not left lairds and nobles behind in the Old Country to be under the thumb of someone like this arrogant man. Saxby took the rebuff in angry silence as he left the gathering, kicking at a stone and swearing under his breath.

From that day forward, they were called the McNair Party. Two days of travel took them to Fort Bridger, where they made final purchases from the meager supplies at the fort. Alice couldn't wait to leave the store with its musty smell and dead flies on the windowsills.

Alice thought back on Saxby's decision to take the cutoff trail and could not reconcile the information she had with Saxby's change of route. It didn't fit. David had warned her it was folly, and she was beginning to agree. Hastings had promised to meet Saxby at Fort Bridger, but he was not there.

Alice worried about Hastings' absence. *I am being led by an obstinate husband and McNair, jovial, but a fool of a man.* What she couldn't know at the time was that an experienced trapper and trailblazer had crossed the salt flats on the cutoff on his way west to Sutter's Fort, but because he experienced so many hardships on that trail, he returned along the Fort Hall trail and met up with the Swede wagon train. When he heard from David that a group of emigrants had left the established trail to take the cutoff, he sent a fast rider from Fort Hall to Fort Bridger to leave a letter for Saxby and any other party with women and children attempting to cross the salt flats.

The letter never reached Saxby.

"We won't be discouragin' use of the cutoff," Bridger told his partner, as he slipped the letter under the counter. "If word of this letter gets out, our business will be ruined. When I bought this darn place, it was on the Oregon Trail, then what's his name found a short cut to Oregon and bypassed us! It's a matter of survival. We don't owe them emigrants nothin'."

Bridger, now in his late forties, was a fleshy man who smelled of liquor and smiled too much. His partner, a thin man with cracked glasses perched on a long nose, was evasive whenever Alice or Dorothy asked about the salt flats and the route over the Wasatch. Alice was certain the owners promoted the cutoff route to increase their business, and cared little for the wellbeing of the emigrants snagged by the promise of a quick route.

I don't trust these men, Alice thought. *Is this not the same Jim Bridger who left the injured brigade guide, Hugh Glass, to die alone without kit or gun or food? Had Bridger not been berated enough for the widespread reports of his callousness to reform him?*

Before leaving Fort Bridger, there would still have been time for the McNair party to head back to the Oregon Trail, but Saxby was not a man who gave up once his mind was fixed, and McNair did not have the leadership abilities to reverse the group's decision.

Even the warnings from an old friend Saxby had met earlier at Fort Laramie did not dissuade him. He advised Saxby not to take the Hastings Cutoff, telling him there was no proper trail for wagons, not enough water or feed for the stock, and no wood for fires.

"You should carry on to Fort Hall, and then head south to California," he urged Saxby. "It is still a difficult trail, but not impossible." Nothing changed Saxby's mind. It was the Hastings route, and that was it.

How many warnings does a man need before he takes a second look at a decision? Alice wondered.

They were stopped for lunch on the trail south from Fort Bridger, heading for the Wasatch Mountains. Amelia missed Louise and Robert, and Alice yearned to be with David. She was fearful for Amelia's wellbeing, and missed the companionship of Anna and Jan.

"Saxby, what's up with this man of yours?" McNair slouched on a supply box by his wagon, digging under his fingernails with a blade. "Hastings says he'll meet you, then he don't turn up. How do we find a trail with no map, no guide?"

"The route is clear, McNair. Just because you were chosen for wagon master doesn't give you a reason to question me. Let's get moving." Saxby strode off, jumped on the seat of his wagon and whipped his team, heading them south and away from the relative safety of the Oregon Trail.

Although McNair was wagon master, it seemed to be in name only since Saxby was incapable of relinquishing control. He bullied McNair and anyone else who opposed him, but finding a trail for a wagon train became difficult as they approached the Wasatch Mountains.

"Saxby, when your man didn't show up at Fort Bridger, you told us Hastings would come back and lead us through the canyons. Where in tarnation is he?" McNair raised his hands in frustration; he didn't wear leadership well.

"I'll ride ahead and bring him back. Hastings told me he is also guiding a group of riders through the mountains and should be a day's ride away."

The party set up camp and waited for Saxby's return.

Saxby caught up to Hastings at Salt Lake. The horsemen were resting at the edge of the desert, preparing to cross that night.

"Hastings, you didn't wait at Fort Bridger as promised! I have a party waiting to cross the Wasatch, and I don't see a route suitable for wagons."

"Well, my man," Hastings told him in a calm, authoritative manner. "I waited a day at Fort Bridger but thought you'd changed your mind. Had to move on myself. I'll ride back a ways with you."

Hastings did not have the appearance of an Overlander. He was closely shaved with a neat mustache, black suit and highly polished riding boots. And what boots! Saxby silently admired Hastings' Albert boots, studded with mother of pearl decorations. A useless adornment, but to Saxby, the ostentatious expense of the boots was impressive.

"Look, Saxby," Hastings said, reining his horse to a halt. "I'm being paid to lead the party of riders. I'd like to help your group, but I am obliged to others. Tie up your horse here. The two of us will climb this peak, and I will show you the route." Saxby puffed behind the younger man, embarrassed by his lack of fitness and impressed by Hastings' confidence and athleticism.

"Look down there," Hastings said as they reached the top. He waved his hand nonchalantly in a general direction. "That's the trail through the canyon. Not a problem." Saxby looked at the rocky barrier. He felt confused and wanted to protest, to insist that Hastings return and guide them as promised, but he also didn't want to appear weak.

"Yes. I see the route," Saxby mumbled, although all he saw was a gorge choked with trees and rocks.

With that, Hastings once again turned his back on the McNair party, leaving Saxby on his own to guide the wagons through the steep mountains and impassable canyons. Saxby doubled back to the camp, where the McNair party waited.

"Is it a flat, clear trail, like they told us at Fort Bridger?" McNair asked.

"It's passable."

"Did you cross through the mountains without a problem?" Alice wanted to know.

"It's passable, as I said." A dark look crossed his face. "Being on horseback, I took the high trail over the mountains. But the wagon route looks flat and clear just as Hastings said."

"We could still turn back to Fort Bridger and join the main trail. Have you considered that?" Alice rarely questioned Saxby, but her concerns for Amelia's safety now trumped her fear of Saxby's temper.

"Enough, Alice! I said we can make it, and we will."

The party hitched up oxen and horses, and moved southwest into the mountains, but it wasn't long before the members of the McNair party began questioning the route. It was obvious that wagons had never passed through the canyon, so choked was it with heavy underbrush and trees so thick that they had to wait while the men went out early each day to clear a path.

On the third day, the party moved forward slowly through the canyon, crossing and re-crossing the stream. Then the route led into a second canyon. Again the men took out axes and saws, and the wagon train came to a halt. They worked for two days until they came to a narrow gap in the canyon blocked by trees and rocks.

"Damn this country," Saxby exclaimed, exasperated. "Hastings said we could make it through this canyon. It's just not possible." He wondered if he had misunderstood Hastings' directions. Others grumbled that Hastings was a charlatan whose claim of a good road to California was nothing but a hoax.

"We'll have to hook up and take the wagons up the side of the canyon," Saxby told McNair.

McNair looked at the steep incline and failed to see anything approaching a trail. Saxby insisted they go up and over the impasse, and ordered the bullwhackers to hook up. A team of four oxen proved unable to pull a heavily loaded wagon along the mountain-side, and Saxby concluded that his team of horses couldn't budge the wagon up the impasse. In order to move forward through the Wasatch, they hooked up twenty oxen to one wagon and laboriously took the wagons across the mountain one by one, once again slowing the party to a crawl.

Exhausted and discouraged, the party finally passed over the Wasatch barrier. Below stretched the Great Salt Basin and Salt Lake. For several members of the party, it was a welcome sight, but for Alice, the miles of barren wasteland in front of them without trees or water sent a cold shiver down her spine. She held Amelia's hand as she stared out across the empty landscape.

I must keep my child safe.

The tired party rested at a spring at the edge of the desert, watering their stock and loading their wagons with a supply of grass. They wanted to take on barrels of water, but water was heavy, and if they filled the large tank, the oxen would be unable to pull the weight.

"You said we would be in California in seven weeks," McNair complained. "We have already wasted several weeks cutting our way through these here mountains, and now we've gotta cross the great desert and the Sierras. I think maybe you got it wrong, Saxby."

"Stop fussing like an old lady, McNair. We'll make it over. Hastings is ahead of us and will leave us messages."

"Hastings ain't traveling with wagons, women and children, and a big herd of cattle and sheep! They're traveling fast on horses using trails over the hills, not needin' a wagon road." McNair looked uncomfortable. "You'd best be right about this, Saxby."

Before moving out of the treed area and onto the loamy alkaline soil of the salt flats, Amelia spotted a note stuck on a tree branch. Part of the paper was torn, so Alice and Amelia patched it together to read the words.

As Saxby had promised, it was from Hastings. Alice read the note: *Two nights and two days of hard driving to reach water.*

"We can make a couple of days with this supply of grass and water," Saxby announced confidently. "There's water on the western edge of the flats and then a quick trip over the mountains."

"How can you say it will be a quick trip?" Alice asked. "Isn't it six hundred miles to Sutter's? It has taken us three weeks to make thirty miles."

"It will be much faster now that we have cut through the mountains. Thirty, maybe forty miles a day."

"Saxby, you don't take into consideration rest days and our problems on the trail. I think we will go ten miles a day. Amelia, you are good at arithmetic. How long will it take us to go six hundred miles?"

"Six hundred miles will take us two months."

"But that means we will be going through the mountains in November or worse, in December," Alice exclaimed. "Oh, my God! Saxby, please let's turn back and rejoin the Oregon Trail. We can't put the children at risk."

"You are wrong. We will be faster now that we are on the flats. Stop putting fear in everyone's heart. If I hear one more word about turning back, you'll be sorry," Saxby countered angrily. "And don't you dare steal off with Amelia. I will tell you only once more: by law, she is mine. If you leave me, I will claim her. Now, pull yourself together."

Alice's heart froze at hearing Saxby's threat spoken before witnesses. *Take my Amelia! How could he be so cruel? He is evil!*

Alice stared at Saxby, stunned by his words. "You will never separate me from my child. She is all I have, Saxby. Please never make that threat again."

"You have a husband whom you must obey," he reminded her. "If you do, you will never have to fear losing Amelia. So stop your worrying. We've been slow cutting a road through the Wasatch, but it's flat across the desert. We'll cover the distance in two days, then cross the Ruby Range to the Humboldt where we join the traditional trail. There, our speed will improve. We will make forty miles a day, and in no time we'll reach Sutter's."

Alice said no more, though she had no faith in Saxby's assessment of the road ahead, and all too soon, her fears were realized. Although the sun bore down on them relentlessly, the underlying layers of soil had been saturated with seepage from the lake, making the trek across the flats proved far more difficult than anyone had anticipated. The horses and oxen sank into the loamy wet ground, forcing the emigrants to push and pull the wagons out of the muck. Riders dismounted and walked their horses, slowing their progress even more.

Alice plodded along, walking with Amelia while Saxby rode in the wagon. She tried to remain positive, pushing herself not to be beaten down by the searing heat. Her lips were parched from the glaring sun, and her eyes burned. But her sole worry was for Amelia, who suffered from the heat and lack of water yet bore the depravation without a word. For two days and two nights, they struggled through scorching heat during the day and bitter cold at night. By the third day, the oxen began to falter, McNair's sheep had perished in the heat, and the horses were unable to pull Saxby's wagon. Alice kept looking to the west searching for her first view of Pilot's Peak, a beacon at the end of the salt flats to mark the end of their desperate trek.

"He told us it was only forty miles without water. That man Hastings is a damn liar. 'T'aint forty. It's twice that fur." McNair scowled, the jovial demeanor he displayed in camp buried under worry and self-recrimination.

At The Parting of the Ways, Saxby had engaged Issachar and a young Irishman, O'Malley, to drive wagons. Saxby's original two teamsters had refused to take the cutoff trail, instead remaining with Swede's wagon train. Issachar and O'Malley tried to urge the horses through the soft soil, but lack of food and water were taking their toll. The beautiful Canadian horses grew gaunt with hunger, and exhausted from lack of water. Crazy for food and weak from thirst, each bit at the horse ahead of it in the traces, drawing bits of flesh and blood. As the horses stumbled and died, Saxby had to abandon all but their elaborate wagon with the roomy interior.

Now, with two of the wagons abandoned, Flynn O'Malley and his young wife Nelly once again had to load their four-year-old son and all their belongings on one mule and one horse. Nelly carried their baby girl. They had joined the McNair party believing in Saxby's quick trip across the mountains, placing their hopes on reaching the green valley of California despite their lack of supplies and no wagon of their own.

"Alice, Amelia," Saxby commanded. "Move the supplies into our sleeping wagon. Stuff as much as you can in the top story and then the bottom. I'll sleep in a tent before I lose one more item."

Alice understood that his supply of wine and opium was of far greater value to Saxby than cornmeal and beans. As she moved the remaining food boxes to make room for Saxby's supplies, Alice's heart clenched.

One half bag of flour, one bag of beans and one of cornmeal. It's already October. Soon the flour will be gone, and in sixty days we'll be lucky if we have a few cups of corn meal and beans. Why didn't I stand my ground and insist on purchasing flour at Fort Laramie? I am married to a self-centered bully who cares naught for me or my child.

Alice fumed as she thought of the disrespect and rebukes she had suffered as Saxby's wife. She remembered something Saxby said at an earlier time, at one of the dinners at her uncle's house: *Give me the fine things in life, and I will give up the necessities.* Now her life and that of her dear sweet daughter were at risk because of a husband who might leave them bereft of the necessities of life.

As they moved west, the exquisite wagon, which had once been the envy of several emigrants on the Oregon Trail, became even more of a burden. Saxby had to hook up the six remaining horses in order to pull the heavy load.

Discontent rose among the travelers as they struggled south of Salt Lake without water, grass for the animals or wood for a campfire, without even buffalo chips to make a fire to boil coffee or cook a hot meal.

One by one, the stock faltered and fell along the trail, often collapsing in their traces. Saxby's beautiful Canadian horses were the first to suffer from lack of water and feed. All but one of his twenty expensive, fine animals, were dead by the third day of the desert march. It was like rubbing salt into his wounds for Saxby to ask McNair for the loan of two oxen, but even the borrowed animals were unable to pull the wagon. Without water and feed, the animals struggled to pull the wagon over the spongy ground. Although the sun bore down relentlessly, the underlying layers had been saturated from seepage that came from the Great Salt Lake.

Saxby whipped the team, cussing at the oxen. They edged forward, trying to move the fancy wagon that was heavily laden with merchandise and Saxby's cases of wine. First one, then the other, grunted, fell and died while still in their traces.

Saxby piled his most precious belongings onto Excalibur, his only surviving horse, and the family started walking west with as much as they could carry. Twenty miles of desolation separated them from Pilot's Peak and the rest of the party, and trekking across the desert without food and water had weakened Saxby and Amelia. Saxby stumbled and swayed from heat and dehydration. Amelia walked alongside her mother, stopping every few paces. It was clear they could not cross the remaining desert without water, and the rest of the group had moved out of sight. Even O'Malley's family pushed forward, leaving them behind in the dessert.

Saxby watched them disappear over the horizon. "Damn it all! How can it be so hot and dry and yet the ground is soaked. This trail is cursed!"

Saxby unloaded the supplies from Excalibur's back and left Alice and Amelia in the heat of the desert while he rode west for water. Alice had hardened even more towards him, but she realized she must face the crisis with a clear head, without anger or recriminations.

For two days, Alice and Amelia shielded themselves from the glaring sun during the day and huddled together for warmth throughout the chilly nights. Alice slept during the day and stayed awake at night. She watched the heavens in wonderment, the beauty of the mass of seething stars above the desert landscape capturing her admiration and curiosity. Alice's mind drifted back to her parting with David, playing over in her mind the warm feelings she had for him. She searched her belongings for a pen and paper. She wrote:

> Dear soul: I am half a person without you. In the beauty of the heavens, I see your face and wonder if you are also watching the sliver of a moon sail across the night sky. Just one warm embrace and I will be healed.

Saxby returned late the second night, riding under a sky awash with stars. Alice recognized his ungainly form on the graceful purebred, a dark silhouette of horse and rider against the black desert horizon. She hid the private poem in the pocket of her smock, and gently shook Amelia.

"Amelia, my sweet, he's back and brings water." Amelia woke. She had no word of complaint, although the girl was hungry, thirsty and shivering from the cold wind that blew across the salt flats.

"Rest here, my darling, I'll bring you some water." Alice picked up her skirt and ran to meet horse and rider.

"Please give me water for Amelia. She is parched and weak."

Alice held the canteen to her daughter's lips and then took long deep gulps herself.

Refreshed by water and a meal of corn grits sent by Dorothy, the trio loaded their supplies on Excalibur and walked through the night towards the strange pyramid of Pilot's Peak that was nothing more than a distant silhouette against the night sky.

Alice, Saxby and Amelia trudged through part of the next day as well before catching up with the rest of their party, who were camped at Pilot's Peak, letting the stock feed, washing clothes and preparing for the next stage of the journey.

Precious days of fall dwindled as the party camped two more nights, but Saxby had been able to strike a bargain with McNair for yet another team of oxen to retrieve his fancy wagon.

It did not require great skill in math to calculate the number of days left before winter would be upon them, and only the small children were thankfully spared the worry. They played happily at this oasis at the western edge of the desert, content to have hot food, shelter from the sun and water to drink.

A series of ridges called the Rubies separated the McNair party from the Humboldt Valley. There were several ridges to cross, and each valley looked the same as the last. It was as if they were in the devil's clutches, made to repeat the same exhausting climbs over and over. The trials of these crossings brought conflicts out into the open. Saxby, with his heavy wagon, had once more dropped behind, leaving the group free to vent.

"Only a fool would say this is a quicker road to California," McNair grumbled to Issachar, "and Saxby is the fool that fell for Hastings' crazy route."

"You can't use a ruler to plan a road through the mountains," the lanky bullwhacker chipped in, waving a sinewy arm towards the blue ridge to the west. "Sure, maybe on a map it looks shorter, but anyone with half a brain knows a pass through the mountains is never straight as an arrow. You gotta take into account how steep the ridges are, and where the low passes can be found. Saxby acts like a know-all, but when it comes right down to it, he's dumb as a sack of hammers."

"A man's got to have a healthy respect for the ways of the mountains. He ain't going to impose hisself on 'em. Them mountains, they put a man in his place," McNair continued, working himself into a lather. Others joined in with further comments and complaints.

"I'd call this Hasting's Longtrip," one of them put in. "'T'ain't no cutoff."

"We're losing a full month. You know where that will put us? Smack into November when we go over the Sierras! And here Saxby is calling a day of rest. The man will kill us all!"

The company faced one final ridge before they reached the Humboldt Valley and joined the established trail leading to Truckee River and the path over the Sierras to California. The party slowed to a crawl as they drove the teams up the rocky incline. Tempers flared at the smallest incident. Saxby, always in command, became incensed when Jake, one of McNair's bullwhackers, insisted Saxby needed several oxen to pull across the rugged ridge that led over to the Humboldt. When the men stood in front of Saxby's wagon demanding he listen to them, Saxby refused to budge. In frustration Jake raised his whip and brought it down across Saxby's legs.

"I'll kill you for that!" Saxby bellowed, drawing his knife. Before anyone could stop him, Saxby plunged the knife into Jake's breast. A gush of blood erupted from the wound and pooled on the ground. McNair and several of the men gathered around. Jake's partner, Issachar, pressed a shirt against Jake's chest to try to stop the flow of blood, but within minutes, the young bullwhacker drew his final breath. Issachar held his friend's bloodied, limp body and wept.

"Jake, you've been a good companion. You didn't deserve to die."
Anger erupted throughout the party.

"Hang Saxby!" Issachar yelled. "Even hanging is too good for
him! I'd cut off his balls and stick them in his bloody mouth."

McNair said nothing. Silently, he raised the tongue of his
wagon in the unmistakable signal among emigrants that the guilty
man should be hanged. If the company voted to hang Saxby, it
wouldn't be the first time an emigrant was strung up on a wagon
tongue. However, the women argued against another such grisly
spectacle of death in a single day. The children had been ushered
into the wagons, but one or two small faces could been seen peeking
out, too enthralled or terrified by the sudden outbreak of bloody
violence to look away.

As the conflict continued, McNair could see that hanging
would split the group further, and the wagon tongue slowly lowered.
"We won't hang you, Saxby, but you ain't goin' with us any further.
You gotta quit us and git yourself over the trail alone," McNair told
him. "Most in the company want ya strung up, 'specially Jake's
friends, but in thinking about your wife and all, others have agreed
that you will be banished. Take your wife and child, or leave her
with us, but leave you must. I'll give you two minutes to pick up
food and water, nothing else, and quit us fer good."

Saxby nodded at Alice, making it clear that she was to stay
behind. He gathered a few belongings, including his supply of opium
and a ration of food and led his horse west up the steep ridge. On his
mind was the gold he had left in his trunk, gold Alice could still
take across the mountains in the wagon. As she watched Saxby disappear over the ridge, Alice felt only relief. She shed no tears at
their parting.

*I followed him on this desperate journey thinking that, at the very
least, I had a husband to help me. Now I am alone with my daughter.*

Others have large, extended families or alliances to protect their children from danger and starvation, but because of Saxby, I am alone. How I wish I could be back with Swede's party with Anna and Jan, following David west to Oregon! If only I had a horse to carry Amelia and a food supply, I would break off from the California Trail and walk to Oregon.

The horses had perished on the salt flats, and no one offered help to the wife of the man who had led them to this dangerous pass. Certainly no one offered up a team of oxen; oxen that would be a food supply for the winter if they could not cross the Sierras before the snows.

No. I have no choice but to stay with the McNair party and hope I can get Amelia safely to California.

Chapter Sixteen
The Humboldt River Valley
Nevada Territory

I t was Saxby's cocksure self-assurance that had led them to take the dangerous Hastings Cutoff. He may have been ignorant and foolhardy, but he had at least been decisive. McNair, weak and easily influenced, delayed making decisions. The company crested the ridge and dropped down into the wide Humboldt River Valley. It had been a dry year, and rather than a refreshing river, the emigrants found that the Humboldt was a series of pools, the water undrinkable.

Everything was covered with a fine layer of dust, blown by the ever-present wind. The emigrants resembled the walking dead, their faces gray masks, but at least the road was fair. They had completed the cutoff and intersected with the California trail that split off from the Oregon Trail at Fort Hall.

They had been on the Humboldt Trail for a week when Amelia looked north, trying to make out if she was seeing a group of Indians or white people. Then she spotted someone familiar.

"Mother! Look! I think I see Robert back there on the trail with four other riders!" Amelia's spirits lifted at the prospect of having a friend join them.

"There's Christian and Addie, but I can't make out the other two," Alice said, peering across the flat, wide valley.

"*By the pricking of my thumbs, something wicked this way comes.* Styles and Finis," Dorothy said wearily. "That is what cometh this way, and they are not welcome." She recalled Annabelle Lee quoting the phrase from Shakespeare's play, *Macbeth*, when referring to men the young girl disliked, men she didn't trust.

"Looks like we have something bad and something good," Alice added philosophically as she walked forward to greet Addie, riding at the head of the group of five riders. "I knew you would strive to reach Yerba Buena, but David told me the old trapper, Bartholomew, would guide you."

"He had another engagement." Addie smiled at Alice, happy to finally be among the company of women. "I told Swede and David that I could travel alone, but they wouldn't hear of it. When Finis and Styles stepped forward, David asked Robert and Christian to watch over me." Finis didn't acknowledge Addie's derogatory remark, but instead remained stiffly erect on his palomino.

Alice's heartbeat quickened at hearing David's name. "Tell us how you left my friends. Anna and Jan! Are they well? And David?"

"They are fine. Anna and Jan send their love."

Christian dismounted and touched his hat brim. "Alice, David sends his affections and asked Robert and I to watch over you and Amelia."

Yes, Alice thought. *He cares for me and sent Robert and Christian, not just to keep Addie safe, but to see to my safety and that of my daughter.*

Alice felt less discouraged now that her friends had joined the McNair party. The trail remained rough, but having Addie to talk to and Christian to lean on, and for Amelia to have Robert's companionship, gave Alice a welcome measure of comfort.

As they trudged along the desolate valley, they were met by a wretched-looking band of Indians.

"Mommy, they don't have any clothes on," Amelia said, staring at the naked Washoe. "Isn't it naughty to have no clothes on?"

"There are many different people in the world, Amelia. Africans wear little clothing, as do the Aborigines in Australia. They're just different, not bad," Alice explained, although she felt her cheeks reddening.

"They are the dirty diggers," Dorothy announced, "and not even ashamed to expose themselves."

Alice remembered David's admonition. "Don't call them diggers. They are Washoe," Alice told Dorothy. "They have a bad reputation for thievery, but they know how to find food when there is no game."

"I don't need no Indian to show me how to find food," McNair barked.

"Styles and me here, we rode out with Addie to join you all, not wanting this young lady to be traveling this here trail alone with Indians on the warpath an' all." Finis lifted his Henry rifle from the saddle and pointed it at the band of Washoe, a silly grin pasted on his face. Styles sidled close to Finis like a dog offering its backside to be patted.

"Finis, put that gun away." Christian's tone was far from friendly. "David asked Robert and I to make sure you don't start an Indian war and put the entire wagon train in danger."

"They don't look friendly," Alice announced. She had learned to read the signs. There was no war paint, but the suspicious looks the Indians gave them led Alice to conclude that they were not to be trusted.

"I didn't say they were friendly, Alice, just that we will not shoot Indians unless they threaten our lives." That night Christian kept watch, chasing a band of Washoe away from the stock, but the next morning when the men changed shifts, the thieves made away with one of the cows.

"McNair, we must place more guards at night," Alice insisted. "The Washoe are trying to drive off the animals. I just watched them cut out one of the cows and drive it away."

"I get more advice from everyone in this company than I can swallow. First, it's your husband, wanting to take over my job. Now that he is gone, you want to tell me what to do. I try to git along with everyone but alls I'se hearin' is complaints. Finis there's a hothead, Styles is less than useless and then I have Mr. Solicitor giv'n me his two cents. I just wish I had never followed that man of yours onto this dad-burn trail.

"I regret mentioning the stock, McNair," Alice apologized, "but I am worried that we will lose too many animals. They are security against starvation, in the event we don't make it to California."

"That's what the Mormons are griping about. They talk of running out of food because they were foolish enough to think there'd be more game. Now they see there's nothing but ducks and squirrels, and no family of twelve can survive on a duck for supper. They want to head back and join with others coming out to form their own country. I told them to go ahead, leave us and maybe they can survive on their own for three weeks through Indian country. Y'all should just leave me be. I tell you, we will cross the Sierras to see a land with rich grass and fruit trees."

But the promise of an easy passage across the mountains inspired no confidence, and though the men took turns at night watch, the Washoe were still able to sneak up to the camp and pilfer animals. Each morning, one or two cattle or oxen had disappeared. Even more irksome was that the band that pilfered the stock drove the stolen animals up the hillside and then laughed and mocked the emigrants below in the valley.

"There ain't anything worse than them Injuns," McNair railed. "They are the wormiest, orneriest filthy thieves I ever set eyes on.

I didn't have no hard feelings towards the Injuns until we met with these thieving, root digging, miserable excuses for humans."

"Our horses are relatively fresh," Christian said. "We'll give chase and try to bring back the cattle." Christian and Robert mounted up and rode along the sloughs, following the Washoe tracks with Finis and Styles tagging along, their rifles ready. The Washoe were not horse people. Footprints were plain in the dusty soil of the Humboldt Valley, but there were dozens of interlacing trails. The men on horses followed the cattle tracks, but soon came upon the remains of the carcasses and signs of butchering. After that point, the Washoe tracks spread out in all directions, useless to follow.

"I'll kill every one of them dirty savages," Finis boasted. "I got me a rifle and a brace of sheilas and will deal with 'dem varmints." He moved his hand onto the belt holding his two sheilas, which were expensive pistols. Like Robert, Christian had trouble believing that Finis had the resources to purchase such pistols, or even the palomino upon which he rode.

"We won't be killing any Indians over a few oxen and cattle," Christian warned. "We'll use our guns to wound any thieves we catch stealing and give them a warning."

"I knows about Indians, a hell of a lot more than a city man like youse." Finis sent a stream of tobacco juice onto the dusty ground. "They need to be kilt to the last baby. Wipe them savages out."

"You will do nothing of the sort. We are not dealing with the Iroquois or Cheyenne. The Washoe are nasty thieves but not a war nation."

The loss of the stock worried the mothers and angered the men. There was nothing they could do but push on. Despite having three more men with long-range rifles, they were unable to stop the thieving, only slow it down. On his watch, Robert wounded one of the thieves, preventing the young warrior from stealing two oxen.

The McNair party plodded on towards the Sierra Mountains without Saxby's strong, though often misdirected, leadership. Fights broke out among the men, and the women huddled together, angry at the men, angry at Hastings, angry at Saxby and even shunning Alice. After all, it was her husband who had led them into this desolate land. On the third night along the Humboldt River, tempers flared. They were at a camp without clean water and with a dry, fierce wind blowing dust. Worn canvas tents tore in the gale.

Alice couldn't wait to leave the inhospitable valley of the Humboldt. Ahead was the Truckee River. If only they could reach fresh water, bathe and wash their clothes, maybe they would be strong enough to cross the Sierras. The next day, they woke to find their belongings scattered by the wind and tents blown away or shredded. Piling more misery on the party, the Washoe had pilfered another ox.

"No one in his right mind would take a wagon train with women and children, oxen, horses and cattle through this godforsaken valley," Dorothy fumed. Although life had never been easy since her marriage to McNair, they had always been respectful of each other. Now, she constantly barked at the children and was moody with her husband and friends.

With Saxby gone, Alice was able to practice loading and cleaning the Colt, filling the four chambers and capping the nipples. Her fingers memorized the movements, and her speed increased. Soon, the metal smell of the Colt was familiar and pleasant. She felt a sense of comfort in having the pistol tucked into her possibles sack. The Washoe continued to pilfer stock, but Alice's Colt was not intended to kill thieving Indians. Despite her increasing skill and confidence, she kept the pistol close at hand, but unloaded.

They trudged along the fetid stream in desperation, no water to drink, and ash and dust kicking up all around them. The rule of the overland trails is "never stop for the night until there is fuel for the fire, clean water to drink and grass for the stock." But the rule couldn't hold along the Humboldt. In this valley, mile after mile was bereft of fuel, feed and drinkable water.

Alice remembered Saxby telling her that Humboldt Lake was at the end of the valley. She looked ahead down the wide valley to Lone Mountain, a desert butte that reminded her of drawings of the pyramids. At the foot of the mountain, they would reach the lake. The promise of clean water kept her walking alongside her team of oxen and kept her mind off her sore, burning feet and the constant thirst.

The oxen suffered from lack of water; their misery pained Alice and Amelia. As they moved slowly towards the Sierras, they grew to love their two oxen that Amelia had named Sally and Sam. Amelia now sat on the wagon seat, calling out to the oxen, encouraging them in her sweet voice.

Moving along the dusty trail and series of fetid pools, Alice imagined bathing in the lake and washing the dirt from their clothes, but when they arrived at the foot of the mountain, there was no lake. Instead, the river disappeared into a sink. In wet years, this would be Humboldt Lake. This year, it was a pool of swampy water.

"Mom! The water is slimy." Amelia cried waving her hands to accentuate her words. "We can't drink this muck, and I'm not even washing my hands in it."

Alice and Amelia stared at the bed of ooze and mud, their last reserves of energy and patience disappearing as completely as the river disappeared into the muddy swamp.

At the end of the sink, an earthen berm held back a small pond of water that was murky, but at least drinkable. Here they filled buckets and even boots to prepare for the next leg of the journey. They would be leaving the Humboldt Valley and crossing another forty miles of desert before reaching the Truckee River.

The company commenced the march across the desert late in the evening to avoid the punishing heat. Walking at night required less water for both man and beast.

Well into the trek, they saw steam pouring out of the desert, white clouds in the night sky. Without a guide, no one knew what they were looking at. Some thought it might be a desert grass fire, but as there was so little vegetation, that seemed unlikely.

McNair led the wagon train. "Holy jumping catfish! What in tarnation is that?"

Soon, others caught up. "It's a hot spring," Christian told him. "If the water wasn't close to boiling, I would jump in and have myself a swim." He laughed as he looked at the amazing phenomenon in the midst of the desert.

"Let's rest and make ourselves a cup of tea," Dorothy suggested, her foul mood of the last few days evaporating as quickly as the steam from the hot springs.

Soon the women were dipping near boiling water from the pools and preparing drinks, and Dorothy, who had a supply of flour, made biscuits, and dropped the dough in the steam bath where the buns cooked in minutes.

This wonder of nature in the midst of their desperate march invigorated them. The women washed clothes and bathed the children, removing the Humboldt dust and the Humboldt misery from their bodies and minds.

But the respite ended all too soon. Again, they had to trek forward through the desert, now under the blazing sun.

As she walked with Amelia through the day and two more nights in the desert, Alice wondered about this man she had married. What drove him? She knew that Americus and Saxby had grown up in poverty, yet both men had pushed themselves to get an education despite their lack of parental support. They were self-made men, cut from the same cloth. This had apparently given them a considerable degree of arrogance, for the brothers believed they could do no wrong, that their judgment should not be questioned.

Amelia ran to her excitedly, breaking Alice's reverie.

"Trees, see the trees!" With her sharp eye's Amelia was able to pick out features well before the others. Alice strained to see the line of trees.

"That must be the Truckee River, my love. At last you will have clean water to drink, and we will wash the dust from our faces and clothes." The miserable, tired travelers felt a surge of energy knowing they were leaving the desert behind.

When they reached the Truckee River, men, women and children waded into the clean, cold water, shedding the dust of their long desert trek. Horses, mules, oxen and cattle walked into the water, drinking till their bellies were full.

"Let's take a day of rest," Dorothy suggested. "We'll cook, mend and wash clothes, and repair our wagons and tents for the final stage."

Alice wanted to protest, tell them they could not lose another day. Instead, she held her tongue, thinking that she was the last person to offer advice, given her husband's folly in leading them on this trail.

Christian was a thoughtful man who kept his own counsel. He rarely entered the arguments regarding the route, but instead waited for his advice to be solicited.

"Christian," Robert whispered intently, "you must urge McNair to carry on. We can't take a rest day. You told me of your summers in the Alps, of the snow so deep it covers treetops, of the storms that pummeled the mountain passes. Have you noticed that it is getting dark earlier each day and that clouds cover the Sierra peaks? McNair has to know that winter will soon be upon us. I'm just a kid. He won't heed me, but he'll listen to you." Robert spoke urgently, his lips tight.

Christian hesitated, wrapping his muscular arms about his chest as he studied the boy. He was reluctant to initiate a confrontation with McNair. Christian never jumped into a conflict unless he had good reason.

"I don't know, Robert," Christian noticed the pain and stress in Robert's face. Christian picked his coffee cup up and sipped before continuing.

"I agree, son. McNair will very likely send you packing." Christian had a kind and thoughtful face. He did not have Robert's fine features and lithe frame, but a rugged, attractive appearance with a full head of red-brown hair and a neatly clipped beard.

"Please, Christian. Talk to McNair."

"He may also dismiss my advice, but I'll try."

"McNair. A word with you, please." Christian spoke in a quiet calm voice. McNair sat on a supply box, sucking his second cup of coffee. His clothes were torn and dirty, and his hat was crusted hard with trail dirt. "It is late in the season. Don't you think we should push on to the Pass, not stop and waste another day?"

"Mister, you did not travel with us and our women across three deserts so don't be joining us and takin' over, making yourself the boss." He kicked at a stone and spat. "We'll stop for a day, just like my woman says we must." McNair walked off, breaking wind. Christian reflected that McNair was the most unlikely candidate for a leader, easily influenced at times, but stubbornly obstinate in the face of measured advice.

Following Dorothy's wish, the wagon train spent two nights at a pleasant campsite on the Truckee River, resting, washing clothes and preparing for the next stage. When they continued their journey west along the Truckee River, the route through the canyon was frustrating. Sections of the river ran through a gully, and the teamsters had to drive their teams and heavy wagons into the stream and up rocky banks, crossing and re-crossing the river in order to find a suitable road.

Alice walked alongside the team of oxen, gently urging Sally and Sam forward, flicking her quirt lightly to get them up the steeper banks. Despite the difficult trail, the Truckee Valley provided campsites that were a haven compared to the dry, windblown sites in the desert with wood for fires and grass for the stock. Most of the company felt energized by the clean, sparkling waters, campfires and hot food. Others were low on supplies. The O'Malleys had only a mule to carry their belongings after the Washoe had pilfered their horse, so the couple walked, each holding a child.

Kraut, a middle-aged single man, had ridden in one of the wagons owned by the Mormon family until two of their oxen died, and they had to ask Kraut to walk. He was heavyset and suffering from an injured knee. Each day he limped into camp later and later. A week after the trail intersected with the Truckee River, Kraut didn't reach the camp. Robert saddled up, riding until dawn. It was a cool cloudless morning when he returned, shaking his head.

"I buried him back there on the trail."

The first death in the McNair party sent a shiver through the emigrants.

"He may be the first of us to fall," Issachar remarked unsympathetically, "but from the look of this lot, he won't be the last." The bullwhacker was a stork-like figure with a gloomy disposition that had become darker since Jake's untimely death.

His words hit Alice like an icy knife in her back. "Stay close by my side, Amelia," Alice cautioned as she kissed her daughter's soft brown curls. "I promise I will keep you safe." As Alice said these words of comfort, her heart felt like a stone in her chest.

Despite the sparkling waters of the Truckee River, despair enveloped them. In the month of travel along the Truckee, four more members of the group died, either by accident or, increasingly, because of starvation.

Alice had a meager supply of food. She offered fifty dollars to McNair for one ox to make dried meat for the journey over the Sierras. McNair doubled the price. Alice agreed, although the cost of a healthy ox in Springfield was twenty dollars, and this one was a bag of bones. She took the gold coins from the stash Saxby had piled in his trunk, leaving four hundred dollars, the last vestiges of the fortune she had inherited on the death of her husband.

"Our cattle, oxen and horses are far more valuable than any amount of gold," McNair grumbled. "Take the scrawny beast, but that is the last animal I will sell."

Robert and Christian could see that the food supply wouldn't provide enough sustenance for the tough climb and the trek to the Sacramento Valley.

"If McNair doesn't move this wagon train faster," Christian confided with Robert, "we will never reach California before running out of food. He has no concept of the problems moving this army of children and sick people over that mountain range will entail."

"My thoughts as well. I want to make a run to Sutter's for emergency food supplies," Robert told Christian.

"You can't go it alone. I'll come with you. No point staying here and using up the meager rations."

With their bedrolls packed at the back of their saddles and a shared bag of jerky, coffee and flour, they left early the next day, heading on horseback towards the base of the Sierras.

By the time McNair and the rest of the wagon train reached Truckee Lake, only McNair retained enough supplies and stock to sustain his family for the final push across the Sierras.

Chapter Seventeen
Swede's Wagon Train

While the McNair party set up at Truckee Lake, the Swede wagon train made its way to a camping spot at the foot of a waterfall on the Snake River. As he crested the hill, David could see a wagon train camped at the site.

We're catching up on the slower parties, he thought. *We're faster, and it's not far now.*

Just as David rode down to the grassy site, he saw a family push off from shore in a raft. This launching spot was deceptive as the river was reasonably calm in the big eddy of the Snake River. However, around the bend, the riverbed dropped over a shelf, and the canyon walls closed in. He raced his horse to the water's edge.

"Turn back! You won't make it!" David yelled, his voice drowned out by the roar of the water. The parents and their three small children clung to the raft as the river took the bend and the current grabbed the frail craft in its grip.

There was nothing David could do. As the canyon narrowed, the current increased, racing between the steep basalt cliffs. The raft picked up speed, passed the bend and smashed into the canyon wall. The man, his wife and the three children flew off the raft and into the turbulent water.

"Oh, Christ! Not the little children!" David thought of his own son, lovingly cared for in a village on the Sacramento River.

Swede joined him, his attention drawn by the shouting and sudden activity, and together they searched out the wagon train captain of the group camped at the Snake River. He was an elderly man whose graying hair blew in the wind, revealing a balding head.

"You should not have let him take to the river! Did you know they planned this death run?" Swede could barely contain his anger.

"They were holding us up. Out of food, oxen dead. Out of will to carry on walking. What could I do?" he whined. He was not a man who would take charge and protect the people under his leadership.

"For God's sake man, it is your job to protect your people!" Swede had watched the tragedy, his normal composure shattered by the senseless deaths.

David had never before heard Swede blaspheme or lose his temper, but now he loomed over the gray-haired man. "Others will hear of your lack of judgment. You are in deep shit and don't have the boots to walk out of it."

David and Swede turned away, disgusted. Despite the beauty of the campsite, a gloomy atmosphere fell upon the Swede party because everyone had either witnessed the senseless loss of life or heard about it.

Anna and Jan had watched as the little children were flung off the raft and into the turbulent water. "The elephant continues to follow us, Jan. Why did the father not realize the Snake River was dangerous, and why in the dear God's name did he take his wee ones? I haven't felt such despair since little Annabelle Lee passed. When will we leave death behind? Will we ever reach Oregon City and have a roof over our heads?"

"Life has its trials, and the Oregon Trail has more than its share, but we are less than a month from the end of our trip. We follow the Snake for three hundred miles, and after we cross the Blue Mountains, we'll reach the Columbia River and our new home.

We are making good time now, catching up with the slower wagon trains."

"Saxby and his fancy wagon and team of parade horses slowed us up some. I don't miss the arrogant know-all, although I do miss Alice and worry about her. She would like this spot," Anna reflected, smiling a little at the thought of her friend. "She always appreciated the beauty of the land we passed through."

Indeed, the camping spot was a respite. Clean water cascaded over twin drops of black volcanic basalt, and a gentle road sloped down to the water's edge where there was grass for the stock and wood for the campfires. Jan and Anna found a secluded spot to bathe while they could, knowing that the Oregon Trail would wind high up along the top bank of the Snake Canyon, with little access to water.

"But I still cannot understand why the father took his family onto a raft. His wife. His wee children." Anna's voice choked.

Jan shook his head. "A good-for-nothing scoundrel talked the father into paying two dollars for a raft that sent them all to their deaths, convincing them that the Snake River would be a safe run."

"If they were in our wagon train, that never would have happened. Swede would never be deceived into letting them take off to their deaths, and neither would David. Our giant wagon train leader may not fit into a parlor, but command rests easily on his big shoulders. Remember how Swede wouldn't let Addie ride off alone at Fort Hall?"

"That plan backfired when Finis and Styles stepped up, saying they would look after the lady, as if Addie wanted Finis sniffing at her skirt all the way to California. Finis, with only one thing on his brain, a hothead quick to draw a gun on the first Indian he spots, and Styles, following Finis like a trained rat. If it wasn't for David, Finis would have already started a war between the emigrants and the Indians. Good thing Christian and Robert agreed to leave our wagon train to keep an eye on those two miscreants."

"David sent Christian and Robert. My thought is that our guide hasn't been the same since Saxby broke off for the cutoff trail and took his beautiful wife with him. He's worried about Alice and the little daughter and sent Christian and Robert to watch over them."

"Unfortunately, Alice has a husband."

"Whether it is willed or not, love fosters in the face of hardship. It is when we are tested that we reveal our true character and our feelings. Look at Swede and Carreena. Who would think that an upper class London woman would be a match for our wagon train leader?"

"He is rough around the edges, but a good man. Swede is a sea captain by trade and has seen the world; Carreena is an independent adventurist. She traveled to see the pyramids of Egypt and the Great Wall of China, always wanting to see far-away places. She's taken up cooking for Swede and keeping him company, but they don't share a bed. Not yet, at least."

"Speaking of cooking," Jan said, "I have the Dutch oven sitting on the fire with a tasty meal of savory beans, onions and bacon."

"I should be hungry, but watching that family go to their deaths lowered my spirits some."

The couple shared a solemn meal. They could not push aside thoughts of the young, innocent children carried to their deaths in the turbulent Snake River.

"At least there are no more worries over Indian attacks, Jan. David tells me there won't likely be any Indian trouble from here to Oregon City. 'Tis the early snowfall that's worrying him now, so time for bed and up early."

The Swede Train followed the Snake River, the road high above the canyon and the river winding below. The cliffs were too steep for human or beast to make it down to the water. Mad with thirst, one of Americus's oxen bolted over the edge and fell to its death.

~

It was late October when the wagon train pulled into the Grande Ronde Valley, a beautiful spot with clear, clean water and grass for the animals.

"This is Paradise," Anna remarked to Jan as she viewed the expanse of green grass, dotted with cottonwood trees and edged by the hills that created the round valley. "Oh Jan, this is the most beautiful spot I have ever seen and a welcome sight for my weary soul. We've been on this trail since I can't remember, and now here we are in this heavenly valley, but the way this trip is going, my guess is that the road ahead won't be a walk in the park."

"We cross the Blue Mountains next."

"At least we have fresh food," Anna said. "I traded a piece of calico and a pot for potatoes and berries. The Indian spoke English, and told me he had stayed at the mission in Walla Walla and that his wife grew the potatoes. David says they are Nez Perce."

"Despite what the likes of Saxby and Finis say about the tribes, Indians are not all savages."

"The Pawnee along the Platte stole our best milking cow, Jan."

"If that is the price of our passage; I can live with that."

"I may have spoken too soon. Looks like we have Indians on the rampage."

A small band of Nez Perce rode into camp, the leader exclaiming angrily and pointing at one of Walter's oxen. He was a handsome warrior riding a black stallion.

"What is this foofaraw all about?" Walter asked, backing away from the armed band.

The Nez Perce warrior pointed again at the ox, exclaiming loudly, then pointed to his chest.

"Are you claiming it's your animal? I bought the ox yesterday from the trader. Paid a hundred dollars."

This did little to lessen the tension because the warrior did not speak English. The Nez Perce lassoed the ox and pulled it away from the herd.

Men grabbed their rifles and rushed to support Walter.

"Hold on!" David yelled, joining the fracas.

"He's stealing my ox," Walter protested.

David approached the warrior, his hands raised in a gesture of peace. The warrior exclaimed loudly for a few minutes while David listened attentively, then spoke reassuringly in Chinook. The warrior and his band lowered their guns as David walked back to Walter.

"He says the same trader sold the ox to him two days ago. Said he traded three fine horses for the animal and the crook stole the ox back from him. Looks like that thieving trader sold the same animal to both of you."

"And you believe him?"

"Yes. I think he's telling the truth. Look. I will pay you back. We don't want trouble with the Indians."

"Walter, don't you be giving up that ox. We need it if we are to make it over the mountains." Penelope had been watching the confrontation from the safety of the wagon.

David wanted to tell Penelope that if she would get off her butt and walk instead of ride in the wagon, their team would have much less trouble on the uphill.

"Penelope," Walter said quietly, "the Indians have a claim on the animal and best we let it go. David will make good the hundred dollars. We'll buy another when we reach Umatilla."

"Giving in to the savages once again! I can't wait to land in Portland and be among civilized people."

"I would have given the Indians the ox without David's promise to compensate me. What sense would it be to pick a fight with the Nez Perce so close to the end of the trail?"

"You are a weakling, Walter. A useless man, not fit to be my husband."

With that, Penelope disappeared into the wagon, the Nez Perce rode off, and Walter walked away, head bent, shoulders slumped.

Walter slept under the wagon that night, covering himself with his coat. The following morning, he ate nothing and said nothing, ignoring Penelope's shrill commands for him to start the campfire.

"Walter, for the Lord's sake, come take some victuals with us," Anna urged, when she noticed Walter's despondency. "You are already thin as a rail and won't make it over the mountains if you don't eat."

"Anna, I thank you. But I feel no need to eat and no desire. Time to hitch up. You're a good woman, Anna. Jan must thank his good providence each day."

From that morning till the wagon train reached the Umatilla River, Walter did not eat and did not speak. He slept on the ground, curled up in his sheepskin overcoat. On the second night, dark clouds gathered over the Blue Mountains, sending fat flakes of snow onto the circle of wagons. Penelope rose from her warm bed and threw a blanket over Walter.

"You are as much a fool as I thought you were. Not even enough sense to come in out of the storm."

Penelope had never given any indication that she cared for Walter. Now she felt humiliated by Walter's rejection and wanted him back with her in the covered wagon.

The wagon train slowly approached the highest point of the Blue Mountains, crossing through the tree-lined trail. At the summit, a coating of snow covered the ground. The oxen were weak, and the emigrants were footsore and ill from mountain fever, scurvy and diarrhea. Charlotte and her children suffered the most. Their remaining team of oxen was so emaciated that only Charlotte was able to ride in the wagon while their bullwhacker drove the tired animals across the Blue Mountains. Louise and the two boys shuffled along the snowy trail, their feet wrapped in rags. Americus drove their other wagon farther back in the wagon train.

Anna and Jan had a late start that day, but with their stronger team and energetic walking, they soon caught up to the wagon train. The day grew cold, and snow wafted down through the fir trees. Anna gasped when she saw a trail of blood on the snow and scuffled prints made by little feet. Soon they caught up to the three children. Louise pulled her brothers aside to let the wagon pass.

"Jan, please stop the team," Anna begged. "We must take these little darlings."

"You children step up into the wagon," she ordered, her heart aching at the sight of their bloodied feet.

Louise choked back her tears as she helped her brothers onto the seats, and Anna covered the children with two sheepskins.

"No need for a thank you, Louise." Anna was close to tears at seeing their misery. "Your eyes tell me all. Help yourself to the biscuits stored under the seat. They are leftovers, and you and your brothers are welcome to them. When we begin the downhill, take hold of the seat as we will be coming down this mountain like butter sliding over a hot plate."

On the descent, teamsters locked the wagon wheels and held the wagons by ropes to keep oxen and wagons from careening down the steep pitches. They were headed for the Umatilla Indian Reserve and more important, a store with supplies.

Louise held firmly onto her two brothers, who had fallen asleep. The boys, weary from walking, were comforted by the food in their tummies. It was their first meal in over a day.

"Look at that, Jan. Is that a house? A real house, or are my eyes deceiving me?" Now the tears trickled down her handsome face. They had been traveling for six months through rainstorms, scorching heat, and dust storms. Tired and hungry, the first signs of civilization moved Anna to tears.

And there it was. The first framed house Anna had seen since leaving the Missouri River, a beacon of normalcy after months on the trail.

"Isn't that a sight for sore eyes? Two stories and a porch!" Anna exclaimed, as she walked beside Jan into the small settlement.

"And there's a trading post here," Jan added, excited at the prospect of leaving behind two thousand miles of wilderness. "I'll buy tobacco, and maybe even a celebratory bottle of brandy."

Charlotte would not be buying supplies at the store. Americus was almost out of money, and Charlotte's supplies were down to a few cups of rice. Charlotte and Americus were ill from scurvy and weak from lack of food. They talked little. What was there to say? The money was gone, along with Americus's infatuation for Charlotte. She had traded on her beauty all her life. Now in tatters, thin and ill, Charlotte was too despondent to care for her children. She held out a small hope that Americus might find some way to save her from this desperate situation, and she was not the only emigrant suffering from depression.

Walter also reached the Umatilla River in deep despondency. He was always an accommodating man, giving in to Penelope's interests and choices. If she wanted to move, he would move. When she decided they should take the Oregon Trail, he left his position as a teacher and joined the wagon train. The journey had convinced

Walter that nothing would ever be to his liking if he continued to share his life with Penelope.

Anna took notice. "David, I am most worried about Walter. He won't make another day unless we can get some food into him. He is not much more than a walking skeleton. You better talk some sense into the man. He went down to the river carrying a bulky, heavy object. How, I can't fathom, as he looks like a feather would knock him over. Please, keep an eye on him."

"I'll go, too, Anna. I've been worried about him." Jan followed David, although he had to stride double time to catch up. He was five foot eight, and David, tall and slim, was over six feet with long, lanky legs.

They reached the riverbank in time to see Walter lower a stove over the river bank on one of the few spots where the water ran deep and dark. Attached to the stove was a short piece of rope, and attached to the rope was Walter.

"My God!" Jan yelled.

"No. Don't!" David called out. But stove and Walter disappeared into the black water. David pulled off his boots, lifted his Bowie knife from its shaft and dove into the water.

"We need help," Jan yelled back towards the camp.

Anna heard the cry and passed on the word. People gathered at the river, some with ropes, others with thick tree branches. For a minute they could see nothing. Then, David popped to the surface, gasped for air and dove back down. It seemed far too long. Surely, they would both drown. No one said a word as they waited, and most of them held their breath. One of the young teamsters peeled off his boots, ready to jump in, but Anna restrained him. "No more of you risking your lives."

When the watchers were sure that the two men could not possibly survive so long underwater, David surfaced, sputtering and gasping, this time holding Walter with one arm and swimming with the other. Men flung ropes to the struggling rescuer and pulled David and his unconscious victim to shore.

The men grabbed Walter, lifting him out of the water and up the bank. Anna stepped into the circle.

"Step back, and give us breathing room."

Anna bent over Walter, placing the heels of both hands in the center of his chest. She began firm compressions, then lifted Walter's chin and breathed into his mouth, still compressing his chest between breaths.

There was no response from Walter. A minute went by, but Anna did not give up. Finally, Walter coughed and drew a ragged breath. Men and women breathed a sigh of relief, and then cheered.

"I never saw someone brought back to life before," David told Anna, with admiration.

"That's my Anna. She read about this way of saving a person and practiced on me till she got used to it. And look a' here. She brought Walter back from the brink!" Jan beamed with pride, and the gathering of emigrants clapped. Anna paid no attention to the accolades.

"Louise, be a good girl and bring that wool blanket from the seat of our wagon," Anna said, as she helped Walter sit up. "Rest here for a few minutes, Walter. Catch your breath, and we'll see you have a good meal of hot soup and Jan's biscuits."

By this time, Penelope had arrived at the river.

"Oh, Walter! I did not mean to say those things! But why would you try and drown yourself? How could you be such an idiot?"

"Leave the man alone, Penelope." David had caught his breath, and now made his way up the bank. "You drove him to take his own life. From here on I will look after him."

"Well, I never!" Penelope huffed. "Walter, you come back to me, or I swear I will take the first ship home to my family."

"If you wish, Penelope," Walter replied.

"I mean it." This time Penelope's voice was shrill and determined.

"I'm sure you do," Walter answered.

"I'll go. And that is it."

"I understand," Walter said, a coy grin on his lips.

~

It was a pleasant camping spot, and the Walla Walla and Umatilla Tribes, inclined to trade instead of steal, offered dried salmon for pots, calico, knives—just about anything the emigrants could spare. The women who had coins to buy flour began to bake bread. One of the bullwhackers brought out his fiddle, and a teamster had an accordion. The Swede party sang the "Old Oaken Bucket" and "Castles in the Air." A young Irish man stepped forward with his fiddle and struck up the tune to the Irish dance, "Siasmas," followed by the Virginia reel. They danced until the rain sent them to their beds.

David engaged Walter to help with the wagon train, recognizing Walter's skill at repairing wheels and harnesses, and fashioning yokes from trees. Walter had an education and made his way as a teacher, but he grew up on a farm: he had also learned to be a handyman, always on the lookout for a wagon that needed axel grease or a wooden wheel that was dried out and required an overnight soaking in water.

"Walter," David admonished. "Take a break! Sit and have a cup of coffee. No need to work every waking hour."

"I don't like being idle. That's the way I am. Keep me busy, and I'm happy."

Similar to Jan, Walter was a capable cook, and in the stretch to The Dalles, he prepared meals for the guide. After his brush with death and his split with Penelope, Walter had a fire in his belly for everything life had to offer.

As the wagon train moved west, they reached a fork in the road. To the left was a newly cut trail heading southwest. Several emigrants from another wagon train were camped at the crossing debating over which route to take.

"It's the Barlow Road, if you can call that trail anything approaching a road, and you have to pay a toll," David explained. "But it does have one advantage. It avoids the river trip."

"We must take this branch, David," Americus instructed David. "I have information from the others up ahead that it is a fair road and will facilitate our early arrival in Oregon City. No boats to worry about, no rough trail for the stock. I've paid to have you guide us, and you must pay our toll and have us at our destination post haste."

"The guide doesn't pay the toll for wagons, Americus. Everyone in the wagon train contributes if they want to cross a bridge or use a toll road. You must know that by now. Besides, I do not advise that route, not this late in the year and not until Barlow lowers his toll."

"But if we go over the road," Jan pointed out, "we don't have to take to the rapids. I've never much cared for fast water or, for that matter, any water deeper than my tin washtub."

"No problem, Jan. You will be walking along the Columbia River herding your stock, and Anna will enjoy a pleasant canoe ride."

It wasn't until the Swede wagon train reached the next camp that Charlotte realized that Americus had abandoned his family and taken the Barlow Road, using the last of their money to pay the toll.

Chapter Eighteen

The Deschutes River
Oregon

The wagon train descended a steep hill to the Deschutes River. The group rested the remainder of the day while David, Swede and Walter scouted along the bank for the safest river crossing.

The next morning, with a plan in place, David and Walter guided the wagons safely over the swift-moving water. Once the wagons were on the western shore, they arranged for the Walla Walla Indians to paddle the women and children across in canoes.

The Swede party was low on supplies, and the stock of horses, oxen and cattle suffered from hunger and fatigue. Only a few miles separated them from the settlements on the Columbia River. The trail crested a hill and, upon reaching the bluff, the tired, hungry emigrants were rewarded with a comforting sight.

"Oh, bless the Lord, the trader's house! I haven't seen anything so sweet to my eyes since Noah last wore shorts." Tears pooled in Anna's eyes as she looked at the modest log house with its garden and fenced yard. It was a a sign that their months in the wilderness had ended. "Oh, Jan! Look, there it is, the Columbia! We'll make it, Jan. It is downhill from here to The Dalles."

The Dalles was a small settlement on the Columbia River, named for the rapids on the Columbia River just upriver from the community. Walter and David watched the seals playing in the waves and chasing the salmon. Both thought about the daring fur traders who took their flimsy canoes through the surging waves.

"You say the Indians and the fur traders run these rapids?" Walter asked.

"Yes, but in high water. I've seen them come through with their long birch bark canoes paddled by those Canadian voyageurs, the Hudson's Bay men. I watched them last year, whooping and hollering as they plunged up one wave and down the other, laughing when they made it safely to shore. It is wonderful how fear can lift the human spirit, that is, providing you survive."

"Not something I want to try," Walter added, with a quick grin. "I've done with dangerous encounters with water, unless it is to wash my face."

"If you want to see killer water, go upriver to Celilo Falls where the canyon narrows to a hundred feet. It is the best salmon fishing site I have ever seen or ever will see. When the salmon are running, the Wasco haul out enough fish to feed an army."

"After The Dalles, the water is calm, is it?"

"It will be a float down to the Cascades, then the river becomes impassable. Before Christian left for the California Trail, he told me that hundreds of years ago, Table Mountain cleaved off and blocked the river. According to him, when the dam breached, the flood waters strew boulders the size of houses all around and created four miles of rapids."

"I gather we will portage the Cascades."

"You could run the section in a canoe, Walter, but I would advise against it. I want to see you catch the steamer to the Willamette Valley and get yourself settled. The end is near, Walter, the end is near. Now, we need to find enough boats to take us to the Cascades. Our wagon train is near out of food."

And, indeed, food was on the minds of everyone in the Swede party, even Anna, who until now had always had more than enough provisions for the journey.

"Anna, they have a store here, so why don't we go along and add to our pantry and sundries? If I don't have my coffee for breakfast, I won't be able to get myself out of bed in the morning."

"They best not charge twice the going price in Springfield or you'll have to wait till Oregon City. Hickory coffee does just fine."

"Not on your life, Anna."

Although the prices were unreasonable, Anna bought coffee and found a few lemons and apples. They had been eating salt pork, rice and beans for months, and several in the wagon train suffered from scurvy, Charlotte more than most. Anna was shocked by Charlotte's appearance when the former beauty approached her.

"Anna, do you have a little lemon juice for me." Her faced was puffy and ugly. This was likely the first time in her life she could not admire herself in the mirror.

"You poor dear," Anna said, noticing that Charlotte's lips were so parched and swollen she could barely open her mouth. "Of course, we can spare a lemon. The fresh fruit in the store is going fast. You must ask Americus to buy apples and lemons. They have fine apples, grown right here in Oregon."

"Didn't you know that he left with the wagon train that took the Barlow Road and with him went the last of our money? I did not know we were so destitute."

"Seems like you've gone from the frying pan to the fire, Charlotte. Didn't you leave a man who could not put bread on the table? Now you have a husband who abandoned you and the children."

"Anna," Jan said. "Don't pour salt on the poor woman's wounds, for God's sake."

"My apologies Charlotte. Here, take this and make sure the children get some. They look like starved chicks in a poor nest with no mother to feed them nor a father to bring home a rabbit. At least you don't have to provide victuals for the children's governess, as I understand you and Americus let her go way back on the trail."

"Swede has been looking after her, and though she wouldn't lift a finger to cook for us or wash dishes, she is making him breakfast and dinner and gives him whatever else he wants, is my guess."

"I wouldn't say a word against Carreena," Anna said coolly. "Not the type of woman to trade her body. Keeps her thoughts close, that woman, but I never had cause to dislike her. Never found her friendly, either. If Swede and her get along well, all the power to her. Now, you should get back to those children. They need that lemon juice as much as you. And Charlotte, here're a few pounds of beans to feed those little ones. Now, try and get well."

"Americus! What a scoundrel!" Anna said, shaking her head in disgust. "Is there no restitution a woman can take to force her husband to provide basic food and shelter?"

"She could take the matter up with the law if she lived in the States," Jan said, as they walked through the small settlement waiting for a boat to take Anna downriver. "What she is able to do in Oregon Country, I don't know. If Christian hadn't left for the California Trail, you could ask him. My guess is that Americus is long gone, and until Oregon joins the United States, there are no laws governing family support."

"At least the Pope is not here snatching souls everywhere," Anna exclaimed as they passed the Methodist mission. "When we settle in Oregon City, it is my hope that the Lutherans will be there."

"With or without the Pope, we will be content," Jan added. "Oh, I see our guide up ahead. Can you pick up the pace, gal? He looks as if his favorite dog just died."

"Folks," David informed Jan and Anna. "I've heard bad news from the locals. Saxby arrived at Sutter's Fort, according to one of the men who works for Sutter. Unfortunately, the others did not make it across the Sierras before the snow closed the Pass. McNair and fifty or so emigrants are trapped on the east side of the Pass. Maybe they are okay. They have stock that should feed them till spring. But still."

"Well I'll be gob smacked," Anna said. "That man Saxby, he should be hanged for what he's done. And him, safe in California, leaving his wife and stepdaughter! I don't understand. I wanted to hog tie Alice and Amelia and take them kit and caboodle with us on the Oregon Trail. Pray to God they survive."

"I have another situation here in Oregon that will occupy me for a few months, but after that I will be going to the Sacramento Valley. Hopefully by that time, they will be safely across the Pass and into California."

Happiness and enthusiasm at reaching The Dalles faded with the concern for their friends caught on the wrong side of the mountains.

As the Swede party waited at The Dalles to arrange for boats to take them downriver, the food shortage became critical, sending more families to the brink of starvation. Even Anna and Jan were down to their last few cups of flour, and the Mission store was out of supplies. While they should have been celebrating the end of the journey, instead they were scraping the bottoms of the barrels for a few beans or grains of rice, and worrying about their friends caught in the Sierra Mountains.

"I've always been a little heavy, Jan. This starvation diet will bring back my girlish figure," Anna joked, trying to lighten the seriousness of their plight. It had been a week since they had enough food to keep their stomachs from growling.

"I like you with those love handles, so hopefully you will not get too thin." Jan laughed and patted Anna's buttocks.

"We will survive. The Nez Perce have salmon to trade, and we have more than enough trade goods. It's the others I am worried about. Charlotte and those poor children of hers have been without victuals for days. Even when they make it to Portland, she doesn't have a penny in her pocket to get them through the winter."

The Swede party had been waiting a week when they heard singing coming from the river. Anna and Jan joined the others to watch a flotilla of Hudson's Bay canoes approach The Dalles from downriver, the men paddling hard against the current, their voices in time with each stroke. It was a mesmerizing sight for the emigrants. As the six voyageurs paddled closer, the emigrants could see what the canoes carried in their long cedar boat.

"Look at that, Jan. They've loaded the canoes with vegetables, fresh vegetables we have not enjoyed for months."

The hungry emigrants crowded at the shoreline to watch the men beach the canoes. There was relief and joy at this unexpected arrival.

Louise and her two brothers stood gaping at the baskets of carrots, potatoes, fresh beans and corn. The children looked so very much like waifs from London's impoverished streets, their cheeks hollow, their tattered clothes hanging on emaciated bodies.

"We might as well not look," Louise told her brothers. "We have no money left to buy even one carrot. Let's go back to the wagon so we don't have to watch."

"How much for a pound of carrots?" Anna asked.

"Not a cent, Ma'am. Oregonian News printed an article about your situation, and McLoughlin, the Chief Factor at Fort Vancouver, along with the good people of Portland and Oregon City, sent the food." The voyageur spoke with a French accent. He was a tall, burly, man, tanned and muscular.

"Glory be!" Anna cried with tears in her eyes. "Bless their hearts, and bless you men for paddling upstream with the food."

Anna noticed Louise and the boys walking away, their thin shoulders slumped, their steps painfully slow.

"Louise! You bring those boys back here. The vegetables are free! You will eat tonight, you dear little ones."

The famished, worn and tired members of Swede's wagon train wept as they accepted sacks of fresh vegetables. The women hugged the rugged looking voyageurs, and the men shook their hands and patted the French Canadians on the back. When they tried to question the voyageurs about Oregon City, they were surprised that most of the men spoke only French.

Louise held her arms out eagerly for the vegetables and smiled at the voyageurs, tears in her eyes. She gave a carrot to each of her brothers then walked up the hill from the river bank, the heavy sack bumping against her thin hip.

Now there were boats to take them downstream, and this was the point in the journey when the Swede wagon train would split up. Anna paid the Hudson's Bay men to paddle her the forty miles to the Upper Cascades and arranged for their wagon to be broken apart and loaded, along with their supplies on a second boat. She offered passage to Charlotte and the three children, seeing that Charlotte did not even have a piece of jewelry to exchange.

Anna was a water person with no fear of the river; Jan preferred to keep his feet on solid ground and, like Walter, was relieved to have the task of driving their remaining stock downriver on the rugged trail. Jan and Walter, along with the bullwhackers, teamsters and several family men, herded stock along the rocky trail that skirted the basalt cliffs on one side, with a steep drop to the Columbia River on the other.

Penelope helped herself to the remainder of their savings and made her own way down the Columbia. She was furious at Walter for leaving her and complained to everyone who would listen. Finally, Walter put a stop to Penelope's harangue.

"We never married," he told Anna and Jan, just before the group split up. "It was always a point of contention between us, but my guess is that I never really felt we were right for each other."

"That is an understatement, Walter. Why did you ever pitch your tents together?" Anna asked.

"Don't you never mind my woman," Jan said, with a big smile. "She seldom chews her cabbage twice." Jan gave Walter a friendly cuff on the shoulder.

David and Swede met them at the riverbank before they boarded canoes.

"Well, folks," Swede said, "we've had our tribulations on this journey, but you have been good fellow travelers. This will be my last trip on the Oregon Trail. I'm back on the sea as soon as I reach Fort Victoria. It's been good knowing you."

"And where are you off to?" Anna asked David.

"I will be guiding a party of settlers north from Fort Vancouver into British Territory. Well, British for now. After that job, I go south to see my son. I will find out what has happened to the break-off party. I know you are both concerned about Alice and her daughter, and the McNair family as well. I expect I will be meeting up with you folks once you are settled in Oregon City."

"Ah! Oregon City," Anna remarked, "where we will prosper and have a good laugh again."

Chapter Nineteen

Truckee Lake
California

Only one hundred miles separated the McNair party from the green valley of the Sacramento River. Surely they could walk twenty miles a day and reach Sutter's Fort in less than a week. But already the nights were cold, and the first icy fingers of winter moved across the mountain peaks. Towering above them were the Sierras, with mountain peaks over twelve thousand feet high and one mountain higher than them all, reaching up fourteen thousand feet.

The emigrants faced a precipitous accent. The Pass over the Sierras was formidable; a hundred times more difficult than the gentle crossing of the Continental Divide. Here, the Sierras tilted to the east, creating a near perpendicular rise of a thousand feet from the base. There was no path for the wagons. A wagon train had crossed the summit a year ago after the emigrants took the wagons apart, attached ropes and cables, and hoisted the parts up the cliff. Ascending the Sierras might be possible in fair weather and with a strong group, but the McNair party were suffering from weeks of reduced rations, and the weather was sharp and cold.

"We have to make it over that pass," Alice said, not really to Amelia, but to herself. "I see snow at the top. Not a great deal of snow. But there will be more."

They camped at Truckee Lake near the base of the Sierras, exhausted from the journey along the circuitous Truckee River, where the wagons had to be driven into the streambed through the narrow canyon that twisted for miles. The oxen and cattle stumbled on the rocky stream bed, their legs bloody from the sharp rocks.

Teamsters had to walk alongside the oxen to coax them forward, each step painful for the poor animals. Now beasts and humans wanted to rest. They did not want to push up the impossible incline. They did not want to hoist wagons and push stock over immense boulders, only to reach snow and ice. Inertia settled into the McNair party.

"McNair, we must begin the ascent of the Pass today," Alice urged. "I am nearly out of food, and I believe we might have another snowfall any day. It is urgent we move along. We've rested enough."

"Do not start in on me, Mrs. Chablis," McNair responded, spitting out his words. "Your husband caused us to be in this pickle. I did not want to be the leader. I don't want to be responsible. But since I was voted Captain, don't keep yakking at me, and close that cake hole of yours."

The rebuff was difficult for Alice to absorb. Pleading to McNair was pointless; she decided to appeal to Dorothy.

"You have four boys, Dorothy. They are still healthy, but if we don't push up the mountain immediately, they will be in danger. Please, urge McNair to move us up the Pass. There is no time to waste," Alice begged.

"Didn't my husband tell you to leave him alone?" Dorothy looked even more drawn when she was angry. "So, leave him to make the decisions, and don't cause friction in the camp. You and your husband have caused enough trouble."

Alice wanted to reply in an equally harsh manner, but instead held her tongue. From that time on, Alice decided to keep her thoughts to herself, and certainly would not share her fears with Amelia.

Alice was not the only one concerned about delays. Siederleggen, an Austrian familiar with mountain territory, eyed the gap in the mountain and watched the dark clouds gathering above the Sierras. Siederleggen was one of the bullwhackers who'd joined at The Parting of the Ways, bringing with him his wife and two small children. He was in his late twenties, medium build and muscular, with blond hair and a neatly trimmed beard and mustache. He and his family had recently immigrated and, although he was educated, he had few resources. He pleaded with McNair to make an immediate assault on the Pass but was rejected as rudely as Alice had been.

Siederleggen studied the approach to the summit, but from the camping spot at the lake it was difficult to determine a route up the impasse. He slung a small pack on his back and walked along the lake.

They follow us everywhere, Siederleggen said to himself, when he noticed the foot tracks along the shoreline that indicated the Washoe constantly observed the McNair party. *We must keep a close watch on the animals we have left, or they will pilfer the entire stock.*

Siederleggen continued along the lake, its sparkling water lit by the slanted late autumn sun, then walked to the base and climbed the steep rocky cliffs to the summit. With only a thin layer of snow, it was a relatively easy ascent for a strong young man. However, Siederleggen realized the climb would be near impossible for the children, toddlers, mothers with nursing babes, the injured, and the sick. Many of the weary travelers had been on short rations for weeks, and with little food left, climbing into the Sierras with the entire party was unthinkable. Then there were the oxen, horses and cattle. The Indians had run off more than half the stock, leaving twenty emaciated animals. This was their food supply, and the stock had to go up over the Pass.

McNair ignored the plight of his party, convinced there was no rush to crest the mountains. Robert and Christian were expected back anytime. That new supplies would arrive gave McNair a false sense of security. *They could give it try in a couple of days once the women were ready and the pack animals loaded with the remaining food and critical supplies.* He delayed the attempt another day.

That night, winds stirred over Alaska's frigid waters, picking up speed and moisture, heading south to Canada's northwest coast, and down across Oregon Country, pelting rain on the Pacific Northwest. The moisture-laden clouds continued east across California, dropping rain on the foothills until the heavy clouds bumped against the peaks of the Sierras. As the storm rose up the mountain, rain turned to snow. A dark bank of clouds crested the Pass, heading for Truckee Lake. First, a few snow flurries, then, heavy, fat flakes descended, covering the mountain pass and the emigrant encampment.

The emigrants woke in their tents and wagons, surrounded by snow. The men who were sleeping out in the open with only buffalo robes for a cover shook off the snow and stumbled towards the shelter of the wagons. There was no place to even build a fire in the whiteout, and little to cook even if there were campfires. It was a dismal morning. It was a day that broke through McNair's complacency. Now he understood that winter storms in the Sierras were unlike the snowfalls in Illinois, where snow depth is measured in inches, not feet.

Dorothy fretted over the delay at Truckee Lake. She had her children to think of. Billy had been saved from cholera, and she would not let him perish from starvation. Alice felt frantic; she had feared that the snow would trap them, and despite her appeals to McNair, he had refused to start up the pass. This time, when Dorothy approached him, he listened.

"The snow could trap us," Dorothy complained to her husband. "We have to start up the Pass today before the snow is too deep for the children to walk."

"Soon. We'll go tomorrow or maybe the next day. We need time to sort through our supplies and decide what we must take and what we can do without." If McNair could find a reason to delay, he delayed. The party suffered from this crisis in leadership.

That night, they slept in their tents and wagons, waking to find their blankets covered in a thin layer of ice, the children shivering under their quilts. Around them, all was white. Two feet of snow lay on the ground and still it kept snowing. Towering above them was the steep ascent leading to a notch in the mountains, a path now blanketed in white. Dorothy dug through the snow to clear a patch for a campfire. Snow continued, sputtering into her smoking fire. *Not sure I can endure this another day. That man of mine has to get us out of here.*

Alice looked out from her wagon and saw a white expanse of swirling snow with a carpet of white covering the ground and gradually burying the smaller pines and the willow bushes. She stepped from the wagon into the deepening snow and looked up at the pass. Fear for Amelia gripped her. *What if we can't continue?* Alice thought about the meager supplies she had. One emaciated ox, a few cups of flour, and enough beans for a week. Looking around, it was clear that game was scarce or non-existent. Even the animals were clever enough to leave the high ground and drop down out of the snowbelt.

McNair had little patience for the emigrants he led, but he did listen to Dorothy. She knew his faults, but felt she must always be supportive and not question him. Now she could not remain silent.

"McNair, listen to me! I will not risk the lives of our children. We have animals that may keep us alive until the spring but I am not willing to spend a winter in this God-forsaken place. We must make an attempt at the pass and get ourselves to the green fields of California. You hear me?"

McNair was taken aback at this unusual outburst from his normally submissive wife.

"You're right, Dorothy. It will be a tough climb, but I agree."

McNair mustered the party, telling them to be ready to try the Pass. Energy surged through the group. Anything was better than waiting as the snow pelted down deeper and deeper each hour.

There were difficult choices to make. Would they be able to carry a supply of tobacco? What about the bolt of calico needed in California? Parting with their family possessions was heartbreaking for some. A few daguerreotypes were too heavy to pack, and yet the photos were all they had of their parents, sisters and brothers back in the States.

Alice was one of the few women able to shed her belongings with few or no regrets and only pack necessities: a few cups of beans, a little sugar, warm clothing and a blanket. Alice removed Saxby's ring and replaced it with the engagement and wedding rings James had given her.

Women carried babes and toddlers, men hoisted packs and tied supplies to the animals. It was late morning before they got underway, walking along the lakeshore with the men at the front, taking turns to tramp down the snow. Although the camp was within sight of the Pass, it was mid-afternoon before they reached the base of the climb. Several in the group lagged behind, especially the children too heavy to be carried and too weak to keep up.

The stronger walkers started up the incline. At times they were on all fours, clambering up the sloping granite rock face, driving the stock with them. As the incline became steeper and icier, the animals could not find purchase and were pushed and pulled up.

The pitiful line of fifty men, women and children, and twenty animals crawled excruciatingly slowly up the nearly perpendicular rock face. The group could only go as fast as the slowest hiker. By the time the vanguard reached the summit, the small children and weaker adults were only a tenth of the way up. Billy and his five-year-old brother struggled to put one foot in front of the other. Snow continued to fall, and the higher they climbed, the deeper the snowpack.

McNair watched his two older sons struggling along through the deep snow and felt proud that they did not whine or complain. *Chip off the old block*, he thought, with a grin on his whiskered face.

As they ascended the eastern slope of the Sierra, fat snowflakes continued to fall. The young and the weak could barely edge their way over the steep rocks, and struggled through the deep snow in the dips. The animals staggered, sinking up to their necks on the few flat sections and losing their footing on the steep inclined face. They had waited too long.

"Oh, McNair. I was mistaken. We cannot make it with the little children," Dorothy wailed. "Oh, what will we do?"

"We go back. What else? It is not your fault, Dorothy. You were right to have us give it a try."

McNair yelled up the mountain to call a retreat and the dispirited emigrants turned downhill.

It was a sorry-looking and despondent party that struggled back to Truckee Lake. Now they faced the gloomy prospect of spending the winter trapped behind the mountains. Divided, they saw others as the cause of the problems. Most blamed Saxby and his imperious leadership, but others eyed McNair as the cause.

There was nothing they could do but seek shelter and dig in, at least until the weather broke and they could cross the Pass. The emigrants who'd spent their lives east of the Missouri felt there would be a thaw, that the snow would pack down and they would cross easily. Others understood that the snow would pile deeper and deeper and that they would stay at Truckee Lake until they died or a rescue party reached them.

At least help was on the way. Christian and Robert would return with supplies. If they carried enough food over the Pass, the trapped emigrants might be able to last until trail opened up. That is what gave McNair hope.

McNair and his family claimed the log cabin that had been hastily constructed by last year's emigrants. Others built log shanties or bush tents and moved their belongings from the wagons to their makeshift accommodations. Alice, O'Malley and Nelly pitched together to build a cabin for their two families. The storm continued, deepening the snow at Truckee Lake. Night after night, Alice heard the animals bellowing, crying for food. She could barely stand listening to their misery.

A week after their aborted escape, Alice looked out from her cabin and could not see her ox, the only animal she had and the sole food supply for her and Amelia. The animal was alive yesterday, moaning for lack of food but staying close to their cabin. Where was it? She could not see a single one of the animals, only a thick carpet of white. Then she knew. The animals were under the snow. They were all dead.

She plunged through the snow, poking down with a stick. As she moved through the deep snow, she had to tramp the snow down, take a step and tramp the snow again. Alice never gave up; she had to find the ox. Hour after hour, she paced through the snow. Finally, she felt something at the end of the stick. Frantically she dug down. There it was. Not a fat animal, but enough meat on its emaciated frame to keep her and Amelia alive for a month, maybe two.

Amelia had kept the fire burning as she waited anxiously for her mother to return, and was relieved when Alice pushed open the door. Beads of sweat covered Alice's forehead, and her skirt and boots were coated with snow.

"I need butcher knives and your help," Alice called out to Amelia, throwing open the door of their rugged log cabin.

They eviscerated the ox, cut it into quarters and the quarters into smaller chunks, pieces that would freeze quickly. Alice laid the meat on a board, separating the pieces to hasten freezing, then buried it in snow, reserving a piece for their meals over the next two days. Before she left her cache, she tore a piece of wood from the wagon and covered the stash with a board and Saxby's heavy trunk. She wasn't going to lose their food supply to the wolves.

Others were not as quick to recognize the consequences of dead animals buried under five feet of snow. Surely it would be easy to find them. What they did not know is the depth of the snow that would inundate the stock. Not five feet or ten feet, but twenty feet of snow would fall at Truckee that winter—snow that piled up and would not melt until the spring thaw.

Eliza, the Mormon grandmother, lost two animals. Even McNair, with his larger herd, only recovered half of his stock. Still, ten oxen and cows should be adequate food for their family of six, at least for now. Soon, parents were knocking at McNair's door, begging for a morsel of food to save a starving son or daughter. McNair refused, but Dorothy could not turn away a mother pleading for her child's life.

The families tallied up their remaining food supplies and knew they could not survive long unless the rescue party returned with pack mules loaded with supplies, enough to feed the fifty emigrants trapped by the Sierra Nevada's vicious snowstorms.

Fragmented and short-tempered from lack of food, fights broke out among the men, and the women yelled at their children. Spirits sank as they waited for Robert and Christian to return with supplies. If only there was a cup of coffee or just one small biscuit. Instead, most of the trapped emigrants were boiling animal hides for sustenance. This gluey, glutinous mush was almost impossible to swallow.

The emigrants suffered through two weeks of misery. There was never enough food. Parents struggled to keep their children fed on the scant supplies from their food boxes and the frozen remains of the oxen. They did not visit each other, spending most of the day in bed, getting up only to cut branches for the fire. Amelia was outside snapping off a few pine branches when she saw them. She turned back to the cabin, calling out as she ran.

"They're coming!" Amelia yelled. "I see three men with packs moving down from the Pass!"

The survivors threw on coats and boots and walked out to meet them. As they got closer to the rescue group, they could see that Christian had not returned. With Robert were two Indian men.

Women carried their hungry babies and toddlers, and starving adults and children struggled forward as fast as their emaciated bodies could take them, all wanting to be the first to reach the long-awaited food supply. Alice hugged Amelia and cried.

Maybe there is still hope for us.

"Christian's feet froze on the way over," Robert told them, "and he can't walk until he is healed. Sutter sent these two men with me. I want you to meet Greasy Joe and Sweeney Scurvy, not what their mothers called them, but I can't get my tongue around their Yana names."

McNair nodded to them but did not offer his hand.

While Dorothy brewed tea for the rescue group, the trapped emigrants gathered about the McNair cabin, crowding into the room or hanging about the door waiting for a share of the food, mothers anxious for a cup of flour to feed their hungry children, men with questions about the Pass.

"We started off with mules, but soon they were sinking up to their bellies in the snow," Robert told them. "I left the mules at Bear Creek along with a cache of food and a supply of feed. From there, we each carried sixty pounds of food. On the way, we cached twenty pounds for the return journey. As we crossed the mountain, each day was worse. We are lucky to have made it."

"How was the trail?" McNair asked, hoping with all his heart that rescue was near, that his family would be safe and his mistakes and delays forgotten. "Is it solid enough to take the children across the Pass?"

"McNair, I am sorry to tell you that the little children won't make it to Sutter's without being carried. There are more children than adults, and we don't have enough strong men and women to carry the children across that pass. We are into November. The snow will become deeper and deeper, and even strong men and women won't make it on foot."

Alice listened to Robert and understood the consequences, but the words were like a cold knife in her belly. They were trapped.

"For now, there is food, and we all thank you. For a sarsaparilla lad still wet behind the ears, you did good." McNair patted Robert on the back.

"Three cheers for Robert!" Amelia called out.

Robert smiled. It was the first smile that had brightened the boy's face since Annabelle Lee's death. Robert held little hope for his own future, but assisting the emigrants offered him a reprieve from his misery. Bringing food for the starving emigrants had given him a slice of happiness.

Greasy Joe and Sweeney Scurvy eyed the pitiful gathering. Both spoke and understood English but did not offer their opinions to McNair and the others.

The two Yana took Robert aside. "We go live with the Washoe," Sweeney explained in broken English. "We have people there who will share their food with us. These white people. Are they crazy, Robert?" Sweeney asked. "Why they bring their babies and old grandparents across the Sierras in winter?"

"Not crazy. They had a bad chief who led them here."

"Yes, sometimes we have bad chiefs too," Sweeney nodded. "Don't starve with these people, Robert. Come live with us at Truckee Meadows till the sun melts the Pass."

"Maybe later. My thanks to you both for carrying food over the mountain."

"We had no choice. Sutter is our boss. When the rich Swiss guy says go. We go."

Chapter Twenty
Trapped

As Robert predicted, the snow continued to fall, trapping the emigrants at Truckee Lake. Alice shared the cabin with the O'Malleys and their two children, who had even less than Alice. Her meat supply was down to a few pieces of jerky and a hide. She had no flour or sugar, and Nelly O'Malley had nothing. Today, Alice boiled a piece of ox hide. At least this kept Nelly's son from perishing. It did not sustain Amelia. She tried to swallow the fetid-tasting mush, but her stomach revolted and she vomited. Alice could not bear to look at Amelia's hollow cheeks and see her daughter grow weaker each day.

Alice did not share her concerns with Amelia. How could she tell her beautiful daughter, the one person in the world she loved with all her heart, that they might not live till spring? The scant provisions Robert and the Yana had packed over the Sierras were gone. Amelia survived on the fish Robert caught through a hole in the ice, gobbling down the life-giving flesh.

Alice kept the fire burning in the hearth while Amelia slept most of the day. Nelly fed her four-year-old the mush made from hide while O'Malley took saw and axe out each morning to gather firewood or ventured out with his rifle in search of game.

Nelly was a talkative young woman, and Alice a patient listener. Each day, to pass the time, Nelly recounted her life in Ireland and the events that had brought her to America. The two women sat on wooden supply boxes, watching the glow of the coals in the hearth. Amelia slept in a cot that Alice had removed from the wagon, and Adam snuggled next to her. After O'Malley deposited his armload of pine branches near the hearth, he took the baby from Nelly, lay down and slept with her in his arms. The fire crackled, and as the dusk fell, shadows crept across the small log cabin.

"In the name of God, why would I stay in Ireland, taking in washing or selling scarves on the street corner?" Nelly told Alice, the firelight touching their faces and the rest of the cabin in shadows. "Then we was so poor, with not even a potato to eat, and there was no selling anything in the streets. There was only begging and starving in the streets."

"We didn't have me no shoes. Me Da, he was a farmer till the potatoes went rotten. We was all starving, the little ones with their bellies bloated, them crying and nottin' I could do for them. 'Twas much like we are now."

"I could 'o moved to London; they were crying for workers to sew! But why would I go to the dirty streets of London and work in a sweat shop being paid a pittance for each piece then marry a brute of a husband who would beat me and take all my earnings to spend on beer? Because that is how it was. Women were nothing, and if me and all me children worked in the sweat trade, we would not have the shillings to put food on the table or shoes on their feet."

"Me Da, he said I must go to the convent. There, I was put to work stitching night and day, making fancy things for the rich ladies. I go to the church and pray, as we was Catholic. They called us Papist, and spat at me on the street."

"The convent could not keep me, so I goes into service. Then I was fifteen. The master was trying to touch me, and I am trying to look plain so he leave me be. I want to save myself for my husband.

I was no longer Nelly; they called me Mary, and that was my name, like it or not. All-purpose maid."

"The Master, he catch me in the pantry and up against the wall he push himself into me and hold his hand over my mouth so I could not scream. This went on for weeks, him catching me and holding me down. Me, I was too afraid to tell the priest, and even if I did, who would believe me? I had enough. I spat and kicked at the Master and ran away." Nelly looked into the fire, reliving the assaults, piling blame on herself when no blame should have fallen on her.

"Then the baby came, and I was in real trouble. Me in a workhouse with a babe to feed and hours at the laundry tubs each day. Next thing I know there's this man at the workhouse looking for girls to ship across the sea."

"In the new world, I would be having me own house and have a sewing machine and the keys to the pantry, almost like the ladies that lorded over us in Ireland."

"My babe could not come. Little Ginny she stays with my sister, and I shall never see her agin." Nelly tried to swallow her tears. She paused before continuing. "At least my little Ginny is in Ireland. There is little enough food there, but I reckon more than here." She paused to look over at the bunk where her husband slept with their baby wrapped in his arms.

"I landed at the docks in New York. O'Malley needed a wife and paid for me. I was the lucky one. Most of the girls on the ship were sold to ugly old men. So here I is, facing starvation and trying with all my heart to save these dear little ones, thinking that this is worse than the Irish famine I left behind. After all the hardship I've seen, I am watching my wee babes get weaker each day." Nelly bent her head, tears pouring down the young woman's cheeks.

Alice took Nelly in her arms, both sobbing, both desperate to keep their loved ones alive.

When Nelly was not recounting her life story, Alice read to Amelia from *Pilgrim's Progress*, and each night they knelt to pray. Occasionally Robert visited to play checkers with Amelia. Robert knew how desperate the situation had become, but did not say a word. He remained stoic, as if he welcomed a death that would reunite him with Annabelle Lee.

Alice refused to accept the inevitable.

"We have to cross the Pass, my sweet girl. Go while we still have a piece of hide to sustain us on the journey."

Alice broached the idea to Robert and the O'Malleys, explaining that she intended to leave even if only Amelia came with her. Robert agreed to make a try at the Pass. The Irish couple thought of the hardship of crossing with a baby and a toddler and opted to stay at Truckee.

It was a cloudy day as the three of them shouldered their packs and wound their way to the base of the mountain, with Robert and Alice taking turns breaking trail.

Robert said little. Alice understood that Robert's role in life had little to do with his own survival. He had abandoned his dreams, along with the girl who'd stolen his heart. Now, he wanted to help others as Annabelle Lee had done during her short life. He knew the chances of reaching Sutter's, traveling with a seven-year-old weakened by hunger, were poor. Just as Annabelle Lee had insisted on caring for Billy, despite the risk of contracting the disease, Robert believed he had to protect Alice and Amelia, though the dangers of the trek were all too obvious to him. He had crossed the Pass earlier and knew its hazards. Now the snow was deeper and the winds colder.

Alice was unusually strong despite the short rations. She had always had a healthy body and more energy than two women. As they moved up the incline, she took Amelia's pack so her daughter could manage to clamber up the steeply sloping rocks. Alice believed that if only Amelia could keep walking, they would reach the summit and begin the descent to the Sacramento River.

What Alice did not know was that it was not just one initial climb. Once they reached the summit, the trail would dip down to Mary's Lake, where they would trudge through deep snow in the valley before facing another steep climb. If the weather held, maybe they would find the headwaters of the Yuba River and follow its path to the Sacramento. However, it was not the weather that stopped them.

They had summited the Pass and could see the snow-choked valley. To the west, the sun's rays turned red across the jagged mountains. A dark, gloomy cloud sat on top of the sunset, creating a blood-red strip of setting sun. The black cloud took the form of a giant monster, its mouth wide and gaping. When the last strip of sunset disappeared, Summit Valley fell into dark shadows. Night would soon be upon them. Alice heard a moan from Amelia and turned to find her daughter had fallen headfirst into the snow and did not have the strength to get up.

"Mommy, I am so sorry. I just cannot," Amelia pleaded. "Leave me and go for help."

"My darling girl, do you think I could ever leave you? We must go back. We will find a way."

They waited until Amelia gained the strength to stagger to her feet. Then, with help from her mother and Robert, Amelia made it back to Truckee Lake. They arrived late that night to find Siederleggen, his wife and two babes taking up a corner of the small cabin. Now there were more people and less food.

Alice's heart was heavy with worry for Amelia, and concern for the four babes who shared the cabin. She knelt with Amelia beside the dying embers of the hearth.

Though I walk through the valley of the shadow of death, I will fear no evil. Alice wrapped the quilts around Amelia and kissed her goodnight, trying not to let Amelia guess how desperate they were.

The next two weeks were wretched as food supplies disappeared, and several of the trapped emigrants died of starvation. It was clear they could not last the winter. Even McNair's supply of meat would not sustain his family.

Robert had been tenting out, surviving on rabbits he managed to snare and fish caught through the ice. He shared his catch with Addie and the families in Alice's cabin, but as the snow piled higher, it became impossible to clear away a patch to reach the ice.

"Mrs. Chablis, the two Yana are lower down at Truckee Meadows because Sweeney has a cousin among the Washoe. I will go there, where I can hunt and dig roots. The Washoe manage, but of course, they put aside acorns and camas roots for the winter. I'll return with roots and whatever the Washoe are willing to trade for. We need enough food so the children are strong enough to walk the Pass. You remember passing through the meadows?"

"Robert, I tried to get McNair to lead us back to the meadows when the first snows trapped us. He wouldn't, of course. Just told me to go it alone with my child."

"Too bad. Maybe everyone could survive if you were out of the snow."

Alice pondered what Robert said about the Washoe.

"Roots. Of course, that is what they brought."

"Who?"

"Dorothy told me, as she put it, some dirty looking Indians, the ones that stole our cattle, opened her door and held out a bag for her to take. It must have been roots. She thought they had come to kill her and the children. She shrieked like a banshee and threw the bag out the door."

"They may be thieves, but David told me the Washoe have helped white people in the past. Yes. They likely brought roots, and if she had smiled and given them a present, they would have come back with more."

"Mrs. Chablis, can you and Amelia survive for a couple of weeks?"

"I have the bones from my ox, and McNair let me have several hides. It is enough to sustain us, providing the children will eat the mush. Dorothy is feeding her family meat, at least for now. Her children gag on the boiled hides. We will survive until you return, as long as Amelia is able to swallow that disgusting glue."

Robert turned to Amelia with a smile on his fine-looking face. "Do me a favor, Amelia, and try to eat. Do that for me."

Although Amelia was years younger than Robert, she had adored him since she first saw him at Kanesville. Now that Robert asked a favor, she promised to hold her nose and gag down the bilious glue.

Before Robert left, Alice rummaged through her belongings for items to trade—a tortoise shell comb, pieces of colored silk, a few knives and pots.

"Would it be alright if I came with you?" Addie had heard of Robert's plan to move to Truckee Meadows. "I cannot bear to have Pierot die for lack of food and be eaten." Addie stroked her beautiful Arabian horse as she waited for Robert's reply.

"Yes. Come with us. David told me you have Indian brothers and a Sioux sister. That should make it easier for you to fit in with the Washoe."

"Did you hear that, Pierot? We are going where there is green grass for you!" She kissed the horse's neck, relieved that soon her horse would regain its shiny coat and its strength.

Over the next two weeks, Alice and Amelia read Bonneville's book till the pages were tattered, and also read verses from the King James version of the Bible. Nelly continued her stories of the hardships she'd experienced during the Irish famine, and each night cried as she watched her babe and toddler grow weaker. Amelia choked down the bilious-tasting mush made from the hides. They survived.

In mid-December, Robert, Addie and the two Yana returned from Truckee Meadows carrying sacks of pine cones and camas roots. It was not food the emigrants were accustomed to, but if they could manage to eat it, they might be able to regain their health sufficiently to hike the Pass.

Robert was too young to be a leader, so O'Malley gathered the able-bodied emigrants to propose an escape. They met in McNair's cabin, standing close to each other in the cramped space. The toddlers and babies were placed on the bunks, the older children bundled up and sent out the door. It was hot and stuffy. The group wanted to finish the meeting as quickly as possible and leave the crowded, smoky cabin. O'Malley spoke first.

"If we all stay here, there is not enough food to take us through to the spring. But if a group of the strongest leave for Sutter's, we could send a rescue party with supplies, and with men to carry the children to safety. There are ten of us prepared to try the Pass. Siederleggen is fashioning snowshoes for the men. One request." O'Malley cleared his throat. He continued with difficulty. He knew that his only chance to save his family was to join the escape group and go for help. He would not be at their side, not be able to protect them. "I must leave my dear wife and my precious children, and I ask that you keep them safe for me."

"And I will be parting from my helpmate and our babe," Siederleggen pleaded in his broken English. "We buried our wee son, and ask you care for my wife and baby girl."

"Of course we will look after them, and Godspeed you safely over the mountain," Dorothy promised.

Along with O'Malley, the rescue group included Robert, Siederleggen, the two Yana, Styles, Finis, and four women, including Addie. Addie had left her horse with the Washoe with a promise of gifts if the Indians would keep her horse alive. She did not expect to get the horse back, only that they would not eat it.

The men and women in the rescue effort headed for the Pass, with the men taking turns to pack down the snow at the front of the file. The day was sunny, and the snow had turned soft along the shoreline. As they climbed to the summit, the air grew colder and the snow deeper. They had not even reached Mary's Lake before dissension broke out among the hikers. Styles, short and stooped, stumbled in the deep snow.

"Goddamn your souls! Slow the pace! I can't stay with you."

"If you can't make it, Styles, go back," Finis snapped. "We can't have you holding us up."

It was not only Styles who struggled. Robert, not even a man yet, was the fittest but suffered from snow blindness so severely that he could not see the person in front of him. The dazzling sun reflected off the white snow, and without any protection for his eyes, Robert was blinded. They had reached the summit, dipped into Mary's Lake and made their way up the next ascent before Robert and Styles could go no further.

"Leave us," Robert told the group. "Styles can gather up wood and make us a fire. We will have to go back to Truckee unless I recover my sight."

"We don't know the route, Robert," O'Malley said.

"Follow Sweeney. He knows the way. We left stashes tied as high as we could reach, so keep your eyes peeled. You don't have enough food to last, so ration yourselves just in case you can't find the food or the animals have found it first."

"We should stay with Robert," Addie urged. "He risked his life to cross the Pass and bring us supplies. If he remains blinded, he may be unable to make it back to Truckee, let alone Sutter's."

"Go," Robert told them. "When I've come this far, do you think I will lie down and die?" Indeed, the escape group believed Robert would die, that he wanted to die and join his beloved Annabelle Lee. The remaining eight bid Robert and Styles goodbye and trudged west into the snow. Addie walked a few steps, turned, and looked back. It pained her to leave them, to see Robert sitting in the snow with his head cupped in his hand, behind him, Styles, his hunched back a black silhouette against the whiteness.

They had walked for an hour when Addie turned back.

"What the hell are you thinking?" Finis yelled. "Git back here!"

"I'm going to help Robert, and if needed, I'll even help that miserable sidekick of yours. Robert saved us. We can't just leave him die in the cold, blind and abandoned."

With that, Addie turned east, reaching Robert and Styles just as the sun sank over the Sierras and the sky turned blood-red.

"We go that way," Sweeney said, and pointed to the undulating ridges. "Hard, but we get there."

The two Yana had passed this way only a month ago. Now they led the party through a low-lying valley and up a steep ascent. The group reached the ridge to see wave after wave of rugged descending mountains, a formidable sight for the weary hikers.

Finis's temper flared. "This ain't the way to Sutter's. You savages are leading us to our death. We should be going down to the Sacramento River, not up ridge after ridge. I'm not following you Indians."

"With Robert gone, all we have are the Indians," O'Malley countered, "and until I am convinced they are leading us in the wrong direction, we should follow them."

"What is worse, following the savages or following a potato-eater from the Wild Goose Nation?" Finis scowled.

It took another week to cross the series of ridges, each time dropping into a gully, struggling through deep snow in the valleys and then up another ridge.

"Shit. Where in the fucking hell is that river?" Siederleggen had been taking the lead and was exhausted from breaking trail.

"Watch your tongue, Siederleggen. There're women with us." It was O'Malley who took offense at the language. O'Malley, like Siederleggen, was a family man. He could cuss in the beer parlor but never with his son listening and never in front of women.

It wasn't Siederleggen's nature to blaspheme, but he had spent days making snowshoes for the men and always took the lead on the steeper pitches. Now he was faltering.

"My apologies, ladies, but maybe you gals should break trail. I've had enough."

"Na," Finis piped up. "Women are only good for one thing. They are useless in the backcountry. Why we took women, I don't know. We are all too tired to fuck them. They be holding us up and eating more than their share. Look at Mary. How come she still has a fat ass?"

"Another remark like that," O'Malley countered, "and I will punch out your lamps."

"Your skinny, starving bag of bones couldn't punch a shadow," Finis fired back.

"Stop this," Mary said firmly. "You waste your energy fighting and squabbling. We must keep moving."

"They start killing soon," Sweeney whispered to Greasy Joe, in their language. "Without Robert, we must watch these skinny white men. The first they kill and eat will be us."

"I don't trust that man who looks like a ferret and has a heart of a wolverine," Greasy Joe told him, glancing nervously at Finis.

"Talk in English, you two," Finis yelled, "so we knows you ain't planning to do us in."

The rescue party disintegrated. No one wanted to break trail. All were hungry. Hiking through the deep snow with only a finger-sized piece of jerky to sustain them sucked their energy.

"Let's call it a day. Dig in. Make a fire and hope to hell we find the Sacramento River tomorrow," Siederleggen grumbled.

Digging in was no easy task. The snow was deep, covering all but the top branches of the pine trees. Both men and women took turns digging the pit and breaking off green limbs to form a platform for the fire. The three women worked as hard as the men to gather firewood, and soon they had a platform for the fire at the bottom of the pit, and a pile of firewood at the top.

The dying sun sent its glorious rays over the peaks. Night fell, and the sky was clear and festooned with stars as brilliant as diamonds. It was calm until midnight, when the wind rustled in the treetops. First they heard the sound of the branches creaking in the wind, then a whistling wind moving up the slopes of the Sierras, picking up speed as moisture-laden air rose up the mountainside and tore across the Sierras.

"Christ!" Finis yelled. "It's a blizzard. A goddamn blizzard!"

The murderous wind raged through the remainder of the night, scouring the summit. They slept fitfully, waking every few minutes from the noise of the storm. The fire sputtered, and their supply of wood diminished. They waited for the dreadful night to end, hoping the sun would return and the winds abate.

"Someone git more wood," Finis ordered. "My feet are freezing."

"Fetch your own wood, Finis," Siederleggen muttered. "I broke trail for hours yesterday. I can barely climb out of this crater."

The men swore and argued until Mary shook the snow from her blanket, climbed out into the storm and passed wood down to

O'Malley. When Mary returned to the pit, she noticed Siederleggen leaning forward almost falling into the fire.

"O'Malley, grab Siederleggen. He's about to fry himself." From that moment on, Siederleggen was unresponsive. Not so long ago, he had scampered up the steep cliffs on the first reconnaissance of the Sierra Pass. Now hungry and worn out, he took ragged breaths and sagged against the icy wall of the pit.

The storm raged for five days. The pit was a dreadful place. They had to relieve themselves at one end, and the stench of excrement and body odor surrounded them as much as the winds trapped them.

Bored and hungry, they could not resist eating their meager rations, telling themselves that they would find one of Robert's caches along the route; that eating their remaining food was not a problem; that once the storm broke, there would be a clear trail leading first to the Yuba, and from there to the green meadows of the Sacramento Valley. It was in this pit of misery that the escape group passed Christmas. Mary led them in prayer, and they allowed themselves a second piece of beef jerky to mark Christmas Day. They thought of the loved ones left behind and the comforts of home back east. Slippers left by the fireplace for presents, roasted goose and mince pies. Mary cried, and others were bitter.

"We gotta have food soon or we're all dead, and I'll never get back to my family." That was from O'Malley, who had left his wife, four-year-old son and baby at Truckee. "We can get out our pistols and fight to the death or hold a lottery like the sailors did when they were starving."

"Hey, we don't need to kill each other. We just kill the savages," Finis added, with a sick grin.

"Stop it!" Mary demanded. "We are not barbarians. No one is going to be killed for food. You men are dumber than a sack of turnips and weaker than the women. I always knew that, but now we see that the proof is in the pudding."

"If you don't shut your mouth, Mary, you may be the first to be fried over the fire."

"Stop it, Finis. Enough. Be civilized," Mary said. "It is Christmas Day."

The most difficult chore for the starving escape group was gathering wood. They had exhausted the initial supply. Now, weakened from lack of food, they had to go farther and farther from the pit to break off branches that were dry enough to burn. No one offered to climb out while the winds tore across the Sierras.

"You redskins. Git your sorry asses up there, and git us some wood," Finis ordered.

Greasy Joe and Sweeney climbed out of the pit. An hour passed with no sign of the two Yana men. They did not bring wood; instead, they walked away into the storm.

"Hey! What the hell!" Finis yelled. "I knew them were useless savages. Good riddance to them. We can find our way without them. But we still need someone to fetch wood. Mary, you're still fat and healthy. You git up there agin."

"Finis, it's your turn. I done my job."

"You bitch! You know what we should do? Cut your throat and enjoy a good meal off your fat bottom. What you think, Siederleggen?"

But Siederleggen did not answer.

"Oh, my God," Mary exclaimed. "I thought he was just sleeping! Holy Mary. He's dead."

"Siederleggen cashed in his chips, did he?" Finis said, with a stupid chuckle. "One less mouth to feed, and one extra set of snowshoes."

The women looked at Finis in disgust.

O'Malley and the three women hoisted Siederleggen out of the pit. It took all the effort they could muster to drag him up the side of the snowy well. They left him only a few feet from the lip. Soon, a mound of snow covered the body.

The food was gone, and so was the wood. It was unlike Finis to offer to help, so the others were surprised when he threw off his blanket and climbed out into the raging storm.

"Grab the branches, you lazy louts, and git that fire a burnin'. I got ourselves a chunk of food."

No one said a word when Finis placed something red and bloody on a sharp stick to roast over the fire. O'Malley shook his head, unable to watch; the women silently accepted pieces of meat. They could not look at each other. They chewed the disgusting meal and wept. The unspeakable had happened, and it would mark them for the rest of their lives.

They endured another day in the pit before the wind abated, and the five remaining members of the escape group climbed out of the stinking hole. They passed the mutilated body, averting their eyes, feeling sick at heart at their transgression into cannibalism.

Silent and somber, they walked west, feeling pain in their stiff muscles and in their hearts. It was a dreary, gloomy day, overcast, with a grey leaden sky. Within an hour, they passed a recently vacated snow cave.

"The bloody, useless Indians! If I catch them, they'll git a bullet in their brains."

"Finis, smarten up," O'Malley told him. "There will be no killing."

"They's just savages. And you think I'll let a dumb Gin Lane Irishman tell me what I cin do?"

Mary and the other two women kept their distance from Finis.

"You two stay with me," Mary begged the women. "Finis has been watching me, and I know what he is thinking. He would kill and eat me without turning it over once in his sick brain."

However, it wasn't Mary who was killed for food. As night closed in on the travelers, Finis spotted footsteps.

"Hey! It's them savages. Look at their footprints. They are done in. I can tell."

Finis had eaten well before leaving the pit, and had regained some of his strength. He hurried along the trail, following the footsteps in the snow.

Two shots rang out. O'Malley and the women gasped. "Oh, my God! What has he done?"

"Holy shit!" O'Malley said, shaken and shocked. "He killed them. Sweeney and Greasy Joe came to rescue us, and Finis thinks it okay to kill them because they are Indian. We are traveling alongside evil."

Chapter Twenty-one
Sweeny and Greasy Joe

The sound of gunfire traveled over the Sierras, amplified by the blanket of snow, ricocheting into the valley where Robert and Addie walked.

"Hopefully they bagged a deer," Robert said.

Addie, Styles and Robert waited out the storm for five days, surviving on spruce gum peeled from the trees. Separated from Finis' influence, Styles was less repulsive and even became a helpful companion to Robert while the young lad recovered his eyesight. When Addie and Robert made plans to continue over the Pass, though, Styles declined.

"I'll return to Truckee. If I come with you, I will slow you down. If I return to the lake camp, I may be of help because I need little food and know something of scratching the earth for crumbs." Once the storm broke, Styles left and retraced his steps to Truckee Lake.

Addie and Robert headed west on a clear day. At the ridge above Mary's Lake, Robert spotted a cache he had left. With food in their stomachs, their strength returned and soon they reached the pit where the others had sheltered out the storm.

"Robert. Come here." Addie was bending over something. She kicked aside the snow and gasped. "Oh, dear Lord! Is this what I think it is?"

Robert looked down. He felt his stomach lurch at the site of Siederleggen's mutilated body.

"Addie, I know this is a shocking sight, but remember, for centuries starving sailors lost at sea have resorted to eating their dead companions. There is even a Navy code of conduct that exonerates sailors in certain circumstances."

"I couldn't. I just couldn't." Addie turned away from the grisly sight, her hand over her mouth. Her stomach heaved, and she vomited. Robert handed her a kerchief to wipe her mouth.

They said no more and continued following the trail left by the vanguard group. Addie and Robert walked on, hoping to catch up before the oncoming night obscured the footprints.

Instead of meeting up with O'Malley's party, what they found on the trail infuriated Robert and sickened Addie. It was clear that Robert's Yana companions had been murdered and their bodies mutilated.

Robert kicked angrily at the snow, feeling betrayed and remorseful for his part in bringing the two Indians across the Pass.

"Finis! He is the only one that would do this. It is on my conscience. I brought Sweeney and Greasy Joe here. Asked Sutter for men to help bring food. They came willingly and were faithful." Robert was near tears as he piled snow over the bodies and erected a cross.

"They were Christians," he told Addie, "and Sweeney could read and write. He wrote poetry, poems that were both heartbreaking and uplifting, always about his people, how they had suffered when the salmon did not return and how they celebrated and flourished when there was an abundance of food."

"How is it he was at Sutter's?"

Robert shrugged. "Sutter, well, he had his ways to get men from the local tribes. Money and booze, and if that didn't work, some say he kidnapped workers."

"Let's pray," Addie whispered. They bent their heads, and the preacher's daughter intoned a prayer for the two innocent victims. "May God bless you, Sweeney and Joe, and I thank you for carrying food across the mountains, food that saved many little ones from starvation. May you rest in peace."

Night fell, and a pure white moon sailed in the sky, glistening on the snow and lighting their path.

"They are headed too far north, following the Yuba instead of turning to meet up with Bear Valley. We must catch them and set them on the right trail."

"I don't want to travel with Finis. He sets my teeth on edge."

"Remember, O'Malley and the three women are with him. We must help them find Sutter's, and we must get there to raise the alarm and get a true rescue party over the Sierras to Truckee."

As they walked through the deepening night, the moon turned orange, still providing enough light for them to find their path. Gradually, a frightening darkness enveloped Addie and Robert as the earth slowly eclipsed the moon, then appeared as a blood-red circle.

"What is it?" Addie, fascinated by the strange red moon.

"It's called a blood moon," Robert told her. "The earth moved between the moon and the sun, cutting off light to the moon. When the earth moved in front of the moon, it created the unusual red color. Beautiful."

Addie and Robert stared in wonder. Addie hastened her steps, wanting to hurry forward and leave the frightening moon behind, fascinated as well as alarmed by the phenomena.

"Beautiful, yes," Addie added, "but strangely frightening, as has been this day." They continued under the light of the blood moon, gaining on the group ahead.

Once Robert felt they were closing in, he whistled, the shrill sound reverberating over the thick blanket of snow.

The vanguard group clearly heard the sound. "Wait!" Mary cried out, stopping on the trail. "It might be Robert. We need him to help guide us."

Within a few minutes, Addie and Robert joined them. Finis did not seem pleased to have Robert back with them, but the women were relieved, as was O'Malley.

"You're going the wrong way, O'Malley. Remember, you mustn't follow the Yuba. It will take you far off the path."

"You should have stuck with us, Robert," O'Malley said. "Once the Yana men left us, Finis took over the lead."

As the footsore, starving survivors dropped down out of the snow and into the Sacramento Valley, no one spoke of the cruel end that had befallen the two Yana rescuers.

"We're close now. I'll go ahead to Johnson's rancho," Robert told them. He looked at his fellow travelers. Gaunt faces and hollow cheeks. Tattered clothes and feet wrapped in bloody rags.

Patches of green grass emerged alongside the trail. They had reached the settled region, for the path was well used by settlers and Native people whose footsteps packed down the scant snow, creating slippery ice. As Robert staggered towards the ranch, he left bloody footprints on the trail.

Finally, Robert spotted the Johnson rancho. It was a small holding with a two-room dwelling built of logs on one side and adobe on the other. Johnson had started his operation last summer, and was in the early stages of developing his land. Robert pushed open the door; Johnson stared, bewildered by the emaciated figure that stood unsteadily in his kitchen.

"My good Lord, son. You've come across from Truckee? Escaped from the McNair party, the ones that are trapped! Are they alive? You must tell me." Johnson took Robert's arm and led the boy to a chair before turning to give orders to his vaqueros. Within the hour, men were mounted and riding towards the survivors.

Johnson brought Robert a dish of beans and listened to Robert explain the plight of the trapped emigrants and the condition of his fellow travelers still back on the trail. When Finis, O'Malley and the women were finally brought to the rancho, there was no rejoicing. They were a subdued group and kept the horrors of the trip to themselves. Some prayed, others isolated themselves, hardly speaking to each other, let alone to Johnson and his ranch hands.

"You are all done in," Johnson said. "I understand. But you must tell us how many are still trapped. There is a rescue being planned by your friend Christian and one of the other members of the McNair group. Saxby's his name, I think."

Robert could not think of a more unlikely person to be involved in rescuing the McNair party. *Wasn't Saxby responsible for getting them all into this? And what on earth was Saxby doing last fall? If he had any interest in rescuing Alice and Amelia and getting food to those he had led, why did he wait this long? Why didn't he send a rescue party last October before the snow closed the Pass?*

The escape party recovered at the rancho for a week, and then, on horses borrowed from Johnson, they rode to Sutter's Fort. O'Malley remained at Johnson's rancho, gaining the strength to challenge the Pass and take food to his starving family. Robert and the four women traveled together. They rode separately from Finis. The blood on his hands was too fresh. No one could bear his company.

The escape group was emotionally shattered and still weak from months of near starvation. They rode silently over the grassy plain, heading to the confluence of the American and Sacramento Rivers where food and shelter awaited them at Sutter's Fort.

After months of cold and depravation, now they suffered from thirst and sunburn under the hot California sun, waiting impatiently to reach the shade and comforts of the fort. At last they reached the outfields of Sutter's land, where cattle grazed and local Indian tribe members and Mexicans worked herding or gardening. Beyond the fields, they spotted the tall, white-washed walls of the fort, with its guns mounted at bastions on each corner.

Robert was the first to reach the immense double doors of the fort entrance. What surprised Robert were the changes since he had left the fort last fall. There was a U.S. Marine in dress blues guarding the entrance to the fort. In place of the Mexican flag were the Stars and Stripes, flying from one of the Bastions.

"Is Captain Sutter about?" Robert inquired.

"Sutter is no longer in charge. The United States under Captain Freemont occupies the fort. We have beaten down the Mexicans, and California is American soil."

Robert had little interest in America's conquests. He needed to save starving emigrants. "I hope to speak with Sutter. We are part of the McNair group trapped behind the Sierras and have been without food and shelter for months."

"Ah. Heard about you. I shall fetch Sutter, although I doubt he has the authority to give you rooms." The sentry left his post and walked across the dirt yard to a two-story building that commanded a view of both sides of the large enclosure. Robert and the women waited under the hot afternoon sun.

Finally, Sutter emerged from the upper story, walking down the exterior staircase and across the dusty yard. Robert watched as Sutter approached the gate. The Swiss entrepreneur was a rotund man attired in a frock coat and neatly tailored pantaloons. Sutter took in the tattered clothes and haggard appearance of the survivors.

"My dear God! What has befallen you? Come in. I give no nevermind whether Freemont allows it," Sutter said, in his heavy Swiss accent. "You must be fed and brought back to health." Sutter graciously kissed the hands of the four women as Robert introduced them. With a wave of his hand, two Mexican women ran over from the kitchen where they had been working. Sutter spoke to them in Spanish, gesturing and pointing to the row of rooms along the outer wall of the enclosure. Within minutes, the four emaciated women had basins of water to wash with, food to eat and beds to rest in.

Satisfied that the women were cared for, Sutter turned his attention back to Robert. "The women will recover soon. It will take longer to fatten you up, young man, and erase the tragedy that has marked you. First, you must come see Christian. His feet have healed, and he is looking well. He is taking a meal in the mess hall. Eating has been his main occupation since he crossed the Sierras with you last fall," Sutter said with a smile.

Sutter led Robert to the center building and into a spacious room. "There he is," Sutter pointed to the robust, big-shouldered man sitting at the far end of the room.

"Christian!" Sutter called out. "I have someone I know you will be happy to see." Christian got up from one of the hand-hewn tables and walked over to Robert, obviously pleased to be reunited with his friend.

"Now, please excuse me. I must return to my ledgers. I'll send the women with a hot meal."

"Hey, young man," Christian said, embracing his former traveling partner. "Why so gloomy?"

"I wish I had died on the Pass," Robert confided in a subdued tone. "What happened is more horrible than any nightmare. After what I have been through, I have no wish to live."

Christian placed a comforting hand on Robert's shoulder. "Robert. Buck up. How bad is it? You brought out survivors. Right?"

"Yes. Four women. They will recover. Siederleggen didn't make it."

"I thought males were the stronger sex. But look at you! Nothing but skin and bones. What about O'Malley and that scoundrel Finis? Were they with your escape group?"

"Finis. I cannot bear have his name pass my lips. He is truly evil. O'Malley did his best. His heart is over the mountains with his wife and babes. He remained at Johnson's rancho and will leave with a food supply as soon as he regains his health."

"And where are Sweeney and Greasy Joe?"

Robert shook his head. "You'll find out in time. Let's make plans for the rescue. I am too weak to be of any use in a rescue but will work at Sutter's till you return. Please rescue Alice and Amelia, and bring enough strong men with you to take out all the children."

"How many?"

"A dozen, maybe more. Many too young to walk over the Pass—babes, toddlers. There are older children who can walk but will need help because they are so weak from lack of food. Then there are some who can't walk and wives who won't leave their husbands. The tragedy is more than I can accept. And that ignorant Saxby! He led them into the trap. And now I hear he is finally mounting a rescue? In God's name, what has he been doing since October?"

"He went to war against the Mexicans."

"He went to war! Really! His wife and daughter are starving on the other side of the Sierras, and he joins the militia?"

"That's not all. We heard that he applied for an extra land grant using Alice's name. That man is the most self-centered bastard I have ever met. Of course he pretends he is now the great savior, prancing up and down the country raising money for supplies. What a braggard!"

News of the trapped emigrants reached Yerba Buena, the Mexican city later to become San Francisco. The *California Star* reported on the tragedy. At first only muted accounts appeared regarding cannibalism, but then the sensational newspapers found the story and soon yellow journalism took over. Reporters embellished the events and exaggerated the horror to make headlines.

Chapter Twenty-two
The Second Escape

As Christian prepared for the rescue mission, Alice was at Truckee Lake preparing once more to cross the Pass. She cut up and dried her remaining ox hide, and packed blankets and warm clothing for herself and Amelia. Over the past few days, Alice had visited the neighboring survivors to ask if anyone would go with her and Amelia over the Pass.

"For God's sake, Alice!" McNair bellowed. "It's February! Our chance of taking all the children safely over the Pass is as slim as a rattle snake."

Again, Dorothy asserted herself. "McNair, we must go. There is less and less to eat. Soon there will be nothing. Annabelle Lee saved our dear Billy with the Lord's help, and I will not have him die of hunger."

This second escape group included Alice and Amelia, ten members of the Mormon family, the McNairs and their four children and Siederleggen's wife Leanne, along with her baby.

Buried in a little snowy grave was the Siederleggen's four-year-old son, and left behind in Truckee were two older men unable to walk, several teamsters too famished to make the ascent, twelve children—many of them too young to walk unassisted over the Pass—and Nelly with her baby and son. Styles stayed, promising to look after the children.

A German family who camped a distance from the lake also stayed behind. The wife would not leave her injured husband's side, even though two of her children were old enough to walk and the mother was strong enough to carry her smallest child. She decided to wait for the main rescue to reach Truckee. Alice knew how they planned to keep their children fed and could not bear the thought of resorting to cannibalism.

As they prepared for the escape, the adults filled their back packs with blankets, hides and any food they had left. Men pocketed tobacco, and the women added jewelry and silver to their loads.

Saxby and Alice had been the most well-provisioned family on the overland journey, with three wagons filled with goods for sale, family heirlooms, books, a pianoforte, silverware and jewels. A small fortune in goods, in fact.

The last of the ox meat was long since eaten, but Alice had saved a few mashed acorns and some hides to sustain them on the walk across the Pass. The trunk that had covered their scant meat supply was the trunk where Saxby had the stash of gold from her fortune. She removed a few coins and a piece of jewelry.

"Dearest Amelia," Alice said, as the group prepared to leave. "Let me put this around your neck. Your father gave it to me, and it is imbued with love, my love for you and the love of your dear father." She kissed Amelia on the top of her head as she fastened the delicate heart-shaped necklace at the back of Amelia's neck. "Now we must cross the steep Pass."

The desperate escape party moved slowly up the ascent. The weather held. It was cold but not snowing, and as long as they kept moving, they stayed warm. Mothers carried babies and toddlers. Small children struggled in the deep snow on the flat sections and crawled on hands and knees up the steeply sloped granite rocks. They reached the summit exhausted. They had crested the highest point of the Pass, seven thousand feet. The sky was clear with a faint moon rising in the evening sky. To the right was the castle-like mountain peak that guarded one side of the Pass, to the left a towering crag. Alice turned to look down at the Truckee encampment, thinking about the souls buried under the snow and the adults and all the young children left behind, clinging precariously to life.

Alice wanted to escape the sight of the misery she and Amelia had suffered. She had hoped to make camp in the valley beside ice-covered Mary's Lake, but the children were too tired to manage the steep descent. Instead, they dug in near the summit, praying that the weather would remain calm.

The morning broke cold and clear, with not a breath of wind. Alice watched the pink glow of the sunrise catch the snow-covered peaks. It was a scene of breathtaking beauty in a land that witnessed such heartbreaking tragedy.

They gathered up belongings, cradled babies and dropped down to Mary's Lake. As they headed up Summit Valley, the snow became much deeper, slowing the group down to the pace of the youngest walker. Alice often had to help Amelia from one deep footstep to another, and Dorothy and McNair took turns to assist Billy and the two younger boys. Dorothy carried their baby with more energy than McNair, who sweated and panted on the ascents and shivered when the path dropped steeply into the valley, his sweat cooling under his sheepskin coat.

Six-year-old Billy encouraged his two brothers. "Keep walking, and Robert will be a comin' down the trail and he will have a pack filled with bread." The boys remembered when Robert had arrived last fall with flour and dried meat and took encouragement from the promise of food.

Leanne suffered more than the others, staggering slowly from one deep footstep to the next, carrying her baby in her arms. Her beautiful son had succumbed to starvation at Truckee Lake, and now she was frantic to save her daughter, Gertrude. Even the little bundle was too heavy for Leanne. She faltered and dropped behind the last of the stragglers.

"Where's Leanne?" Amelia was the first to notice that mother and child did not catch up when the group stopped to rest.

"She can't make the Pass, and now she is on the trail, dead," McNair blurted.

"McNair! You must not speak in that way," Alice admonished. "Look! I see her. She needs help."

Alice looked back along the trail at the frail figure moving slowly towards them, pausing every other step. Alice walked back to meet Leanne and steadied her, then reached out to take the baby.

"Let me carry Gertrude. Soon we'll have a fire and a morsel of food for you."

Alice took the child in her arms, but gasped when she discovered the little bundle was cold. Tears brimming in her eyes, Alice looked at the sweet face, now blue and still. "She's left us, Leanne. Gertrude is with the angels."

"No. It can't be true. Give her back."

Leanne pulled the child from Alice and held the cold little body to her chest.

"Your babe is gone, Leanne. Do not burden yourself by carrying her. You must let her go."

"No. I'm walking out with her. I won't leave her. I won't." Leanne's tortured sobs weakened her, and the distraught mother fell to the snow, then wrenched herself up, first onto her knees and then on to shaky legs. She struggled forward, holding the dead child in a fierce grip.

Alice wrapped her arms about the anguished mother. "No, dear Leanne; Gertrude is with us no more. You must let me make a wee grave for her. You will slow the group down, and the other babes need us to keep going."

This argument resonated with Leanne, who loosened her hold on the child and gently kissed Gertrude's cheek, her tears falling on the baby's cold little face.

"Yes, dear Leanne. Now give her to me, and let's make a cradle for her in the snow."

With tears pouring down her thin face, Leanne passed the bundle to Alice, then broke a branch from a tree and fashioned a cross over the mound of snow. She sobbed uncontrollably when Alice insisted she leave the tiny grave.

"Her soul is now in Heaven," Alice comforted her. Seeing that Leanne was so stunned by her loss she was unable to move down the trail, Alice took Leanne's hand and led her along the trampled snowy path, reaching the others as they made camp for the night.

Leanne sat still at the camp, her head resting on her chest, occasionally emitting a muffled cry. Sometime during the night, the young mother took her last breath, leaving the cold, snowy mountain to join her husband, her beloved daughter and her little son. Dorothy and Alice lifted Leanne from the shelter, placing her body a few feet from the top of the pit. No one had the strength to cover her or place a cross. Someone solemnly whispered a prayer.

"Hail Mary, Mother of grace, blessed art thou and the fruit of thy womb."

Before returning to the pit, the two women broke off branches for the fire, piling the supply at the top of the pit. Earlier, the adults had built the fire on green pieces that did not burn well. This way, they prevented the fire from sinking into the snow and being engulfed.

As the night deepened, Alice, Dorothy and the Mormon grandmother shared the task of fetching the firewood from the top of the pit. McNair slumped down in the pit, unable to help. Billy held his baby brother and kept an eye on his other two siblings, warning them to keep their feet warm but not so warm that their boots caught fire. Night fell on the camp as the winds picked up and raced along the western slopes of the Sierras.

"Oh, Alice!" Dorothy wailed. "We should have stayed at Truckee! We will die here!"

"Shush, Dorothy," Alice whispered. "Never give up. Don't let the children hear your worst fears. We must persevere, and take them all safely across the mountains."

That night fierce winds moved across the lowlands, and the storm clouds met the high Sierras engulfing the mountain pass in a whiteout. Soon Alice could not see where the snow on the ground ended and the sky began. It was all one sheet of swirling white.

The survivors huddled about the fire, covering their heads with blankets as the snow plummeted down. No one wanted to climb out into the blizzard.

"We must take turns to fetch wood for the fire," Alice suggested. "I will take the first shift. McNair and Dorothy, try to sleep. Amelia, please watch over the little children. See that their feet don't get too close to the fire, and also make sure their feet don't freeze. And don't let your feet freeze. We are going to walk out of here, and no one can do that with frozen feet. We must not lose anyone else."

Alice was thinking of Leanne in the snow at the top of the hole. Each time someone climbed out to gather wood, they passed her. And each time they passed her, the pile of snow rose higher. By the third day, it was a mound of snow that they stepped around on their way to cut wood.

They became entombed in the snow pit, growing weaker each day. Alice removed the laces from her boots and cut them into strips. "Roast these, and eat them." She gave each child a few inches of leather to chew on. On the fourth day trapped in the pit, there was not even a shoelace to stem the hunger. Their faint hope was that the rescue party would start up the Pass from Sutter's Fort with food and enough strong men to carry the smaller children and help the weak.

The following night, two babies died in their mother's arms, and then all four of the Mormon men died. Alice was frantic, knowing how weak Amelia was. There was no food, and if they didn't eat, they would all starve to death.

The storm abated. Alice climbed out of the pit, Amelia so weak she had to be dragged up the incline. McNair and his family refused to move. "We will stay here," McNair said. "I can't walk."

"Please come with us," Alice begged. "Don't stay here to die."

"Leave us be, Mrs. Chablis. Leave us be." McNair pulled his blanket over his head, the icy wall at his back and the fire at his toes.

Alice shook her head, then shouldered the two packs and took Amelia's hand.

"Mother," Amelia said. "Let me stay with them."

"No, my darling. We must walk and meet the rescuers." Christian had told Alice that when the cold burned through your body, it was easier to go to sleep and let death erase the pain. She would not let her child die in that pit.

"Come, my sweet girl. I will help you."

Amelia staggered, one foot sunk deep into the snow. She tried to pull her foot out, but fell back.

"Oh, dearest!" Alice cried. She pulled Amelia out of the deep, soft snow, but her daughter was limp.

"Here, take this." Alice had saved a few grains of sugar folded in a cloth. She dipped her finger in the sugar and forced open Amelia's lips.

"Please, my darling. Please," she entreated. Amelia slumped in her mother's arms and drew her last breath. Alice placed her ear against Amelia's lips, praying there would be a faint breath.

"Oh, Dear Lord! No!" Alice screamed in anguish. Her child, her reason to live, was gone.

Chapter Twenty-three

The Miwok Village

Two weeks later, the second escape group reached the last of the descending ridges. Spread out below them were the green plains of California. The starving emigrants dropped down into the Sacramento Valley, staggering forward on weak legs and blistered feet, first through slushy snow and then onto grassy patches that emerged out of the receding snowbelt.

They followed a well-trodden trail through the pine trees, but Alice was too traumatized and heartbroken to feel any relief as they left the snow behind and walked into the California sunshine.

Two Miwok children dressed in rabbit skins watched them from behind the bushes. Frightened by the appearance of the survivors, the boys ran back to camp, calling out an alarm. A Miwok woman who had been gathering acorns in a nearby copse walked out to meet the survivors. What she saw were skeletal figures walking, their cheeks hollow, their faces waxen. The middle-aged Miwok woman cried out at the sight of them and hurried to their aid.

She spoke gently in her language as she led them into camp. The Miwok village consisted of several cone-shaped structures built with poles and bark, and two houses built partially underground and covered with dirt. As they approached the camp, one of the men walked to meet them.

"You come from mountain?" he asked in broken English. "Why you go over that with little children and old people?"

None of the survivors felt they could respond to this question. Indeed, why had they followed Saxby?

He shook his head. "Come, sit. I am Watu and this is my wife, Owoo'yah. She and the other women, they look after you."

Then Watu spoke in his language to the Miwok woman who still held Alice's hand.

The Miwok women placed robes on the ground and helped the weak to lie down. The Mormon grandmother accepted a bowl of fish soup and was soon able to sit by the fire.

Alice curled up weeping and shook her head when Owoo'yah offered her a cup of broth.

"Tell the woman she must eat," Owoo'yah said to her husband.

The Mormon grandmother watched Alice then spoke to Watu. The Miwok chief listened intently while the Mormon grandmother explained what had happened—becoming trapped by heavy snows, the starvation and the death of Alice's daughter. Whenever the grandmother paused, the Chief interpreted to the others. Some took the news with compassion; a young Miwok spit.

The chief approached Alice and knelt beside the anguished woman. "You drink broth. Owoo'yah hurt if you die. She lost daughter to white man's disease. A daughter with years like daughter you lost to mountain's anger."

Alice gradually choked back her sobs, sat up unsteadily on the robes, and finally held out her hand for the cup, tears still streaming down her gaunt face.

"We feed you till you walk to Sutter's. He got all land, all food." He paused and took in the miserable conditions of the emigrants. "We feed only little. A white man came over the mountains. He walk days with no food. He filled his belly died screaming."

By the end of the day, the Miwok had erected three more pole houses, placing deer and rabbit skins on the ground for the survivors. The Miwok fed them, allowing each of the starving people only small quantities. When the oldest of the Mormon grandchildren tried to sneak another piece of roasted deer, Owoo'yah slapped his hand and pushed him away, scolding him in her language. She mimicked with sign language what would happen to the starved boy if he gorged himself.

Owoo'yah helped Alice to one of the houses, speaking in a kind voice and patting the distraught woman's back. Alice lay on the robes sobbing until she finally dropped to sleep.

The next morning, Alice accepted a bowl of mashed acorns but did not leave the house. Instead, she sat on the robes, keening. This is how Saxby found her.

She heard his voice and shuddered. A dark shadow fell across the entrance to the house and there he was, looming over her. She did not look up or stop crying. Here was the one person she could not bear to see. Her hatred for him was palpable.

"What is the matter with you? Get yourself up." He grabbed her arm, trying to pull her to her feet.

Alice, who had not spoken since Amelia's death, pushed his hand away, shrieking at him.

"Don't touch me! I am not your wife! Leave me be, or I will take a knife and sink it into your murdering heart! You've taken all I had!"

He grabbed her arm again, this time pulling her to her feet and shaking her. "You're crazy, Alice! Pull yourself together. You are my wife and always will be mine."

Alice shrieked, trying to push him away. His hands on her felt like the devil's touch.

Owoo'yah heard the commotion and ran to Alice, who was crying and fighting off Saxby. The kindly Miwok woman pulled on

Saxby's sleeve, telling him in her language to leave Alice alone. Saxby raised his fist, about to strike Owoo'yah when Alice bit his wrist. Saxby yelled in pain and released her, anger rising in him. Owoo'yah held Alice in her arms and moved her away from the man.

"If that is the way you want to be, then sink in your despair for now, but you best snap out of it when I return. I'm crossing the Pass to rescue the survivors and bring out our valuables. I have men hired to help me, and soon others will come to rescue the rest of the Truckee survivors. You are beside yourself now, but you will get over Amelia's death and be an obedient wife to me. I will be back to fetch you."

Alice looked at him coldly. "Never will I be your wife. I will kill myself first." She knew he had not come to rescue people, he'd come for his possessions. He was returning for the gold, the jewelry and her.

"One more thing, Alice. Why didn't you bring my gold across the Pass?"

"Gold?! Do you think I was concerned about gold when my daughter had not a crumb to eat?"

Saxby finally left her, heading across the mountains. The Miwok and Alice were relieved to see the back of him.

The Miwok diligently nursed the survivors, feeding them on dried salmon, deer meat and acorn mush. On the third day, the Miwok Chief told them they must walk out to Johnson's rancho, and from there to Sutter's. The Miwok women gave each survivor acorns and dried salmon for sustenance during the walk to Sutter's. Owoo'yah spoke kindly to Alice, both women with tears in their eyes. The compassion of the Miwok woman healed a small slice of Alice's immense pain.

It took the survivors a day to walk the ten miles to the rancho. This was the first summer for his gardens and crops, so there was only a meager supply of food and little room for the survivors in the two-room cabin. He housed them for two days, then loaned them horses and mules for the trip to Sutter's. From Johnson's it was still another forty miles to Sutter's.

Alice was a healthy woman and able to survive physically, but emotionally she was dead. Her reason to live lay in a snowy tomb on the Sierra summit.

On the well-worn trail to Sutter's, the survivors were pleasantly surprised to see Christian and a rescue party approach. Except for Alice, the riders dismounted, dropping the reins. The Mormon grandmother and her daughters had recovered their strength and were relieved to meet rescuers heading for their loved ones still trapped on the other side of the Sierras.

"There are many in need of rescue. You must go back for my grandchildren at Truckee, and if God in His mercy allowed them to live, save the McNair family left up on the summit in the snow cave."

Alice remained on her horse, numb to the appearance of the rescuers. She did not even react to the sight of Christian, despite the fact that they had been close friends. He noticed the vacant look in her eyes.

"Alice, where is Amelia?" he inquired, puzzled. Alice looked briefly at Christian with empty eyes and turned her head.

"Her little girl died up there at the pit. Alice suffers most terribly," the Mormon grandmother told him.

"Oh, Alice! I am so very sorry," Christian said soberly. He opened his arms to help her down from her horse so he could hug and comfort her, but the stricken women turned away, unable to accept compassion from a friend she had cared for.

"You must try and survive, Alice," Christian said with compassion. "That is what your dear girl would want."

"That useless, lying husband of hers met us at the Miwok camp and frightened poor Alice. I understand her pain," the grandmother told him. "I lost two sons-in-law and two sons, but no daughters and no grandchildren. I worry about the little ones left behind, the ones too young to walk but too big to carry. If you reach Truckee, please carry out my grandchildren." She reached out, pressing Christian's arm firmly as she pleaded. "I place my trust in you."

Christian left, feeling overwhelmed by the task he faced. He was exceptionally strong, but how much could he do when so many needed help?

The California sun warmed the soil, its dazzling rays melting the snow on the west slopes of the Sierras and eating away at the snowpack on the summit. Christian and his men rode east into the snow; the survivors walked west, each day warmer as they crossed the green Sacramento Valley heading for Sutter's Fort. Life held no warmth or sunshine for Alice.

~

Christian, O'Malley and two hired rescuers with six pack-mules wound up the ridges towards Bear Valley and the snowpack that encased the mountaintops. O'Malley had recovered from his ordeal. As he walked the trail, his thoughts were with the wife and two children he had left at Truckee.

Please, they must be alive.

When they reached Bear Creek, the snow was so deep that they were forced to lead the pack train laterally along the ridge. Christian knew that they could not take the animals any further, and left supplies and feed for the pack animals at Mule Spring, a staging point on Bear Creek.

The men shouldered as much food as they could carry and continued east over the ridges and deep valleys that separated Bear Valley from the headwaters of the Yuba. They wore snowshoes, and the weather held. The men were all strong and determined, covering three times the distance the survivors had managed each day.

When they saw smoke rising near the summit, they thought it was Saxby and his men making camp. It was the McNair family, all six of them alive. At the top of the pit were the mutilated bodies of those who had perished, so Christian knew how they had survived.

The signs of cannibalism pierced O'Malley's heart.

"Dorothy, did my family survive?" O'Malley asked, his pain and worry palpable. *If they had died, was this their fate? If they were alive, had their survival depended on human flesh?* He felt sick waiting for Dorothy's reply.

"They were alive when we left, and I gave Nelly a hide," she assured him.

While Christian paused to talk to the McNair family, O'Malley hurried along the trail, praying that his sweet Irish wife, his beloved baby and his son were still alive.

"McNair," Christian urged, "you must start down now. I will give you enough food to sustain you and your family until you reach the food cache at Mule Springs. The trail is packed down, and you should be able take your children safely to Johnson's and then Sutter's." Christian said nothing about the cannibalism, but Dorothy had to divest herself of the guilt paining her.

"I know it seems barbarian to you, but what were we to do?" Dorothy told Christian. "I had to save my family." She had remained stoic until this moment, but as she confessed to Christian, tears welled up and she sobbed on Christian's shoulder.

Through her cries, she continued, wanting to share the burden of the terrible act. "Billy's friend Avery told him. You know boys, they want to impress each other with grisly stories. Back in Truckee, Avery's mother was boiling something in a pot and asked the children, 'What do you think we are having for dinner? Issachar's arm,' she told them! We will be damned forever," she sobbed.

Christian held her and patted her back. "You did not kill any-one. Yet you and your children are alive. Now you must walk out while the weather holds. Follow our tracks to Mule Springs where there is food and tents. If we have not caught up to you by then, continue until you leave the snow behind. Alice and the others, including the Mormons, are at Sutter's. You can make it."

Christian shouldered his heavy pack, soon catching up to the two hired men and O'Malley. The four men walked east, up the ascending ridges and into the snow-choked valleys.

Christian saw fresh footprints. Saxby and his two men were not far ahead. McNair had informed them that Saxby and his sidekicks had passed the snow cave without a word or an offer of food.

"That son of a bitch is not here to rescue survivors; he is here to loot!" Christian stormed. "Twelve children! We will need Saxby's men, or we will never get them all across the Pass."

Christian and his men reached Saxby at noon, and found him sitting and staring at the fire. His two men were gone, heading for Truckee.

"I cannot continue," Saxby moaned. "I did not understand how difficult it would be. It is all her fault; she insisted on dragging Amelia over the Pass. On top of it, the stupid woman left our gold behind for the Indians to scavenge."

Get up, man," Christian ordered. "You are well fed and strong. We need every able-bodied man if we are to rescue the children."

"I organized a rescue party. A navy man is sailing up the Sacramento with a boatload of supplies—flour, sugar, shoes, clothes, even ladies' small things. Captain Woodworth will cross the Pass with mules and bring out the survivors."

"I've recently been at Sutter's," Christian said angrily. "There is no rescue party on the river and, even if there were, how would your navy friend get boxes of supplies over the Pass? Saxby, you don't understand that mules cannot cross; they sink up to their necks in the snow! We must have men. Now, get on your feet. We will pass through Summit Valley today, and tomorrow make our way down to Truckee. We must hurry. Lives depend on it."

Saxby could not keep up with Christian and his men, but trudged along in their path, dropping farther and farther behind.

As Christian suspected, Saxby and his men were not rescuers. Since Californians had heard of the entrapment, there had been much talk of the riches left at Truckee—jewelry and thousands of gold coins. The riches seemed to increase with every telling, and Saxby brought two treasure-seekers with him. Healthy and greedy, Horace and Ferris reached Truckee ahead of the rescuers and Saxby.

They did not visit the occupied cabin and tent where starving people waited for food and rescue. Instead, they ransacked the abandoned shelters, hoping to find Saxby's gold stash and pocket a share before Saxby arrived.

"Christ, this place smells!"

"If you look in the bed, you will know why." Horace pulled aside the blanket. There was O'Malley's dead wife, and in her arms lay the body of their baby.

"Let's git out of here. It's a graveyard."

"Hell. They told us this Saxby was crazy. We ain't goin' to find anything? Them wagons are all covered in twenty feet of snow. We were as dumb as Saxby to think we would find jewels and gold."

"Saxby told us about another family with money," Horace reminded Ferris. "They must be the ones camped up yonder on the creek."

Horace and Ferris reached the German family's camp that night. Herman was bedridden, but Marguerite was healthy and capable of making the trip.

She greeted them warmly and was surprised when they offered only a small portion of beef jerky.

"You said they would bring bread," Marguerite's six-year-old girl pouted. She had watched the rescuers approach their tent and believed they would end her suffering. Now there was only a thimbleful of food, hardly enough to stem the hunger of a mouse.

"My little ones," Marguerite told her children, "there will be lots of food once you walk across the mountains. I must stay with your father." She turned to Horace. "You will take them, please. I have one hundred dollars for you, and another hundred if you deliver them safely."

"I will care for them like a father." Horace's smile was like greased oil. "You must get them ready quickly before another storm hits." Marguerite did not care for these men, but she dressed the three girls and choked back her sobs as she kissed each child. "God keep you safe, my little ones."

"Mommy, please come too! We can put Papa on a sled and pull him up the mountain. Please Mommy! Please!"

"My darling girls, don't worry yourselves. Your father and I will come later. You must be brave and walk over the mountain where you will find food and a warm house. Now, goodbye, my dearest hearts."

Horace and Ferris led the children to the lake encampment and opened the door to the Mormon cabin. Four emaciated children sat on the bed, and here was Styles, stoking the fire.

"You're the rescue party," Styles said hopefully. "Give the little ones food. They have had nothing all day, not even that slop I make from the hides."

"I am giving you these three girls but cannot spare any more food. Others are coming."

Horace and Ferris abandoned any thought of rescue and headed back to Sutter's, leaving Saxby to fend for himself and cursing him for leading them on a wild goose chase.

By this time, Christian, O'Malley and the two rescuers had arrived. O'Malley rushed to the cabin, throwing open the door. The cabin was dank and the smell of death permeated the room. He stepped forward slowly, his heart heavy, tears welling in eyes. *Were they all gone? His sweet boy, his little daughter? His beloved Nelly?*

He knelt beside the cot and lifted the blanket. "Oh, my God. No!" His dearest Nelly was dead, and in her arms she cradled their baby daughter, now dead and cold. There was no sign of Adam, their four-year-old son.

O'Malley searched the cabin, wildly pushing aside the debris, looking in every corner of the small cabin before running through the encampment calling out his son's name. As he searched the tents and cabins, he was certain that his son had also perished and was now covered with layers of snow. The thought of never finding even his body filled O'Malley with the utmost sorrow. At last he spotted McNair's former cabin, and there was Adam, sitting on the roof, kicking at the piles of snow that reached to the eaves.

O'Malley had rarely cried in his life, but at the sight of his beloved son, he burst into tears, sobbing with joy as he lifted his boy from the roof and pressed him to his chest.

"Da. Don't cry. I am so happy to see you! And Christian gave me bread."

O'Malley could not stop his tears as he clutched his son in his arms. "Dear God, thank you for saving my boy."

O'Malley left Adam with Christian and returned to the cabin where he knelt beside Nelly and their daughter, praying for their souls. He did not blame Dorothy, who had promised to keep them all alive, and he even felt relief that his dear ones had not been mutilated. He looked for a resting place for his dear wife and babe. He could not dig a grave because twenty feet of snow covered the ground, and he couldn't leave her in the fetid cabin. He picked up his wife and baby and carried them to a mound of snow, digging down until he found Saxby's wagon, where he placed them on the leather seats. He covered them with blankets and buried the wagon in a pile of snow. It was fitting that Nelly, who had been deprived all her life, should have the fancy wagon as a tomb.

Meanwhile, Christian and his two men were making the rounds of the lake cabins, gathering the children.

"We must leave within the hour with all the children and every adult capable of walking," Christian told O'Malley and his two hired men.

While Christian and O'Malley organized the final rescue, Saxby rummaged through Alice's abandoned cabin, swearing when he realized the trunk was not there and cussing the dead for the stench they had caused.

"Damn her to hell! She must have left it in the wagon. I'll whip her for this." As he left the cabin, Saxby walked over a mound of snow, unaware that the gold lay under his feet where the Washoe would find it in the spring.

Saxby noticed the recently disturbed snow that O'Malley had piled up. He dug away and uncovered the entrance to his expensive wagon. The trunk was missing. Instead of his gold, he found the bodies of Nelly and the baby, wrapped in a brightly colored quilt. He swore and kicked snow at the dead mother and child.

Christian and his two men led the weak and starving survivors up the steep incline of the Sierras, bringing out the adult survivors and children. Behind, in the snow-filled encampment of misery, were Marguerite, Herman and Heinz. Marguerite had refused to leave her bedridden husband, although Christian had begged her to save herself. Why Heinz stayed, Christian did not know. He could have walked out. He suspected Heinz intended to rifle through the belongings, having believed rumors that there was a fortune in gold left behind.

The trail was well tracked as there had been no fresh snow since Christian's men crossed two days earlier. He tried to hurry the group. Always, looming over them was the threat of a storm. They had to lead the survivors out of danger while the weather held.

Two rescued bullwhackers each carried one of the smaller children but were weak and could barely keep up. Women carried their babies or toddlers, Christian carried a three-year-old and herded three walkers, all under the age of seven and one as young as four. Christian gave Saxby a child to carry, a task he took up reluctantly. Saxby resented Christian's leadership of the rescue and was still angry over his missing gold.

Christian encouraged the children, hoping the escape group could make twelve miles a day and reach Sutter's in a week. As they trudged through the snow, Christian told them stories to keep the tired little tykes walking west. He lifted the youngest walker over the steep pitches and at times carried her along with his other little burden. However, they were not making anything close to twelve miles a day; they barely covered five miles the first day and were forced by the oncoming night to camp in Summit Valley.

The next morning, each person was given a finger-sized piece of jerky to last all day, not enough food to fuel a child climbing over the Sierras, let alone an adult. The deeper snow in the valley also increased the difficulty for the young walkers.

"Keep walking, my little ducks, and look for the food I cached, food hanging on trees," Christian told them the next morning. The little walkers struggled on, their eyes on the trees, their thoughts on food—fresh bread smothered in thick butter, hot apple pie topped with cream. The promise of food kept the children shuffling forward.

The escape group moved slowly along the trail, weak from hunger. Christian, O'Malley and the two rescuers were still healthy and able to assist the others. Styles, surprisingly robust despite his months trapped at Truckee, carried a toddler. He was not much taller than the oldest child, yet his years in the coal mine had made him wiry and muscled. He did his best to keep up with the group in spite of his short legs and crooked frame.

Saxby was the enigma. He had not suffered from lack of food; he was stout and healthy, yet he could not keep up to the women and faltered carrying one small child. Christian noticed that Saxby often dropped back and placed his little burden on the trail for several minutes before picking the child up and carrying on.

"That man would grow tired carrying his blanket," Christian told Styles. "And look at you, carrying on without complaint, with that crooked back of yours, not much flesh on your bones and half Saxby's bulk."

"I'm tired, too. But I got me a chore to do, and I'se goina do it."

For his entire life, Styles had been a pariah; now, embracing the role of rescuer, he was treated with more kindness than he had ever received during his hard life. The misery of his childhood as a breaker boy in the mines, the destitution his family had suffered and the taunts from the other boys all dropped away from him as he walked across the Sierras carrying the little child in his arms, a warm bundle that filled Styles' heart with comfort.

At one time, he had gravitated to Finis, repeating the evil that had once fallen on him as a child. Now Styles found redemption in the rescue effort.

On the sixth day of the crossing, a wild storm struck the mountain pass as night fell upon them. The icy wind howled across the Pass, stinging through their wool coats and burning their faces. Christian, O'Malley and the two rescuers dug a pit and built a fire. Christian said nothing to the others, but knew that if the blizzard continued, the bag of food would be eaten and there would be no possibility of reaching the cache at Mule Springs or reaching Sutter's without someone dying of starvation.

As the adults dozed beside the fire, a six-year-old Mormon boy snuck over to the food and gorged himself on hard tack and jerky. His stomach cramped and he groaned in pain, waking the adults.

"Quick, make him vomit!" Christian stuck his finger down the boy's throat and one of the men held the child, letting his head drop. The boy gagged, vomited and moaned.

"What a stupid little ass," Saxby growled. "I suppose the little bugger ate all the food and then puked it up, leaving us to starve until we reach Mule Springs."

"I hope to find a cache, providing your so-called rescuers did not steal it," Christian said, annoyed at Saxby for his lack of compassion. "Besides, we still have a small supply to take us to Mule Springs where there are boxes of food."

"No need to blaspheme," one of the mothers told him, "especially in front of the children."

"I meant no offense, Ma'am," Saxby mumbled.

"No offense taken," the mother replied with an edge to her voice.

On the second day in the pit, the clouds dispersed and the sun glazed the ridges of the snowy Sierras. William had recovered and the last escape group ate a minute piece of jerky each and gathered up their belongings. The blizzard had ended, and the day promised to be calm and clear.

"Now, let's climb out of here and be off," Christian said. "Two days of walking and the women will cook you little ducks fresh hot biscuits and make me a pot of coffee strong enough to put hair on my chest." The big man chuckled as he lifted the youngest walkers up out of the snow cave.

One of the older walkers tried to climb out of the pit, but slipped down the icy pitch, landing near the one of the bullwhackers.

The man did not move. He had carried a child from Truckee, but the effort and the months of starvation were too much. During the night he had ceased breathing.

"We can't carry all the children," Saxby insisted. "Leave one here. If we try to carry them all, none of us will make it to Sutter's. Be sensible, Christian."

"We will bring them all out, and that is the end of it. I will hear no more." Christian felt a shiver run through his chest at the thought of losing even one of the children he felt so responsible for.

"I agree with Christian," one of the mothers added. "Too many children died at Truckee. These must be saved. With the Lord's help, we will carry them all to safety."

"I, for one, will not be held up." Saxby placed the two-year-old girl he'd been carrying on the snow and without another word left the group, heading out to civilization.

"I did not expect much from Saxby," Christian said, "but refusing his duty? How could he? The little we asked of him has unmanned him."

"This trail of sorrow tests us, bringing out the worst in men like Saxby and bringing out the best in others." She smiled at Christian, wondering why this man who had no children or wife would risk his life to rescue them.

"I will try to carry another child," the youngest mother offered, although she already carried her six-month-old. "The elephant follows us, but we won't let it harm another child."

"That is good of you," he said, smiling at the young woman.

They left the dead man in the pit, covering him with the remaining wood before piling snow into the cave. "Rest in peace," Christian said solemnly.

"God be with you. Amen," echoed the others, many with tears in their eyes. This was a man who had driven their oxen across hundreds of miles, laughed with them, and shared their pain. A big strong man, so suddenly taken down. If this man could perish so quickly, what about the little ones, struggling along the trail with only a morsel to eat?

Christian carried a toddler in his strong arms and a child on his back. He looked back at the young ones who followed in his tracks. "You little ducks," Christian said to the three, a big grin on his handsome face, "one more sleep, and we will have bags of food."

Christian was of average height, but his back was broad and muscular. The rigors of the trail had strengthened him, ridding his body of the extra weight he'd gained while working as a successful New York solicitor, enjoying dinners at expensive 5th Avenue restaurants. Now in his late twenties, he had regained the youthful endurance he'd had during his years at Oxford when he climbed in the Alps each summer and rowed on the Thames. While O'Malley and the two rescuers puffed and paused on the steep pitches, Christian's stride was almost effortless as he carried and assisted children up the steep ascent.

The trail dipped into ravines and rose steeply up the undulating ridges of the Sierras. Christian could see that the young mother struggled trying to carry two children, and took the toddler from her. Christian now had the care of three toddlers too young to walk, and the three walkers. Six children in all. As the sun dipped below the ridges, the youngest walker could no longer move from one deep foot hole to the next. He already had two children in his arms and one on his back, but Christian knelt down.

"Climb on my back, little duck, and the turtle will give you a ride up the mountain." The other two stood waiting to see what would happen.

"You little ducks, keep walking up the trail, but stay together and look after each other. I will come back and pick you up. When you tire, sit on the snow and eat your piece of meat. Don't worry,

I won't leave you behind. Will you be brave little ducks while I am away?"

The children nodded and watched Christian stride up the steep pitch with his burden of children.

Christian walked for a mile at a pace twice as fast as the main group. He put the four children down, gave each a piece of jerky and walked back for the other two. He found them sitting on the trail, making little snowmen and laughing.

"My little ducks," Christian told the six youngsters as they rested with the main group of hikers, "if my back were broad enough, I would carry all six of you, and in no time we would see the green fields of California and you will be fed apple pie and drink milk, rich in cream. It is time for me to carry three of you little ducks forward and leave three of you resting on the trail, with the man in the moon to look after you."

The children looked up through the clear night at the half moon.

"While I am away, promise you will look after each other." The three staying back nodded and smiled. The children loved their broad-shouldered rescuer and he them. Christian left the three toddlers on the trail and walked west with his burden of three children.

He worried about leaving the little ones on the trail as night enclosed the mountain, but he hid his worries from the children, thinking only that they had to reach Mule Springs that night, where there was food to nourish the survivors and mules to carry them to Sutter's. Christian soon reached the vanguard hikers, left the three children in their care, and hurried back.

Christian covered the distance fast, leaping along the trail, now solid in the cold night. He was anxious and the light was dim, making it difficult to spot the children ahead on the trail. Finally, he saw them lying motionless on the snow.

"My God! No!" Christian ran to them, an overwhelming pain of worry in his chest, but before he reached them, one of the boys stirred, sat up and smiled sleepily. They were alive!

Christian scooped them up, two in his strong arms and the oldest on his back. It was pleasant for him to feel their reassuring weight on him. In no time, he'd retraced his steps and reached the main group resting beside the trail.

"If you three walk, we will reach the food before morning," Christian said to the three oldest of his charges. The moon dropped below the snow-clad peaks as they struggled west. The last mile was slow and tortuous for the weak adults and the small children, but they kept going. As the tired group shuffled along under a sky of dazzling stars, the leader spotted people ahead, sitting beside the trail.

"It's McNair and his family," O'Malley told them. "They will be wanting food and encouragement to get them moving on."

Dorothy stood to greet them. She held the baby, and three curly heads popped up from their seats on the snow. Now there was one more child too young to walk. It was clear McNair was too sick to carry the child. He was wrapped in a blanket and stood up, shaking from the cold.

"You can't carry the McNair children," one of the six children pouted. "You carry us, not them."

"Only the youngest McNair needs a piggy back," Christian said.

"I'll carry the McNair child." It was Styles, the most unlikely rescuer.

"Not you," Christian said warm-heartedly. "You are doing your share. I will take another child." Christian sat on his haunches to let the youngest McNair child climb on his back. Billy and his five-year-old brother walked with the other three little ones, all proud that they could carry on.

"There it is, my little ducks!" Christian told them, in an emotional voice. "Do you see the mules and the shed filled with food?" Christian's heart filled with relief, and his voice choked with emotion. *The children will live!* "There are boxes of food there, and those mules will carry you out of the mountains." They reached Mule Springs as the first rays of sun lit the summit of the Sierras.

Relief surged through the tired survivors. Food and rest and the end of starvation. Christian and Styles handed out hard tack and raisins, and O'Malley and the two hired men erected tents and handed out blankets. Soon the survivors were asleep, warm and content, thoughts of a hot breakfast in their minds. It would be the first nourishing food the survivors had had for months.

The exhausted hikers slept until the warm spring sun blazed through the canvas tents. The women made biscuits and brewed tea, coffee and hot chocolate, insisting that the survivors eat small portions. They rested for a day, and the following morning they prepared for the journey out of the snow. Christian and O'Malley helped the children and the weaker adults onto the mules. The trail dropped down into the green Sacramento Valley. Their ordeal was over.

The escape group reached Sutter's Fort as the spring sun melted the snow on the western slopes of the Sierras. Alice and Mary now worked at the fort as cooks and were charged with the care of the survivors. At first they only allowed the starved people soup and porridge. Then, as the survivors gained strength, Alice brewed thick meat stews, sweet currant cakes and apple pies topped with cream. Baking and cooking at the fort deadened only a shred of the pain that engulfed her every waking hour.

Chapter Twenty-four
The Yana Slaughter

Word of gold reached Sutter's Fort in the spring of 1847. Men dropped their farm tools, sailors abandoned their ships, and clerks packed in their jobs, all heading east to the gold strike.

"I'm for the gold creeks," Finis told Sutter. Saxby, following his aborted rescue attempt, had immediately made his way to Yerba Buena to purchase supplies on credit. He, too, was drawn in by the fevered promise of endless gold.

Farmers and gold seekers alike gathered at a farm on the fertile land along the Sacramento River. Higgingbottom, the owner, had been railing about the Indians going on the warpath, and had Saxby and Finis, among many others, worked up. Along with Saxby were Horace and Ferris, the two men Saxby had brought with him across the mountains, the men who'd taken money from Marguerite and rescued no one.

"The savages are all gathering up there at the headwaters, starting some kind of war dance," the farmer told them. "Neighbors here been telling us we gotta take action, or we'll be wiped out and have our scalps hanging from some buck's lance."

"How do you know they are planning to attack the settlers?" Robert asked. He now worked for Sutter and had been tasked with driving a mule train to the gold-bearing streams. He took a cautious approach to Indian fighting, caution he had learned from David and Christian.

"Them Injuns will be attacking us," Higgingbottom repeated. "They're having a war dance up there on the Sacramento headwaters."

"Sure, the Blackfoot have terrorized the plains, but in Bedford, where I come from, we farm while the Assiniboine hunt and trap nearby. There need be no war between settler and tribesman."

"You are too young, kid, and know nothing," the farmer told Robert, in a condescending tone. "This here is the wild west, boy, and I don't plan on having my family killed by no Injun. Farmer Lassen and his neighbors are palavering with that Captain Freemont, the one they call the Pathfinder. Some say he has Kit Carson with him, a man that knows something about Injuns killing. We are asking him to take his men to that Indian camp and wipe out them savages."

The prospect of warring against the Indians immediately got the attention of Saxby and Finis. Finis had been hankering for another chance to kill Indians, and Saxby saw himself as a land baron who had to drive the Indians out of the fertile Sacramento Valley if farming was to prosper. Alice's false accusations against him rankled, but he would reclaim her and she would bear him many children. He was convinced that he would be an important member of the new state of California, with land holdings and a reputation greater than Sutter's.

"You give us horses, and we'll git ourselves up there and help out," Finis offered. "What you say?"

"Since I got myself a bum arm and wun't be no use shootin', you all are welcome," Higgingbottom told them, leading Finis to the corral.

The planned attack would take place in the valley of the peaceful Yana, who were celebrating the return of the salmon. It was this gathering of the three tribes at the headwaters of the Sacramento that had frightened the settlers and angered the gold seekers.

The farmers who had recently settled in the valley were seeing hundreds of Indians travelling up the river valley heading in the direction of the settlers' newly established farms and feared that they were preparing to attack. Farmers from Illinois, Iowa and Missouri never seemed to learn how to spot when an Indian was approaching to trade or to kill. Many of the new settlers and miners brought with them a shoot-first-and-ask-later attitude.

Saxby and Finis, along with a group of farmers and miners, rode east to join Captain Freemont and his army contingent. Finis, who thought the only good Indian was a dead Indian, would get his chance to kill and mutilate.

Kiowa, the Yana Chief's wife, and her young daughter, Blackberry, were gathering fiddleheads when they saw the soldiers cresting the hilltop above the Yana village. Kiowa grabbed Blackberry and pulled her deep into the bushes.

"Hide, and if I don't return, run to Sutter's and then find your way to the mission at Yerba Buena. You are a Christian. Tell them. They will protect you."

Kiowa ran for the encampment, screaming as she reached the first of the houses. "Soldiers! Hundreds of them! Not just soldiers but others, all armed!"

There were no warriors to take up arms; they were not a war tribe, they were fishermen, hunters and acorn and berry gatherers.

"It must be Freemont," the Chief told his council. "He's been camped at Lassen's farm. But why would he be armed and ready to fight?" The Yana chief searched through the house, looking not for his musket but for a way to save his people.

"Ah, there it is. I don't have an American flag, but a white flag that Freemont will honor." The Chief held up the flag, sure that he enjoyed protection.

A few of the younger braves had muskets. They were mounted and looked anxiously up the hill where the militia formed up. The women gathered their children into the houses, while the older men took up lances forming a second wave behind the young men on horses. The Chief walked through the line of young horsemen, speaking in a calm voice, telling them that soldiers would not attack someone holding a flag of peace. He knew about these matters.

An old Yana woman held her blue-eyed grandson in her arms. She watched the militia and renegades, her heart pounding in fear. She kissed her grandson on his fair hair, her eyes teary. She had no faith that a white flag would stop the militia.

The ground was to the advantage of the soldiers, armed farmers, miners and sundry recruits. Freemont had positioned his raiding party on the hillside above the tongue of land at the bend in the river and watched through his spyglass as the Chief moved ahead of the young horsemen.

"He's waving a white flag, Freemont," a young soldier informed his captain.

"It's a ruse," Freemont replied and gave the order to fire.

From the high ground, the trained and well-armed militia rained bullets down on the Yana. The Chief holding the white flag was the first to fall. The advance guard mowed down the mounted young braves and, in the second volley, slaughtered the older men.

"Men, do your duty!" Freemont ordered.

Soldiers, miners and farmers stormed down the hillside into the village. The raiding party rode into the camp, sabers raised. They cut down anyone still standing and set fire to the village. Mothers with babes in their arms and children at their skirts escaped from the burning houses only to be cut down by gunfire and sabers. Among the dead were the old grandmother and the small boy with fair hair.

Blackberry did not run for safety. *How could I leave my parents and my little brothers and sisters?*

A greasy-looking man raised his pistol and shot Kiowa as she fled. Blackberry ran to her mother, crying out her name, but it was too late to save Kiowa. The man stood over her mother, blood dripping from his knife. Held in his hand was the pudenda sliced off Kiowa.

Blackberry wailed in anguish and fell to the ground beside her mother's butchered body. The young girl was defenseless against the raiders. Two men grabbed her arms and lashed her wrists with a rawhide rope.

"I'm taking her first!" Finis yelled. "I ain't had myself no cunt for months."

The greasy-haired miner held the young girl and watched Finis rape her. Blackberry wept, her eyes wild with fear and disgust. Before the miner could take his turn, a soldier interrupted.

"Get off that girl! We kill Indians on the warpath. We don't rape their women." He aimed a weathered boot at Finis, tumbling him off the terrified girl.

"There wouldn't be any nits left," Finis complained. "You think we was goin'a to let her live?"

"Exactly what we will do. Let her go so she can tell the tribes what happened here, and maybe they will have the good sense to move out of the valley."

"We should kill her and take her breasts and that thing between her legs," Finis mutinously told the militia man. "Them trophies fetch a good price. Folks'll pay money to see a piece of Indian hangin' on a nail on the wall. I see you got yourself some scalps. Why you want to meddle with our fun?"

"There has been more than enough butchery here," Finis was told bluntly. "We took a river of blood for the spoonful they took from us. I am sick to my stomach." A survival instinct urged Finis that meddling with the tough-looking ranger would end with his own blood spilt on this field, so he did nothing but scowl as Blackberry was seen off by the soldier.

"Who is that? How does he get off bossing us around?" Finis piped up, once the man was out of earshot.

"Maybe Carson. Looks like him anyhows," the greasy-looking man said. "Met him back on the Sante Fe trail once. He is an Indian killer alright, but they say he's gone soft on 'em. Lost his nerve for killin'."

The soldiers, farmers, miners and recruits saddled up and left the killing ground. Fires burned throughout the village but, aside from the crackle of the flames, there was not a sound to be heard. Not even a dog whimpered. Blackberry didn't move from where the soldier had left her. She lay in the bushes, curled into a ball, too traumatized to make a sound. Eventually she crawled away, staggered to her feet and walked to Yerba Buena. She was the last living Yana. She found her way to the mission in the city that would soon be called San Francisco, where a kind minister welcomed her into his family to be a big sister to Ruth and a little sister to Addie.

Sutter sheltered and cared for the Sierra survivors until they were healthy enough to travel. The McNairs and Alice remained at the fort working for Sutter, filling in for the men who'd abandoned their jobs to join the gold rush.

Alice had always been a hard worker, but now there was far more work than workers. She ate little and slept only a few hours each night. Alice was a favorite of Sutter, a Swiss man who admired hard workers. It was Sutter who met the tall guide at the gate of the fort.

"Ah, another one of the travelers that cross the country. Welcome to America." Sutter stood at the large gate, one of the two entrances that led to the interior of the fort. David dismounted from his stallion to stand outside the high, white-washed walls that enclosed the fort.

"So the Americans defeated the Mexicans," David said as he stood at the big gate to the fort.

"It matters not to me. Mexicans, Americans," Sutter went on in his Germanic accent, "as long as they leave me my fort and let me do business. What I need now are strong men to work for me. It's spring, and we need to plant crops. Guess where the men are?"

"I know, Sutter. They are off to the gold creeks. I did not come here to work. I made good money on my last trip on the Oregon Trail and north to the San Juan Islands. I am here to look for the survivors of the McNair party."

"Then you've come to the right place! But please don't take away my hard-working women," he smiled.

"I am searching for Mrs. Chablis?"

"No one of that name here," Sutter said impatiently, anxious to return to his office and his ledgers.

"Alice."

Sutter looked at David, sizing him up.

"That bastard of a husband of hers hung around pestering to see her. I sent him packing along with the other good-for-nothings he hired for his so-called rescue. I'll send you packing as well if you come here to cause her more pain. Tell me why you should see Alice."

"I was the guide on the wagon train that took her as far as The Parting of the Ways. I worried about her when Saxby chose to take a wagon train across the salt flats. How is she?"

"She lost her daughter and is gravely wounded, not in a physical sense but in her soul. A good worker, but never have I seen a sadder person. She cries each night. I caution you; she is not healed. No stranger sees her without my approval. She is fragile and in my care."

"Please tell Alice I am here. She will see me."

Sutter looked carefully at David and nodded his head. "Step inside the fort; I will talk to her." Sutter walked across the open courtyard, dust swirling in the hot sun. Inside and opposite the south gate, David saw a two-story building that appeared to contain an office on the second floor. Sutter did not go to the office, but walked to the right, passing an outdoor oven before making his way to a row of buildings against the exterior wall. David inhaled the smell of freshly baked bread wafting across the yard.

David watched as Alice emerged from one of the rooms and walked slowly towards him, crossing the open yard. She was thinner, but even more beautiful. He removed his hat as she approached.

"Oh, Alice. My God. What has happened?"

Alice was too traumatized to speak but fell into David's arms sobbing.

"Your daughter. Tell me, Alice." He took the kerchief from his neck and gently wiped her tears.

"I couldn't save her," she sobbed. "My dearest child collapsed and couldn't carry on. I tried to put sugar in her mouth to revive her, but I failed."

"Oh, my poor, poor Alice. I can't imagine what you and the others have endured."

"The unspeakable has happened. My soul will never mend. I live, and that is all. My life is over." Alice lowered her head, grief lining her face.

"Alice, please don't give up. Sutter told me the McNairs all survived, and that is a good thing." Alice gave a choked sob, a dead look on her face. David understood.

"I must go to my wife's village. I have not seen my son for a year, and I worry about him."

"Yes, you should go. Robert returned from the headwaters with word of trouble between the farmers and the tribes. Ask Sutter. He has the latest news. Take care of your son, and may God watch over you." Alice felt safe with David. He would comfort her and not make any demands.

David shared a meal with the McNairs and Sutter, listening to Dorothy and McNair describe their escape and the suffering of those trapped. Alice remained in her room.

"Christian was our savior," Dorothy told him. "I have trouble choosing between Jesus and Christian as the greatest savior. His mother named him correctly. He carried out the children, and refused to leave anyone behind. Dreadful, unspeakable things happened, David, but there were courageous people like Christian who saved us."

"Where is this man who walks on water?" David asked, the hint of a smile in his eyes.

"Christian left for Oregon City, and Robert followed. Christian told us he was disgusted with the treatment of the tribes, and Sutter has hired Robert to pack supplies to the gold diggings. Robert made good money working here for Sutter, but the boy wants to read the law, so Christian took him on as an apprentice. Christian will be opening an office in Oregon City."

Sutter shook his head briefly at the mention of Robert, as if the thought of missing out on his continued labor pained him.

"What of the Truckee survivors? Are they all safely across the mountains?" David persisted.

"Herman and his wife stayed behind; I can't believe they would have survived long. Marguerite stood by him, sacrificing herself so he would not die alone. Christian saved their three girls."

"Then there is Heinz," Dorothy continued. "They say he stayed to eat the dead, steal from the dead and maybe even kill to eat. The Lord may forgive us for saving our children, but someone who kills to survive will face hellfire. What horrors befell us and all because of that scoundrel, Saxby! He and that lowlife Finis joined up with Freemont against the Indians, as if the murdering fiend hadn't caused enough suffering already."

"What Indian tribe?" David's voice was tense, his entire body alert.

"The Yana," Sutter told him, in his Germanic accent.

"Tell me, man," David demanded in a frantic voice. He'd leaned forward towards Sutter, startling the man. "In the name of God, what happened?"

"Freemont, along with the farmers and miners, raided the village. They saw the Indians gathering at the river to celebrate the spring salmon run. The newcomers are ignorant of the Indian ways, and Freemont is a bloody murderer. Freemont had other reasons, or so he says. One of his men had his skull opened up by a Klamath warrior, but the so called Pathfinder had to take out his revenge on innocent women, children and old men of the peaceful Yana. Are you alright?"

"His little son is there," Dorothy informed Sutter, her voice a whisper.

"I am so sorry," Sutter told David. "They are all dead. All except one young girl who fled."

"They killed everyone?" David moaned, standing up, his hand on his brow. "Those bastards! Those Indian-haters! My little boy! How could this happen to peaceful people?" David stumbled across the room, shaking his head in anguish.

"One survived. One young girl," Sutter said again. "She came to the fort, weeping and distraught. Her entire family, her entire tribe wiped out. Alice cared for her before the girl left for Yerba Buena. I gave the girl a horse, and Alice told her to find Reverend Appleton. You remember Addie? They took the young girl in. The good Reverend already has three Sioux children. The Yana girl will fit right in and be a good little sister to Addie."

"One person out of a village of forty peaceful Yana, people who fish and grow potatoes!" David cried. "People who never fight."

He fell to the floor, weeping and pounding his fists until his knuckles bled.

When he came to his senses, David left Sutter's to make his way to the village to see for himself. He rode hard, a faint hope burning in his heart.

He smelled the smoke before he saw the village, but he still rode down the hill through the charred remains of the houses and into the stench of the dead. It was a killing field. He found his four-year-old son, his little face hardly recognizable from the shotgun blast.

David buried his son and rode for the Sierras. At the summit, he stopped for a day to gather the bones of the victims of the Sierra disaster. He buried them and planted a cross. So much suffering and misery in a single year, and for what?

He rode past the Truckee cabins without stopping. Only one man had survived over the winter, and Heinz was not someone David could bear to see. After the death camp of Truckee, David traveled north up the Humboldt Valley and then east on the Oregon Trail, heading back to Kanesville to guide another wagon train.

News of the gold in California creeks reached the other states. Thousands of miners stampeded west to the gold fields, and thousands of settlers took to the Oregon Trail, driven by the promise of free land in the territory America had grabbed from the British. Experienced guides like David were in demand.

I will not turn into a killer to avenge my loved ones.

Alice learned that David's son had been slaughtered, news that sent her deeper into depression. She kept up with her work, but spoke to no one. When left alone one day, she took David's pistol from the dresser and cleaned the gun, comforted by the sweet, oily smell of the Colt and the cool, smooth surface of the steel. She moved the revolver to one of the four loaded chambers and lifted the gun to her mouth.

Chapter Twenty-five

Settling In
Oregon City, Oregon

North in Oregon City, Anna and Jan enjoyed the warmth of the long spring day, sitting on the porch of their restaurant, watching fairy fingers of pink clouds stretching across the western sky. While most of the emigrants who traveled with them on the Oregon Trail were busy in the fields planting their first crop on the rich soil of Willamette Valley, Anna and Jan discussed their thriving restaurant business.

On their arrival, Anna and Jan immediately understood that what Oregon City needed was a restaurant that served good food. Although Anna disliked cooking, she was a smart entrepreneur. They used the last of their savings to invest in a building, and within a week the Emigrant Cafe was open for business. During the first month in Oregon, Jan pitched in as the chef and Anna served food and washed dishes. Once the business was established, Anna hired a cook and servers, and Jan found a job in the bank. While most of their companions on the Swede wagon train prospered in the new land, some failed, and others could not wait to take a boat back to the States.

Penelope arrived, angry at Walter and bitter over his rejection. She never saw herself or her ways as the cause of the break up and continued to blame Walter. She'd even convinced herself that it had been Walter's idea to emigrate to the West. Now, at twenty-eight, she would have to return to her parents without the intricate quilt her mother had made for her as a wedding present. Even worse, she would have to admit that Walter had never married her.

Penelope boarded a boat in Portland and sailed south around the Horn, planning to return to her family in Springfield. Anna wondered if the needy woman would be welcomed back to her parents' home, but at least Walter was making a life for himself in the new land.

"Jan, can you ask Walter to sell me enough wood to build a good-sized bunkhouse? Each day, I have at least one miner asking me where he can find a room to rent, and there just aren't any. What would you think if I had some rooms built?"

"Soon you will own all of Oregon City. Remember though, don't work Louise too hard. That girl has her studies on top of waiting table and the care of those two rapscallions." Louise now attended the County Female Seminary and still cared for her brothers, along with waitressing in the Emigrant Cafe.

"Jan, you just look after our money in the bank, and I will look after the business. I'm fair to the workers, Jan, more than fair. I've even been giving Louise a little something to take to her mother. She walks to the asylum every week, although I doubt Charlotte is sane enough to recognize her own daughter."

~

Anna and Jan were well settled in Oregon City when two survivors from the Sierra Crossing sought them out.

"Christian, I hear you are the saviour of the Sierra rescue," Anna said warmly, hugging the big-shouldered man. "And you, Robert, with your black suit and vest, a fine young man you are! You've left behind the skinny lad who ran from the Missouri River to catch up to the wagon train to ask David for a job."

"Christian has taken me on as apprentice so I can read the law. When I come of age, I hope to be a solicitor."

"Robert studies all night and toils for me in the office all day. He's smart as a whip, that boy," Christian said, smiling. "However, it is hard to get him to show customers his disarming smile." Christian cuffed Robert on his arm.

"I'm smiling at the sight of you two," Robert pointed out, opening his arms to embrace Anna and then shaking Jan's hand.

Anna and Jan knew better than to mention Annabelle Lee. The pain of his loss still clearly marked Robert's handsome face.

"So, what is the latest news in our new state of Oregon?" Christian asked.

"Being a law man, you likely know that the boundary between Oregon and the Brits was settled the year we arrived." Jan placed his hand on his forehead, trying to remember other news that might be of interest. "Since the Whitman Mission was attacked, and his family and those poor Sager children murdered by the Cayuse, there's been hell to pay. Settlers are killing the first Indian they see, Indians are being herded off their land to make way for farmers, and now the tribes are fighting back. It is a sorry situation that will only get worse."

"The Cayuse who attacked the Whitman Mission should be brought to trial, but whites who kill innocent Indians should also face justice. The United States extended the North West Ordinance to protect Indians, and that is now the law in Oregon," Christian told them.

"What about Oregon's Law of Land Claims?" Robert asked. "I read that it is illegal because it allows settlers to take up a section of land without considering the use of the land by Indians."

"If you talk like that on the streets of Oregon City," Jan replied darkly, "they will laugh in your face, or worse, take you down a dark alley and give you a hiding. The settlers are delighted that Congress raised a regiment of the Mounted Riflemen to protect wagon trains from Indian attacks, but they will ignore the law that supposedly protects Indians from being killed without cause."

"Jan and I love it here, but we don't support herding Indians onto reservations and sending the poor starving souls eight hundred miles across the desert. The Oregon Tribes are being removed from the coast and sent to the other side of the Cascades."

"The militia is relocating all the coastal tribes, sending them east to land no one wants. Did you hear about the Trail of Tears? Kit Carson was along on that tragic march. The old Indian-killer switched horses in mid-stride, saying the Government's treatment of the Indians was inhumane. He had to obey his commander, of course, but he later said that removing Indians from their lands and sending them to a reservation, where they could not hunt or fish, would kill them."

"Oregon is not all that bad. They voted to abolish slavery in the new state," Anna told them. "At least we will not have that abomination. Did you know that my family had slaves back in Washington? I was too young to think anything about it, and my nanny and our gardener were welcome at the dinner table with us. It was only when I was a young woman and learned about the atrocities of slavery—the beatings, men, women and children in chains, babies taken from their mothers...." Anna gulped a breath before continuing. "Even worse, the Church of England says nothing from the pulpit about slave owners breeding black babies for sale."

"Now that Anna has started, we will get an earful about slavery." Jan raised his hands in a mock gesture of frustration.

"We should all know what is going on," Anna proclaimed, launching into her story. "Have you heard the story of Burns, the fugitive slave from Virginia who was beaten almost to death and fled his master?" Anna did not wait for an answer, but continued relating the story ardently.

"He stowed away in a boat going north and ended up in Boston, the Cradle of Liberty. The slave owner had posted a reward for his capture, and a greedy good-for-nothing turned the young fellow into the authorities. The law allows slaves to be captured in slave-free states, even though most northerners abhor slavery. They marched Burns in chains through the streets of Boston, where thousands of anti-slavery protestors watched the young black man dragged onto a boat destined for Virginia, where he was put in a slave pen and whipped to the point of near death. Boston people paid for his rescue, but it was too late for Burns. He fled to Canada and died shortly afterwards, a victim of this country's inhumane laws. 'My bones are my own.' Those were his last words to his Boston rescuer."

"Anna is passionate about anti-slavery," Jan said. "In Washington, all Anna's parents talk about is the slavery question. Adding California to the Union brought the issue to the forefront, with northerners accusing Polk of grabbing California to expand slavery from Texas to New Mexico and all of the Sunshine State."

"My father is deeply involved in Washington politics, and keeps us up to date with the issues back home, although his letters travel for an entire year to reach us."

"A year! Why so long?" Robert asked. "If the letter came on the Oregon Trail, it would arrive in a few months. Am I right?"

"Yes, Robert, but until they get the Pony Express operating, the mail goes by ship to Panama, fifty miles overland by mule, rail to San Francisco and boat up the Pacific Coast to Oregon," Anna explained raising her hands in frustration.

"In his last letter," Anna continued, "he wrote that it meant everything to Polk to expand north into British Territory and then win California. But did Polk appreciate the men who fought the Mexicans? No! He distanced himself from that war. Deceit walks boldly through the halls of Congress, according to Papa."

"Anna, you might be interested to know that I defended a woman enslaved in Oregon, even though the State had abolished slavery. I successfully sued for her freedom."

"Well, bless you, Christian. Your good deeds continue! You are the savior of the Sierras and of the dispossessed." Anna smiled warmly and looked at him, sizing him up. "You are also a handsome-looking man. How is it that a fine man like you is not married?"

"I like women fine, but I get little return of it. I was married for five years, but we divorced. My wife was a beauty and enjoyed her life of tennis and riding. She cared naught for children, and told me that a family would marinate her in milk and tears. I did not insist on children, nor did I restrict her in any way, but the unfaithful woman ran off with her riding instructor. I have no wish to be entangled again." Christian raised his muscled arms in resignation.

"Oh, Christian. Life takes many turns," Anna said with a smile. "As sure as God made little green apples, you will find a true and faithful love. I promise you."

Chapter Twenty-six

Sutter's Fort
California

Alice moved her finger onto the trigger, and placed the gun in her mouth.

"Don't you do that, Mrs. Chablis! You best not play with a gun." It was Billy, who had walked into the kitchen to see what Alice was preparing for dinner. At the young age of nine, he was a considerate child. His mother often told Billy of his brush with death and of Annabelle Lee's sacrifice, and his trials had turned him from a regular, carefree boy into a thoughtful lad, sensitive to the pain of others.

"Amelia and Annabelle Lee, they were my friends and now they are gone. Maybe you suffer because you think we disturbed Amelia's body when we were in the snow camp. It is not true, Mrs. Chablis. We covered her with piles of snow, and my little brothers and I placed branches over her grave and built her a cross. Amelia whispered to me from Heaven, telling me to look after you. She told me to be like Annabelle Lee and save the sick and the sad people."

Alice lowered the gun. Yes, she had believed that Amelia had been cannibalized, a thought that disturbed her sleep, that had filled her every day with anguish. Knowing now that this was not so gave her more than relief, it marked the beginning of her healing. A large slice of her pain left her.

She looked at Billy, overwhelmed with relief. Here was a child sent to save her, to prevent her from committing an egregious sin.

"Oh, Billy!" Alice cried, throwing her arms around the boy and choking with emotion. "I won't hurt myself. It is wrong to take a life, even if it be thy own."

She pressed the little boy against her chest, weeping for the beloved daughter she'd buried in the Sierra Mountains. Billy did not mind at all to have Alice's arms about him.

"You'll get better, Mrs. Chablis. It will help you to have a good cry." He patted her back to comfort the distraught woman.

From that day on, Billy shadowed Alice like a protective dog. He comforted her, gauged her emotions and cheered her up when she seemed depressed. Alice was most content when she cooked; she loved preparing delicious food and serving it. Billy often watched her working in the kitchen because he loved good food. Despite his age, he had a keen sense of flavors and spices and often made suggestions about what to add to the stews or soups.

"Mrs. Chablis, you must make those meat pies you made for us on my birthday after we walked over the Pass. I know it is a lot of work, but I will help you."

The ordeal at Truckee and on the Sierra crossing did not leave any visible marks on the McNair family. Billy had become more sensitive, while his three younger brothers remained carefree and happy. McNair was loud and jovial, and Dorothy was content with her work at the fort, surrounded by her four healthy boys. It was as if the tragedy had never happened to the parents.

Over the following winter, Alice recovered enough to join in conversation at the table. Once again, it was Billy who intervened. Alice was about to eat by herself in the kitchen when Billy took her hand and gently led her into the mess hall. Here, it was noisy with the sound of forks on dishes and lively conversation. She sat at the long wooden table beside Dorothy and the youngest McNair child, now a big toddler with a loud, demanding voice.

Alice was still slim as a willow, but she regained her strength working in the fields and cooking for Sutter. She often thought about David, worried that he might seek revenge for the death of his son, for the unforgivable and brutal massacre of the peaceful Yana. Alice believed that men who suffered loss or fear were more likely to hate and settle scores, while women who have lost their loved ones tumbled into a well of despair. She hoped he would not become a killer.

More than a year passed before David returned to the fort.

He found Alice in the kitchen kneading bread, her hands sticky with dough and a dusting of flour on her cheek. She wore a white apron over a blue smock of plain homespun. A strand of dark hair fell loosely over her forehead.

"You look well, Alice. Stronger, and I must say more beautiful. California sunshine must be good for you." He wanted to hold her in his arms, but David sensed that while Alice wanted her friends about her, she would reject intimacy.

"I am so very sorry about your son." She wiped her hands on the kitchen towel and tucked the strand of hair under her bonnet. "Please join us for coffee in the mess hall and tell me how are you managing?"

"I keep moving. I've crossed this country so many times I could guide through the dead of night with a blindfold over my eyes and still not miss a river crossing or a steep hill. I've just come from Oregon City. I have a message for you," David told her, as they walked out into the bright sunshine to cross the yard to the mess hall.

They sat at one of the long wooden tables that held a metal jug of hot coffee. Alice poured the coffee and sat down across from David.

"What is the message?" Alice asked, looking at his tanned face and noticing new lines at the corners of his mouth. She thought he was the finest looking man she knew. Ruggedly tough, yet handsome.

"Anna and Jan are in Oregon City, and Anna is feeding the miners. She is busy making money and asks that you come to Oregon and work for her. If she is able to find employees for her business, she will make even more money, and rival McLoughlin in terms of wealth and property."

"Who is McLoughlin?"

"You will meet him when you get there. They call him the Lion of the North. A big man in the Hudson's Bay Company. With the fur trade disappearing, McLoughlin put his mind to building Oregon City. He owns the grocery store, sawmill, gristmill and shipbuilding, and likely most of the land in the city."

"I care little for men who are rich and powerful, but I do hope to see my friends again. What about Carreena?"

"She went north to Fort Victoria. We heard she is Swede's intended."

"The aristocratic, independent woman marrying a rough-around-the-edges sailor! I never would have guessed those two would be attracted to each other. Christian with his fine language and manners, yes, but Swede who could swear like a..." Alice paused and chuckled. "I was going to say drunken sailor, but he really is a sailor."

"Robert and Christian are also in Oregon City, and they send their love. Their law firm does well. Christian has a farm, and Robert hopes to put in for his land claim when he comes of age. McNair has also told me he plans to move to Oregon City. You should go too and be with your friends. Anna needs workers and misses you."

"I would like to see Anna again, but I am not ready." Alice hesitated, thinking that the days on the trail before leaving with Saxby on the cutoff were the only happy days she had enjoyed since her fateful marriage to Saxby. She missed the feelings she had had, the love she'd once felt for David and her enjoyment of Anna's friendship.

"Maybe next year. I am safe here. Sutter must be like that Lion of the North. He has immense land holdings, but he is not one to look to his baubles. He is generous to a fault, taking in the survivors, feeding us and looking out for my wellbeing. Sutter protects me and won't let Saxby through the gate."

"You haven't told me what happened to Saxby," David said, a grim look on his face. "I am not sure where he landed. I hope in Hell, and if he isn't, I would like to send him there."

"He has a ranch in the Sacramento Valley, thousands of acres of land. He is like the devil cat. Despite all the deaths he caused, it appears he will land on his feet. He threatened me, saying I must come and live on his holdings. Be a true wife. Never! Never!"

"I wish I could put a bullet in his miserable skull. He was with Freemont and the murdering scum who massacred my family and were never held accountable for their crime, but if I kill Saxby for massacring my son, the law will hang me." A hard look crossed David's face.

"Please don't turn vengeful. I could not bear it if something happened to you." Alice's face softened, and tears pooled in her eyes. She paused, the pain of her loss returned, and her mouth tightened. "Of course, I would not shed a tear if Saxby died, and I hope never to look on his evil face ever again. He is a monster. He was responsible for the unthinkable tragedy. My soul will never heal. Some mornings I wake up, and wish I were dead." Alice's despondency enveloped her again, as it had since the day she lost Amelia.

"I want you to live and once more be the woman I first met on the Oregon Trail, the one with a smile on her face and hope for her future, despite the troubles with Saxby."

"That woman is gone. I cannot blame Saxby alone; I sent Amelia to her death. I did not have the courage to oppose Saxby and protect my daughter from his rash decisions. I berate myself for my submissiveness, for not standing up to him. There is more," Alice sobbed, and continued. "Did you know that Amelia asked to stay with McNairs at the top of the Pass? But I made her come with me, and led her to her death. I cannot live with myself. The McNairs survived, and if I had left Amelia in the snow cave, she would be with me today."

"Dearest Alice, please don't torment yourself. You are not to blame for Amelia's death." David looked at Alice, her eyes wet with tears and a tortured look on her beautiful face. "Come here. I need to hold you and show you there are people who love and care for you."

"Don't you be looking at me. I don't want you to remember me like this. Close your eyes and hold me close. I need comfort, like a sister needs a brother. Make the pain go away."

David enveloped Alice in his arms, then lifted her face to his and gently kissed her wet cheeks.

"I must go east to bring a wagon train across next spring. When I return to Oregon City I hope you will be there. Please take care of yourself, Alice. Do that for me. I lost my child, too. We both suffer."

David pulled a red kerchief from his vest pocket and wiped the tears from her cheeks. "There, that's better." He lifted her face to look at her. "You are strong, Alice, and if you learn to smile again, it would please me." She did not smile, but rested her head on his shoulders, feeling a sense of comfort she had not felt since Amelia's death.

"I know you can't feel anything for me now," David said, his voice soft and emotional, "but I do want to help you. I won't let Saxby take you, and I hope someday you will love again."

Chapter Twenty-seven

The New State of Oregon

Robert waited at the docks in Portland to meet survivors from the Sierra tragedy. He saw Alice disembark, followed by McNair, Dorothy and their four boys.

"Mrs. Chablis, may I carry your bags?"

"Robert, you've become a fine-looking young man," Alice said, with a warm smile. "Where's the skinny lad who helped pull our wagon out of the ruts and looked after us at Truckee?" Indeed, Robert was handsome beyond words. Now in his twenties, he attracted the attention of every young woman who chanced to look into his startling blue eyes or admire his well-tailored and slim-fitting vest and jacket.

"Looks like your family recovered from the Sierra ordeal, Mrs. McNair," Robert said to Dorothy, "and your boys, grown so tall." Billy was in his teens, tall and strong for his age. Near starvation and his brush with death hadn't stunted his growth.

"And you look very fine, Alice." Although Alice's beauty had returned, Robert could see that she still held onto the pain of losing Amelia, just as he could not forget Annabelle Lee, not for a day, not for an hour, despite the years that had passed.

That night, they gathered at Anna's restaurant for a feast. Jan and Anna did not ask about the crossing of the Sierras or the continued suffering of the survivors. They understood the experience was too raw, and that events on the trail of misery had been more than a human could bear. Christian had told Anna and Jan the tragedy suffered by the escape groups, including the murder of the two Yana and the unthinkable way in which some of the trapped people had survived.

"We welcome our friends from the Oregon Trail and thank the Lord that those of you who crossed the Sierras are with us tonight. May you find prosperity and happiness in this new land," Jan said, raising a glass to the gathering. They tipped their glasses. McNair and Dorothy joined heartily in the celebration, McNair's voice rising in volume in pace with the wine and food he consumed. Robert and Alice remained subdued; celebrating was impossible for these two survivors.

"Did you hear about the Grattan Massacre up there near Fort Laramie, and all of it started over a cow?" Jan asked them. "When David dealt with the Indians over a stolen ox, he did not let matters get out of hand."

"You siding with them savages?" McNair's voice grew even louder. "They slaughtered Grattan's men, but the army will settle with them. Indians won't get away with killing white men." McNair pounded his fist on the sturdy wooden table in Anna's dining room.

"Grattan shot Chief Conquering Bear in the back and ignored the treaty provisions," Christian reminded him.

"How'dya know that?" McNair was now worked up over the topic, his voice too loud for Alice.

"He's right," Robert added. "Under the Treaty, U.S. soldiers are not allowed to settle disputes. Conquering Bear offered a horse in place of the stolen cow, but instead of negotiating, the soldiers shot the Chief in the back. The young warriors retaliated by slaughtering the soldiers."

"Now we have Indians raiding settlers," Robert continued, "and the army wiping out Indian villages. Up on the Sacramento River,

Freemont and his militia slaughtered an entire village. They killed David's son and left only one person alive."

"My guess is that David won't be a peacemaker no more," McNair proclaimed, with a self-satisfied grin.

"David will not kill to avenge his child," Alice told them. "He would like to bring Saxby and Finis to justice, but there is no justice for those killers."

"This craziness won't stop until the Indians lose all their land," Christian added. "I don't believe it is right to steal people's land. For the last fifty years, the Hudson's Bay Company, the Asters and North West Company lived peaceably with the tribes because the Indians trapped furs and bought supplies. Now that farmers want the Indians' lands and the miners want the creeks, the Indian tribes face a choice of leaving their homeland or being killed."

"Christian represents the tribes who signed the Yakama Treaty," Robert informed them.

"I find myself across the court room from the Government," Christian explained, "reminding our own officials that they violated the Yakama Treaty a mere twelve days after it was signed. We will see more violence if we continue to let settlers move onto the Treaty lands. You would think it would be enough to move the tribes east of the Cascades, leaving all the rich land for settlers."

"They don't farm the land. They don't have title." McNair was angry, unable to understand why anyone could defend the tribes once the U.S. went to war against them.

Alice did not want to listen. She whispered her apologies to Anna and slipped out into the clear night. She knew of the slaughter at the Sacramento River and kept imagining the screams of the mothers as their children were knifed or shot. Sutter told her that Finis had bragged about the massacre, the mutilation and the children he'd shot.

"I hated it so when my rifle shattered their little bodies," Finis had told Sutter, "so I dispatched the adults with my rifle and the children with my pistol." She wanted to take the Colt David had given her and shatter his evil face.

Why can't I find peace? No war between Indians and whites. No starving, dying children.

The discussion around the dinner table continued, with McNair's bellowing voice, insisting that he would never kill a dog-gone Indian without cause, but everyone knows they are thieving sneaks who are better off on a reservation where they can't harm the good folks trying to settle the land.

McNair was a good father and a law-abiding man, Christian thought, but held the same view as most of the settlers who believed Indians were inferior and had no rights to land and little right to a fair trial.

Robert joined Alice on the porch. "Alice, I am going back to the Platte River."

"You are going to visit her grave," Alice guessed. "Am I right? I can't go back to the place Amelia died. It is too hard for me, but she is in my heart every moment, just as your Annabelle Lee is with you." Tears filled her eyes. Robert opened his arms and held the mother who mourned for her child just as he mourned each day for his young love.

They could have stopped my breath, and I would have missed it less than losing Annabelle Lee.

For the moon never beams without bringing me dreams
Of the beautiful Annabel Lee;
And the stars never rise but I feel the bright eyes:
Of the beautiful Annabel Lee.

PART III
GOLD RUSH

Chapter Twenty-eight
North to the British Colonies

The sternwheeler landed on the Portland docks. Crowded onshore were hundreds of miners pushing to get passage on the ship. A new gold rush was on, and this time in Canada. New Caledonia, it was called.

"We are heading for the Fraser River diggings," they told Christian, when he asked about the hullabaloo. Christian brought the news to Anna's restaurant that evening.

"It looks like all the men of Oregon and California are going north to the new gold strike on Fraser's river. Are you and Jan thinking about joining the rush to find gold?"

"Jan and I prosper because we don't run off to dig gold with the crazies," Anna said, her hands on her substantial hips. "Instead, we may go north to sell shovels to miners, then buy them back and sell them to the next yokel that believes there is easy gold for the taking."

"I might go to the British Territories," Christian said. "I've prospered here, but there is war with the tribes, and I have seen enough Indian killing."

At this point in the conversation, McNair burst through door, a look on his face as if he had witnessed the resurrection.

"Californians are going mad about gold in Queen's country— New Caledonia it's called, just north there of the boundary. A boat comes in to San Francisco, I hear, and this steamship, *The Otter*, it's loaded with gold dug up by the Indians way north on Fraser's river! Now hundreds are crammed onto the steamship Commodore, and they're all headin' to Fort Victoria. There's more gold to be had up there on Fraser's river than there were in forty-nine and just laying there for the takin'."

Since crossing the continent twelve years ago, McNair's hair had receded further, and his round paunch had expanded with the plentiful food of Oregon. The lure of fortune was irresistible. Since he had left his extensive farm holdings in Illinois, McNair's desire for free land and adventure hadn't abated, and the lure of gold drove him.

"I missed out on getting ourselves a piece of good land in Oregon," McNair complained, as he settled himself on a table in Anna's restaurant. "Settlers poured into Oregon like locusts to a grain field. By the time we arrived from California, there were no more good land left for the takin'. I regret staying at Sutter's so long and losin' out on a spread along the Willamette River. Is there land to be had in the British Territory, good prairie land?"

"They say you can apply for land on the island but not sure about the mainland. It's still ruled by the Hudson's Bay Company," Christian told them. "I heard that the Hudson's Bay Governor does not let settlers or miners on land the tribes use. Appears it is different in British Territories than America. There is protection for the natives, not like here where the Yakama were moved off their land to make way for the settlers."

"I don't approve of removing these people from their own land," Jan said. "The Yakama woman who works for Anna must have a pass to work here, and if she doesn't return to the reservation at night, she can be arrested. Her family lived here for centuries. It is their homeland."

"It is my belief that the Indians own their tribal lands," Christian added. "When I applied and received title to the land from the Oregon Provisional Government, I figured the land was not the government's to sell. I paid the local tribe more than a fair price for my four sections of land."

"You're out of your mind, Jan. Their land!" McNair blustered. "They have no rights. They are savages and will disappear back into the jungle and die off. By the end of this century, America will be quit of them for good. Their land! What nonsense comes out of the mouth of an educated man! You're throwing good money away on them savages. What percentage is that?"

"It has worked out just fine for me." Christian replied calmly. "The Yakama Indians will never burn down my house and farm buildings." Christian politely excused himself from the table, not wanting to carry on a discussion that was leading nowhere. Changing settlers' views of the tribes was like trying to convert the Pope to the Protestant religion.

He did not bother telling McNair that his firm prospered because of his friendship with the tribes. The Walla Walla, Yakama and Cayuse came to him for assistance when their young men came up against the law or when the government failed to live up to the treaties.

～

"We're taking the next steamship to Victoria," McNair told Dorothy. "There's a fortune to be made in gold. It will set us up for life." He plopped down in one of the comfortable big chairs in their modest frame house.

Dorothy studied her husband for a minute, a cross look on her face. She put down her needlework and walked over to stand in front of McNair. "I've come across the continent with you. We almost lost our oldest boy. We were close to dying of starvation. The unspeakable happened to us. No, McNair, I will not go north to Queen's country, nor will our sons." She turned from him, to indicate that there was no more to be said. Before she was able to sit back down and pick up her needles, McNair was on his feet, protesting.

"It is safe," he argued, his leaden voice louder than Dorothy could bear. "Not like the Sierra Crossing or the salt desert. Just a boat trip to Fort Victoria on Vancouver Island, then by canoe up Fraser's river. And there's land to be had there. Good land, and no trouble with Indians. They are peaceable tribes, not like these savages here, burnin' farms and massacring people."

Dorothy turned back to McNair, shook her head and placed her hands firmly on her hips. "No, no, no. I will no more leave my home than take my dear children and drown them in the Columbia River. Go, McNair. Find the gold, and come back home when you are through with your wanderings. I am happy here in Oregon City. "

Dorothy held her ground as McNair prepared to leave on the next steamship bound for Fort Victoria. However, striking out alone was not part of McNair's character.

McNair and the survivors of the Sierra disaster were accustomed to gathering at Anna's restaurant for a late Saturday evening meal, but Dorothy declined to go. She knew that McNair would be boasting about the buckets of gold just waiting for him to pick up out of the gravel beds of Fraser's river. Sure enough, McNair broached the subject to Jan.

"Us men should go to New Caledonia and leave the womenfolk and children in Oregon. What say you all come with me? After we land in Fort Victoria, I'll get us a canoe and some Indians to take us up the Fraser. We'll be digging gold from the river bank and filling pickle jars with gold dust. We'll be rich before you know it."

"You mean leave my soul mate," Jan protested. "Leave Louise and the boys just when they are finding their way? Not in my life." Jan put his arms about Anna's firm waist and brushed her cheek with his lips.

"Where himself goes, I go," Anna said. "Where I go, Louise and the two boys go. We are a family, and we stick together like mussels to a rock. And it isn't digging gold we will be after, it'll be the gold the miners drop in my pocket for food and boarding. Our business will suffer when all the miners go north, so I think it would be smart to pull up stakes and relocate to Queen's country. I'm for another adventure," Anna continued, a smile on her lips and a sparkle in her eyes. "My one condition is that Alice agrees to come and help me set up my restaurant."

"If Anna is all for heading to Fort Victoria, I am for it too," Jan said. "What do you say, Alice? Will you come with us?"

Alice sat quietly for a few minutes, trying to process all the information. Years ago she had been forced by a domineering and careless husband to cross the continent. In the process, she had lost everything: her child, her family home and her fortune. "Jan, of course I will come with you. Anna and you are my family now." Alice gave her friends a rare smile.

McNair was among thousands excited beyond reason over the gold strikes. The *Pioneer Democrat*, an Oregon newspaper, told its readers that the Hudson's Bay Company had traded with the Indians for over a hundred pounds of gold and that three miners had dug up eight hundred dollars of gold in ten days. As news of the gold strike spread across the continent, sailors abandoned ships, farmers sold out and businesses closed. Anna put the restaurant and boarding house up for sale and prepared for the steamship journey north.

The date for departure was quickly approaching. Alice packed her meager belongings, happy to move north into British Territory and put distance between herself and Saxby. Shortly after their decision to move to Fort Victoria, Anna and Jan had engaged Christian and Robert to look after the sale of their properties and were kept busy every waking hour, tying up their affairs.

"What about you, Robert?" Anna asked, as they sat in the comfortable, richly furnished law office. "They'll be needing solicitors to register mining claims and settle disputes, and I know the Indians Wars have troubled you and Christian."

"What do you think about going north, Robert? Should we take the steamship to Victoria and find you a wife?" Christian gave his partner a warm grin.

"You are more in need of a wife than I, Christian. Wait much longer, and you will be too old to attract the fair sex," Robert teased, a rare smile on his handsome face. "In any case, I doubt there is even one maid in a gold rush town suitable to be your wife. Remember 'forty-nine? Men swarmed into California, but single women were as rare as hens' teeth."

"The bachelor life suits me. I don't want to be like Walter, who was chained to the wrong woman for years. Speaking of Walter, I hear he got the jump on us and will be landing in Queen's country before we have packed our bags. Like you, Anna, he knows how to take coins from gold-crazy miners."

"Walter will not be digging in the creek beds," Anna agreed. "He will be hacking down those giant cedars and building houses. Whatever is needed, that man will do."

~

The Saturday before their departure to Fort Victoria, the friends met for a last time at Anna's restaurant. "Dorothy, I believe you will be traveling to The Dalles to visit your sister. Am I right?" They were seated at the largest table in the dining room, while Alice moved from kitchen to table with bowls of beef stew.

"Of course, I wrote her about Annabelle Lee's death, but until now I could not face her." At the reminder, Anna noticed the change in Dorothy, as if it were just yesterday that Annabelle Lee had succumbed to cholera. Dorothy nervously kneaded her hands on her lap and bit her lower lip.

"Stop treading on eggshells, and tell your sister everything," Anna advised. "She will be glad to see her flesh and blood again, and hear firsthand of Annabelle Lee's courage on the trail. They are doing well in their business, making money hand over fist, or so I have heard through the moccasin telegraph."

"You haven't told me what happened to Charlotte and Americus," Dorothy said, changing the subject. "Last I saw them was at The Parting of the Ways. The children were surviving on a diet of rice, ignored by their mother while young Louise was being ogled by Americus. I plain forgot to ask after them."

"The young girls on the wagon train had to keep their distance from that stepfather with the wandering hands," Anna told her.

"I recall Americus telling Annabelle Lee he was a phrenologist or something weird like that. He wanted to run his hands over her head to determine her personality. Young Annabelle Lee, bless her soul, knew what he was up to and come a-running to me."

Hearing Dorothy talk about Annabelle Lee was too much for Robert. "Thanks for the dinner, Anna. You have the very best scratch in all of Oregon. I would love to stay for coffee, but I have a file to work on in the office."

"That young man can't let go," Anna said, after Robert had left the restaurant. "Maybe someday he will find another love, but just now he works night and day, shuffling papers for Christian. On weekends he plows and plants on his farm. He has already banked away more money than most of the older men. He will send for his family as soon as the railroad reaches Oregon City."

"You asked about Charlotte," Anna remembered. "Sadly, she passed away. It was a nasty bit of business. Americus sweet-talked himself into a job teaching in Portland and abandoned Charlotte and the children. He was a good-for-nothing son-of-a-bitch, excuse my language, just like his brother Saxby. Charlotte arrived in Oregon City with her three hungry children and nary a cent. We helped her unload her belongings from the boat to the riverside. She just sat there on Abernathy Green surrounded by her meager goods, not moving, not able to care for the children or find shelter for them.

"Settlers got together and built a little cabin for Charlotte and the children, but the poor woman went mad and couldn't care for a kitten, let alone three children. When I visited her one day to drop off a dinner, the house smelled like a wet dog. Charlotte was on the bed, lost in her own world of misery." Anna paused, thinking back on the tragedy that beset the once beautiful Charlotte. "Louise visited her mother in the asylum every week until Charlotte died. The children have been in our care since their mother's illness."

"What about Americus?" Dorothy asked, intrigued by the story of beauty and wealth turning to dust.

"Americus taught for a year until he was discovered fondling one of the girls. The girl's father didn't ask any questions, just took his Winchester and shot Americus dead. The father got off scot-free as no court in Oregon would convict a father seeking revenge against his daughter's abuser, so that chapter closed."

"And Louise? I noticed she occasionally works in your restaurant." Dorothy commented. "And how did the children come into your care?" Dorothy asked hoping to catch up on years that the McNair family remained at Sutter's.

"Louise has grown as beautiful as her mother was," Anna continued, "but without her mother's weak character, thankfully. Louise attends the female seminary here in Oregon City and works hard. Not a brilliant student, but hard-working. The girl's heart is steady. I figure she's been in love with Robert since we crossed, but he pays her no notice. For that matter, he pays no mind to any of the eligible women here."

That all changed the next day when Robert spotted a familiar woman sporting long, dark, curly hair and walking with the most graceful posture. His heart missed a beat. He could not believe his eyes, and practically ran across the street to greet this beautiful vision. His heart pounded in his chest, and the emotion he felt overwhelmed him.

"Annabelle Lee?" Robert's voice choked.

The woman turned to Robert with a quizzical gaze. "No. I'm Elizabeth. My sister passed." She had the same liquid eyes and dark lashes as Annabelle Lee, and Robert was entranced.

"My apologies, Miss," Robert said softy, still gazing into her eyes. "You look so alike, I thought you had returned from Heaven's Gate to be with me again. I knew your sister and loved her dearly." He felt tongue-tied, just like the first moment he'd looked at Annabelle Lee and love hit him like a bolt of lightning.

Robert could not take his eyes off this apparition, this beauty who had shared the womb with Annabelle Lee, the twin survivor of the cruelest separation.

Elizabeth eyed Robert with a puzzled look on her face.

"Ah, now I know you." A cautious smile lit up her beautiful face. "She left her diary, and our aunt sent it to us. Annabelle Lee's journal was filled with her gushy infatuations over you."

Robert smiled, flushing a little at hearing her speak of the love he and Annabelle Lee shared years ago. Now he was transferring his feelings to this identical copy of his childhood love. His heart beat as he spoke. "I want to tell you about Annabelle Lee and her courage while on the Oregon Trail. Could we meet and get to know each other?" He finally remembered himself, straightened up a little, and inclined his head. "Would you do me the honor of having tea with me tomorrow?"

Elizabeth was delighted. She had never met a more handsome, well-mannered man. Later, as Elizabeth dressed and primped in the room she shared with another boarder, she told her roommate Molly about Robert.

"He actually asked you for tea!" Molly exclaimed. "He's never even taken a second look at any of the eligible young women. And him so handsome! I could just eat him with a spoon. And here you are, only one day in the city, and you've caught his eye! Lucky you!"

Molly had a pile of wild red hair and a pleasant face with cheeks sprinkled with freckles. She had lived at Fort Aster on the west coast since she and her family arrived by ship when she was still a toddler, and after arriving in Oregon City, she had catalogued all the unmarried young men. She was not shy about sharing her views with Elizabeth, despite their having just met. Molly was a talkative young woman with an outgoing personality but not someone who monitored her words before speaking.

"Not really luck, Molly. He was in love with my sister, and I am her exact image. But I agree he is beautiful beyond words, if a young woman is permitted to describe a man in those terms."

Robert and Elizabeth met the next day and the next, sharing their memories of Annabelle Lee. Robert wanted to hear about their life in Springfield before the girls were parted, and Elizabeth was desperate for news of her sister on the trail. At last Robert could open up to someone, and he poured out his pain over the loss of the one they both had loved most in this world.

Robert could not stop looking at Elizabeth. Every glance brought back the sweet and cherished memories of Annabelle Lee.

"You are staring at me again," Elizabeth said, with a wry smile on her beautiful lips.

"I am fascinated. When I look at you, it is if Annabelle Lee had not died on the Platte River."

"I am not Annabelle Lee. I loved my sister dearly, but she and I are as different as the blazing sun and the cool moon. She was a dreamy girl, her head always in a fantasy novel about heroines. That is why she risked her life for that boy. She was living some romantic notion, not willing to be realistic about the danger it imposed, putting herself at risk for our cousin."

"I tried to warn her, but she believed it was her destiny."

"My destiny is to be rich and have a grand house up there on the hill, across the street from Mr. McLoughlin," Elizabeth informed him with a confident manner, as if she had her life carefully planned.

Robert thought about his farm on the Willamette River with the log house, vegetable garden and sheep pasture.

"So you can't see yourself on a farm? I was raised on a farm; it is the life I love, and I could not see myself a city dweller." His face lit up as he spoke of his love for the rural life. "The first year I planted a garden, the vegetables were luscious and so abundant I had to give most of it away! In summer, I swim in the river and in winter, I like to cut wood for the fireplace. It is a great life, balancing out all the long hours I spend at a desk."

"Why would you live on a farm when you have a practice and must be at your situation each morning?"

"I am up early and ride to the office. It is the perfect life for me. I have all the delights of the country, with all the advantages of town. I am a patron of the arts and don't miss a play or a concert. That reminds me. There is traveling company performing *Romeo and Juliet*. Would you be my guest at the theatre?"

"I am not that fond of Shakespeare, but I would be delighted to go with you."

"It's a company from San Francisco. I hear they are excellent Shakespearean actors."

The night of the performance, Elizabeth wore a long green satin skirt with a bodice decorated with glitters, and Robert a top-coat, with a velvet grey vest and white cravat. As they walked to their seats, eyes turned and the theatre patrons murmured, wondering who the beautiful woman was. An elderly woman watched them and whispered to her equally elderly husband, "At last, the handsome young solicitor is squiring a lady."

Robert listened and watched the performance with rapt attention, while Elizabeth shifted in her seat, at times in boredom and once to move closer to Robert. He did not take her hand as she hoped.

As the two handsome young people exited the theater, Elizabeth noticed Robert wiping tears from his eyes while she felt relieved to hear the end of the melancholy tale. *If only he would take me to the vaudeville where we could have a good laugh.*

Elizabeth took Robert's arm as they walked to his carriage. It was a warm June night. Finally, the persistent rain had ended and the city felt clean and fresh. Robert saw a pale moon rise in the east. *At last, might I be able to stop grieving over my love and transfer my feelings to her lovely sister?*

They rode in silence to the ladies' boarding house. Robert jumped from the carriage to help Elizabeth down, offering his hand. She stepped down and purposely fell against him.

"Elizabeth! Let me help you." Robert felt her slim body against him. Rather than desire, he felt awkward and wished she would be less forward, waiting for him to make the first advance.

Elizabeth smiled at Robert, forming her lips in a way that she knew was the most attractive. She pressed closer to him and lifted her face to his.

Robert bent to kiss her. She was so beautiful, his first love reincarnated. He meant to kiss her lightly on the lips but Elizabeth opened her mouth, wet and sensual, and pressed against him.

Robert pulled away, feeling uncomfortable. Elizabeth could not believe that her ardent advances were not reciprocated. Men always desired her, always pressed her for kisses that she did not want to give. Now, the handsomest man she had ever walked with was quite obviously not taken with her.

Their parting was polite. As Robert walked her up the pathway to the boarding house, Elizabeth held out hope that he would ask to meet her again. *Perhaps he is shy and needs more time. Surely he must love me.* At the door, Elizabeth turned, smiling hopefully at Robert. She wished he would kiss her fervently and fall in love with her. Instead, Robert planted a quick kiss on her gloved hand and bid her goodnight.

It was the last evening they spent together.

Chapter Twenty-nine
The Queen's Country

The steamship landed on Vancouver Island, and passengers from all over the world disembarked—Americans, Scotsmen, British, Chinese, Hawaiians, and a smattering of others from around the world. There was even a large party of African Americans fleeing the discriminating laws in California.

The Songhees Native people gathered at the dock, offering to transport the newcomers' goods into the city. A young Songhees man approached Jan as he and Anna walked onto the dock. He wore an intricately decorated woven blanket over cotton trousers and shirt, and a new Stetson hat. His black hair was neatly pulled back in a ponytail, and an engaging smile lit up his face.

"Sir, would you like assistance to transport your goods to the city?" His manner was confident, and he spoke with a strong British accent.

Anna, Jan and their adopted family stood on the docks, waiting for their trunks and numerous boxes of supplies to be unloaded from the ship. The dock was noisy and crowded with anxious miners, impatient to be on their way to the gold fields.

"My wife and I hired two Wells Fargo wagons, but we could use help loading our goods and need transport across James Bay to Fort Victoria." Jan told the young man. "What's your name, lad?"

"Yoletan. I live here long time. Our village is just across the water from the fort, and we have big canoes and take you fast across water. Work for the Bay, learn how you speak the English."

"We'll pay you one dollar to load up these crates and help us move into the Royal Hotel on Wharf Street. This is my wife Anna, our friend Alice, and our children, Louise, Jimmy and Michael."

Yoletan went right to work, finished the job quickly and competently, and gave Anna a wide smile.

"Jump into the wagon with us," Anna invited him, "and tell us about this place. It looks like the entire world is on its way to the gold diggings."

Yoletan took a seat beside Jan and Anna. Alice, Louise and the boys climbed into the back of the horse-drawn carriage. A Wells Fargo man drove the second wagon, piled high with trunks and supply goods.

They travelled on a rough road from the docks at Esquimalt to the bustling community of Fort Victoria. On the road to the fort, miners carried their meager belongings. Others, like McNair and his friends, loaded their household goods and supplies in carts and horse drawn wagons.

Anna, the consummate entrepreneur, had brought goods to sell, and before they even reached their lodgings, she'd sold a dozen pairs of gumboots to miners traveling the road between Esquimalt and Fort Victoria. Anna not only sold the goods quickly, but received several times the going price in Oregon. It took them an extra hour to reach Victoria, and by then Anna had gold coins and pound notes stuffed in her purse.

Yoletan helped Jan guide the horse drawn wagon through the Songhees village, smiling and nodding at friends and relatives as they passed the longhouses. Women sat outside the immense cedar houses spinning wool into capes and blankets while children ran excitedly through the village. Anna did not appreciate the noxious stench of smoke and fish that wafted about them.

Jan and the Wells Fargo driver brought the wagons to a halt above the beach where thirty-foot-long dugout cedar canoes were lined up near the water. Soon several Songhees men arrived, offering to help move their goods into canoes, and an elderly man picked up a paddle to help Yoletan take the family across to the fort. Two other paddlers took the canoe with the trunks and supplies. Jan gave each of the helpers a tobacco plug and a gold coin.

The beach was busy with miners arriving and bargaining for passage across the narrow strip of water that separated the Songhees village and Fort Victoria. Children ran over and around the boxes of supplies, curious about the strange items and the strange people. The Songhees were accustomed to the Hudson's Bay men and the strong voyageurs at the fort. They worked for them, and while the fur traders did not treat them as equals, they treated them with a degree of respect. These newcomers were very different, with some of them dressed in finery, but most in rough clothing and poor shoes. Many of the newcomers looked at them with disdain instead of a smile or a polite gesture. Not all, but most of the new arrivals were pushy and disrespectful.

Anna, Jan and Alice were among the few newcomers who met the Songhees people courteously and with a smile. Anna gave a bag of candy to Louise to distribute to the children and very shortly, there was a crowd of youngsters at Louise's feet, their dirty hands held out, big smiles on their dark faces. The children continued to follow Louise until she stepped into the big canoe along with her two brothers. A strong Songhees man on shore pushed the boat into the water, and the elder steered them into James Bay. The ocean was clear and calm, and the day so warm the three women wished they had dressed in lighter clothing instead of the wool traveling suits. The boys cared little that it was hot; they were fascinated by the fort across the water.

As they crossed the water, Anna saw the high bastions of the fort, with its six-pounder aimed out to the channel. Fort Victoria was a substantial structure sprawling over, what appeared to Anna, an entire city block.

Alice quietly watched as the fort drew closer and felt a sense of renewal. She was leaving Saxby behind in another country, and now she had a real chance for a new beginning.

"Do you remember Fort Vancouver?" Anna asked Jan. "This Fort looks the same. High walls, bastions to protect the Fort, and gardens to provide food for the fur traders."

"Both forts were built by the Hudson's Bay Company, which might explain the why and wherefore," Jan replied.

"We built the fort. I mean my father and grandfather," Yoletan told them proudly. "Our people cut the trees and built it. Blankets. That's what the Hudson's Bay Company paid. But we're proud that we built the fort, and it is important to us. We trade salmon and game and furs for pots, knives, clothing, everything."

The two Songhees paddlers brought the canoe alongside the wharf, helped the family out, unloaded the supplies, and carried the boxes and trunks up the rocky incline to Wharf Street and to the hotel.

"There is certainly gold to be made," Anna said, after they'd had a few days to settle into their lodgings. "First order of business is to hire Yoletan's friends and relatives to build us a decent place to open a restaurant. I'll offer twice the going rate for their work and outbid the others. The flea-infested places up for sale won't suit me, but I saw an 1856 map of Victoria with all the land surrounding the ocean, marked off in lots. Amazing that the British foresaw the need for land before all but fur traders had even heard of Fort Victoria!

Tomorrow I'll see Governor Douglas about purchasing land. If all goes well, we should have our establishment up and running in a couple of weeks. Alice, I am looking to you to run the kitchen and serve, at least until I can hire a waitress."

"Won't Jan want to look after the kitchen until you establish the restaurant? He did that in Oregon City, I recall him saying."

"Oh, no. Himself will be finding a position in the bank. Put your welfare in two pots. That way, if one fails, the other will put bread on the table. Louise will be finding a job as a tutor, and can only work on weekends and evenings. You'll be on your own during school days."

"I like to be busy, Anna." She smiled, thinking that it was a wise choice for her to pull herself out of Sutter's protective care and throw her future in with this smart but caring entrepreneur.

Over the next month, twenty thousand miners descended on Fort Victoria. During the day, miners lined up at the Hudson's Bay fort to obtain their mining licenses. McNair waited in line with thousands of prospective miners.

In the absence of direction from England, Governor Douglas, the chief official at Fort Victoria, assumed control as the influx of miners crowded into the city and up Fraser's river. He'd published a proclamation requiring all miners to be licensed and had also posted gunboats on Fraser's river where British officials stopped the miners and extracted the license fee. However, Americans entering from the Columbia River and making their way north did their best to avoid the fee.

Louise had completed her education in Oregon City and advertized for a position as a tutor. The wife of one of the Hudson's Bay officials hired Louise to teach her two daughters. They were Anglicans and refused to send their daughters to the nuns at the Catholic School or to the fort, believing that their children should not mix with the offspring of the rough French Canadians or be taught by Catholic nuns.

A tent city grew up overnight. Miners, waiting for licenses and transport across to the mainland to Fraser's river, crowded into Anna's restaurant.

Alice was at work before the eastern sun lit the canvas tops of tent city. She set the bread rising, whipped up the dough for pancakes and cut the bacon into strips. Cooking, baking and serving fell on Alice. Without Yoletan's help, she would have been swamped. Anna had hired Yoletan to shop for food supplies as well as purchase potatoes, game, fish and seafood from the village people.

When the restaurant closed late, Jan, Alice, Anna and Yoletan finally had time to sit down. They were joined by McNair, Christian and Robert as they sat around the long table in the dining room, where coffee and desserts were spread out on the white linen table cloth.

"We are very busy, Anna," Alice said, in her quiet voice, "and now that Louise has a teaching position, I'm not sure I can manage to look after the kitchen and the tables. Won't you need more help?"

"I've placed an ad in the *Victoria Times*, so not to worry. I won't overwork you. I want you to smile again and maybe find a new husband to keep you company. Are you quits with that murdering Saxby?"

"Saxby. I could never abide living with him again. He is to blame for the death of my darling Amelia." Alice's voice broke as her daughter's name passed her lips. She composed herself and continued, now with anger in her voice. "On his head are the deaths of the poor souls who were trapped in the Sierras. Worse than that, he was with the renegades who slaughtered David's wife and son. Is there no judge who will hang him for his crimes, or at the very least, put him in jail? Christian, you are a man of the law. Could he be brought to justice for massacring the Yana Tribe?"

"In California, I doubt it. For that matter, anywhere in the States it is most difficult to get justice for the Indians. That is one reason Robert and I moved our practice to the Colony of Vancouver Island and under British law. Governor Douglas is Creole, and his wife is of mixed blood. Hopefully he will be better at protecting the Indians."

"A customer told me that the governor appointed Judge Begbie to keep the peace and punish murderers," Alice continued. "If Saxby follows me, can't we ask this judge to bring him to justice for massacring the Yana tribe?"

"Begbie will be a tough judge, but he will hang innocent Indians without a second thought. Even Douglas is changing his views towards the tribes, siding more and more with the miners. Besides, we are under British Law now, and Saxby's crimes were committed in the United States. I doubt Saxby will ever pay for what he has done."

A knock at the restaurant door interrupted the conversation.

"Can't they read the sign?" Anna asked in tired voice. When there was a second and louder knock, she sighed and got up. She opened the door to find Walter and an attractive Aboriginal woman.

"Walter! Well, I'll be! All of us wondered where you'd gotten to! Come in, and introduce us to your friend."

"Anna, this is my wife Maggie," Walter said, putting his arm around the handsome, dark-skinned woman. "She is Musqueam. Her people live at Chilukthan, their village near the mouth of Fraser's river."

The round-faced, pleasant-looking woman smiled and nodded. Maggie wore her hair in a neat bun and was dressed in a simple but clean calico shirt and skirt.

"Maggie is the Chief's niece. She speaks a little English, and I speak a little of what they call Chinook." Walter smiled at his wife, who bowed her head slightly, nervous in the company of so many white strangers.

"Where did you meet each other?"

"I hired her brothers to paddle me across the straits to where the Fraser flows into the Pacific. I met her relatives, and we all got along. I asked her family for her hand, and we were married in her village, a beautiful spot near the mouth of the river. Now I look after the sales for our sawmill here in Victoria, and Maggie manages the Musqueam workers. Well, at least until our baby is born," Walter remarked, a wide grin on his face.

"Congratulations, Walter!" Jan said. "Now I recall hearing about her, when Yoletan bought cutboards for me. This calls for a celebration."

Anna disappeared into her office and returned with a bottle of whiskey. She poured a shot for everyone.

When she passed a glass to Maggie, the woman shook her head. "No." Her voice soft and barely audible.

"Maggie's people are opposed to the drink, or at least the Chief and his advisors," Walter explained, "but I will drink my glass and hers too. I thank you, Anna, for including us. Fort Victoria is no longer friendly to her people. Several establishments refused us service, and many of the newcomers stick their noses up in the air when they see us together. Only the Hudson's Bay men are accustomed to intermarriage."

Anna noticed a significant change in Walter since the days on the Oregon Trail, in both manner and looks. He wore wool pants and a beaded vest now, and on his feet were beaded moccasins. Although still muscular looking, he had filled out and looked prosperous and content.

"Walter, you gotta come with me up the Fraser," McNair announced. "I'm heading out in a few days. You might be making money here, but you will get rich overnight from the diggings."

"I'll think on it, McNair. I suppose those miners will need a roof over their heads. Nobody wants to stay in a tent with winter bearing down. Trees here are as tall as the highest mountains back East. Enormous trees. Enough wood in one cedar tree to build a dozen houses! Now I must ask Maggie's people to teach me how to cut those monsters down."

The next day, McNair and Louise's brothers picked up their licenses and joined Walter, who had hired Maggie's brothers to take them across the Georgia Strait in a canoe and up Fraser's river.

Miners continued to arrive at the docks, overtaxing the few businesses that had been established in Victoria. It was a weekend, and Louise arrived early to help Alice prepare for the onslaught of customers who lined up at the door each morning. Louise had grown into a beautiful young woman, with eyes as brilliantly blue as her mother's. She wore a simple dress of blue and white gingham, an outfit that accentuated her slim waist and enhanced her blue eyes. In character, she was very much like Anna, practical and organized. Her pale beauty attracted the miners, the businessmen, the old men and young men alike, but Louise paid no attention even when her admirer was handsome and young.

"I will not end up like my mother, dependent on a man who cares for me just because of my looks," she told Alice, as they set the places for dinner. "I will be independent. Maybe I could be a solicitor like Robert and Christian. Are there any women solicitors?"

Anna was walking through the dining room, checking the tables, and overheard the question. "Not yet, Louise; however, Christian told me of three women who applied to the New York law school. They were refused, of course, but I can see a time when women will become doctors, solicitors, whatever they choose! This is a new country, and you will have many possibilities." Anna smiled at Louise, pleased to have the beautiful, thoughtful girl as her adopted daughter.

"What do you think of Robert?" Anna asked, wanting a life of happiness for Louise.

"We don't want to tease and embarrass you, Louise," Alice said with a smile, "but both Anna and I noticed it was not just Annabelle Lee who was sweet on him. My Amelia, despite being years younger than Robert, couldn't keep her eyes off him, and you were often huddling with Robert and Annabelle Lee, laughing and telling stories."

"Robert will never care for another," Louise said wistfully. "His heart is back on the Oregon Trail, buried with Annabelle Lee. Even Elizabeth, Annabelle Lee's twin, could not capture Robert's heart."

"And my heart was left in the snows of the Sierras." Alice turned away, tears in her eyes. She busied herself in the kitchen, frying bacon on the big, iron-topped stove and checking on the bread in the oven.

That morning, Alice and Louise could not keep up with the orders.

"Hey girl, git me a coffee, and hurry the cook with the bacon and eggs!" a whiskered miner yelled across the room to Louise. "We're a headin' for the gold fields, and this will be my last meal under a roof!"

"I'm doing my best, mister, and so is the cook," Louise replied, thinking that he did not belong in a restaurant; he belonged in a barn.

"Louise, I'll help serve the customers." Anna came down from her office, donned an apron and carried plates to one of the tables.

"Anna, you must have enough money to buy all of Victoria. Why are you waiting on this riffraff?" Christian and Robert were seated at their usual table.

"A rolling stone gathers no moss, Christian. I won't be sitting about while Louise and Alice are run off their feet. What will you have, Robert, oatmeal, or would you like to try Alice's flapjacks this morning? And Christian, Alice has rolls fresh from the oven."

They ordered, but before the food arrived at their table, two women walked into the restaurant as opposite in appearance as a pig and a swan. One woman was repulsively ugly and heavyset, with a pudgy face and small eyes buried in fat cheeks. The other had a classic face framed by coal black hair, which she wore modestly wrapped in a bun. She had coppery skin and the darkest eyes Christian had ever seen, set off to great advantage by long, black lashes. Although she was short and slight, she had long slender legs and arms, looking more like a ballet dancer than a woman born on the plains. She wore an ankle-length skirt and a striped muslin shirt with long sleeves and high neck, polished black boots, every bit as modestly and well attired as a young woman from the most prestigious sections of Upper Canada.

Christian watched the dark-skinned beauty with an emotion he had not experienced since his youth. *Have I ever seen such a beautiful creature in my life?*

Anna brought breakfast to the table and noticed Christian looking across the room at the young Métis woman.

"The new waitresses are here, and I see they did not walk in unnoticed. Are you spellbound, Christian, or just too sleepy to take your eyes off that girl?" Anna placed a dish of fried eggs and fresh rolls in front of Christian.

"What? Oh, thank you, Anna," Christian said, distractedly.

For a man with such a constant, steady demeanor, seeing him flustered made Anna chuckle.

"Glad to see you are still alive to beautiful women! There have been times I thought your only interest was in the law and saving wee children. I figured you'd never let your guard down when it comes to the fair sex," Anna teased. "Now, enjoy your breakfast. I must find a place for the new girls to set themselves down until I have a minute to talk to them."

Anna returned after leading the two women to her office. "Her name is Rose, daughter of the Hudson's Bay factor in Rupert's Land. Her mother is Cree. She was born in Fort Edmonton, raised by the nuns and educated at the Catholic Convent in Upper Canada. Rose's father sent her to Toronto to be schooled by the nuns at an expense of sixty pounds a year, and according to Rose, he felt it was well worthwhile to give his child a good education. The other lady is Ella, arrived here from San Francisco. I can really use some help…"

"Is Rose married?" Christian asked, interrupting Anna.

"Ah, so the sworn bachelor has a serious interest in the dark-eyed beauty from across the mountains," Anna commented, with a smile. "You will be pleased to know that she is not married and has no intended. She comes from a fine family and knows little about the world outside the church." Anna paused and scrutinized Christian.

"I know you are a good man, Christian, but others in this rowdy town may not be. I will keep a close eye on her."

"Anna," Christian was now serious. "Please understand, my interest in Rose is entirely honorable."

Anna turned to Robert with a little chuckle. "What do you think of your law partner swooning over a woman who has not given him as much as a howdy doo?"

Robert smiled, showing a flash of the cheerful youth Anna had met at the beginning of the Oregon Trail. "I recall the day I saw Annabelle Lee for the first time. It was like being struck by lightning." His lighthearted mood disappeared, and the melancholy returned as Annabelle Lee's name crossed his lips. Years had passed since the death of his dear love, but the pain of her loss clearly haunted him still.

"You'll be seeing Rose soon enough, Christian, as she and Ella start work tomorrow. Now, I must ask the young women a few questions, so will bid you handsome gentlemen a good morning."

Although Rose and Ella worked together, they were not friends. Ella's father was a slave owner who had brought his family and slaves from Virginia to California in 1847, after the Mexican War. California was a rich plum grabbed from the Mexicans and ready for the picking by Easterners weary of the growing opposition to slavery that swept the northeastern states.

Ella had been raised with a sense of entitlement. She was an only child of indulgent parents, accustomed to getting what she wanted. At twenty-five, what she most wanted was a husband. Not just any man, of course. She wanted a wealthy, educated man of society, someone who would spoil her just like her father and mother had fêted and indulged her.

Before Ella had decided to leave San Francisco, her parents had hosted a coming out party for their daughter in hopes of advancing her prospects for a husband, but given Ella's pudgy appearance, none of the suitable young men were interested. The son of a bankrupt businessman took an interest in Ella or, that is, an interest in her inheritance, but was roundly rejected by Ella and her parents.

"If I am to find a husband," Ella told her parents, "I must go north to the British Territories where there is only one woman for every hundred men. Men are advertising for wives there, and I will find myself a handsome, educated man, maybe a Brit from the Royal family! California has nothing for me, only a passel of gold-hungry miners who don't know how to use a knife and fork or select the proper wine."

Ella had taken up lodging in the Island Hotel and took her meals at the Saint George Hotel, where the restaurant had recently engaged a French chef. Life in Victoria was pleasant and comfortable until a letter arrived from her father informing Ella that he had invested heavily in a ship carrying supplies around the Horn, and the ship had been lost at sea along with his fortune. Her allowance ended abruptly, although he had enclosed sufficient funds for Ella to book passage home to San Francisco.

Ella had no wish to return to her parents' home and face the prospect of life as a spinster. Instead, she decided to seek work.

The first day she and Rose arrived at Anna's restaurant, Ella spotted Christian and Robert. Both men were dressed in tailored suits of fine wool, looking prosperous. Ella surveyed the two men, Robert, who was a few years younger than Ella, and Christian, a decade older. She wanted a husband with a substantial fortune, not a young man still making his way. Ella was immediately attracted to Christian, admiring the handsome profile framed by red-brown hair and his neatly trimmed beard. Although it was clear from his expensive suit that he was a professional, he was as fit, robust and muscular as a logger.

It did not take Ella long to find out that Christian and Robert were successful solicitors, and it took her even less time to arrange her shifts and select the table where Christian usually took his meals. He was a regular at Anna's restaurant, and as he entered the door, Ella was there, guiding him to one of her tables. She did not pick up on the fact that Christian's eyes were on Rose. She spent a long week of frustrated attempts at engaging Christian in conversation before Ella figured it out, and it did not improve her mood.

The next morning, as usual, Ella marched up to Christian the minute he and Robert entered the restaurant.

"Take a seat, sir. I will bring your coffee," Ella said, pulling a chair out for Christian and nodding to Robert.

"Thank you, Ella. We'll sit over by the window this morning," Christian declined politely, moving over to the table where Rose busied herself clearing off the dishes.

"Good morning, Rose," he said, smiling and seating himself.

"My apologies Sir," Rose said in a soft voice. "Perhaps you would like to take a table that is already set?"

"I will sit here, as this is my very favorite table," Christian smiled, and sat back in his chair to watch this vision move about clearing the dishes. He wanted to tell her how beautiful she was, but intuited that Rose would feel offended by any impropriety.

Rose carried out the tray of dishes and returned shortly, quickly removing the tablecloth and replacing it with fresh linen and napkins. All her actions were efficient and graceful. She did not appear rushed, yet the table was set, cutlery placed and water glasses filled within minutes.

Christian was flustered as he gave Rose his order, first asking for bacon and eggs, then changing his mind twice and settling on Eggs Benedict, a breakfast dish that only Anna's restaurant offered.

Robert had his usual breakfast of oatmeal porridge.

"You don't seem yourself this morning, Christian," Robert smiled, as he added a large scoop of brown sugar to his bowl of hot cereal. "Could it be the beautiful girl from Rupert's Land has taken over your mind?"

"Robert, I think it is time for both of us to socialize. I've been a single man for a decade, and I'm tired of the lonely life. What about you? With your looks and hair fair as a mermaid's, you could entice every maid that glances your way. You could find yourself a wife with your first smile."

"I doubt it, Christian, but I see no reason you should refrain from pursuing the dark beauty from the Territories."

Rose returned to the table to ask if she should top up their coffee, and noticed that Christian had barely touched his breakfast.

"Is your breakfast to your liking, Sir? May I bring you something else?"

"My breakfast is wonderful. Thank you," Christian said, looking at her with a warm smile. "Miss Rose, I have a question for you if I may impose. What does a young woman like you do for entertainment? Do you attend the concerts? Go to the library?"

"I work, Sir. I design and stitch my wardrobe. I make hats, write letters to my family in Fort Edmonton, and I read. I like to ride but sadly I couldn't bring my horse." She smiled, remembering her rides on the plains. "He was a beautiful palomino, gold with a white main and tail. I called him Wind because he galloped like the wind."

"I would like to ride with you but am without a horse as well. But also enjoy a Sunday walk." He smiled at her, a little nervous, thinking that she would view him as too old. "Would I be dismissed if I asked to walk with you on your day off?"

"Thank you. That is most kind of you. However, I am obliged to refuse this time as I am not ready to go out in company yet. You may ask me again in a few weeks, if you still wish to."

"And may I ask what it is you are working so hard for, Rose?" Christian asked, while indicating that Rose could take his uneaten breakfast away.

"I am saving money so that I might buy my own property, and then I will open a hat shop." Rose answered Christian's questions while removing the dishes onto a tray she balanced in her left hand. Christian could see that Rose was concerned that her work duties might be derelict.

"Please, give me just a second of your time, as that is a matter I can help you with," Christian said with a smile, relieved at finding a common interest with Rose. She paused and turned back to hear him out. "When you find a property or stake a claim for your preemption, come to us and we will file the papers for you. I will see that you are not overcharged or cheated."

"I will take you up on that offer. That is most kind of you Mister…?"

"Please call me Christian."

"I should use your surname, Sir," Rose said lowering her eyes.

"It is Martin. But would it not be appropriate for us to be on first name basis?"

"I think not, Sir. At least not yet." Rose turned and walked quickly through the swinging doors of the kitchen.

Ella had watched from across the room, a worm of panic slithering up from her gut. *Christian avoided me to chat with a squaw?* Ella's mood grew dark and hateful as she cleared one of the tables left after the morning rush. Instead of quietly removing the dishes, she hastily cleared up, not caring that her actions were noisy as she clumsily clashed dish against dish. *That little slut! How could she proposition him right here in the restaurant? I always knew she was nothing but a whore, just like all those squaws.*

Ella could not let this happen. She could not bear having Christian snagged by a woman Ella believed was inferior, and at the end of her shift she stormed into Anna's office.

"She's selling herself right here in your establishment! You must do something." Ella's fat face was beet red with anger, and she trembled with pent-up hatred and frustration.

"What in the good God's name are you talking about, Ella? Who is selling herself? Surely, you are not accusing Rose of impropriety?"

"Rose. That's who. She cozies up to Christian and is making plans to meet him!"

"So?"

"I heard them discuss money that would pass between them."

"I will talk to Rose, but you say no more. Save your breath to cool your porridge. I don't hold with malicious gossip, especially if your words defame a respectable woman."

Before the lunch crowd arrived at the restaurant, Anna asked to talk to Rose in the office, telling her of Ella's remarks.

Rose could not believe the charge being laid against her.

"Miss Anna! Never ever in my life would I do such a sinful act," Rose protested, tears streaming down her beautiful face. "I have never so much as kissed a man. I have not even walked with a man. How could she think this of me?" Rose broke into sobs.

"Now, don't you take on so, my dear Rose. I knew it wasn't true, but I had to ask you because Ella was so very certain about this claim. She wanted me to fire you. Instead, it is Ella who will be dismissed."

A week later, Christian brought the *Gazette* into the restaurant to show Anna.

"Did you see this?" Christian stood in front of Anna, waving the newspaper with a stern look on his face.

"Do I look like the kind of person who sits about in the morning reading that rag? I have better things to do with my time."

"This, you should read."

Dear Editor,

Citizens of Victoria take precautions so your husbands are not ruined by adulterous half-breed women. I warn you that we have a woman of questionable morals working at the James Bay Restaurant. All proper patrons should insist that she be fired on the grounds that she sells herself. I have proof of this. Lenora knows what she is saying and will stand by her words.

Signed, Lenora Baines

"This refers to Rose, a young woman of strict morals. I'll get to the bottom of this malicious libel!" Anna stormed into her office, picked up her satchel and left the restaurant, slamming the door behind her, so infuriated she could barely contain her anger. She returned to her house, put on her Sunday hat, a modest but expensive walking suit and strode purposely to the office of the *Gazette*.

I know exactly who wrote this garbage, and it wasn't Lenora Baines, who cannot write her own name without misspelling it.

At the office, Anna asked to see the editor and was admitted immediately. The editor and owner of the newspaper was a middle-aged man with receding grey hair and a full beard and mustache. The hair on his face more than made up for the absence of hair on his head, but he wore a neat grey waistcoat, a black cravat and pressed black trousers. He rose up from his desk to greet her, a look of concern on his face.

"My dear lady. Please sit down. May I offer you a sarsaparilla or lemonade?"

"What you can offer me is an apology and a public retraction in this rag. If I don't see it in the next edition, I shall be pulling my advertizing from your newspaper. That letter was not written by Lenora Baines," Anna said emphatically, her hands on her hips. "You should have known that, and you should never have printed it. In fact, I am half inclined to hire Messrs. Martin and Ackerman to sue you for libel. However, I have never been a vindictive woman; I am simply a business person who doesn't want to lose money and who gets incensed when she comes up against prejudice and malice."

The matter was settled and a retraction printed the following week.

"Rose," Christian said the day after the retraction, "I am so very sorry the malicious letter was printed. I should be pleased to represent you, should you wish to take action."

"I will do nothing. I don't wish to be the center of attention and have colonialists gossiping about me. My wish was to live among the white people as if I were like anyone else. I see that is not possible. I am viewed as Indian even though my father is a chief factor from a wealthy British family, and my mother comes from a respected and prosperous family of fur traders. People with a different skin color are no longer welcome in this society."

"Pursue your goal of a hat shop. Show them! That is the only way attitudes will change."

"I have a mind to return to Fort Edmonton. I wonder now why I ever crossed the mountains in the first place."

"How did you cross from Rupert's Land? I traveled on the Oregon Trail and then over the Sierra Mountains, and that was very difficult. Many people died. I hear the Rockies are impassable."

"I am part Cree, and over the centuries, our people have traveled over the mountains. I came with a group of my people led by a Hudson's Bay man, James Sinclair. We took the Kananaskis Pass. It was difficult, but no one died. No one starved to death, and no one ate human flesh to survive. That, I cannot imagine. Our people are able to find game where even an old frontiersman like Sinclair could not. When I heard about the emigrants in the McNair wagon train starving at the foot of the Sierras, I wondered why the leader did not turn to the Indians for help. Certainly some rob and pilfer, but they have always offered food to starving whites. The local Indians call you people, Xwelitiem. Do you know what that means?'

"You are about to tell me," Christian said with a warm smile.

"It translates as starving people."

Christian could not help laughing. "The white people believe they are superior. It is hilarious to learn that the Indians view the newcomers as destitute and incapable of feeding themselves."

"My father relied on the Athabaskans at Fort Edmonton. The explorers and Hudson's Bay men would never have survived without my mother's people guiding them and hunting for their food."

"I am pleased to hear you voice an opinion. I am also encouraged that you no longer believe I am a threat, and perhaps even understand that I am a gentleman. If you would accept my offer to walk with me, I would be a paragon of propriety. You may even bring along a companion as a chaperone."

"Louise," Rose decided. "She will come, especially if you talk Robert into joining us. No one will gossip when they see four of us out for a stroll. Besides, I understand from Alice that Louise has been most taken with Robert since their days on the Oregon Trail."

Chapter Thirty
Rose and Christian

Over the summer, Rose and Christian walked together each Sunday, taking the ocean trail up Beacon Hill while Robert and Louise followed at a discreet distance.

"Louise, let's sit for a spell and let Christian and Rose walk ahead. I want to allow them a little privacy today because it is my belief that Christian hopes to ask Rose for her hand."

"He is besotted with her, and so distracted he can't eat his meals," Louise confided, thinking how happy she would be if Robert had similar feelings for her.

Louise sat primly on a rocky ledge on Beacon's Hill overlooking the Pacific Ocean and opened the sketchbook that she carried with her on her walks. An eagle flew above, catching the high winds, and Louise had captured its likeness within a few minutes.

"You are an amazing artist," Robert told her, as he looked over her shoulder at the pencil drawing. "Have you heard of Audubon?"

"Why, yes! Carreena spoke of his wonderful prints of birds and animals that hang in the Library of Congress."

"Perhaps you will go there someday. In fact, if I become well off, it would please me to pay your passage around the Horn just to watch you enjoy the Audubon prints."

Color rose in Louise's cheeks at this unusual offer. *I believe he may become wealthy, but he will never take me on a trip to Washington.*

When she turned her head to look at Robert, he held her gaze for a moment.

Louise blushed and averted his eyes.

If only Robert would care for me as Christian cares for Rose.

As Robert and Louise sat in the brilliant sunshine on rocks warmed by the sun, Christian took Rose's hand and drew her close to him, shielded from view by bushy pine trees. Rose leaned against the trunk of the pine tree, shivering with anticipation of her first kiss.

"I know you have never kissed a man, and I don't want to pursue you beyond what you feel comfortable with. But I should so very much like to kiss those beautiful lips of yours."

"That would be fine with me, Christian." She lifted her face to him. Christian trembled as he bent to kiss her. It was the sweetest kiss in his life. Her lips were soft and warm, her kiss modest. He wanted the kiss to last forever, but she placed a cool hand on his forehead and gently pushed him arms length from her.

"Your kiss is wonderful, Christian," she said, smiling lovingly at him, "but since it is my first kiss, I have nothing to compare it to, only that it felt amazing."

"Rose, you must know how much I love you. May I ask if you return my feelings?"

"I do, my dear Christian. From that very first day we met, I thought to myself what a fine man you were, the type of man I have dreamed of, gentle and kind, yet muscular and strong. What more could a woman want?"

They walked hand in hand back towards Robert and Louise.

"I believe love prevailed," Robert said, smiling. "Come, let us join the happy couple." Robert offered his hand to help Louise up. Again, their eyes met. This time Robert squeezed her hand and his face lit up with a smile.

How many years have I waited for Robert to realize I exist? But he would never seriously love me. He is simply caught up in the love radiating from Christian and Rose. Robert's feelings for me will disappear as quickly as that majestic eagle catching the winds wafting above Beacon Hill's rocky coastline.

It was the end of a long and busy day at the restaurant when Rose asked to speak to Anna.

"Anna," Rose said, standing in the office and smiling at Anna who sat at her big walnut work desk. "Christian and I are to be married, and I hope that you will be my matron of honor. I have asked Alice and Louise to be my bridesmaids."

"Rose, what wonderful news! Christian will be a fine husband," Anna smiled and got up to take Rose in her arms. "I know you will be happy. He is the most honorable man in this city...well, other than Himself," Anna chuckled.

"Robert will stand up for Christian, and needless to say, I will not be inviting Ella." Rose gave an uncharacteristic chuckle. "I hope to ask Jan to take me down the aisle as my father cannot come. Mother has been ill. I would not ask her to make that difficult trip across the mountains, and my father would not think of coming without her."

The following weeks of preparation occupied all the spare time of the four women. Rose ordered cloth of the finest quality from San Francisco and designed and stitched her gown. Alice and Louise made their own gowns from blue satin they purchased in Victoria, and Anna spared no expense. She ordered the suit for Jan and her Matron of Honor dress from the best shops in San Francisco.

The day before the wedding, Anna and Jan closed the restaurant and hired staff to prepare a wedding feast.

Christian cared little for the clothes he would wear or the food to be served. He thought only of the night he would hold his dear love in his arms. Robert checked on him to make certain that he purchased the appropriate frock coat and cravat for the wedding, and that he had the ring on the day of the wedding.

The ceremony took place in the small Victoria District Church, and the reception and dance in a spacious Hudson's Bay warehouse. Alice, Robert, Louise and Yoletan had decorated the dreary, dark space by hanging British and American flags, and cedar branches festooned with bright yellow ribbons on the ugly log walls, completely transforming the cold, bleak space into a ballroom.

Yoletan brought two fiddlers over from the Songhees Village, musicians who had entertained the Hudson's Bay men for the past ten years and were delighted to be asked to play at the wedding of the beautiful Athabaskan woman.

The newlywed couple opened the dancing, Christian holding Rose in his arms, their eyes locked, both happier than they had ever been. Then Jan danced with Rose, and Christian took Anna onto the floor. Throughout the evening, Christian and Rose danced, holding each other closer and closer.

The music livened up, and the voyageurs took their Native partners onto the floor for the French Canadian folk dances. Christian and Rose sat out these dances, instead watching their guests and holding hands, touching every chance they could.

Robert and Louise sat side by side throughout the celebration. Several men approached Louise to ask for a dance. She declined with a smile and turned back to her conversation with Robert. Both were reserved at the beginning, but that changed as the evening progressed.

"I promised my mother I would complete my education and prosper," Robert told Louise. "I have accomplished some of which mother asked of me, but I have no wish to live in a big house in the city. I want to continue my work as a solicitor and look after the farm animals and tend the vegetable garden."

"I don't desire riches. My mother traded her life to have a mansion by the sea, yet ended destitute and out of her mind. I want a simple life, and although my mother taught me naught about homemaking, I've learned from Rose how to sew my own clothes, and from Alice how to put up preserves and bake bread." She paused and listened to the music, now slow and romantic, a song she would have liked to dance to with Robert.

"What about your family?" Louise said, turning back to Robert. "I remember you telling us that you would bring them west once you were settled."

"My father passed away five years ago. Since then, I've been sending money to help my mother look after the children. Only when the rail lines reach California will they join me because my mother does not wish to take the ship around the Horn or risk bringing the children across the Panama route. You would like my mother. She makes everything for the home herself, from candles to soap, fine lace and even shoes."

"I hope to meet her and your siblings."

"I have eight sisters and one little brother. I miss them."

"My brothers are much like our father," Louise told him. "Not Americus, but our real father. They are after the gold in the Fraser, and they inhabit the beer parlors. I prefer the theatre and concerts. Most men in Victoria are either old and greedy, or too rough around the edges. You are different."

"And you are very much like me," Robert replied. "We should dance and see if our steps match as well." He offered her his hand, and his face lit up with the beautiful smile that had captured Louise's young heart many years ago on the Oregon Trail.

As they danced, Louise rested her forehead on Robert's shoulder. At last, the ghost of Annabelle Lee took flight and Robert opened his heart to a new love.

"Dear Louise, I cannot understand why I never noticed you before. All those years, you were right here." Robert knew it was too soon to propose. Too sudden for a young woman who clearly loved him. *I will give her time. Give myself time to be sure of my heart's desire.*

Robert thought of the Bible he had passed to David. David and I will share the Ackerman Bible that crossed the ocean over two hundred years ago. *Yes. Louise is the woman whose name I will write in our family's old Bible.*

Robert was once again filled with hope for the future, for him and for his family left behind in Iowa, and for this beautiful fine woman who loved him.

The musicians played waltzes as the evening came to a close. Robert and Louise continued dancing, not too closely, because neither of them wished to move the relationship too quickly. Christian danced with his bride to the "Yellow Rose of Texas," holding her tightly against his chest, her head nestled on his shoulder.

"We have stayed long enough," Christian told her, as they left the floor holding hands. "We can bid goodnight to our guests and slip away."

Once in the finest room in Bayley's Hotel, Christian could hardly contain his desire. His love and physical feelings for Rose overwhelmed him.

"My sweet girl. My dearest heart. Have you any idea how much I love you? It is almost unseemly for a man of my age to love with such abandon. You complete me, my lovely Rose." They were both so overwhelmed by love for each other, that his voice choked, and Rose's eyes filled with tears.

"You have my heart, my soul and soon will have all of me, my dearest husband."

Christian slowly loosened her wedding gown, undoing the pearl buttons down her back. As each button was unhooked, he gasped at the perfection of her body.

"I can hardly bear to look at such beauty. I have never imagined a back so perfect, such lovely arms. Oh, Rose, you are more than beautiful."

"And that will be all you may see, my dearest husband. I shall retire to the water closet to change into my nightgown. I will allow you a minute to put on your pajamas, if pajamas there be."

She stepped out from the folds of her white satin dress. Christian lifted the dress from the floor and placed it over the chair. He watched Rose walk across the room, admiring the curves of her body, modestly clothed in a light blue satin lace top and bloomers. He could not even allow himself to think about being intimate with Rose as it sent such a wave of desire through him.

Rose returned, wearing a white silk nightgown, with long sleeves and a high collar of fine lace. Christian lay naked under the sheets, watching her cross the room. In a second she would be in his arms.

Rose lifted the satin sheets and slipped into bed to lie facing Christian. He reached out, enclosing her in his arms. He ran his fingers lightly over her bare neck before moving his hand down her back, feeling the warmth and smoothness of her body through the thin layer of silk.

"My love, I want to touch every part of you. Your toes are exquisite, your ears beyond description. You are a work of art."

"And you are fooling with me, dear soul mate. I am a simple girl from the plains of Rupert's Land."

"There is naught that is simple about you, dear one."

Chapter Thirty-one
The Fraser River People

The week after Christian and Rose exchanged their vows, they moved into a two-story frame house a stone's throw from Anna and Jan's impressive mansion on Government Street. Belleview and Government Streets formed the center of the burgeoning residential district, while over by the fort, miners threw up canvas and clapboard shelters. The week Christian and Rose said their vows was also the week mining fever reached a pitch.

A group of miners, including both Americans and Brits, met for breakfast at the Brown Jug Saloon, which reeked of bacon grease and burnt biscuits. The men gathered around a long table. Most wore rough denim pants, a cotton shirt and gumboots on their feet, their unkempt hair crowned with wide-brimmed Jim Crow hats. Saxby was attired in a dark wool suit and stood out in this group of rowdy adventurers who met to make plans for the trip to the Fraser gold diggings. All were as greedy as pigs at the trough.

"I heared that the governor won't let us mine if there is as much as an Indian fishing shack on the banks of the Fraser," the former Hudson's Bay man said, sucking at his drink. Recently, he had been released from the Hudson's Bay Company and was anxious to make a fortune mining gold.

"I heared that too, but ain't goin to happen. We can do what we want without regard for the Indians." Finis squirted a stream of tobacco juice onto the floor, adding to the fetid smell of the room.

"No Indian owns land," Saxby added.

"Changes are coming. The Hudson's Bay boss won't rule for long; the colonialists and miners gotta stand up for what is right and good for this here country!" The Bay man knocked his fist on the rough-hewn table to emphasize his point.

"According to the strict rule of international law," Saxby told them, "the territory occupied by a barbarian or wholly uncivilized people may be rightfully appropriated by a civilized or Christian nation."

"That ain't what the governor says," the Bay man continued. "He has rules about which land is available and won't let the settlers take up land when there is just some Indian shack or useless potato field there. Then we gotta apply for a mining claim the size of a piss pot. Twenty-five square feet ain't nuf for a rocker, a tent and a shit-house. Then we gotta pay for the claim, for what is rightfully ours. He spouts out about protecting them Indians. What a pile of shit."

"They are just savages and must give way to the bustling sons of civilization," Saxby added, smoothing his dark, clipped beard. "I heard about this Governor Douglas and his protection of Indians. He married a darkie, so he's just another Indian-lover like that squaw man who guided us on the Oregon Trail."

"Us Americans know how to deal with them Indians: wipe them out, and what's left send to reservations. Leave the land to those that put it to good use." This was one of the American miners recently arrived from California and wild about the prospects of gold in British Territory.

"Douglas thinks he can give land to them Indians," the recently arrived miner continued. "Did you see that mess across the inlet where them Indians have their village? We settlers need land for our families. Douglas, he done give the good land on the water for them savages. I come up to the British Territory because I was told that I can get myself a quarter section if I swear allegiance to the Queen. That were just a lie. It rankles me some 'cause I've had practice at swearing and thought it would be easy to move them Indians back into the bushes where they belong."

"The governor is making a big mistake giving land to the Indians," Saxby added, "land right across from the fort, and even paying each family! What for, I don't know. If I didn't want to find my runaway wife, I would return on the next boat to Sacramento, where we rid ourselves of the tribes and put the land to good use." Saxby thought of the sunny land far to the south, land where Indians had been massacred or pushed out, sun-bleached land so different from the British Territories with its dark forests, gusty winds and sudden downpours.

"Did you read what Douglas posted?" The Bay man read from a wrinkled slip of paper. "Land available for pre-emption must not disturb possession of village sites and enclosed fields, and Indians are allowed to hunt and fish as before." He crumpled the paper and threw it on the table. "What stupidity that man has," the Bay man said, anger simmering close to the surface.

"I heared them Indians is buying guns from the Chinese and arming themselves up there in the canyon. If we gonna git to the gold, we need to fight." Finis's normally taciturn nature was enlivened by the prospect of killing Indians.

"We will find out when we get there. I've hired Indians with one of those big canoes," Saxby said. "They will take me across to the mainland and then up Fraser's river until the current is too swift. They know how to handle the tides and gales in the Georgia Strait. There's room for one more. Finis, you care to pitch in with me?"

"Before you leave, Saxby," Finis told him with a smirk on his weasel-like face. "I am betting you want to check on that wife of yours."

"Alice! Where is she?"

"She's working with Anna at the James Bay Restaurant," Finis answered. "I heared that the last person she wants to see is you. But youse are her legal husband, and you got your rights. They also have a beauty of a squaw serving table there, but she is one of them uppity Indians. Wouldn't give me the time of day when I propositioned her. Indians putting on airs as if they was like us."

"Finis is pissed off because Anna kicked him and me out, and said we'd better never darken her doorstep again," the Hudson's Bay man added. "Now we gotta eat in this greasy joint. Anna will likely boot you out the door as well, Saxby. She got a lot of power around here, what with her money and her buying up half the town."

The news about Alice threw Saxby. He had searched for her in Sacramento, then Oregon City, where just by chance, Saxby had met up with Billy and Charles, Billy's younger brother. The boys worked at the docks in Oregon City, and Saxby did not recognize them from their days on the Oregon and California trails. They were only little boys when Saxby had led the emigrants onto the Hastings Cutoff, but Billy immediately recognized Saxby. He was not pleased to meet up with the man who was responsible for so much misery and so many deaths.

"You're Saxby," Billy said, in a cool voice. "I remember you, as do all the poor souls who lost their loved ones because of you."

"You're Dorothy's son?" Saxby asked, ignoring Billy's allegation. "I am very pleased to see you boys have grown up strong and healthy. I just have one question for you. I will give you twenty gold coins for an answer. Tell me where my wife is."

Before Billy could stop him, his younger brother put out his hand for the gold. "Up north in Queen's country. Not sure exactly where, but north."

"Shut your trap, Charles. And don't you dare take his money." Billy grabbed his brother's arm and pulled him away from Saxby. "You know who that is? The monster of the Sierras. The lying bastard who is responsible for Amelia's death, and for many more besides."

Charles looked at Billy, surprised at the fury in his brother's voice, a brother who normally had a happy disposition. Charles no longer wanted the gold coins.

"Alright then, boys. Don't take my money. I'll find the bitch just the same, and she'll be sorry for running away from me." *I'll get her back and show her who's boss!*

~

"So when we leaving, Saxby?" Finis asked, getting up from the table and wiping the grease from his mouth on his sleeve.

"I'll be in touch. Find me at the Royal Hotel."

Saxby walked through the town, anger growing with each step. *Who does she think she is to run from me? I bet she's taken up with that squaw man, David.*

Through the streets of Victoria, there was the air of men whose minds were occupied with thoughts of gold. Saxby passed dozens of miners, bundles slung over their shoulders, some with wooden packing boxes weighing them down with their supplies, and Songhees people carrying baggage for the newcomers.

Knowing he had finally tracked down Alice, Saxby's interest in gold diminished. *I'll get her back, take her to my ranch on the Sacramento and teach her a lesson.*

"Where's Alice?" he blurted, after slamming the restaurant door behind him.

"Well, look who the cat dragged in," Anna said, crossing her arms over her ample chest. "There was a rumor that you were in Victoria. Looking for more defenseless women and children to slaughter? Killed all the Indians in the States, have you, and run out of victims? They don't truck with killing innocent people under the Queen's laws, so you might as well get yourself back to the States."

"Stop flapping your lips, Anna, and tell me where I can find Alice."

"Gone, Saxby, gone. And you will not find her."

"Anna. You tell me where she is or else…," Saxby stormed across the room, raising his fist. He was within a foot of the tall restaurateur when Anna picked up a plate of eggs and bacon and threw it at Saxby.

"You! You!" Saxby fumed, wiping the mess from his fine wool suit. "I'll have you in court for this."

"Go to court, Saxby," Christian said sternly, as he crossed the room to confront Saxby. "I will testify that you threatened Anna and that the plate of eggs was defense. Not likely your case will hold. And as for Alice, she's applied for divorce, and I will be serving you papers. After your absence all these years and your lack of financial support, the courts will rule with Alice."

"So it's the hero of the Sierra Pass, is it? I suppose you have a mind to take my wife."

"I have a wife, and my interest in Alice is to provide legal advice. All Alice seeks is to find peace of mind after all her suffering. Her daughter died in the Pass, your stepdaughter whose protection you had an obligation to provide. Do you know how many people starved and froze to death because of you?"

"It was their decision to follow me. I didn't put a gun to their heads."

"Maybe. But Alice had to follow you, and because of you she lost her daughter and her love of life. She will never recover, and

I place the cause of her misery at your feet. I warn you. Stay away from her."

"She is mine, and I intend to track her down. There is only a smattering of white women in this Territory. I *will* find her." Saxby paused at the door. "Rose, you said. You married that squaw, didn't you?"

"Take that back!" Christian yelled, charging across the room towards Saxby. "Say one more word about my wife, and I will smash your miserable face to a pulp!"

"No longer the calm solicitor, are you? I see that your liaison with Indians reveals your true nature. You were always siding with the savages, causing problems for me and Alice."

"Christian," Anna interjected, stepping between them. "Let it go. He is not worth it. And you, Saxby. The door is at your back. Get out."

~

As Saxby crossed the alley beside the restaurant he saw the Chinese laundry man leave from the back door of the restaurant, carrying a basket of white table linen.

"Hey, man," Saxby called out. "Tell me where Alice went!"

"We told to say we don't know."

"Here's a gold piece. Will that loosen your tongue?"

"Anna said she pay me more than you pay if I say nothing."

"Well, maybe this will convince you." Saxby drew a knife and backed the laundry man further into the alley.

"Is it worth your life to keep the information? Will Anna give that back to you after I slit your throat?"

"Don't. I tell," he pleaded, backing away from knife. "Alice, she's on the mainland. Not sure where, but she crossed last week. Now, you leave me?"

"I'll leave you, alright." Saxby sliced the knife across the little man's throat. He fell over the laundry basket, his blood soaking into snowy white sheets and tablecloths.

Saxby, Finis and two other miners waited on the banks of James Bay, watching as a long, sturdy cedar canoe, paddled by several Songhees, crossed the bay through the gray fog hanging over a granite sea. The bright carvings on the bow stood out against the gray water as the Songhees men beached the canoe and tied it up at the dock. The man in the stern was an elder, thin but with strong, sinewy arms. In the bow of the canoe sat a boy in his teens. Saxby took charge, loading the bags as if it was his boat. The Songhees men stood beside their boat watching the miners. The older man pointed at Saxby, talked to the younger man in Salish and laughed.

"What the hell did you say?" Saxby yelled. "Speak English, for Christ's sake."

The older man looked at Saxby with a blank expression.

"What the hell is this? I arranged for a boat with King Freesy. He's your chief, right? He sends me dumbass boatmen who can't speak a word of English? Well, so be it. You best be able to paddle."

Saxby boarded the boat, along with Finis and the miners. The older man untied the rope, got in the stern and pushed the canoe off from the dock with his paddle. A graceful heron lifted off the dock, startled from its perch. A light wind blew across the bay as they left the protected water and turned north, heading out of James Bay. Within an hour, they passed through channels separated by offshore islands. When night fell, the winds increased. The boatmen beached the canoe on one of the islands, where they camped for the night. Saxby grumbled, and Finis refused to eat the meal of salmon and baked potatoes the Songhees had prepared. A few hours of sleep, and they were back in the canoe.

Hours passed before they left the protected waters of the channel and turned into the Strait of Georgia. Immediately upon entering the wide strait, the waves and winds increased. The heavy canoe rode up a wave and plunged into the trough of the next, water crashing over the bow, soaking the bowman and the gear and feet of the passengers. The paddlers never paused. The old man steered the boat into the waves, and the younger Songhees kept the bow from sinking into the trough. Saxby and his group huddled in the canoe, silent in their misery.

Vancouver Island became a faint outline against a darkening sky. Hours passed as the wind tore across the ocean, kicking up waves that grew higher with each gust of wind. Still the boatmen held the course, pointing the boat east to the mainland. Clouds obscured the sun, and all was gray. A steel gray sky and the dark gray outline of the mainland. The storm never let up.

As the night wore on, Saxby could see the mainland, but could not make out where the river entered the ocean. Night fell, and still the boatmen continued northeast, with a stiff wind blowing them along. Then the wind abated, and a steady drizzle settled in. Finally, they entered a channel, whereupon Saxby, Finis and the miners gave a sigh of relief.

"Well, men," Saxby said, puffing out his chest. "We've made it. This must be Fraser's river, and soon we'll hop out of this bucket of misery and get our legs onto terra firma."

The boatmen brought the canoe alongside a rocky shore forested with towering cedars. Near the entrance to the channel, they passed a prominent rock outcropping, feet from the shoreline.

"Skalsh," the elder Songhees said, pointing to the rocky prominence rising out of the sea. After passing the unique rock the boatman called Skalsh, they entered a sheltered inlet with land on both sides. A brackish smell blew up the channel, and gulls swooped above the canoe. As the boat moved up the inlet, they passed fishing skiffs. The salmon were running and Native fishermen were out on the water, gaffing the Chinook salmon from the nets and tossing the fish into their boats. Hundreds of salmon, maybe thousands were caught during the run, and the smell of gutted fish wafted from the nearby shore.

"Whoi. Whoi." The old boatman pointed east at a sandy beach on the south shore of the channel.

"What are you babbling about? Is this Fraser's river?" Saxby yelled at the old boatman.

"Whoi. Whoi." Now Saxby could see the beach, cedar canoes lined up on the shore and, on the rise above the beach, a Native longhouse. The village, a hive of activity. Fish being gutted and smoked.

"This isn't Fraser's river, you numbskull. Where the hell did you take us?"

The Songhees ignored Saxby and paddled hard, driving the big boat onto the sand. Curious children, eyes dark and beautiful, ran to meet the strange white people, broad smiles on their faces. The adults followed, with welcoming smiles for the boatmen.

The leader of the welcoming party, a tall impressive man, approached Saxby and spoke in English. "Welcome to our village. Come, we feed you baked salmon and fresh berries, and you sleep in our longhouse."

"Where are we? Where the hell is Fraser's river?"

"Not the Fraser. You are at Whoi.Whoi. Could not go to the Fraser. Too big wind, too low water, too big waves. You want to get to the gold diggings, yes?"

"We paid money to be taken to Fraser's river. I should give that old man a boot in the ass."

"You not talk that way. He the brother of my father. Good man, and the best boatman you find. Show respect. Tomorrow we take a different route to the gold diggings. Old Squamish way. Better. Faster. Part trail. Part by boat. Go to place you whites call Lillooet."

"I paid to go up the Fraser, and the old man better take me up the Fraser." Saxby swiped angrily at the mosquitoes. It was bad enough to be wet and cold. Now pesky bugs landed on every piece of exposed skin.

"Better our way. Eat and sleep. Then we go early."

The Chief walked away, shaking his head and speaking to his people in Salish.

Saxby and his group made camp near the shore. He was sullen. Angry at the boatman, at the mosquitoes, the rain, the brinish air, and the stench of fish entrails.

"Them Indians cheated us, Saxby." It was Finis who reached for his pistol and brandished it. "If there weren't so many of them, I would kill them all just like we done to the Yana. Who do they think they are telling us civilized people the way to git to the Fraser?"

"Finis, shut the fuck up," Saxby growled.

The miners refused the lodgings and the baked salmon. Instead, they brought out dried meat and biscuits from their supplies, ate quietly and slunk off to a sheltered spot under the towering cedars where they rolled out their bedding.

Winds blew from the north into the Strait of Georgia, bringing clouds laden with moisture. Rain pelted down, soaking Saxby and Finis. A gray light fell on the wet shoreline as Saxby shook off his oilskin sheet, crawled out of his wet blankets and woke Finis.

Saxby gathered up his kit and motioned to Finis to be quiet. Saxby walked over to where the two miners slept in the shelter of a towering cedar tree. He kicked one of the miners. "Wake up. We're leaving."

Saxby led his men to the boat and climbed into the stern. "Which one of you varmints can handle a paddle?"

Among the miners was Etienne, a French Canadian and former Bay man. "I paddle across Rupert's Land from Upper Canada and never tip the canoe." He moved to the back of the canoe.

"Get your ass at the front of the boat, Froggy," Saxby ordered. "I'm steering."

"You crazy Boston man. Not easy out there in the wind."

"Finis, push us off, and all of you keep your traps shut." The wind kicked up a light froth as they steered the long cedar canoe out of the inlet.

~

They paddled south through the waves and wind. The sky and the sea were dismal.

"Sacré bleu! Saxby, steer this boat into the waves or you tip us! Ma mère, she paddle better than you."

Saxby dug his paddle into the waves but failed to bring the boat around. A rogue wave hit the canoe sideways, tipping the boat to a dangerous angle. Water shipped over the side.

"Vite! Vite! Lean into the wave." The French Canadian made a powerful high brace on the wave and brought the boat up. "Saxby, do as I say, or you put us all in the ocean. You make a strong draw on your right. Strong, not grand-mère type. Strong."

Saxby was shaking and nervous, his mouth dry from fear. He followed the instructions and drew the paddle towards the stern while the French Canadian reached out over the bow with a powerful left draw. The heavy canoe swung perpendicular to the waves and, with a few strokes, the French Canadian brought them onto the sandy shore of the Fraser River delta. Seagulls rose up from their perches, catching the wind above the delta.

"We take a pee here." Etienne said, a worried look on his face. "Then I get another man in the bow to paddle up the Fraser and you, Saxby, sit but no paddle. Bon Dieu, Saxby, we this close to swimming." The French Canadian raised his hand, his thumb and index finger a fraction of an inch apart.

Saxby stepped ashore on shaky legs. An eerie light fell on the granite sea. He walked along the spit, swearing under his breath, furious at the diminishment of his self-importance. "Damn him to hell." He looked at the flat, sandy expanse of the Fraser delta and thought back to the rocky hills on the Hastings Cutoff.

This is the second time I've been deposed. First it was that bumpkin McNair taking over as captain of the wagon train. Now I am humiliated and replaced by an uneducated know-all from the boondocks of Canada —a stupid Bay man who thinks he is better than me. Saxby kicked angrily at the sand and shuffled slowly back to the shore where the men waited impatiently. The tide was low and the expanse of the delta immense. Saxby hated this land of sucking tides.

The canoe wasn't about to tip. He's a bloody liar. I did not cause the problem. I'll put a knife through the throat of that French Canadian smartass. And McNair, it was all his fault I was banished and separated from Alice. But I am close now. She's on the river. I will find the bitch and beat the hell out of her.

The Frenchman steered the canoe past the Musqueam village of Chilukthan and up the north arm of the Fraser. Fishermen in their skiffs and on riverbanks stood gaffing the heavy run of salmon. Gulls swarmed over the boats, snatching pieces of the rich meat, then with cries reeled off into the blue August sky.

~

At the same time, Alice, McNair and Walter disembarked at Fort Langley. They had packed their boat to the gunnels with supplies: tools for Walter's lumber business, pots, iron frying pans, a Dutch oven and sacks of food for Alice's roadhouse.

They replenished their food supplies at the fort, supplementing their root vegetables and dried food with fresh beans, corn and

Brussels sprouts grown on the rich Fraser River soil. The fort was a busy place, with miners landing every hour. Most spoke little, bought their supplies and hurried on, driven by the lure of gold. McNair was anxious to get underway, but Alice and Walter lingered. Walter talked with the Hudson's Bay factor, and Alice listened, interested in the news.

"So you say that Douglas will be in Fort Langley soon to declare the new Colony of British Columbia?" Walter repeated to the factor who managed the fort.

"It is big news for the Hudson's Bay Company. They will no longer be owners of Rupert's Land. It marks the end of our rule over these lands, lands we have controlled for two centuries. As the men tell me, HBC doesn't mean Hudson's Bay Company, it means 'here before Christ,'" the Hudson's Bay factor chuckled. "It will be a little sad, but then us Bay men will take up land and settle in the new crown colony."

"After my trip to the gold diggings, I hope to have enough money selling lumber to develop my properties at Fort Victoria. My wife, she is Musqueam. We have a lumber mill in Fort Victoria and we want to work the farm as well as cut lumber for houses."

"I see you have Elswa and his grandsons and family members as your boatmen. Old Elswa is one of the strongest men I've ever seen behind a paddle, and those Musqueam know how to get through the canyon to the gold diggings. Good men. Not all the Indians are to be trusted. Some have taken to drinking. The liquor is destroying the people, and disease kills them. The Musqueam, they're smart. Stayed away from the booze, even agreed to vaccinations and saved most of their people from smallpox. You folks will be okay with them. Upriver we have a few renegade Indians that may give you trouble."

The Musqueam boatmen loaded the canoe with supplies and paddled out from the shore at Fort Langley and north towards Yale.

Elswa spoke broken English and had already mastered the art of telling jokes in a language foreign to his tongue. He had a pleasant disposition and spoke both Salish and English. Alice was not always quite sure what he said, but the grin on his face was enough to bring a smile to her face.

"You like my brother's sister, Maggie. She not scared of water, and when we hunt the whales, she the best paddler. I bet you know how to hold a paddle. Yes, lady?"

"I've never paddled a canoe, but I want to learn. Would you let me help, and I'll paddle you all the way to our campsite?"

"You paddle. I sleep, lady. Remember, you and the other paddlers control the canoe, not let the water tell you where to go. Strong and steady."

The river was low and the current lazy. Alice took the paddle and stepped into the bow. She dug into the water with deep catches and strong strokes. Elswa watched her for a few minutes then fell asleep sitting up.

"You so strong lady, you become a boatman, yes?" Elswa said, waking up and grinning at Alice. "You skookum lady."

"I am done in and happily give up the paddle."

Alice handed Elswa the paddle. "Want a bite to eat?"

"Cookies. I like them cookies you Xwelitiem bake."

"Xwelitiem? What does that mean?"

"Starving people. You people come across the mountains with no food. We feed you salmon. Now upriver you come thick like pack of rats, starving and soon freezing your backsides."

Alice chuckled at this description of white people. "That may be, but today I am feeding you." She laughed, her face lighting up with a moment of peace and happiness at being on the water with this congenial boatman.

She dug through the food bag and passed each person a chocolate cookie and a chunk of cheese. Elswa never slowed. He paddled with one hand, grabbed the snack with the other and, in a moment, smoothly returned to full power paddling.

"Kloshe," Elswa, said with a grin, as he held up one of her cookies.

"Excuse me," Alice said, puzzled.

"He says your cookies are *kloshe*, meaning good in Chinook language," Walter explained.

Alice smiled. She remembered David conversing with the Tribes. "Chinook. That is what David spoke."

"Along with signing, it is the common language among the tribes, French, Scots and Brits ever since the beginning of the fur trade," Walter told her.

Alice was tired from her time as bow paddler. The August sun reflected off the river so brilliantly that she had to pull her bonnet over her eyes. The splash of the paddles and the green banks of Fraser's river soothed her. She yawned, put her head on a flour sack and dozed until the sun descended in the west. She woke when the canoe scraped over a rocky outcropping in the riverbed.

Above the river, she saw green forests and towering above the trees, rugged peaks. To the west, the setting sun turned the wide, flat surface of the river to gold. Alice felt a sense of peace she had not experienced for years. *I might be fleeing from Saxby, but with every mile I travel into the wilderness, my heart sings with the beauty of the land and the peace that water brings me.*

They camped on a grassy beach next to the river where Alice built a fire and had a meal of fried beef, potatoes and fresh vegetables ready before the men had finished putting up the tents. They used supply boxes as seats and sat enjoying the fire, a comforting pod of light and warmth. The massive cedar trees created a bank of darkness against the night sky, and the jagged mountains towered in the distance.

"Three trails to the gold diggings, and all start here at Hal'emeylem Ts'go'. The Brits call it Fort Hope," Elswa told them. "The Hudson's Bay brigade trail, it goes back of the canyon, the Kem'loop way is easier but long, and you can take pack horses. Maybe, you bringing your horses over Kem'loop way," he commented before continuing. "The fast way is the canyon, but it is tough for you Xwelitiem—steep trail high above the falls. You visit the fort now?"

"I don't need anything at Fort Hope," Alice told Elswa. "I am anxious to see Fort Yale and decide if I should open my restaurant there."

"If you visit Fort Hope, Chief Factor Walker," Elswa told her, "he tell you about the bags of gold dust the river tribes are bringing out in their canoes. Even the women are sluicing ten to twelve dollar a day."

"I don't believe them Indians are capable of digging up the gold. Where you git these stories, Elswa? Maybe them Indians stumbled on the gold and started all the excitement, but learning how to sluice it?" McNair blustered, "There ain't no way that will happen." Elswa had learned to ignore McNair's racist comments and changed the subject.

"Seems like them Boston men are around every bend from Fort Hope to Fort Yale, naming every gold-bearing bar. Tomorrow we pass New York Bar. Then we got American Bar and Texas Bar. Can't believe no more that this is our land and that we are in Queen's country. Can't even remember what this village was called before the Hudson's Bay men renamed it Fort Hope."

"I'll have to call the place Hope as I can't get my tongue around the local names," Walter said with a smile. "Those French Canadian voyageurs risk their lives every year paddling canoes through the canyon and then carrying their supplies and gear across the cliffs.

I bet'cha they likely *hoped* with all their heart that they would survive till they reached *Hope*." He chuckled and lifted his cup in
a salute to the mountains. "And me, well I *hope* to fill this canoe
with gold from the miners who need houses."

They woke before the sun ascended over the high mountains to
the east. The morning was crisp as they sat on packing boxes sip-
ping coffee and warming their hands over the dying embers of the
fire. As shafts of light lit the river, they packed up camp, and Elswa
pushed the canoe into the Fraser River.

"River, it gets stronger now. When we fight through the current, we need skookum woman and Walter to help paddle and
maybe McNair learn Musqueam way to handle paddle."

By midday they reached swifter water where all the paddlers,
including McNair, worked to keep the canoe moving upstream.
After passing a set of rapids, the river calmed and the Native paddlers were able to handle the canoe without help.

"Are we walking the canyon tomorrow?" Alice asked. There
was a hint of concern on her pretty face.

"We stay two nights in Nlaka'pamax. They call it Fort Yale.
Big place soon with miners and more Xwelitiem than we like to
have visit. White people, they like relatives who do not leave, take
over everything, kick our people out of little fishing houses. They
burned down upper river people's rancherias, took food from their
cache and they throw rest of berries and salmon in the river. The
river people soon homeless in their own lands."

"And here we are, more white people," Alice said smiling
warmly at Elswa.

"You okay. Walter, he is family. You good woman." Elswa
looked at McNair and made no comment. McNair knew better than
to continue to express his views about the Indians in Elswa's company, and in fact, the longer he spent with the accomplished Musqueam boatmen, the more his views about the tribes changed.

Chapter Thirty-two
Chief Spintlum

Elswa and Walter walked Alice to the Hudson's Bay Post in Fort Yale while McNair headed off in search of an establishment that offered meals and, McNair hoped, something to wet his whistle. The town was bustling with miners, some in poor garb, some in fine woolen suits and some in U.S. military uniforms. They gathered on street corners talking loudly in agitated voices. It was clear from their tone that these men were angry and in a fighting mood.

"Be watchful, Alice," Walter advised. "I don't care for the mood of the miners."

"Did you hear what one of them yelled at you, Elswa?" Alice said, not waiting for an answer. "They said, get out of here, you dirty savage."

Elswa shook his head, but did not appear to be surprised. "There will be trouble with the Indians upriver. I know that. And Walter is right. You nice lady, be careful. Well, here we are. We go in to talk to Chatelain."

The trading post was a single-story log building constructed on Front Street as part of the expansion of the fur trade. It formed the center of Fort Yale, a fur trading post that grew up overnight in 1858, not with substantial stone and brick, but clapboard shacks thrown up in haste and a sea of tents pitched on every available piece of reasonably flat ground.

While Alice shopped, the manager of the Fort Yale post, Ovid Allard, a French Canadian with a strong accent, offered a running monologue regarding the problems Yale faced. He had a bushy beard and his clothing was clean but worn out, with several patches and mends. His vest stretched over his round stomach. What was unusual about Ovid was his ability to speak with the local tribes, and his passion for the town soon to be part of the new Colony of British Columbia.

"Dere's trouble comin' to our remote fort. A young girl from the Nlaka'pamax tribe, she was taken by one of dem miners," he told her with a look of abhorrence. "My wife Justine, she is from dat tribe, and she hears stories the white folks don't hear and don't care to hear. Da chief of the Nlaka'pamax Tribe dere in da upper Fraser has gathered his people, saying he gonna turn the miners back. Why not? They've been here forever, and the miners just pour in, disrespectful of the locals or our laws. Many are part of dis here Vigilance Committee or a rival contingent, the Law and Order group. De're Californians, or a good bunch are. Dey want to push up the canyon, all in here telling me I gotta sell dem guns. I told dem no. But they be back." Ovid uttered a tired sigh and took a deep breath before continuing.

"Dey don't understand dis here is British Territory and dem Americans have no authority to wage war in our country or set demselves up as law makers. I've never seen da like of it since crossing the continent and landing in New Caledonia." He wrapped his arms about his chest in frustration. "You must watch out, little lady. Those vigilantes are out for blood, Indian blood, but they are a danger to the peace lovin' people of our little town and to a pretty woman like you." He offered her a kindly smile.

"Thank you, Ovid," Alice said politely, trying to process all the information he had poured out. "I will stay in my room, and you look after yourself. Don't be a hero when the vigilantes come. You have a wife and children, and no harm must come to them." Alice smiled at one of the dark-eyed children peaking at her from behind the counter.

"Ovid, or are you called Chatelain?" Alice asked him.

"Chatelain, my lady. Dat is my French name, and my wife, she likes dat name."

"Well then, Chatelain, my goods will be picked up by our Telt'Yet porters who will pack over the brigade trail. I bid you goodbye and warn you to keep your family safe."

"Farewell for now." He gave her a warm smile.

Alice walked out from the dim interior of the fort and stood at the door of the log building looking out to the river that was flowing high up on its banks, the recent rain having raised the water level. *The miners will not be pleased*, she thought, *because they needed the river levels to drop before they could work on the sand and gravel bars.*

The sun scorched the town, lighting up Front Street. As she watched from the shadows of the log building, she saw a tall figure along the river trail that led to the Fort. Alice recognized the familiar gate and form of the man before he was clearly in sight, and although her capacity to feel for anyone was damaged, her heart beat faster. *I loved him once*, she thought. *I loved him so much that the smallest touch of his hand aroused me.*

Alice remained near the fort, watching David take long slow strides towards her. He was still a fair distance away when he recognized her. His face lit up with a smile as he came towards her.

"Mr. Ackerman! I didn't expect to see you in the British Territories." David looked different. Except for a neat beard and small mustache, he was clean-shaven and his blond hair shorter. She noticed that he had replaced the decorated Indian vest with a black vest and jacket, his badge clearly displayed. Two Colt peacemakers hung from a belt around his waist. His black boots were polished to a fine shine.

"Alice. You look well." David took in her healthy appearance, the simple blue smock she wore and the blue bonnet covering her dark locks. "How are you feeling?" He opened his arms to her, but Alice stepped back, instead offering her hand.

"Healing a little, Mr. Ackerman." She spoke softly and had a wistful look about her. "I wish I could have remained with Anna in Victoria, but when I got word that Saxby was in the city, once more I had to flee." Alice stepped out from the shade of the fort and walked alongside David, heading back to the makeshift buildings and the tent city that made up the town.

"I saw Christian and Rose in Victoria. They crossed the Straits two days ago and asked that I warn you and tell you that Saxby searches for you and may be heading up the Fraser River."

"That man will never leave me in peace." Her voice had a bitter harshness, and her body stiffened.

"He views you as his possession and will resort to violence if he can't get you back. Christian told me your divorce will be decided soon."

"I doubt if Saxby will let me go based on a pile of papers." A dark look crossed her face at the mention of Saxby's name. Alice placed a hand on her forehead as if to brush away his memory. She needed to talk about something else. "Why is Christian coming to the gold diggings?"

"He is going upriver to help sort out trouble in the canyon with the tribes. Governor Douglas hired him as a special deputy. Rose is traveling with him. They came upriver in style, taking the steamer, staying in a cabin and eating chef-prepared food in the dining room."

"Rose. Of course, she would not stay in Victoria," Alice said with a sweet smile, as she thought of her younger friend. "Where Christian goes, she goes."

"Love will heal many wounds, Alice. Christian struggled to bring the children across the Sierras, gave up on finding a companion, and look at him now filled with love and hope. And Robert, he has opened his heart to Louise, and we thought he would mourn Annabelle Lee forever."

"Love. I loved Amelia with all my heart, and she was taken from me. I cannot bear thinking of it." Alice bowed her head. Even after all the years, tears pooled in her eyes as the painful memories flooded back.

"I know you are wounded," he said with compassion, pausing along the trail to look at Alice, to hope that she might leave behind the misery of the Sierras. "You cared for me once, Alice, although we never declared our affections. I saw the way you looked at me. It was unmistakable, and I felt the tears on your face when we parted." David looked in her eyes, believing that he saw something of the affection she once held for him. "Think on it, and try to open your heart once again, if not for me, then someone else who will care for you as I would."

"If it is all the same to you, Mr. Ackerman, I prefer not to speak of love. I insist we change the topic." Her words sent a cold splash on his face.

"Forgive me, Alice. I did not mean to intrude on you."

"Nothing to forgive," she said softly. "Now, please tell me why you are in Yale?"

"I've been appointed by Governor Douglas as a special constable to help keep the peace. War has started on upper Fraser's river, with tribes keeping the miners from working the gold bars, and miners burning down their rancherias. Killings on both sides. Maybe a dozen."

"I heard that three bodies floated into Yale, with their heads severed. Is that why you were sent here by Governor Douglas?"

"The Brits don't want Indian wars to break out in Canada. They saw what happened in Oregon and Washington: settlers burned out of their homes and scalped; the tribes slaughtered and their villages razed to the ground. The Brits don't intend to see whites kill Indians or Indians kill settlers in the new British Colony." He paused, noticing Alice's look of concern. "And what will you be doing, Alice?"

"I'm going upriver to the gold-bearing bars with McNair and Walter. I will cook for them and maybe anyone else who will pay me in gold. I hired Telt'Yet Indians to pack our supplies to the gold diggings. As well as cooking, I will be selling flour, bacon, beans, and whatever else they need. Do you realize the miners will pay forty dollars in American money for one pair of gumboots?"

"When did you acquire an interest in gold, Alice? That doesn't sound like you." David offered a wry smile at the thought of Alice, who distained material things, now speaking of earning riches.

"I know you are laughing at me," she said, returning his smile. "I care little for fine things. I want my independence. Saxby squandered my fortune, and when I rid myself of him I don't want to be beholden to any man."

Alice noticed the sad look on David's face and immediately regretted her words. She had loved him once.

"I'm sorry, David, if my words wound you. I need a friend, nothing more. I still grieve each day for Amelia. I blame myself."

"You still blame yourself, Alice?" David said, astonished. "You were not at fault! Saxby led you on that desperate trail. Failed you and Amelia in every way."

"I could have saved her, I know that. But please, let's talk of something else. I could use a friendly shoulder."

"As a friend, I hope you will join me for dinner," he said with a warm smile. David offered his arm to Alice. She placed her hand lightly on his arm, comforted by the warmth she felt through his jacket. They walked to one of the few eating establishments in Yale, a new log building with rooms for rent and a dining area. It was a good deal more substantial than the other kitchens operating out of canvas tents. "We won't be dining on gourmet food, just simple fare, but it will give us a chance to talk and give me time to learn how to be your friend."

They entered the roadhouse where they were served a meal of beans and bread. David ate heartily while Alice picked at the beans, thinking that she could prepare a far tastier dish. They sat at long tables along with miners from countries all over the world, miners who had not seen a beautiful woman in months. Alice did not go unnoticed.

David looked over the motley gathering at the eatery. "Alice, please be careful while you are here, and don't walk the streets alone. The newcomers are liquored up, talking of killing Indians to get onto the gold bars. Who knows what they might get up to having found a beautiful woman alone in their midst?"

"Not to worry, Mr. Ackerman. Although the day is early, I am retiring to my room to make plans for my roadhouse and to read until nightfall."

Alice did not sleep well. Late into the night, miners wandered the streets, drinking and yelling. Every time she dropped to sleep the noise woke her. Finally, as the eastern sun lit up the town, Alice fell into a deep sleep and woke at the sound of a knock on the door.

"Alice. It's me. Rose. Join us for breakfast downstairs in the dining room. I need your company."

Alice found Christian and Rose sitting side by side at the table.

"Your cooking is far better, Alice," Christian told her, as he pushed his leathery eggs to the side.

"And you look exceedingly well, happy and prosperous." Alice noted Christian's fashionable frock coat of fine black wool and his velvet waistcoat with a white silk stock tied in a flowing bow at his neck. A thick gold watch-chain hung across his chest. "Rose, are you sending Christian to the tailor so that his attire might be more suitable to yours?"

"My dear husband could wear torn pants and a frayed shirt, and he would still look handsome to me. In fact, when we take to the canyon trail tomorrow, he will leave behind his fine clothes and wear an outfit more fitting for the rough trek along the Fraser." Rose wore a practical walking outfit of light blue wool and elegant buttoned boots, her black hair in a modest bun.

"What are your plans, Alice?" Christian asked, while he held Rose's hand.

"I will continue upriver and open my own kitchen near the gold diggings. I could use your help, Rose. Would you consider going in with me?"

"That will be fine with me," Rose replied, "as long as I remain near my dear husband."

"I won't be too far away from Alice," Christian said, "because I want to give warning if Saxby seeks you out, and of course, I need to be near my dear wife. I cannot be far from her for more than a minute," he smiled and squeezed Rose's hand.

"Will I have to be on the run from Saxby for the rest of my life?"

"He is determined to find you, Alice," Christian told her in a somber tone. "He's telling everyone that you are his lawful wife and that he has rights."

"Rights! What about my rights? What about the poor souls who died in the Sierras because of his foolhardy decisions? Christian, the divorce will be heard in court soon, won't it? Once it is finalized, then I can ask for protection from Governor Douglas. Walter heard that Britain is sending a militia to keep the miners in line. Am I right about that?"

"You are correct. The Royal Engineers will be here soon, but please understand that the militia has only recently arrived on the lower Fraser River and will have all they can handle with the conflicts between Indians and miners."

"What are these Fraser River Indians up to?" McNair held a cup of coffee and pulled a chair up to their table. "They should be like the Musqueam and work with the miners instead of fighting us. That Elswa is one good man, but I hears them Indians upriver are nothing but savages."

"Have you learned nothing, McNair?" Christian asked. "The river people have been here for centuries. They discovered the gold on the Fraser; now the miners want the tribes to move aside. They live off the salmon. Didn't you see them on Transformer Rock, with their long spears bringing in the salmon and the women drying them on the shore?"

"The rock you speak of, my dearest husband, is the home of the underwater bear, T'itequo Spa'th," Rose told them, a sweet smile on her lips. "Not only is it one of the most important fishing site on the Fraser River, but it is a spiritual site."

"Thank you, my linguist wife. Home of the underwater bear," Christian said, smiling. "I like that legend, and it is one to remember as all will be changed by the newcomers. Already, miners are taking over land that is occupied by the tribes and has been for hundreds of years. I'm going upriver to defend their rights, and I hope that if you are going to pan for gold, McNair, you will respect British law."

"Ain't it the same as U.S. law?"

"There's more protection for the tribes under British law, at least for the present. Governor Douglas says no one can take over land that shows occupation or use by the Indians. Of course, the American miners, crazy for gold, are ignoring the laws. Well, not just Americans. We have gold-hungry people from all over the world. Many Chinese, but mostly Americans who ran roughshod over the Yakama and believe they can run roughshod over the Queen's Indians." Christian frowned and opened his palms in a gesture of hopelessness.

"Well, Saxby has been running roughshod over me, Christian, so I hope you can help me."

"Your best chance is to keep your distance from your former husband."

"Well, not former yet, so I need to be constantly vigilant. Soon we will go up the canyon trail. Walter befriended the Indians; he gave them rough lumber at no cost. He is protected by them."

"David and I need to get to Spuzzum where the Telt'yet and several other tribes are mustering, hoping to stop the miners from going farther upriver. I'll ask Walter if his Telt'Yet friends will guide us through the canyon. Without the protection of the river people, it is impossible to get through the barricade."

Christian and David worried when they saw the mood at Fort Yale. Three thousand miners were gathered there, armed, and too many were ready to kill any Indian they found. Once again Ovid refused to sell rifles, but within the hour a band of angry miners had charged the door, threatening the clerk and his family. Ovid had no recourse but to hand over the arms to Captain Graham and his band of vigilantes.

Captain Graham led the group of armed miners, mostly Americans, who were preparing to force entry beyond the falls. Captain Snyder led another group of miners but differed in his approach to dealing with the tribes. Snyder argued for talks before use of arms.

Both American militia men intended to gain entry beyond to the falls using whatever it would take.

Upriver from Yale, the tribes were armed and waiting for the miners, prepared to fight for their rights to the gold fields, their salmon fishing spots and their villages. At the Indian barricade, there were both chiefs fired up to fight and chiefs cautioning against war with the whites.

Captain Graham was used to using force against the tribes in the States. He believed that counseling negotiation over violence was weak and would not give them access to the gold-bearing bars.

"I am ready to take my men up the canyon and wipe out every man, woman, and child!" Captain Graham told a contingent of armed militia. "Kill those murdering savages and teach them a lesson." Graham was a spit and polish militiaman who had fought Indian wars in the States. "Upriver, a band of Fraser River Indians beheaded three miners and sent the mutilated bodies floating to Yale. We will take the heads off the savages and see how they like that."

"You'll start a war, Graham," Captain Snyder said, stepping into the discussion. "First, try to get the tribes to stand down. I propose to take my men up the canyon and parlay with the chiefs. Make a show of force but harm no one. The Bay man Yates speaks their language. We need to convince the Indians that war with us will only end in the death of their people."

"My men are armed and ready," Graham argued. "We don't parlay with savages, Snyder. Have you gone soft since you landed in the British Territories?"

"You can't gain entry by shedding blood," David countered. Christian and David had joined the mob. "Blood of the river people and blood of the miners. It may start a war between the tribes and whites, just like the wars in Oregon and Washington. There is a better way."

"Don't listen to them, Captain." It was Finis, armed with a rifle, a silly grin pasted on his face. "They's were with us on the Oregon Trail. They's nothing but Indian-lovers. We gotta wipe out the Indians if we want to civilize this country."

Finis had joined the militia, which had only added to the simmering anger. Very few of the miners accepted that the Native people had any hold on the land, the gold in the river or the fishing sites. They coveted the gold bars in the Fraser River.

"Kill the savages! They have no right to stop us. Who do they think they are?" Finis expressed the views of the armed militia. David had not seen Finis since the massacre of the Yana, and he moved his hand to his sidearm, struggling to contain his fury.

"Don't return violence with violence, David," Christian whispered. "I know how hard it is for you to show restraint, but restraint we must demonstrate, or the canyon will be filled with blood."

"I want to shoot him in the face like he shot my little son; I want to slice off his ears and his testicles and stuff them in his ugly mouth. No, I will be lenient and take him into the woods and cut his throat. That is what I should do. No one would know, and would the world miss that evil man?"

"We are here to keep the peace, David. I don't want violence. I have a wife with me, and you want to ensure Alice's safety. We can't convince the miners to stand down entirely. There are too many of them, and they have no respect for British law. We must show patience in the face of these vigilantes."

"You talk to them, Christian. I cannot bear to look at their evil faces. You have the gifts of a peacemaker."

Captain Snyder's contingent took the old Native trail that led to Spuzzum and then to the canyon. A hundred of Snyder's militia men followed him, walking in single file. Christian and David joined the march, falling in at the end of militia. As representatives of the Queen, they were greatly outnumbered. They could observe, but if war broke out, there was little they could do. Stay out of sight, and if a conflict broke out, they could only hope to stop a slaughter.

David and Christian walked the trail in silence. What could Christian possibly say to an American militia man who intended to take over lands the river people had used for centuries? What would David say to an American soldier who was so much like Captain Freeman, the man who'd led the massacre against the Yana? What would Christian, who adored his Aboriginal wife, say to a soldier who had disdain for the Natives? They kept their own council, thinking ahead to the inevitable confrontation with the river chiefs.

They walked towards the canyon, stopping at a ransacked Native village. The fishing shacks had been burned, and among the destruction they found two dead Natives and one miner. "This is the fate of the river people," David said, stopping to check the one shack left standing. The small shelter was dark, and they waited until their eyes adjusted. As they walked through the door, a woman clutched her two children and screamed.

"Don't be afraid," David said, in sign language and Chinook. The mother looked suspiciously at David. He signed that he would not harm her and offered her bread and smoked salmon, smiling and speaking in a soft voice. She took the food and gave some to the oldest child. He grinned at David, his eyes dark and beautiful.

"Tell us what happened." The mother seemed less afraid now.

"The miners were here," she said in her language. "We told them to go. There were about a dozen, and we were mostly women and children. Our men wouldn't let them on the river to get the gold." She paused, looking toward the dead bodies that lay near the shack. "That is my husband and my brother." Her voice choked. "We told the miners to leave. They refused, and they fought. They killed my husband. My brother killed a miner; the miner killed him.

Then the miners threw all our winter food in the river and burned our houses. The miners went upriver. Our people ran into the woods."

David and Christian left food with the mother, cautioning her to stay away from the miners. She picked up her baby and took her son's hand. "I'll try and make it downriver to Yale. Ovid will help me."

Christian and David joined the end of the contingent, disturbed at what they had seen. "It will be just like the Yakama War. Native villages burned to the ground, the river people as well of miners dead. It makes me sick," David told Christian.

"If Graham gets ahead of Snyder and engages the river tribes, it will be a massacre," Christian agreed, as they hurried up the trail.

"He had better keep his war-mongering men on the other side of the Fraser like he agreed and give Snyder time to negotiate."

They camped overnight in a gully and woke to a clear sky and a bright sun rising across the mountains from the east. They took a hasty meal and were soon on the trail. It wasn't long before they smelled smoke from the campfires and heard a commotion ahead on the trail. It was Spuzzum, a major village before the canyon.

"Stop. This is our land." It was Spintlum, Chief of the Kumsheen at The Forks. He was an impressive man in his middle years, one who commanded respect. His people stood defiantly with him, and beside Spintlum were the Native chiefs from Kem'loop and the upper Fraser. They were armed and angry, facing white men who intended to breech the barrier of logs erected across the trail.

All were anxious as they viewed the angry and armed bands— more than one hundred Natives, most with muskets, a few with axes, spears or bow and arrow. Many had war paint and looked fierce and unbending.

"I am Captain Snyder, of the American Pikes Guard. Mr. Yates will speak in your tongue and will interpret." The tribes knew

Yates. He was a good man who treated them fairly. "I propose a treaty—an agreement the tribes and the miners can all live with." Snyder's men took up their position, prepared to fight should the Natives attack.

David moved towards the assembly of chiefs and warriors so that he could hear. He could feel their hatred for white men.

"We know about the treaties in Oregon," Spintlum said, "broken before the next moon. The Cayuse and Yakama moved off their land. Why should we trust an American soldier?"

Tensions were high. And indeed, why was an American proposing a treaty in Queen's country, the chief wondered? Had America taken over New Caledonia? The river people were used to dealing with the Hudson's Bay Company. They cheated the Indians, but did not threaten them with guns. It had been peaceful for the past fifty winters. The tribes were encouraged to pan for gold, and the Hudson's Bay bought everything they produced. Now they were using rockers and making even more money. The chiefs grumbled, thinking that the only way to stop the Americans was to fight.

"There is an army of miners gathered at Yale," Snyder informed them. "They are a militia numbering in the thousands and are ready to storm through and kill every Indian in sight. The Hudson's Bay clerk would not sell guns to the militia, but the miners threatened Ovid, and now they are armed and dangerous." He had killed many Indians in the dreadful Yakama war. Now, for the first time in his career, he was intent on avoiding war.

"We also are armed and dangerous," Spintlum countered. "We can fight. Protect our land with its gold, our salmon-fishing spots, our women and children." Chief Spintlum of the Kumsheen spoke with fervor, knowing that many of the other chiefs intended to fight the miners, and that if peace was to be achieved, it would be at great cost.

"If you choose to fight, many will be killed," Snyder told them, speaking slowly but with a hard, unbending edge to his voice. "I come to tell your people to step down. You don't want to fight the Americans; they successfully fought many tribes. Now the tribes across the border have conceded." The captain paused to give time for Yates to interpret.

"That is no peace," the Chief countered, now speaking in English. "We give up our river. You miners come from America, you push us away, dig our gold, ruin salmon fishing, destroy salmon pots, take our women?" He was a tall, strong man with an imposing voice. "A young girl, the daughter of my brother, only twelve winters was taken by three miners. We killed miners over that and miners killed my people. We already at war."

"No harm will come to your people if you stand down. Your fishing sites will be protected." Captain Snyder promised, even though he knew he could not control the miners. They were empty words given out to encourage the tribes to stand down. Let the miners dig the gold. Gold that belonged to the tribes.

Christian's stomach tightened. *Would Captain Snyder keep his word? Won't the river tribes be overrun, their land taken, their lives changed forever?* Christian felt he should be the one to speak for the Governor, not the American. Although he knew in his heart the tribes would soon be overrun, and nothing would stop it.

"We had promises before." Chief Spintlum faced the American Captain. "Promises given, promises taken away."

After Chief Spintlum spoke, the tribes left the barricades to meet the following morning at The Forks. Eleven tribes faced Captain Snyder and the militia. Below, the clear blue water of the Thompson River joined the silt-filled river of the Fraser. A slight drizzle came down, and a gloom settle over the tribes.

The Kem'loop chief, anger burning in his breast, faced Snyder. "We are many and have already suffered from strangers taking our gold, harming our land. You killed unarmed people at Okanagan Lake, shooting them as if they were ducks while they pleaded for their lives. You destroyed the winter food supply. Now we kill the white miners to keep our river, save our villages, our gold."

"Try and kill a white man. See where that gets you. You kill a white person, and the entire country will be against you. Best you negotiate a peace," Captain Snyder told them. "If you don't, I will kill all the old people, and only the women will be spared. Your peoples' blood will fill the canyon. If you kill the miners, there will be war, and you will not win. More and more white people will come." His hard countenance so unlike the fur traders the tribes were accustomed to deal with.

He waited until he had the full attention of Chief Spintlum and the other chiefs from the Fraser and Thomson Rivers. "This time we come in peace, but if we had to come again, then we would not, come not by hundreds, but by thousands and drive you from the river forever." His voice held no pity. His demeanor was stiff and unyielding.

The chiefs did not need to wait for the translation to understand. An angry murmur rippled through the tribes. David heard the Kem'loop chief demand they fight to their deaths. The war chief raised his voice, telling the others to refuse to listen to promises from white men who never kept promises.

It was Snyder's threat of annihilation that gave them pause. Chief Spintlum understood that his people and the many other tribes along the gold-bearing rivers would not win a war with the militia. The militia had superior guns and outnumbered the river Indians.

Chief Spintlum spoke at length to his people and to the other tribal chiefs in a calm but sad voice, arguing for a fractured peace over a hopeless war. Yates interpreted, acknowledging that while they may be saving lives, the agreement benefited only the newcomers, not the Fraser River tribes.

Snyder offered nothing to the river people except their lives. Christian and David felt sick over the negotiations.

What kind of treaty was that?

Snyder puffed up his chest like a mating rooster, extolling his role in ending the blockade, smiling and self-satisfied that he, and only he, had won the day. But Christian and David were well aware that if not for Chief David Spintlum, there would have been no agreement to lift the blockade.

Having settled with the chiefs at The Forks, Snyder and his militia continued north upriver, visiting villages with threats and shows of force, convincing the chiefs to stand down.

Christian and David turned back to Yale, relieved that they did not have to travel with Snyder, whom they knew would not stop boasting and congratulating himself. They made their way back to Fort Yale to rejoin Rose and Alice, not pleased with the settlement and all too aware that the miners would overrun the river people.

Reluctantly, the tribes as far north as Fort George stood down, letting thousands of miners push past the falls and into the gold-bearing upper Fraser and Thompson Rivers, changing forever the lives of the river people.

~

Elswa led the group out from Fort Yale early on a misty morning, heading for the canyon while Telt'Yet packers carried their supplies, taking the Hudson's Bay trail to the east of the canyon. Alice and Rose followed Elswa, walking briskly along the old Native trail. McNair puffed and struggled up the steep ascents from the creek beds. Walter and Christian were in the lead, close behind the guide.

"What about Alice and Rose?" Christian asked Walter. "Can they manage the trail along the canyon wall? I read Simon Fraser's account. He wrote about ropes made of cedar branches swinging above the drop to the river."

"Christian, your wife crossed the Rockies with Sinclair. No one was injured. She is more agile than the rest of us."

They walked for a day along a trail that wound through tall cedars. At times, the trail dropped close to the river, but other sections were on high benches above the canyon.

"Soon we are at the canyon wall. There you are mountain goats," Elswa told them, a sweet smile for Alice. "First we camp. Eat Lady Alice's wonderful steak and cookies."

The sun set behind a dark bank of clouds, painting the sky in hues of purple and red. During the night, thunder rolled across the sky, and a sheet of lightening flashed above the tents. Alice woke to the sound of rain pelting onto the canvas.

Today I will be walking on a steep cliff that is not just dangerous but also slick with rain. It was a hard rain till midnight, then a drizzle.

A gloomy fog hung over the canyon. Alice could not see the river, but she could hear its roar. The narrow trail above the Fraser canyon was only comfortable for a tightrope walker, and today the footing was slippery from the overnight downpour. As the fog lifted, Alice could see the river boiling through the canyon far below. She moved onto the narrow trail, carefully clinging to the edge of the cliff, not looking down. Halfway through, they crested a steep section at the top of which was a flat area where they rested and ate lunch. Far below, the water raged through the narrow canyon, the roar so loud the travelers could not hear each other speak. The sun warmed their lunch spot and created a partial rainbow in the canyon.

The most dangerous section of the trail lay ahead, and Alice did not want to think about it. She looked down into the gorge, a sheer drop to the canyon floor where the Fraser River seethed between rocky walls. Up ahead were the falls where the river pushed through a narrow chasm that the miners called Hell's Gate.

Elswa noticed Alice staring at the footpath winding along the canyon wall.

"You skookum woman," Elswa told her. "You have no problem on trail. Just step on ropes with feet and hold on with hands. Don't look down. Keep eyes where you put your feet and hands. You be fine. It is big men with big feet who have trouble, not little lady like you and Rose." He smiled. "Someone coming." Elswa said, glancing back down the trail.

She felt chilled, despite the warm sun striking the canyon walls. A chill in her fingers, a chill running up her spine. Her stomach clenched with anxiety. "We must go," Alice said, looking to see who it was.

"Better stay here, lady, and let him pass. Not room for two pair of feet on the trail ahead. I take Walter up ahead. We fast. We be through the canyon before that man catch his breath."

Walter and Elswa disappeared around the cliff.

Alice watched anxiously a sick feeling in her stomach. Saxby emerged onto the clearing, gulping air like a wind-blown horse, his face red from the exertion, his skin mottled.

Alice backed away from the man she despised most in this world. "Saxby! Let me be."

"Let you be? I'll let you be, alright!" he yelled, his face dark red with exertion and anger. "You will be my obedient wife. That is what I will let you be, you bitch."

Christian stepped between Saxby and Alice. "Your wife has filed for divorce on the basis of cruelty; Judge Begbie has agreed to hear the case. She should be free of you within the month. Turn back, Saxby, and leave Alice alone."

"I will fight the divorce. She is mine by rights."

"She has suffered enough, Saxby. Leave the country. No good will come of this."

"Get out of my way!" Saxby yelled, lunging at Christian who held his ground between Saxby and Alice. Saxby raised a fist at Christian, who easily fended if off before pushing the enraged man back to the edge of the clearing. He clenched his fists and glared at Alice, anger and frustration building in him. "You are nothing but a whore. A bitch who should be knifed from neck to cunt."

Saxby reached for the gun in his holster, but McNair had watched the confrontation and had his rifle ready. He cocked it and aimed at Saxby.

"Don't make another move, Saxby. You've caused enough misery to Alice. Now leave Alice alone, and git yourself back to the States."

Saxby glared at McNair and backed away, moving closer to the canyon drop.

"It's all your fault, Alice!" Saxby yelled, his face contorted in rage. "If you had supported me, none of this would have happened!" Anger erupted in him, and spittle flew from his mouth as he yelled at Alice. "You should have been a helpmate instead of questioning my judgment, opposing me at every turn. You have no right to question me!"

He turned and scowled at McNair, who held the gun steadily, pointing at Saxby's chest. Saxby was filled with pent-up anger. *That bumpkin who took my place as captain then banished me, and that bitch who thinks she can divorce me.*

Saxby, energized by his blind rage, moved with unbelievable speed for a heavy, unfit man. He snatched Alice's arm, pulling her to the brink of the precipice.

"Step away, all of you, or Alice will go over the cliff with me."

"My God. No!" Alice screamed, teetering above the abyss.

"Don't shoot, McNair," Christian cautioned. McNair lowered the rifle, and Christian inched towards Saxby and Alice. The savior of the Sierra Pass had one more fellow traveler he felt compelled to rescue.

"Christian, go back," Rose said in anguish. "Saxby will pull you over, too."

"Yes, Christian," Alice pleaded. "Don't come closer. I fear for you."

Christian was now within arm's length of Saxby, all three in danger of plunging over the canyon wall, but Christian was not only strong, he was also swift. He grabbed Alice by the arm, and with a left hook punched Saxby. The blow stunned Saxby, forcing him to release his grip on Alice. Christian pulled Alice to safety.

Rose ran to her friend and wrapped her arms about Alice, leading her away from the sheer drop.

Saxby swayed above the abyss. His feet gave away and he slipped, catching the rim of the drop with big hands.

"Save me!" Saxby screamed in terror.

"Let the bastard go!" McNair yelled.

"No!" Alice yelled. "Christian, please help him! I cannot bear to see another death, even if it be Saxby!"

Christian looked back at Rose. She nodded. "Do as Alice wishes, but please take care, my love."

Stretched out on his stomach, Christian reached out with strong arms and grasped Saxby's wrists.

"McNair, hold my feet firmly. Don't let me slip towards the canyon. Gradually pull back on my feet, and I'll pull him up." McNair and the two women pulled on Christian's legs, dragging both men slowly away from the drop. Christian continued to grasp Saxby's wrists until both men came away from the abyss.

Saxby lay on the rocky clearing, gasping and cussing under his breath.

"When you find your legs, Saxby," Christian told him angrily, "I want you out of this Territory. I swear to God that if you ever set foot above the U.S. border again, I shall see you are tried and convicted, and it seems I have my pick of crimes. The police are investigating a dead Chinaman in Victoria, and a man fitting your descripted was sighted in the area at the time of the murder."

Saxby scowled at Christian, but turned back and headed down on the trail towards Yale.

"Come, take my hand, Alice," Rose said. "Let's climb out of this canyon. Steady yourself. You're shaking like a leaf." Rose led her friend along the canyon wall, watching closely to make sure Alice placed her feet and hands carefully on the ropes that formed a web across the cliffs.

At first, the trail was reasonable before the canyon walls closed below and above them. Ahead on the trail, Alice could see the narrow path above the steep drop into the canyon. Rose stepped lightly along the rocky path, sure-footed as a mountain goat. She looked back often to assure herself that Christian and Alice were safe.

"Rose, please stay with me. Hold my hand; I am so worried about you," Christian said.

"Dearest, don't worry about me. I am tiny and could cling to a rock face with my fingers and toes. Let me worry about you, the husky Scot, the good man who carried children to safety, but maybe doesn't have the rock climbing skills of his little wife. I will watch you, my love, so step cautiously."

"And I will watch you," he replied. She lifted her head for a kiss, shouldered her pack and moved nimbly up the trail.

Alice watched the kiss, a pang of loneliness settling on her.

"Elswa tells me it is not far before we are out of the worst part of the canyon," Christian said.

Rose and Alice moved along the narrow trail, clinging to the canyon edge and clutching the ropes. Finally, they left the steepest section of the canyon and arrived at the forest trail on a bench above the river. They reached a Native village where a stream created a large sand bar far out in the river where American miners panned for the rich gold dust. The Telt'Yet called them Boston men. It was the sand bar known as Boston Bar.

Chapter Thirty-three

The Roadhouse

The miners took up claims along the river from Hill's Bar and further north, working their way upriver, searching for the richest bars. A few continued upriver to where the Thompson and Fraser Rivers converged, the Native settlement where Chief Spintlum made his home—The Forks, they called it. The small village quickly expanded with tents, rugged pine log cabins and a few substantial buildings.

It was here where two great rivers converged that Rose and Alice opened the Gold Poke Roadhouse, offering bunks for one dollar a night and a fifty cent meal of stew, baked beans, bacon, coffee and bread. Their pickle jar quickly filled with gold.

Walter and his Native workers built the roadhouse using the pine trees that covered the surrounding hills. It was a two-story building with a large dining room filled with long wooden tables and an efficient kitchen with shelving, a huge wood stove, and a pump providing water. A wooden staircase led to the bedrooms upstairs. Beside the roadhouse, Walter and his workers built a twenty-person bunkhouse, a blacksmith shed, a stable, and two outhouses.

In the stable were two saddle horses, a pinto that belonged to Alice, and a palomino that Christian had purchased for Rose as a wedding gift. Rose had spent her early years riding with her father and could gallop with the best of them, and Alice, had ample opportunity to ride during her the months on the Oregon Trail. Now Rose enjoyed her free time riding the hills around The Forks, and Alice used the pinto for practical trips.

Alice and Rose put up the money for the enterprise, certain that the thousands of miners arriving would provide enough customers to make the investment worthwhile.

After completing this job, Walter set up a lumber mill farther downriver at Boston Bar and was soon pocketing gold in exchange for rough-cut lumber. David and Christian moved into the Commissioner's cabin, filling in temporarily until the Royal Engineers arrived from New Westminster, the new city near the mouth of the Fraser River.

"There is a bit of life coming back to your eyes, Alice," Rose said with a smile. "I think you will learn to laugh again and maybe even love once more." They rose early and were both busy in the kitchen, Alice mixing cake batter and Rose setting the tall coffee pot on the stove to boil.

"Never. I am quit with men." Alice paused in her work and thought for a moment about David, then shook her head. "Being tied to Saxby and allowing his rash decisions to rob me of my child has closed my heart."

Just then David and Christian entered the roadhouse. David was not smiling or joking as was his usual demeanor. Alice immediately noticed the worried looks on both their faces.

"Why, Mr. Ackerman, what might be the matter?"

"Rose, Alice. Take care when we are not about. A Victoria man brought horses and a load of liquor over the Kem'loop trail and opened a saloon, called it the Bucket of Blood. That tells us something. Drunken miners have no respect for the law, and they are out for blood, Indian blood."

"The miners got what they wanted," Christian added, in a sad tone. "They don't give a damn for the people who've lived along the river for centuries. I knew this would happen, but did not think they would threaten women, and certainly not white women."

"How quickly they forgot about the treaty Snyder brags about," Alice said. "I thought he promised Chief Spintlum peace, and that he agreed to use only one side of the river."

"It is similar to the confrontations in Oregon and Washington." David said, "Indian lives mean nothing to the greedy miners. I knew in my heart that the treaty would soon be broken."

"Do you still have that Colt I gave you, Alice?"

"Yes, of course." She thought back to the day she intended to take her life and the young boy who saved her. She had been so grief stricken she did not wish to live.

"Please keep the pistol close to you. If the miners find Rose unprotected, they may be a threat to her. I have heard them at the saloons. Some of the men will kill the first Indian they see, and I heard from Chief Spintlum himself of a young Indian girl violated by a drunken miner."

While David was speaking, Christian kissed Rose lightly on her lips and held her hand. "I have to go downriver a few miles, Rose, but I will return before noon. Be vigilant, my love. David will be in the Commissioner's Office. Run to him if there is any trouble."

"And you, Alice," David said, his eyes catching hers, "with your beauty, you are also at risk. I could not bear for anything to happen to either of you, and Christian would die if Rose was harmed."

"I know," Alice answered. "I can hear their rowdy, drunken voices all the way from the river. We'll be careful. What really worries me is Saxby. Are you sure he left?"

"He would be stupid not to leave; as there is a warrant out for his arrest. He is a coward and would not want to face British justice.

For my thinking, he is most likely on a boat to San Francisco. You should not worry about him."

"Unfortunately, we must go," Christian said, before giving Rose a farewell kiss.

"And you be careful, my dearest Christian, and return before the storm descends," Rose wrapped her arms around him. "Did you see the black clouds gathering in the west? You will get drenched if you don't hurry back."

"Do not worry about us. Christian and I are accustomed to riding through storms. Alice, you likely remember the day the rain came in sheets when we traveled along the Platte River, and I recall you walking in the downpour with a blue bonnet on your head and a white smock tied to your waist. You sang and lifted your arms to the rain."

"That was a different woman, David. Today, Rose and I will be under a roof, busy preparing dinner for you and our guests and will stay dry in the roadhouse. Walter's workmanship will be tested today; I feel there is a good soaking on the way. The rain will be a blessing. This country is so dry and hot, even a grasshopper would wilt."

Christian rode off to inspect the mining claims, and David went back to the office to register claims while Alice and Rose returned to the kitchen. Alice had a cake to bake and ice, and Rose had the chore of watching over the stew and setting the tables.

As Alice predicted, the storm descended with fury. First the wind came, rattling the windowpanes before the first early drops of rain pattered against the glass. Within the hour, the rain came down in sheets, pounding on the shake roof, but inside the log roadhouse, Alice and Rose stayed warm and dry. Alice wondered about the men at their rockers, sluicing for gold, tired men who would return to a wet campfire and a small, leaky tent. If they'd hit pay dirt, they would be celebrating at the saloon, and later looking for food and a room at the Gold Poke.

The stew bubbled on the iron cookstove, and the aroma of chocolate cake wafted through the roadhouse. Alice read Jane Austen's *Pride and Prejudice* while Rose took out her sewing. She was stitching a new shirt for Christian. Alice enjoyed the sound of the rain on the roof and the comfort of the sturdy four walls. After a time, Alice put down her book and walked to the windows to look out at the gray day. The rain was so heavy, she could barely make out the road that led through the town, connecting the Commissioner's Office, the Roadhouse and scattered log shacks and tents.

"When are Christian and David coming back?" she asked Rose.

"Soon, I hope. They planned to be away for the morning"

A crooked splash of light slashed through the window, and thunder roared as a second rainstorm hit the valley.

"Looks like customers are coming our way, I see men on horses." Alice pressed her face to the window, trying to see the group more clearly. "Not many miners have horses. They must have brought them in on the Kem'loop trail, along with the whiskey." Alice and Rose watched the band of riders move out from between a row of tents and log shacks.

"Do you have enough stew in the pot to feed this bunch?" Rose asked.

"I always make more than needed. We could feed fifty."

A blue flash of lightning lit the ground in front of the roadhouse, illuminating the riders. Under dark clouds, it was difficult to be certain, but the man at the tag end of the horsemen reminded her of Saxby. The man had the same shape and posture of Saxby as he'd ridden towards her and Amelia across the salt flats when they were on the Hastings Cutoff. The sight sent a shiver down her spine.

The band of riders emerged from the trees, allowing Alice to see them clearly for the first time. She spotted Finis and, riding a few feet behind him, was Saxby.

We're in trouble.

The men were not hungry for stew and biscuits; their appetite was for women and revenge.

"Rose. You stay inside and lock the door!" Alice said, as she stood on the porch, sheltered from the rain by the roof overhang. "I have my Colt." Alice felt the smooth, cool steel in the pocket of her smock, hoping that she didn't have to use it, praying that they would see reason and leave. Her experience and instincts told her that she and Rose were in great danger. She also knew that Christian and David were too far away to hear a gunshot or a scream for help. She thought of barring the door, but knew nine or more crazed men would soon find a way to break in. Instead, she decided to reason with them. She stood her ground on the porch.

"Where's the squaw?" It was Finis, who had a smirk on his face as he dismounted and shifted from foot to foot near the cabin porch. Saxby stood with the other renegades. All were armed but had not raised their guns. Alice guarded the door and faced Finis. Her heart pounded.

"We have hot stew and fresh biscuits," Alice said calmly, although her stomach tightened and she felt sick with tension. "Why not have yourselves a tasty meal, and go in peace? Don't cause problems, Finis. You harm Rose, and Christian will see you hang. And you, Saxby. You were ordered out of the country. Christian and David will return any minute, and you will spend the rest of your lives in prison. Think about it. Do not pile more evildoing on your souls."

Stall them. Reason with them. I can't face a posse of nine armed men. I can't outgun them, but I must save Rose, or I won't be able to live with myself. I could not save my darling Amelia, and I won't allow any harm to come to Rose. Alice stood straight and steady, but the blood raced through her veins.

"I'm taking that young brown-skinned girl," Finis answered. "You go bring her out here. And Saxby, he gits to take you back to where you belongs."

"I will die before I go with you, Saxby, and, Finis, I will kill you before I let you come within a foot of Rose."

"We come for youse two, and we ain't stopping because of some skinny sheila standin' in our way."

"Go back to your tents. The peace officer and solicitor will be back shortly. They have the authority to haul you in chains to Victoria if you break the law."

"What law says we can't have a squaw?" Finis stepped closer to Alice, a malicious smile pasted on his lips.

"Get back, Finis. I warn you."

"This time I git the girl. Last time I was cheated out of a good fuck." Finis raised the rifle, pointing it at Alice's chest. Alice felt panic rise in her throat, but did not flinch.

Saxby stepped in front of Finis. "Alice is my property. If someone is to whip her good, it will be me." Saxby pushed Finis' gun aside.

"Be reasonable, Alice, and no one will get hurt." Saxby stepped towards Alice, his face hard and mean. "You come with me and let Finis have the squaw."

Alice pulled the Colt from her pocket. "I am never going with you, and no one is taking Rose." Alice planted her feet firmly and pointed the gun at Saxby. She steadied herself, holding the pistol with both hands.

"Don't take another step. Either of you." Alice had never before aimed a gun at either beast or man. The situation was so foreign, she felt as if she were watching herself from outside.

Stay calm, Alice, she told herself. *I can face him down.*

Saxby had a cruel smile on his face as he chuckled. "You don't have the guts to fire that gun. Killing isn't in your blood. Drop it." Saxby stepped closer. His gait was unsteady, and his skin had the dyspeptic look of an habitual alcoholic.

"I may not be able to kill, but I can shoot." Alice took a deep breath, aimed at Saxby's boot and fired.

"Damn you, Alice!" He crumpled to the ground, blood seeping from his foot. "Damn your soul and the soul of Amelia!" Hearing him blaspheme the one she loved most, the daughter whose death he had caused, filled Alice with rage. She wanted to empty the gun into this evil man. She raised the pistol, held it with one hand and pulled the trigger without preparing for the shot. The bullet spattered on the gravel, missing the target. In her fury at Saxby, Alice had forgotten about the Colt's powerful recoil. It threw her off balance. She teetered backward and placed her hand on the door to keep from falling.

Finis used this to his advantage and lunged at Alice, bludgeoning her on the head with the butt of his rifle. Alice fell onto the steps of the roadhouse, blood oozing from her forehead. Finis walked around Alice's body and pulled at the roadhouse door.

"Help me out here, youse louses." Three of the miners rushed forward, one picked up a log and together they battered down the door. Rose stood in the kitchen, a cast iron frying pan in her hand.

"So the little squaw wants a fight, does she?" An alcohol-fueled grin crossed on his lips. Despite Finis' poor fitness, he moved quickly, snatching Rose's wrist and squeezing until she dropped the pan.

"You come with me, and we'll all have some fun with the pretty Injun."

"You are nothing but a filthy white man." She beat him with her fists furiously but with little affect. "You will hang for this."

"They have to catch me first. Even if they track me down, what jury will sentence a man to death 'cause he had hisself a squaw? Never happened, never will happen." Finis gave a sickening chuckle as he dragged Rose from the cabin.

"You let me go! Christian will kill you!" She screamed and kicked but was defenseless against a posse of men. Finis lashed Rose's hands together and slung her onto a horse, fastening her wrists to the saddle horn. She was so small and light, despite her flailing feet and arms, it was like lifting a small dog onto the horse. Finis grabbed the horse's reins, mounted his horse and prepared to ride off, pulling horse and terrified young woman along behind.

"Finis, you bastard!" Saxby yelled between moans, "didn't I tell you I am the one to give Alice a beating? She's mine! If she is dead, it is me who should have delivered the blow! You get yourself back here and help me onto my horse!" He lay groaning, his foot wound gushing blood. "Leave me here, and I'll make sure the law finds you, and we'll hang together."

"He's as useless as nun in a whorehouse, but we gotta take him with us. Sling him up on his horse, and let's vamoose!" Finis yelled to the men. Two men lifted Saxby onto his horse, and they galloped up the well-traveled trail along the banks of the Thompson River hooting and hollering. Saxby followed slowly, blood dripping onto the rain-soaked ground.

Alice gained consciousness and saw the battered door. She staggered to her feet and searched the roadhouse for Rose, although she already knew her friend was gone. "My dear God, no!" she screamed, feeling sick with anguish and blame.

Alice pocketed her pistol, mounted her horse and raced to the mining office, yelling for help and ignoring the blood oozing from her head wound. Before she sighted the office, she fired her gun in the air. As she rode frantically forward, brushing the blood from her eyes, she saw David galloping towards her.

"My God, Alice! What happened?"

"Rose! They took her! Finis, Saxby and a pack of drunken miners! Christian will go insane. Where is he?"

"Sorting out a dispute downriver. Did you see which way they went?"

"The gun recoiled and the next thing I remember is waking up on the porch." Alice's chest heaved from anxiety. "Come quickly. You can track them. Finis and Saxby with seven other men. All on horses."

They galloped to the cabin, urging their horses. David easily spotted the tracks leading out of town and onto the trail that led along the banks of the Thompson River.

"We must save Rose." Alice could barely keep from crying.

David dug his boot into Lightning's flank and raced upriver, gravel and dust flying from the horse's hooves. Alice followed, keeping him in sight.

"I might know where they are going!" David yelled back. "There's a mining claim beside the waterfall, and it has a cabin. The claim is held by one of the troublesome newcomers. May be Finis and Saxby have been hanging out there."

An open forest of pine covered the hills above the valley where the two rivers met. From the hill, David could see the kidnappers' tracks but no sign of the men themselves.

"They must have veered off through the trees, into that gully!" David yelled.

Alice caught up to David, and they turned their horses down a bank and through a narrow border of trees and willows, where a creek rushed over a gravel bed. They splashed through the shallow river that flowed into the Thompson, icy water racing against the horses' fetlocks.

"I see them at the base of the waterfall!" David spurred his horse, galloping through the shallow creek, spray kicking up from Lightning's hooves. Alice spotted the drunken party far up the creek, palavering while they let the horses drink in the pool created by the waterfall.

"Stay here, Alice. This is not a fight I want you to be in. If it goes bad for me, find Christian. Get him to form a posse."

"Two shooters are better than one," Alice protested.

"Yes, Alice, but I will be taking shots from five hundred feet. Your Colt doesn't have the range. You will be of more use here."

Alice understood. "Save her, David. I cannot lose another one I love." She was close to tears. "You must be careful. Don't let Saxby or Finis near you."

He rode out of the creek bed and dismounted. Quietly and slowly, David led his horse uphill through a gully and made his way to the top of the waterfall.

The horse whinnied. "Easy now, Lightning." He dropped the reins to let the horse graze and stealthily made his way to a point above the waterfall. The stream dropped down a hundred feet into the Thompson River Valley. David positioned himself on his stomach, shielded by pine trees and an outcropping of rocks and watched through his spyglass. He could see Rose with her hands tied to the saddle horn. Finis held the reins to her horse.

"I'll kill that bastard Finis."

He was America's top sharpshooter, a man who'd bested two thousand men in a military shooting competition. David would not miss a shot like this, but just as he readied for his shot, Finis turned his mount and led Rose's horse out of the river bed. Saxby and the band of men followed, now heading towards the mining shack.

David held his breath, aimed and fired. Finis released the reins on Rose's horse and slumped into the saddle as his horse galloped back into the riverbed. For a minute, Finis managed to hang on, then he lost his grip and slipped from the saddle. His boot caught in the stirrup and the horse pulled him through the rocky creek bed.

The horse dragged Finis over rocks and gravel, his shrieks filling the gully. Finis was helpless as his body scraped on the gravel and bounced over rocks. Finis let out a final scream before his head smashed against a boulder. It was a fitting death for a man who'd killed and raped, David decided, and for the man who had been with the vigilantes who'd murdered his child.

"My beloved son," he whispered, "your death has been avenged."

David took aim again and picked off two other men. The others, except for Saxby, turned and fled from the gunfire. The miners had not counted on a fight, especially with a sharpshooter they couldn't see.

Saxby raced his horse into the river and grabbed the reins on Rose's horse. He needed a bargaining prize to get Alice back.

"You will live if Alice comes with me!" he yelled at Rose. "We're going to get her."

"She won't ever be yours, you monster! She hates you."

"Shut up, you little squaw." Saxby pulled on the reins, urging his horse along the creek, heading back towards town, towards Alice who stood concealed by trees.

Alice's chest ached at the sight of her dear Rose, now Saxby's captive. She would easily give her life for the young woman, so long as she could save Rose.

Alice stepped out from behind the copse of trees, pistol in her hand. Saxby reined in his horse, keeping a firm grip on Rose's horse.

"Let her go, Saxby. You have so much blood on your hands. The blood of my daughter, the deaths of the innocent people you led, and who knows how many others. Release her, and go back to the States."

Saxby slid awkwardly from his horse and moved behind Rose, using the young woman and the horse as a shield while he pointed the gun at Rose's chest.

"Oh, Alice, be careful!" Rose's eyes were wide with fear, not just for herself but for Alice.

"A bargain, Alice. I will let her go if you come with me." His voice was unsteady from the liquor and the pain from his leg wound.

Alice steadied herself and raised the pistol. She felt calm and in control. With the gun pointed at Saxby, she walked towards him.

"I'll give you one chance to release her," Alice told him calmly. "If you don't, I will put a bullet through your evil brain."

"You missed me before. You will misfire again. Be reasonable, Alice. If you try to shoot, you'll hit Rose, not me. Put that gun down, and leave with me."

Saxby held the reins tight, his left hand visible just under the horse's neck. It was a shot Alice knew she could make. She had loaded the chambers and cocked the gun. She was ready. Alice took a deep breath, bracing for the kickback. She aimed at Saxby's hand and fired. A puff of smoke obscured her view for a minute, but she heard Saxby's scream and knew the bullet had hit its mark.

The gun shot startled Rose's horse, spooking it into a dead run. Rose gripped her knees tightly to the horse's flanks, fighting to stay in the saddle. As the gelding galloped down the creek bed, she spoke to it, keeping her voice calm and reassuring. Gradually, she urged the horse into a gentle trot. She wheeled the horse, turning it with her knee and headed back up the creek, letting the horse choose its gate. The horse stopped to drink, putting its muzzle into the cold creek. That is where Christian found her.

Farther up the creek, Saxby stood unprotected, with a bloodied hand and bloodied foot, aiming the gun at Alice while Alice pointed her pistol at Saxby. They eyed each other silently. Saxby wanted Alice alive, and Alice had no wish to kill Saxby now that Rose was free. It was a standoff. Minutes passed until they heard hooves and splashing water from upstream.

David was racing towards the gunfire, his horse kicking up gravel, his rifle raised.

"Drop your gun, Saxby!" David yelled as he reined in Lightening.

Saxby looked bewildered and shaken. His right hand was still holding the gun, still pointing it at Alice.

"Drop it, I said!"

"The Indian-lover thinks he can stop me from taking what's mine." Saxby's voice slurred as he moved closer to Alice, dragging his injured foot, a trail of blood disappearing in the wet gravel.

"You drop your gun, or I will kill her right here!" Saxby's gun arm shook from pain and fear.

He stumbled toward Alice, swaying from loss of blood, and collapsed on the ground moaning.

David dismounted and ran to Alice. He gently folded her in his arms. Alice felt an unusual sense of happiness. She felt redeemed.

"Oh, David." Tears of relief pooled in her eyes. "I did it. I shot that monster's hand."

David looked at Alice and saw that the misery she had held for years had lifted. A slight smile crossed her lips. He wanted to kiss her, but holding her and comforting her felt right.

"You used my pistol. I knew when I gave it to you that it had a destiny."

"It's done. I will be better now that he will face justice. I did not want to kill him unless I had to. I want him to answer for his crimes."

"Judge Begbie will see to him." David tied Saxby's hands and hoisted him onto his horse.

"Please go to Rose and help her," Alice pleaded.

"Rose doesn't need me. Christian is with her."

I saved her. An enormous weight lifted from her tortured heart. *I would have died if Saxby had killed Rose; she is my friend, but more than a friend. I love her like a mother loves a daughter.*

"My sweet love! We should have stayed in Victoria." Christian's voice trembled with emotion as he gently lifted her out of the saddle and into his arms, untying the ropes binding her hands. They clung to each other, Rose sobbing and Christian kissing her tears. He stepped back to look at her, his hands patting and touching her everywhere to assure himself that she had not been harmed. Realizing that she appeared to be unscathed, his heart filled with overwhelming relief.

"I am fine, my husband. I am unharmed other than the rope burns on my wrists. Alice saved me with an unbelievable shot. My dear friend can shoot a pea off a stump from a hundred feet."

"Miners told me about the raid on your roadhouse. I came as soon as heard. Is Alice unharmed?"

"See for yourself." They led their horses back along the creek and found David and Alice waiting for them. "It looks like Saxby is trussed up and ready for a jail cell," she said, glaring at her former captor.

"Alice, Rose tells me you saved her life. I am indebted to you forever." His eyes were full of the gratitude he could barely express, but when he turned to his friend, a bit of a teasing light came into them. "David, I thought you were the sharpshooter."

"He took out Finis with a shot you would not believe," Rose told him. "Then Saxby grabbed me, trying to trade my life for Alice."

Christian turned to David, "I owe you for taking out Finis."

"Rose, come ride with me." He swung effortlessly into the saddle, then reached down and pulled Rose up behind him, her weight as light as a pillow in his strong arms. "Hold me tight, my darling. I need to feel you're still here and safe."

He kissed the rope marks on her wrists and turned back to kiss her lips. "I'm so sorry I had to go the mining claims," he said as he spurred the horse into a gentle trot. "I was called to settle an urgent matter that could have ended in violence."

The four friends rode down the creek bed, turning their eyes away from Finis, who lay mutilated in the shallow creek, his blood turning the water pink. David led the horse carrying Saxby.

"I am so relieved that Alice will be okay." Rose held Christian firmly and rested her head against his broad back.

Chapter Thirty-four
The Angel at Peace

The rain clouds had dispersed as they rode back to the roadhouse, arriving in late afternoon. Rose and Alice tidied up the roadhouse, while David repaired the door and Christian carried out broken furniture. Alice had a clean white bandage tied over her forehead and a white apron about her waist. David thought she looked as beautiful as she had in the early months on the Oregon Trail. He listened to her melodic voice as Alice sang softly, moving from stove to table and back again with bowls of stew. This brought back memories of Alice singing around the campfire as she'd baked bread. David gazed reflectively at Alice.

Is it possible Saxby's capture is mending her pain?

"You're looking at me, David, and I wonder what you are thinking." Alice had a sweet smile for him and clearly appeared more at peace.

"Tell me if I am wrong, but I believe you will recover from the tragedy that had stolen your smile." David and Christian sat on the smooth pine bench next to one of the smaller tables. The aroma of stew filled the room. The door remained open, and a cooling breeze, freshened by the recent rain storm, wafted into the roadhouse.

"Don't expect me to be healed just because Saxby is facing justice for his crimes. I think of Amelia every hour of my day. It will take more than Saxby rotting in jail to put laughter back into my life. You misunderstood my singing. I sing when I cook because I love to prepare food for my friends.

"Yes, it is a relief that I no longer have to run from Saxby," Alice continued, "but if I think of all that has happened since leaving Springfield, there is far too much death and suffering, and there will be more suffering to come. The tribes who put their guns down, what will happen to them? Will there be a true peace for the people of the river, for Elswa's village on the Fraser River, for Yoletan's family on James Bay? I think not."

"There will never be lasting peace for the river people," Christian said. "They bought peace at a great price. They were wealthy tribes. They never suffered from hunger as long as the salmon ran upstream every year, and they prospered with the gold they found. Now the miners will take their gold diggings and ruin their salmon pots and fishing areas."

"As the Queen's representative, Christian, there is something you should know." David paused, waiting till he had Christian's full attention. "Captain Graham led his forces up the west bank of the Fraser, and Snyder was on the east. He had impressed upon Graham not to start a conflict with the river people unless the tribes refused to stand down. So what did he do after a runner informed him that a truce had been reached?" David's face became red with anger as he continued. "His militia ignored the truce and prepared to storm a peaceful village. When the local chief raised a white flag, Graham killed him in cold blood. What kind of peace is that?"

"Graham is an Indian killer. That's all he knows," Christian said, shaking his head.

"One of his militia retrieved the white flag and slept with it to protect the peace," David added. "Not all gold miners are out for blood."

"I heard that Graham was killed later that night," Alice told them. "No one knows who fired the shot, and we don't care. Justice was meted out."

"You both did your part, you and David," Rose added, "and Captain Snyder, as well. Without his effort to offer peace to the tribes, there would have been war."

"Captain Snyder may present himself as a hero," Christian continued, "claiming he averted war with the tribes, but I know different. If Chief Spintlum had not persuaded the war chiefs to stand down, Snyder, Graham and a thousand miners would have stormed through Hell's Gate and murdered every Indian in their path. I read his self-congratulatory words—eleven pages extolling his triumph over the tribes, in the letter he wrote to Douglas. He proudly admits that he would have wiped out every man, woman and child if the tribes refused his treaty."

David paused, a look of regret and sadness on his fine features. "The tribes gave up their land, their fisheries, and their way of life to prevent a war with the whites. Life will never be the same for the Queen's Indians." David thought of the massacre of the peaceful Yana and wondered if the price the river tribes had paid was worthwhile. He paused for a minute before shaking his head and continuing.

"But we are being so very solemn when we have cause to be light-hearted," David said. "Enjoy this tasty stew and rejoice that the two women we care for are safe."

"I, for one, look forward to a peaceful life in Victoria once more, with my husband by my side. Alice, I am sure we have enough gold in our pickle jars to return to Victoria. Christian, haven't you and David fulfilled your duties to Governor Douglas, leaving us free to depart this rough country?"

"Well, my dearest wife, if you wish to return to Victoria, I will go with you. What about you, David?"

"I have plans for Alice."

"No one has plans for me," Alice retorted. "I am my own woman, and I make my own decisions."

"Hear me out, Alice. Come, let's walk along Fraser's great river and watch the sunset on the water." The storm was over, and the haze of the setting sun sent golden rays across the water. "Maybe you would even take my arm if I promise not to press my case for your love. I have a proposal. Not a marriage proposal, but a request for you to consider."

"And what would that be, Mr. Ackerman?"

"My first request is that you call me by my given name, David. The name means beloved. If you recall, we were once close friends, and at one time I believed you had strong feeling for me. Now we can be friends, and what a good friend does is help mend someone's tortured soul."

～

Alice and David boarded the steamship bound for Portland, then another for San Francisco. They traveled in separate cabins, ate together in the dining room, and walked the deck arm in arm.

"You must tell me where we are going," Alice demanded, on their last day on the ship.

"When we reach San Francisco, we will take a boat up the Sacramento River. I hope you will agree to visit the site of my son's resting place. I will borrow horses from Captain Sutter, and we will ride to the summit."

"The Sierra Pass. No! I cannot go there." Her voice broke and tears pooled in her eyes. "I could not bear it." Alice burst into tears at the thought of the tragedy on the Sierras and the death of her beloved child.

"Trust me a little. I believe I know how to lessen your suffering."

The valley of the Sacramento River had changed drastically since the survivors had struggled out of the mountains. Sutter's Fort was now in the thriving city of Sacramento, and Bear Creek was the relay point on the route to the Pass, a busy town.

They rode horseback from the Sacramento River to the site of the Yana village and there, under the pine trees, David knelt beside the cross marking the grave of his little son. He did not shed tears this time. Alice picked wildflowers and placed them on the grave, then put her hand on David's shoulder.

He has suffered as much as I, yet I never thought to comfort him.

Alice knelt beside the grave of his child, and shed tears for David's loss. Her compassion lessened her own pain.

Their journey took them up the gentle western slope of the Sierras, the trail worn by the footsteps and wagon wheels of the thousands who had crossed into California for gold. Ahead lay the summit and the place Amelia had died.

With each step, Alice's heart grew heavier, tears flooding down her cheeks.

At the summit, Alice stood sobbing. Finally, she was able to talk through her tears.

"This is where we stayed in the snow cave. Amelia died in my arms here, although I tried to save her. I covered her with pine boughs and then heaped snow over her and built a little cross with branches. At least her body was left unmolested. Others who died here were mutilated."

"It is not evil when there is no other way. It is only evil to kill."

"Oh, David. It broke my heart, and I will never be the same again. I could not save her life, not even a proper grave for my darling child." Alice's voice broke again. She stood, rooted to the spot, her body shaking in remorse. "It was my fault, not only Saxby's. Don't you understand? From the very beginning of my life with Saxby, I was submissive, never standing up to him, refusing to listen to Anna and Jan who counseled me not to take the Hastings Cutoff, not even heeding your warning, and taking that trail of death instead of staying on the Oregon Trail."

Her sobs racked her slender body. David wanted to take her in his arms to try to comfort her, but she was in her own world of pain and regret. David knew Alice needed this cathartic cry. The violent sobs subsided, and Alice wrapped her arms about her chest, trying to sooth the pain in her heart.

"Alice, don't torture yourself with the past decisions you made. You had no resources; Saxby had made you dependent on him, and McNair was a poor leader. Then there was the severe winter with snow up to twenty feet deep. There was little you could have done. Please, dear, see that it was a dreadful turn in your life, but that Saxby was pivotal in the tragedy, not you. Come here, my dear friend."

She walked to him and placed her head on his shoulder as he held her comfortingly. Her body still shuddered from her outburst of tears. Gradually she calmed and stepped back from David, shaking her head to try to cast off the past.

Alice's sobs subsided. She looked around at the site of the death of so many. "David, I don't understand. So many died here, yet there are no bones scattered about. Has someone taken them?"

"No one took, them dear Alice. I buried the bones years ago, and while gathering the bones, I found a necklace."

"What necklace?" Alice asked, remembering with a heavy heart the day she had placed a necklace around Amelia's neck before her darling daughter had succumbed to hunger and cold.

"Heart-shaped and delicate. You had given it to Amelia. Right?"

Renewed tears trickled down Alice's cheeks, the memories still so raw. She nodded her head.

"It is not just Amelia buried, but all the poor souls who perished at the summit." David looked at her grief-stricken face, feeling immensely sad for this tortured lovely woman, hoping that somehow he could lessen the sorrow and anguish. "Now come, and I will show you." The aroma of mountain flowers wafted on the light breeze.

"This is where they rest," he told her, reaching out to hold her hand. Alice looked at the crosses covering the mound. The grave was shaded by a pine tree.

Alice knelt, her head on the sweet flowers, letting her tears flow over the mass grave. Peace descended on her, wiping away another lump of the dreadful injury she had carried for years.

"I have something for you and Amelia." In his pack were two packages. One was the old Bible Robert had insisted he take, assuring David that the Bible must be shared by the two Ackermans and that Alice would someday be his wife. *I know it is too soon to mention the Bible to Alice.*

David took out the second package and unwrapped the cloth. He handed Alice a small stone angel carved in white marble.

She gently held the angel in her hands and read the inscription: *Here rests Amelia, age eight, beloved daughter of Alice. May the angels care for her.*

Alice buried the necklace in the grave, placed the gravestone over it and gathered alpine flowers to scatter on the graves.

"Now, my dearest Alice, say your farewell to Amelia. May you both find peace."

They walked their horses down the mountain until they were out of sight of the summit. David took her hand in his and drew her into his arms. Alice placed her head on his chest and felt the pain lift from her heart. She did not feel joy, but finally she was at peace.

"Dear Alice. My wasted heart will love you always, even if you can't love me back."

Alice slipped a crumpled paper into David's pack. It was the poem she had written to him while she had watched a sliver of a moon and the canopy of stars, and her heart was his.

I do love this beautiful man. Someday, maybe not too soon, I will want him again. I once desired him more than anything. I hungered for his kiss and, God willing, soon I will be strong enough to open my heart to him again.

Acknowledgments

I received assistance from so many people during the preparation of this book. My sincere thanks go out to Dr. John Harris, Marina Michaelides and Kaija Sproule for their advice and editing and to Shane Kennedy for his unwavering support. I would also like to thank Dr. Kathryn Bridge of the Royal British Columbia Museum for advice on the gold rush.

The main research was assisted by the wonderful archivist Marian Tustanoff of BC Archives. I also want to thank the members of the staff who were so generous with their time. Thank you to Barb Buxton of Port Moody Public Library, Anne Dottington of Vancouver Public Library, and Kathleen Wyatt and Debra Duncan who assisted me in interlibrary loans. Karen Rehkop, the Donner Museum in Truckee; Norm Sayler, a Donner tragedy expert; and Mr. Norden, a Route 40 historian, all helped me with the research.

I owe thanks to many sources including Sean from Seattle's Greatest Hat Shop to David of the Lion Heart Book Store in Seattle.

I want to thank my friends who contributed to the story: Michelle and Gary McKill, Lynn Meehan, Rob Ackester, and history buffs Brian McConnell and Jim Verner.

Main Sources

The wonderful museums and interpretive centers along the Oregon and California Trail were an excellent source of information, as was the British Columbia archives. Although I read over one hundred articles, letters and books in preparing this historical novel, there are several main sources. They are:

Bridge, Kathryn. *Extraordinary Accounts of Native Life on the West Coast*. Canmore, AB: Altitude Publishing. 2004

Campbell, Marjorie Wilkins. *Savage River: Seventy-one Days with Simon Fraser*. Calgary: Fifth House. 2003.

Cowie, Isaac. *The Company of Adventurers: A Narrative of Seven Years in the Service of the Hudson's Bay Company During 1867-1874, on the Great Buffalo Plains (1913)*. Ulan Press. 2012

Darwin, Hanna and Mamie Henry. *Our Tellings: Interior Salish Stories of the Nlha7kamax People*. Vancouver: UBC Press. 1995

DeVoto Bernard, ed. *The Journals of Lewis and Clark*. Mariner Books. 1997.

Downs, Art. *Cariboo Gold Rush: The Stampede that Made BC*. Victoria, BC: Heritage House Publishing Ltd. 2013

Fawcett, Edgar. *Some Reminiscences of Old Victoria*. William Bridges. 1912.

Hanson, T.J. *Western Passage*. TJ Hanson. 2001.

Holmes, Kenneth L. *Covered-wagon Women: Diaries and Letters from the Western Trails, 1840–49*. University of Nebraska Press. 1995

Lindsey, F.W. *Cariboo Yarns*. FW Lindsay. 1974.

Mallandaine, E., T. N. Hibben and Co., and A. Roman and Co. *First Victoria Directory*. BibiloBazaar. 2010

Marschner, Janice. *Oregon 1859: A Snapshot in Time*. Timber Press. 2008.

MAIN SOURCES

McGlashan, C.F. *History of the Donner Party: A Tragedy of the Sierras.* Dover Publications. 2013.

McMurtry, Larry. *Oh, What a Slaughter: Massacres in the American West, 1846–1890.* Simon & Schuster. 2013.

Meeker, Ezra. *Personal Experiences on the Oregon Trail: Sixty Years Ago (1912).* Kessinger Publishing. 2009.

Murphy, Virginia. *Across the Plains in the Donner Party 1846–1847.* Outbooks. 1995.

Newell, Olive. *Tail of the Elephant: The Emigrant Experience on the Truckee Route of the California Trail, 1844-1852.* Nevada County Historical. 1997.

O'Brien, Mary Barmeyer. *Heart of the Trail: The Stories of Eight Wagon Train Women.* TwoDot. 1997

Osborne, William M. *The Wild Frontier: Atrocities During the American-Indian War from Jamestown Colony to Wounded Knee.* Random House. 2001.

Parkman, Frances. *Oregon Trail.* Dover Publications. 2002.

Reed, Victoria. *The Way We Were.* Unknown.

Schlissel, Lillian. *Women's Diaries of the Westward Journey.* Schocken. 2004.

Settle, Raymond. *The March of the Mounted Riflemen: From Fort Leavenworth to Fort Vancouver, May to October 1849.* Bison Books. 1989.

Swanky, Tom. *The True Story of Canada's "War" of Extermination on the Pacific.* lulu.com.2013

Thornton, J. Quinn. *Camp of Death: The Donner Party Mountain Camp 1846 to 47.* Vista Publications. 1978.

Vancouver, Captain George. *Voyage of Discovery to the North Pacific Ocean and Around the World.* Sagwan Press. 2015.

Yvonne Harris is an avid outdoorswoman and marathon canoeist who has competed eight times in the longest canoe race in the world, an event in which she and her partner have held the women's record.

To write this sweeping saga about the Oregon Trail and the Fraser River gold rush, Yvonne traveled the trail and the old trails along Fraser River attempting to recreate the passage across virtually unknown country. She wanted to understand the hardships that the emigrants endured on their journey to a new home in the West.

Deeply interested in the natural and human history of North America, her work shows a respect for Indigenous peoples and an appreciation for the natural environment. She has used her wide outdoor experience hiking many trails in both Canada and the U.S. to help her understand and shape the characters she has written about in *Redemption*.